Arthur William Upfield is well known as the creator of Detective Inspector Napoleon Bonaparte (Bony) who features in 29 crime detection novels, most set in the Australian outback. It is not well known that he also wrote more than 200 short stories and articles, drawing on his experiences in the bush between 1911 and 1931.

Up and Down Australia is the first published collection of Upfield's short works. Kees de Hoog has selected 33 fiction stories, including the only known Bony short story, and has added the unfinished first chapter for another Bony novel. There are also humorous yarns, crime stories, comedies, and dire tales about the dangers of living and working in the bush.

You will not simply be entertained and informed by reading these stories, but you will sample life in the Australian outback during the early decades of the twentieth century.

Kees de Hoog lives in Australia, and has been researching Upfield' ''`` ``` ```` in his spare time since 20(

GW00728841

Up and Down Australia

Short Stories

by

Arthur Upfield

Collected, Selected, Edited and Introduced by

Kees de Hoog

Published 2008 by Lulu.com (Lulu Enterprises Inc, Suite 300, 860 Aviation Parkway, Morrisville, NC 27560.)

ISBN 978 1 84799 413 4

The front cover is a photograph of a well on the Canning Stock Route in the Murchison region of Western Australia.

Contents

Contents

Introduction

Arthur William Upfield is well known to aficionados of crime detection novels as the creator of the Australian Detective Inspector Napoleon Bonaparte (Bony) who appears in twenty-nine novels written over forty-two years from 1924 to 1966. It is not so well known that Upfield also wrote six other published novels, as well as many short stories and articles published in magazines and newspapers in Australia and other countries.

He was born in 1890 into a family of drapers at Gosport on Portsmouth Bay in England. An avid reader of the boys' adventure magazines popular at the time, Upfield did not do well at school. Apprenticed to a firm of estate agents, auctioneers and surveyors just before his sixteenth birthday, he was more interested in writing novels and other, more daring, escapades. In despair his father sent him to Australia in 1911, allegedly saying: "It is so far away that you will never save enough money to return."[1]

Arriving in Adelaide, Upfield soon went to the outback where he worked in a variety of jobs including fence building, boundary riding, droving and opal digging, and carried his swag to all the mainland states and the Northern Territory. He quickly developed a lasting passion for the Australian bush that laid the foundations for the rest of his life.

On the outbreak of World War I in 1914, he joined the Australian Imperial Forces and served in Egypt, Gallipoli, England and France. Returning to Australia in 1921, and probably still suffering from shell shock, he "went bush" again soon afterwards to find work as he could not tolerate working in a Melbourne factory and missed the outback lifestyle.

Upfield had continued to write desultorily, and in 1924 was persuaded by friends to "have a go" at writing professionally, drawing on his experiences in the bush.

While working on the rabbit proof fence in Western Australia in 1929, he devised, with the help of workmates and friends, a

---

[1] Hetherington J, *Forty-two Faces*, Melbourne: Cheshire, 1962, p21.

way to dispose of a body without trace - the perfect murder - for his second Bony novel, *The Sands of Windee*. Fact and fiction collided when one of those "mates", Snowy Rowles, employed that method when committing at least one, possibly three, murders. Upfield was almost charged with criminal offences, and was summoned to give evidence at Rowle's trial in Perth in 1932.[2]

After four of his novels and several short articles and stories had been published, he left the bush in 1931 to write full time and live in Perth. Two years later he moved to Melbourne to join *The Herald* newspaper, but he resumed freelance writing about six months later.

His production of short stories and articles was the most prolific from 1931 to 1940 as he sought to supplement the income from his novels. Of almost 220 published between 1917 and 1951 that I have found, about 170 were published during those nine years.

Upfield became a censor with Australian military intelligence during World War II, and in 1943, with much less time for writing, he sent some of his Bony novels to a publisher in the United States of America. The books proved very popular as Americans had become aware of Australia through their troops stationed here during the war. Most of the earlier Bony novels were published in the USA within a few years, as were those he wrote later. The extra sales allowed Upfield to live comfortably from writing mainly Bony novels until his death in 1964.

This collection contains thirty-three of his short stories. It was not always easy to determine whether an article is an autobiographical anecdote or fiction. I finally decided that if the major element of the plot could be found in either Upfield's unpublished autobiography or his official biography[3], then it should not be included in this collection.

Three of the stories, namely "Mirage Waters", "A Waif on The Nullabor" and "Four Gold Bricks", were originally published

[2] See Walker T, *Murder on the Rabbit Proof Fence*, Perth: Hesperian, 1993 for more details.
[3] The autobiography is *Beyond the Mirage*, National Library of Australia, Manuscript MS9590, 1937; and the biography is Hawke J, *Follow My Dust*, Melbourne: Heineman, 1957. For a more comprehensive and accurate biography see Lindsay T, *Arthur William Upfield: A Biography*, wwwlib.murdoch.edu.au/adt/browse/view/adt-MU20051003.113934, 2005.

under a pseudonym, Frederick Barmore. There is no doubt they were written by Upfield, as Barmore was his mother's maiden name, other unpublished articles with the same author are in his archives, and the themes and settings of the stories are similar to many others he wrote.

The stories are presented in five groups. The first nine are humorous short fiction set in the Australian outback. They read like autobiographical anecdotes as the narrator is called 'Ampshire by other characters in some of the stories, and Upfield's birthplace, Gosford, is in Hampshire County in England.

The second group of five stories explores serious themes about the hazards of living and working in the outback, themes that also permeate Upfield's novels and non-fiction.

The next seven can loosely be described as crime fiction. The first, "A Lovely Party", claims to be based on events at a Queensland station in the 1830s or 1840s, with the names of the place and the people changed. The others are clearly fiction.

There are nine stories in the penultimate group. They are comical tales written in the first person, the narrator being one Joseph Henry. The narrative style of an uneducated story teller is a feature of these stories, and the highly improbable plots leave the reader in no doubt they are fiction.

The last three are crime detection stories. Upfield enthusiasts will be pleased to read two more of his stories of this genre, but will also be disappointed that my research seems to confirm that "Wisp of Wool and Disk of Silver" is the only Bony short story he wrote. It was sent in 1948 to the *Ellery Queen's Mystery Magazine* in New York as a competition entry, but was mislaid there until 1979 when it was first published. Although it merely recycles the "perfect murder" developed for *The Sands of Windee*, a collection of Upfield's short fiction would be incomplete without it.

For Bony enthusiasts I have added the unfinished first chapter for another Bony novel. It appears Upfield started writing it on 5 September 1962, and had given it the same title, *Breakaway House*, as a novel first serialised in 1932 but not published as a book until 1987. They have nothing in common except for the titles and being set in Western Australia. Bony's wife, Marie, is the main character in this partial chapter from which we learn more about her than from all the twenty-nine finished Bony novels.

Upfield is now recognised as the first Australian writer of crime detection stories. But his books were never critically acclaimed here during his lifetime, despite their popularity in North America and Britain where crime detection had become an established form of literature. When asked, shortly before his death, about his place in Australian literature, Upfield replied:

> "I haven't one, I'm not literary – and don't want to be. I'd rather have people read my books, understand them, enjoy them. I don't want to be consigned to the oblivion reserved for our great literary figures. I'm a storyteller, not a bloody amateur writing high-falutin' rubbish."[4]

An overstatement, perhaps, but readers who empathise with that view will enjoy this collection at face value. Those who look for more in literature will find typical Upfield traits.

In all the stories he evokes contemporary speech by recording the language as spoken. His gift of painting scenes with simple words is displayed in "My Money on the Rain" where he wrote about an afternoon's fishing:

> "The fish were not interested in mutton but the turtles were, and after a little I gave up the labour of feeding them and settled to watch life about me. Along the upper reach, sand formed small islands along the edges of the lazy waterway. On many of these, cranes and storks stood on one leg and dozed; a native companion – beautiful bird! – was preening itself; and a party of red-billed, red-legged, grey Queensland ducks was fossicking among the weeds in the shallows. Now and then a solitary shag whirred by, or a wedge of teal ducks."

Upfield showed his ability to enliven action scenes in "Frozen Pumps" where he describes crossing the flooding Paroo River:

> "Grey rubble! Loose, iron-hard, baked-mud pebbles crowning wide stars of sun-baked mud, each separated by three-inch-wide, fathomless cracks. Our boots slipped on the surface rubble, gained no firm purchase for frantic feet hurrying, hurrying to Ma Slavin's pub and nearly 4,000 schooners. Above us, the relentless sun. About us, the already heated and motionless air. Below us, a strange gurgling noise as though there had come to

---

[4] "He Won't be a Literary Man", *Readers Review*, vol 10, no 12, Oct 1963, p5.

the Paroo all the giant earth-worms from Gippsland. Winded, legs like cooling lead, I fell, crawled, lurched up, fell again, crawled, again lurched up to run after the lank man who never knew fatigue."

Like his novels, Upfield set his short fiction in places he had visited while travelling around the outback, or in imaginary locations based on those places. For example, "Mice and Men", "Rainbow Gold", "Laffer's Gold", "The Demijohn" and "New Boots on Old Feet" are all set in the Murchison region of Western Australia. It is also the settings for two of his novels, namely *Breakaway House* and *Bony and the Mouse.*[5] Many other stories are set in western and northern New South Wales where Upfield spent much of his time in the bush.

They share many themes and events with his other works. There is a drought in "Why Markham Bought a Radio Set"; there are sandstorms in "The Dream That Did Not Come True", "The Mover of Mountains" and "Willi-Willi"; there are rabbit migrations in "The Grousers" and "The Great Rabbit Lure"; the risk of getting lost in the bush is highlighted in "A Waif on the Nullabor"; and the dangers of working and living alone in the bush are brought home again in "The Stalker of Lone Men" and "Hullo, Mate!"

Upfield's versatility as a writer is more clearly demonstrated in his short works than in his books. The stories in this collection range from humorous yarns to sombre tales of near death from dehydration, and from farcical comedies to deadly gun battles.

One the great values of these stories is their contribution to the chronicles of life in the Australian outback during the early decades of the twentieth century. Those lifestyles have now vanished, and the people of today are richer for being able to sample the life of those times through its literature, as well as being entertained by it.

The stories in this collection also reflect the attitudes and the ways of talking about women and Australian aborigines in that period. By selecting them I do not endorse those attitudes and opinions.

I am grateful to the late Arthur Upfield for writing the stories in the first instance, and to Bonaparte Holdings Pty Ltd for

[5] Also published as *Journey to the Hangman*.

permission to publish them. I thank the staff of the Battye Library in Perth, the National Library of Australia in Canberra, the State Library of Victoria in Melbourne, and the Mitchell Library in Sydney, who helped me to find them. And last, but not least, I am grateful to my wife, Margaret Robertson, who advised and encouraged me throughout the search and the publication process.

I hope readers enjoy these stories as much as I did collecting, selecting, editing and introducing them.

Kees de Hoog
Perth Western Australia
January 2008

The Man Who Liked Work

A boisterous gale from the Antarctic made the red gums bordering the River Darling not a little dangerous to passersby for, even on a still day, branches will fall for no apparent reason. The British elm has the same peculiarity.

It was July in New South Wales, and a most unpleasantly cold night to men whose blood had been thinned by many blistering summers. Old Joe Avery, however, was warm and contented in a roomy dugout he had built on high ground overlooking the river. Beyond the entrance was a wide shelf; beyond the shelf a drop of twenty to thirty feet to a deep hole gouged out by past floods; on the shelf itself, and opposite the dugout, a huge wood fire blazed and sang its song of companionship.

Sitting on a petrol-tin just within the dugout, Old Joe used a long sapling to lift a blackened billy-can back from the fire; and, having thrown a handful of tea into the boiling water, he pushed the billy near again to the fire, allowing it to boil till the liquid became as black as liquorice.

Dyspeptic? Decidedly not. Old Joe was eighty, and would live to be a hundred. In a not unmusical voice he told the story of The Man Who Liked Work.

I cannot honestly say (began Old Joe) that even I liked work - I mean for its own sake. I have knocked up many a good cheque by working like a maniac for twenty hours every day over a period of weeks, while on contract. But that was for good money, not because I liked work.

With Richard King it was different. To him, swinging an axe or using a pick and crowbar was a joy of which he never wearied. Even at the close of a hard day he would jump on a cook's wood-heap and make the axe sing for an hour without a stop. Work! He had work on the brain.

By birth he was a Tasmanian; by speech and manners an educated man. He was good to look on, possessing a perfect body and a face like Atlas. You would have liked Richard King, or proved yourself singularly unappreciative of the best human qualities. When he laughed, you laughed. A roaring, jumping tooth would not have stopped you laughing with him. The impish flash in his blue eyes, and a trick of raising one eyebrow almost to his hair and lower the other almost to his cheekbone when he was amused, would have made my Aunt Jane smile when she was talking about her dear departed.

We were working on Wombra Station, below Menindee, when one evening he said to me: "Joe, old pirate, the boss has offered me fifty miles of fencing at sixteen pounds a mile. What about coming in with me?"

He stood looking at me, with his eye brows all awry; but I was not going to be caught so easily, having worked with him on contract before, and knowing what it meant to keep up with him post for post. A man's pride won't let him fall behind, but there is a limit - and I had reached it.

"I will, if you agree not to work more than sixteen hours a day," says I. "I am not going to do with less than eight hours' sleep even for £100 a mile."

He laughed at that and agreed, and two days later we had established a camp at the back of the run in the pine country, and started on the post-cutting. I am not going to tell you how many posts we cut daily, because post-cutting tales cause Truth as many blushes as fish tales. But we did work those sixteen hours in the day, seven days in the week. I had been a fool in not stipulating meal-times, so that two hours were added to the sixteen, and I got only six hours' sleep.

Even that amount of sleep was too much for Richard. When I turned in he was sharpening the axes ready for the following day; in the morning, when I awoke, he was cooking the breakfast and sufficient tucker to last that day. The harder he worked the happier he became, the more he sang and laughed.

At the end of six weeks we had thousands of posts littering the country all around, which two bullock-teams carted along the line of fence. By that time I had become a human machine, beyond feeling, beyond thinking. Money? Damn the money! I wanted sleep. I wanted rest and peace, the everlasting peace beside this old "Gutter."

"Come on, old pirate!" I kind of dreamed hearing him shout at four in the morning. "Down tools, poor tired dear!" he would gibe at me at ten o'clock at night.

All day long he would sing, keeping time with his axe-strokes, whilst the white chips flew out before him. A yell of supreme happiness preceded the crash of every falling tree. In spite of midsummer heat, he worked only in trousers and boots, his body becoming as black as his sunburned face. He dwelt in paradise, I in hell.

Following the post-cutting came the erection of the fence, marked with tall sighting-sticks set by the boss. We sunk post-holes one day and stuck up the posts the next, wiring and straining the third day. The next we would sink post-holes again, and so on. Every week we built six miles of fence. Every third day we moved camp, and the camp-moving was done in our meal-time. I could have yelled for sleep. I believe I slept occasionally whilst I worked.

To give the devil his due, Richard wanted me to rest up on Sunday, being much older than he. You may be sure that I was dead game - if he would do likewise.

"Couldn't," says he. "I'd strain myself stretching."

Naturally I could not allow myself to be beaten. If he put up a 150 posts in a day, I was not satisfied with one less.

The boss - manager for a Miss Thynne, of Adelaide - paid us weekly visits, and was astonished at our speed. At first he thought we were skimping the job, not putting the posts into the ground the stipulated two foot. But he soon gave up testing them and, instead, looked at us like an asylum visitor watching a lunatic figure out on paper the number of times "Come and have one!" has been said in Australia since the War.

Came the day when we had but ten miles more to complete the job, and I was looking forward to a month's solid sleep without even waking to eat, when who should come out with the boss but Miss Thynne herself!

She was about thirty, a pretty woman, but a woman whose eyes were too steady, and whose chin had a little too much out-thrust to gain my admiration. At least that is how she struck me through the veil of sweat dropping before my eyes.

Stepping out of the buggy she gave me the kind of look a woman gives to a beetle she has trodden on, and from me her gaze wandered to Richard in the act of jamming a post into a hole.

It not being his custom to cease working when the boss spoke to him, Richard did not see Miss Thynne. He was made aware of her presence when she asked: "How many posts do you put up in a day?"

"Lost count," says he, turning towards her.

I saw the laughter die out of his face. I saw his blue eyes shine like stars. I saw her look at him with the same stunned bewilderment. For ten seconds each stared at the other.

It was a picture I shall never forget. She in her cool, white muslin dress, tall and imperial in bearing, her face slowly becoming dyed with pink, her eyes misty and large; he semi-naked, his magnificent body, arms and head bared to the sun and the wind, the muscles rippling under a rosewood skin, his head thrown back and his powerful, handsome face alight with a dawning glory.

Her lips parted, but she hardly breathed. Suddenly he sighed deeply, and then literally flung himself onto the next post to be erected.

So it was they fell in love. Three months later they were married.

There never had been any necessity for Richard King to work for a living because his interest in a chain of stores in Melbourne, left him by his father, made him independent. But, like many more, the bush had got him so hard and fast that he was never happy out of it.

Consequently, when he married Miss Thynne who hated the bush which provided her with a large income, he was compelled to sacrifice many things, the greatest being his love of work.

I quite think, when he wrote me the invitation to attend his wedding in Adelaide, that he did so with his eyebrows all aslant and a twinkle in his blue eyes. Probably he bet that I would never get there, and he would have won. With a whole week to spare I drew my cheque and started off.

I remember distinctly leaving Menindee by coach for Broken Hill, where I would train to Adelaide. I have a dim recollection of arriving at Broken Hill. There then followed a kind of blank, and when I woke up the wedding was passed by two weeks and the shanties had every penny I possessed. It is a long way from the Hill to Wombra Station - all of a hundred miles. I walked it.

I wrote a polite letter explaining that I had been taken with sudden illness at Broken Hill, and enclosed with it a private note to Richard telling him the nature of the illness. Man proposes, and Mister Booze disposes.

His reply letter read like a book, saying how sorry he was to hear of my indisposition, and telling me how, after a short honeymoon in Tasmania, they had settled up in the Adelaide Hills, about a mile beyond Glen Osmond. In another letter, later, he wanted to hear how the fellers were whom he knew.

When I wrote and told him that they were all well with the exception of Dan Riley, who had accidentally shot himself in trying to get a bead on a ten-armed man with pink eyes and blue hair who followed him for miles from Murphy's shanty, he wrote back for further particulars.

So I sent for more writing materials and set out that Dan looked a lovely corpse when we planted him, and that we had subscribed nearly sixty pounds for his poor old mother in Menindee. The next week Mum Riley was in receipt of a pension of three pounds a week for life. That was the kind of thing Richard would do.

Time passed - it might have been a year. He wrote me about once a month, being hungry for bush news, wanting to know how the river was running, and how Bill Smedley was getting along on his contract of sinking a dam on the next run. Reading between the lines, I guessed what was happening to him. The bush was beginning to pull.

They had been married eighteen months when I received a letter from Mrs. King, telling how Richard was very poorly and wanted an old bush-friend to visit him. She enclosed bank notes for twenty pounds to pay my expenses. I sent them back and said I would pay my respects the following week.

And because Richard, the blackguard who laughed at me because I could not keep his pace at work, wanted me to cheer him up, I went on the water-waggon - a thing I had never done before and have never thought of doing since. I did it because only on the water-waggon would I get beyond Broken Hill.

Reaching Menindee, I was obliged to stay at Holland's shanty for the night because the horse-coach did not leave till ten o'clock the next day. In the bar were Ted Williams and Ned McCormack on their bi-annual bender.

"Come and have one, Joe," says Ted, before I could get properly through the door.

"Right!" says I. "Mine's ginger-beer."

Ted gasped and his eyes circled about eleven times. Ned began to cry, and Bill Holland behind the bar gazed at me as though I was Lazarus.

"Ginger-beer!" I repeated. "I'm on the ice-cart, and if either of you urges me to take a man's drink I'll knock his head off."

So it was that this time I did reach Adelaide, but at what cost I could never describe. To me Adelaide always was the back-door of South Australia. In those days there was only one street worth walking through; they tell me there are now three. Wasting no time in the city, I hired a cab to take me out to Richard's house - a long, dry, thirsty drive.

We came to a large bungalow overlooking a deep gully on the one side, and on the other the city of Adelaide, with the glimmering sea beyond. Paying off the cab at the white gates, I walked up the short drive, and, coming to the deeply shaded stone verandah, I saw Richard King watching me from a wheeled invalid-chair.

Richard the axeman; Richard the lightning fencer; Richard the man with a mania for work. Yes, he sat in an invalid-chair, a rug covering his knees, wearing a flash suit and a collar. A collar, mind you, on him, Richard! One of those things, stiff as bullock-hide, with an edge like glass.

Standing on the verandah-edge, looking at him with astonishment, I saw his left brow rise to his hair and the other move downwards, and into his ghastly face came a smile of welcome. He was so altered, so utterly different from the splendid man I had known, that I could have howled. It was worse than coming across a racehorse so tangled in barb-wire that one had to shoot it.

"Well, my dear old pirate," says he, in a haw-haw tone of voice his wife must have taught him in the belief that the Governor-General spoke like it, "I'm immensely pleased to see once again that old mug. But I did not expect you."

"But I said I was coming," said I.

"You said you were coming to my wedding," says he with

dancing eyes. And to change an awkward subject I says: "Well, and what's wrong with you? Are you dead?"

"Not quite," says he seriously, looking steadily into my eyes for a full minute. "You have brought the smell of the pine and the needlewood with you, Joe. In your eyes I see the wonderful dear bush which tugs so hard at my heart. The breeze through your hair makes it shimmer like the top of a mirage in the great distance. God! I wish I were back."

"Well, why in hell don't you go back?" says I bluntly.

"Hush!" he warned. "My wife."

Following the direction of his gaze, I saw Miss Thynne that was, coming along the verandah. She was little altered, having lost none of her looks and freshness. But somehow she made me nervous.

You see, the women I knew well enough to say "How-de-do?" to were of the bush; plain, jolly women who laughed at and with you with their eyes as well as their faces. This one minded me of a school-marm who used to cane us boys harder than the master whose place she took. When Mrs. King looked at me I felt as though all my clothes had fallen off, and the feeling did not leave me when she smiled with her lips only, whilst her eyes said: "What a dreadful person!"

"This is an old friend of mine, dear," says Richard. "You will remember Joe Avery? We were together when you and I first met."

"Oh, yes! I am delighted to see you, Mr. Avery," says she.

"Don't mention it," says I, flabbergasted at the "mister."

Wheeling Richard to a small table on which she had placed a tray containing a cup of beef-tea and a biscuit, she told me: "You may talk to Richard for twenty minutes, but no longer, as he is not to be excited."

When she went into the house I felt like I used to when sent to a corner by teacher.

Looking at the beef-tea Richard was drinking out of a spoon, I says: "What's that?"

"Beef-tea," says he.

"Faugh!" I snorted. "What you want is beer, more beer, and still more beer, to put colour in your checks and strength in your limbs. What's wrong? Have you got consumption, lumbago, or shearer's knee?"

"I don't know," says he with a sigh. "Maybe it is this easy life. You see, I have nothing to do. I must not even dress myself. I can do nothing that can be tainted by the name of work. I can't fence, or dig the garden, or swing an axe. I mustn't smoke, nor must I, on any account, drink - as those vices affect my heart. If we go to Adelaide we have to use the carriage. No - I am done."

I looked at him in astonishment. Says I: "But why don't you do as you please?"

"I must do those things a gentleman should," he sighed.

Bending towards him I whispered with amazement: "Do you mean to tell me, Richard King, that you're afraid to please yourself?"

"I never please myself when by so doing I would displease my wife," says he. "At least, that has been my policy. You see the result."

"She must be doping you," says I.

When I understood properly what Richard had come to, I wanted to run amok. Barring his pale face and a flabby softness there appeared nothing wrong with him, that I could see. It struck me that he was mesmerised into believing he was ill, through lack of exercise and his wife's will-power. His love for her demanded that her slightest whim must be satisfied, and, in the greatness of his heart, he had repressed his mania for violent action to an absurd extent for her sake. He was fading away like an old lion caught and caged. Like Samson of the Bible, a woman had stolen his manhood.

At the end of twenty minutes to the second I was ordered off by Mrs. King, and conducted to a bedroom by a manservant who told me lunch would be served in half an hour.

Lunch! It was a lunch! Mrs. King ate a small portion of a mixed salad. I got down on what there was to be got, but poor Richard was given a wing of a pigeon, a thin slice of bread, and a cup of milk. My mind pictured Richard in the old days cleaning up a leg of mutton and a two pound loaf of damper at his evening meal, helped along by tea as black as coal. And now, pigeon-wings and milk. Jumping ants!

I was not allowed to see him again till after dinner, when we sat on the verandah whilst the shadows crept up to us out of the gullies. Every time I looked at Richard I felt like crying; when his wife looked at me I wanted to scream like a trapped rabbit. Yes, I felt trapped.

On the rare occasions, during the following week that I was able to talk alone with Richard, I tried with gibes and sarcasm to rouse him from his lethargy. He was being treated like a baby by a woman with a passion for nursing. A baby would have saved him. It would have taken her mind from him. As there was no baby, the saving business was up to me.

And the way came to me in a flash when, on returning from a stolen visit to the pub at Glen Osmond, I saw an old buffer divining for water in a small paddock adjoining Richard's house. Climbing through the fence, I asked him if he had located water.

"Yes, I have," says he. "I am trying to discover the direction of the stream-flow.'

"Give me the wire," says I, reaching for the copper wire on wooden handles he was using. "You are not holding it right," and I showed him the way the stream was running, and estimated it to be between sixty and eighty feet below the surface.

"I see you know something about water-divining," says he, looking me over.

"I know most of what there is to know," says I. "I've done little else but sink wells all my life. If you want a well sunk on contract, I'm on."

"Well - well," says he, looking up at the sky.

In less than half an hour I had contracted to do the job at thirty shillings a foot, plus another pound per foot when I struck solid rock, if I did. He was to supply the tools, gelignite, and sawn timber. I told him that I would work at night on account of the day heat, and would want lamps. And the less he poked about, the quicker I would do the work.

The next morning, when looking out of my window, I saw two drays unloading timber on the site, which was about 400 yards from the house. After lunch I went to Adelaide and bought two suits of dungarees, and a suitcase. On the way home I filled the suitcase with bottled beer, and planted it in the timber-stack. I was thinking that someone would want something stronger than milk and beef-tea to work on.

Now, Richard slept in a bed on a corner of the verandah, and I woke him about eleven o'clock that night, saying: "Hist! Keep quiet! Put on those dungarees. Don't argue!"

And, being used to obeying his wife, he obeyed me without hesitation. Poor devil! He could hardly stand, having almost lost the use of his legs, but I got him at last into the working togs, and, leaving our boots till we were well away, I led him back to work like leading a bullock to the abattoirs. Arrived at the timber-stack, I unearthed the suitcase, and, knocking the tops off two bottles, handed him one, saying: "Drink, pretty puppy-dog, drink!"

His eyes flashed and his jaw protruded when I lit the lamps, but I had no mercy.

"You give me any of your lip," says I, "and I'll knock you rotten - you lump of putty, you! Drink that man's drink, quick, 'cos I got a contract sinking this well here, and you're going to do your share in sinking it."

"Joe," says he, "I think you're mad."

"Richard," says I, "I know you're become a weakling. I'm going to make a man of you or kill you stone dead - so help me Bob, I am! Take this shovel and stand by."

It must have been eleven-thirty when I started picking over the first foot of earth. It was quite an hour after that that Richard had shovelled out the earth. In the lamplight his face shone with cold sweat, and was as white as his flabby arms. He tottered on his feet and his breathing came in wheezy gasps.

"Sit down, Richard, and watch me pick over the second layer," says I. "Here, have another man's drink, and take a chew off the tobacco-plug."

Without a word and in a kind of daze he took the beer and the pannikin, and drank deep. Whilst I worked I watched him regard the jet-black tobacco-plug and shudder. Then, putting it down on the suitcase, he leaned back against the timber-stack and closed his eyes.

Supposing there was something seriously wrong with him? I began to worry as I leisurely worked in the warm night air. Yes, supposing he had consumption or cancer or something? I never heard of those complaints being cured by hard work. Suppose he were to die there against the stack? A cold shiver ran up and down my back at the thought of his wife looking at me over his dead body. I'd sooner face the devil. Then I heard him mutter:

"Come on, you old pirate! Are you going to lay in bed all day?"

He was asleep. He was back again on that fifty-mile fencing-job, calling me to work when I was paralysed for the want of sleep, when I wanted to sleep for ever and ever. Like Pharaoh of old, I hardened my heart.

"Hey!" says I. "Get a holt onto that shovel and do your turn instead of loafing on me."

Again I saw the sweat streaming off him, his lips, his knees, and his hands trembling like whipped jelly. And, sitting back, I drank beer and laughed and taunted him with his weakness.

It was almost two o'clock when he had thrown out the second foot of mullock, making our total earnings that night three pounds. It was not too much, because we would slow up the deeper we went, and in well-sinking the first fifteen feet has to pay for the remainder.

Anyway, I decided to knock off. Richard was all in, and I still considered it likely that he was dying of consumption. Allowing the shovel to drop from his cramped hands, he straightened and made a half-hearted attempt to stretch his body like of old. Then, coming over to me, he sat down and says in kind of a whisper between pants: "Give me a drink."

"Glad to see you're taking a dislike to the germ-filled milk," says I. "How are you feeling?"

"Bad-d-d, bad, Joe," says he.

"Ah, well! There's consolation in knowing that you'll make a very handsome corpse," says I. "Still, don't throw a seven till you're back in bed. Come on! We'll get along home and have a hose-down from the pipe I've fixed up at the back of the stables."

Arrived at the hose-pipe, I left him, sneaking round to his bed for his pyjamas. Then, with the towels out of my room, I crept back to him, stripped off his dungarees, hosed him down like a horse, and flayed him with the towels till his skin was scarlet. Quietly I escorted him to his verandah bunk, helping him into it, and neither speaking a word. And, as I was leaving, he grabbed my hand and squeezed it.

In the morning he was still alive. He appeared quite cheerful when I asked him how the pains were that day. After lunch I slipped along to the pub with the suitcase, bringing back the lubrication for the night.

We sunk the well a further three feet that night, and the next night we put her down to eight feet. Richard still lived, and if he improved in health it was too slow to be noticeable. We started to line the sides with timber, and build a windlass, putting in about five hours every night. At the end of the week we got the well down twelve feet, and the old buffer who came messing about on Sunday was delighted.

After that first week, Richard appeared to grow stronger. We were drinking most of our earnings in bottled beer, but I cannot say if it was the beer or the work which was the actual cause of his improvement. From one suitcase full of bottles a day, I got into the habit of fetching two.

It was at the beginning of the third week that Richard refused point-blank to sit in his wheeled chair. His wife at first was astonished, and then looked as though she wanted to cry. Finally, when Richard walked up and down the verandah, head back and swinging his arms, she would have fainted had she not remembered in time that she was the strong, unbending oak.

She found it a waste of energy telling Richard how ill he was, how ill he had been, and how ill he would be. With his dressing-gown flapping against his pyjama-clad legs, he went on walking up and down, and repeating: "I'm all right, dear. You go and read your novel. Please don't worry about me."

Quite possibly she thought that the strong, unbending oak might snap off at the roots, because suddenly she bolted, and, when she had disappeared within the house, I took from my pocket Richard's eleven o'clock bottle of beer. He drank the contents out of the bottle like old times, and winked when he handed the empty bottle back to me.

Came a night when we had the well sunk to forty-seven feet. Richard was doing his two-hour spell below whilst I manned the windlass, pulling up the mullock. There was never a doubt that he was rapidly returning to his old form. No longer did he sweat like a duck shedding water. At one o'clock I called down to him: "Hey, Richard, your time's up!"

"Is it, you old pirate?" says he. "Well, I'm going to do another two hours. Beginning to enjoy myself."

"Right-oh!" says I with a grin, feeling terrible proud that my cure for general debility was working full strength.

It was a very quiet night, and the moon was near full. I never heard a sound, but I suddenly sensed that someone was behind me, and, turning my head, I found myself being regarded by Mrs. King. I sort of went icy cold all over, and the windlass crank nearly slipped out of my hand, to let a full bucket down on Richard. When I got the bucket up and pulled aside, I waited with great calmness for the end of the world; waited for the sky to pour fire and brimstone upon my uncovered head.

And then from the well came Richard's deep voice.

"Hi - Joe!" says he.

"Hullo!" says I in a kind of croak.

"Send us down a bottle of beer!" says he, loud enough to be heard down in Adelaide. "You'd better send down two bottles. I'm getting d-d-dry. And - Joe!"

"Yes," I whispered.

"Send down the tobacco-plug. I could do with a chew."

I saw stark, naked horror come into Mrs. King's wide-staring eyes. I saw a pulse in her throat throb like a twitched violin-string. When she spoke it was with effort, and her voice was no louder than a zephyr through spear-grass.

"Tell him to come up," says she.

So I hollered down the well like a drowning man yelling for help: "You've got to come up, Richard. Your wife wants you."

"Hell!" says he, looking up startled.

When he had climbed into the bucket I pulled him up, and when he reached the ground surface he gave his wife an impudent wink. Then, stepping out from the bucket, he hitched up his trousers higher round his vestless body, streaked and smeared with clay, and stretched himself like a giant. He was a man once again. He was cured.

"Hello, Edith!" says he.

"Richard," she whispered, "how long have you been doing this?"

"Ever since Joe came," says he, stooping and picking up a crowbar. "I do believe I am getting my manhood back," and he bent the bar double across his knee, whilst his eyes bored deep into hers. I saw her wilt beneath that look. The oak suddenly fell, and after all she was a woman.

"Oh, Richard!" says she, with a kind of sob. "I didn't

understand. I wanted to be a mother to you, but - but - oh, Richard, I love a man!"

And, in front of me, he took her in his arms, and, crushing her against his earth-stained chest, kissed her upturned lips. Then, when her head fell forward on his shoulder, he looked over it at me. And, with one brow raised and the other lowered, he nodded slowly towards the suitcase.

Yes, he manages Wombra these days for his wife, and he has his time cut out preventing his son becoming the occupant of the invalid-chair. His wife still has a passion for nursing.

My Money on the Rain

It had been a long, dry summer, and the anticipated usual rain in March and April had not materialised. Throughout the whole of May the sky had been cloudless.

The cook offered to bet any amount of money at even odds that it would rain on June 4. The old hands, wise in droughts, wrote I.O.U.s, and predicted that, as the autumn rains had not come, it would not rain until September, and that even if it then rained the country was faced by a drought. When the cloudless days passed in monotonous succession the old hands were joined by the young men in writing I.O.U.s for presentation to the kitchen book-maker. To vary the betting, I laid a pound at even odds that it would rain before June 4.

The Midnight Mail made a second bet on June 1, this time to coincide with mine, and the cook accepted it as cheerfully as he had accepted all the others. The Midnight Mail came to suspect the cook of having received a mulga wire concerning the rain. Even the boss became a little more confident that the dry spell would end on June 4.

June 2 was a Sunday, and, as was usual, I took a fishing line and a piece of mutton for bait up along the river to a deep hole at a bend so far removed from the track and its traffic that it was a fishers' paradise. It was a paradise, too, for the birds.

The afternoon was hot. June the second - and a hot day! I threw the baited hook into the stream just above the hole, eased myself against a grand old red gum, made a cigarette, and decided that I would not change places with an emperor.

The fish were not interested in mutton but the turtles were, and after a little I gave up the labour of feeding them and settled to watch life about me. Along the upper reach, sand formed small islands along the edges of the lazy waterway. On many of these, cranes and storks stood on one leg and dozed; a native companion - beautiful bird! - was preening itself; and a party of red-billed, red-legged, grey Queensland ducks was fossicking among the weeds in the shallows. Now and then a solitary shag whirred by, or a wedge of teal ducks.

A hot day in early June - as still and as silent as only a bushman can know it.

Quite abruptly, the sun went out.

Looking to westward I saw my pound plus one of the cook's pounds, sweeping across the sky towards me in the form of a knife-edged bank of dark clouds.

The shadow which had fallen on the river produced strange results. A pair of unsuspected kookaburras in a tree above me burst forth in high glee. A flock of galahs in an opposite tree took to the wing. The cranes and the native companion casually walked off their sand banks into the shallows. Beyond them appeared nine pelicans, swimming to the centre of the stream. On the surface of the water above the great hole for a moment swam a cod as long as my arm.

And then, looking at the darkening sky through the trunks of the red gums bordering the far side of the river, I saw fall a huge living branch.

Knowing how the red gum's branches will fall without warning on hot days - due, I think, to the sap being driven out of the branches into the trunk - and looking upward to discover that I then lounged beneath a three-ton branch, a change of position was clearly indicated.

The ducks were waddling over the sand banks. The native companion and the cranes were standing like statues, or as though in the mirror-like surface of the water they saw the head of Medusa.

Actually, they were tensely waiting.

The cook's pound and my own were coming nearer to my hand every second. The edge of the cloud belt had reached the zenith. Still the wind delayed in ruffling the water - even the ducks were now motionless, crouched on the sand-banks. The kookaburra chuckled as though wanting to scream, yet they dared not for fear of being fooled. A wagtail danced on a twig almost touching my boots. Nothing in all the world could keep IT still.

Then, along the skyline presented by the top of the opposite bank, rose swiftly a red-brown fog against the black clouds. Dust! Wind! That was what the birds were waiting for - the wind. The wind would lash the surface water into foam, and the big fish would come up out of the deep hole to chase the turtles into the shallows where the wading birds waited with such confidence.

The blue sky was now a swiftly narrowing strip. A drop of rain fell upon the stream sending outward a ring to rival those made by the now active small fish. My pound and the cook's were within my greedy grasp.

When the dust cloud was higher than the opposite trees, the moment had come to seek shelter. The wagtail and I climbed the steep bank together, for the bird took but half-foot jumps. Looking back, I saw that the water birds were still motionless. The stump of a great red gum provided shelter in its lee.

Abruptly the wind rose. It came from the east with steady pressure sweeping countless leaves and small twigs into the sullen river. Every bird in the branches of the river avenue rose to wing and to scream defiance. When the east wind died, as suddenly as it had risen, the birds at once settled again among the foliage. The water birds were hidden from me, but I knew that they were banqueting. Two seconds later the west wind arrived - and the dust.

A red-brown fog rolled across the world. I thought the wind had swept away the wagtail which had been dancing beneath a shrub, but I discovered him dancing on the ground in the wind shelter formed by my boots.

Another drop of rain fell. It was the second - and the last. The fog thinned, vanished among the trees eastward. The wind died down. The sun came out again two hands' breadth above the western horizon. The cloud bank passed, its western edge as clear cut as had been its eastern edge.

The cook said: "I told you it wouldn't rain before June the fourth."

What the Midnight Mail said cannot be recorded!

About two o'clock on the morning of June 4 the cook came into the bunk-house to invite all hands to: "Come out and see 'er coming."

We went out. The moon, then two hours to setting, shone on a pure white, mile-deep cloud which sailed the eastern sky. In that great aerial iceberg lightning flickered. The quietness of the night permitted us to hear the roar of the water falling from it nine miles away.

As we breakfasted, black clouds were racing across the sky beneath a dark, grey pall. It began to rain at eleven o'clock. It rained incessantly for three days and nights.

"'Ow jew know it was gonna rain?" demanded the Midnight Mail.

"It always rains on me birthday," the cook replied, licking his lips. "There's never no drought till all a dry winter 'as gone."

Mice and Men

With Bill Townley and Niagara Spence I was sinking a well on station property bordering the 1300-mile-long No. 1 Rabbit-proof Fence in Westralia. The Coffin Maker was riding that section of fence which passed close to the job, a section of 163 miles, with the town of Burracoppin on the south end and the Government Camel Station marking the north end.

Son and grandson of an undertaker, he had deserted the family calling, but could not throw off its influence. He carried the atmosphere of the churchyard with him, and at all times his aspect was funereal.

Niagara Spence was old in all bar muscles and voice. He was white-haired, blue-eyed, pink-complexioned, and fourteen stone in weight. When he conversed, one could hear him distinctly at a distance of a hundred yards; when he raised his voice at the bottom of a sixty-foot well, the sides threatened to cave in. An airman a thousand feet up could have heard him.

As for Bill Townley, he was nothing much to write home about. After the holiday he took subsequent to selling his share in Townley's Reward for £7,000, he seemed never to be of this world. He had no opinions about anything. To everything said by his friend of many years, Niagara Spence, he would reply without enthusiasm: "Too right."

The Coffin Maker arrived at the camp on December 10 with his covered two-wheel cart drawn by two camels in tandem harness. Then, on his way north, he was to reach the Camel Station the following day, stay there for four days - one day for each Sunday he had spent on the track - and return on December 16 on his way south to Burracoppin.

Having worked all this out with the aid of stones, Niagara Spence suggested that, if The Coffin Maker would be so obliging, we could leave with him on his southward trip and reach Burracoppin in time to be properly drunk on Christmas Day.

"Too right," agreed Townley in a manner which was not exclamatory.

The Coffin Maker looked gloomily into the fire, sadly cut

tobacco chips from his plug without once looking at it, and after a period of inward calculation gave his verdict.

"Well, I leaves 'ere on the sixteenth. I gets to the 144-mile the next day; the 126-mile the day after that; the 96-mile on the nineteenth; the 69-mile on the twentieth; the next day the 46-mile; the day after that the 27-mile; the 9-mile the on the twenty-third; and we goes in on Christmas Eve."

"That ain't no good! We'll want a day to get heated up properly," objected Niagara Spence, as though The Coffin Maker had offered insult somewhere among his careful calculations.

"Too right," agreed Townley.

With unrelieved gloom The Coffin Maker indulged in further thought. Then still without hope he said:

"If you blokes could be ready on the track with the billy boiled when I come along on the sixteenth, I'd get away from the Camel Station early, and we could make the 144-mile that night instead of me campin' 'ere. Then we could hit Burracoppin the day before Christmas Eve."

That night the conversation was kept to the one subject - alcoholic refreshment as represented by pubs and shanties, cheques and chequemen, the best bedroom for the spender and the woodheap for the stiff. This subject, with its sub-points, enabled Bill Townley to open out and describe how he spent his £7,000 in eighteen months on whisky and "a widder woman."

And throughout the evening The Coffin Maker sat on his tuckerbox, smoking and gazing at the heart of the fire, as though the world were lost and damn well lost.

He was well on time when we saw his camels and cart coming down the breakaway at the 154-mile post on the sixteenth, and when he reached us, waiting beside the road with the tea made and lunch ready and the swags rolled, it was not much after twelve o'clock,

"I put in two flash 'uns," he explained when the leader was dancing on electrified feet, and the shafter was formed into the letter S so that he might look back at the cart and at us,

I assisted The Coffin Maker to rope the leader by the neck to a stout mulga, and to short-hobble them both, and whilst we ate the shafter pulled the wheel-locked cart forward and threatened to spear the leader with the point of one of the shafts. The leader twisted herself round the tree like a grape-vine. Without the slightest doubt they were, indeed, "flash 'uns."

Even the casual Coffin Maker thought it wise not to lounge at the dinner camp for a smoke, but to get away along the track before either camel lost its reason altogether. Having packed the tuckerbox and the swags into the cart, and having instructed Townley and Niagara to climb up and take their seats, we unhobbled the mokes, disentangled the leader from the tree, straightened up the team and let them go.

The Coffin Maker had locked the wheels, but this was as nothing, for with mighty plunges the camels got into a gallop in three yards. I grabbed at the tailboard as the vehicle passed me, and The Coffin Maker then climbed up the one back step into the cart and took the long reins attached to the leader's halter from the calloused hands of old Townley. The speed being greater than a man could run, I, too, climbed up on the back step, resting there with my right foot on it and with my left ready to move the brake-handle. Before me, through the tall cart-hood, rose and fell the swell of galloping camels' humps.

"This'll do us," remarked Niagara Spence, quite pleased that we were doing about fifteen miles an hour despite the locked wheels.

"Too right!" agreed Townley with remarkable fervor.

"Pull 'em up!", I urged. "If you don't they'll blow out."

"Pull 'em up, be cursed! Sool 'em up, you mean. We'll get to Burracoppin tomorrer at this rate," remarked Niagara.

"It'll take the sting out of 'em, any'ow," predicted The Coffin Maker, as though he referred to the weather reports. "Ease orf that brake, 'Ampshire."

When I made a further plea for sanity, I was roundly cursed, so I eased off the brake and the wheels began to revolve. The speed then rose to about twenty-five miles an hour, and the endless fence posts flashed by.

Three miles were covered thus, the shafter skillfully keeping the cart-wheels from striking the fence on the one side and the mulga trunks on the other. I blessed Irish, the man who originally had broken him in.

Bill Townley was loading his pipe and settling down for an afternoon's gallop, and I could see Niagara licking his upper lip as though there clung to it the foam of beer, when the shafter abruptly faltered. As though it spoke to the leader, the leader pulled up to a walk.

Then they stopped, fell on their knees and relaxed.

As I had predicted, the camels had "blown out." And no method conceived by man could make camels in that condition get up before they chose to do so.

Those two camels did not get up for two night and two days. For the latter part of one day and throughout the whole of the second day we sat with our backs against the fence looking at them.

We arrived in Burracoppin just in time to celebrate New Year's Day.

The Dream That Did Not Come True

The reason why the Midnight Mail married the Paroo Parrot always remained obscure, for through marriage both appeared to lose much more than they gained. There was the Midnight Mail knocking up good cheques; leaving a job when he wished to walk hundreds of miles with his swag lashed to his pedal-less bicycle; as free as the birds and as unmindful of the future.

And there was the Paroo Parrot, who, with her tribe of children, drove small mobs of sheep to the Burke butchers, or took young rams from the railway station to the stations through which runs the Paroo River - about once every eighty years. It may be that she was more far-seeing than the birds and the Midnight Mail, but, for all that, one could not see how she gained through marriage.

In a roundabout way we had heard about the wedding, and of the home the Midnight Mail made for his bride on the outskirts of Wilcannia; and then, to our further astonishment, in less than a month from the wedding day, the bridegroom turned up to accept a fencing contract at Momba.

To Momba came the Midnight Mail with his pedal-less bike and much gear loaded on the buckboard formerly belonging to the Paroo Parrot. He wanted a mate, and it happened that I wanted a change of scene.

"I got eleven mile at eighteen pounds a mile," he explained while carving my tobacco plug. "I've got the plant and we'll go fifty-fifty in tucker, drill bits, and the cheque. It's easy country, and we'll slip through it like a hot knife through fat."

"What do you want to take a fencing contract in December for?" I asked him complainingly, when, a week later, we were slaving from dawn till dark cutting pine posts.

At that his eyes lit up and the hairs of his grey moustache trembled like cats' whiskers. For an instant his long, wiry form relaxed against his axe, and down his face and chest ran glistening drops of sweat.

"Can't beat the summer for hard work," he replied, cheerfully.

"A man likes tea-drinkin' in summer better'n in winter. In winter 'is muscles is too cramped up."

There was no possibility of cramped muscles during three months.

"Come on! Day's breakin'! Breakfast's ready!" invariably was his morning greeting; and at the end of that long day, when I was so tired that to move was painful, when my hands were smeared with mutton fat and wrapped in rags, he would cheerfully set to work making a damper and boiling salt mutton for the morrow.

"When we gits through this job, 'Ampshire, you and me will go inter Wilcannia, and you can come an' camp with us. We got a good 'ouse with a south verandee, and on that verandee we'll lie in deck chairs and drink nice cold beer," was the vision he constantly created when the temperature was around 100 and from the flies there was no escape. "My ole woman ain't one of them miserable souls, an' we can send young Alf to the Globe with a cuppler jugs. Come night we can take a stroll round the town and have a schooner or two with any of the boys 'appening to be on a bust."

"Sounds good."

"Good! Course it's good! Here's me, sixty-two come next May. For nigh forty years I been tearing up and down Noo South. No comfort, no ease in me old age. Marriage! Why, marriage is the greatest invention of any. What more can a man want that a lovin' woman ministerin' to 'is needs?"

I agreed – even though I had known the Parroo Parrot for several years.

Every night did the Midnight Mail discourse on the haven on that south verandah in company with jugs of beer. I got to know the habits and the dispositions of the many step-children, and I came to know more about the Paroo Parrot than an unmarried man should have known. I dreamed about the deck chairs in which I need not move one solitary muscle for hours, and of the cool verandah and a team of bare-legged youngsters carrying away empty jugs and returning with jugs capped with foam.

"You'll be all right once we get 'ome," the Midnight Mail assured me when, our contract finished, we drove away from Momba on the forty-five-mile journey to 'the Queen City of the West.'

"Ah! A lovin' woman's gentle 'ands arrangin' the cushions and puttin' a jam case under your feet! A table between us and jugs of ale at our elbows!"

Ah, rest! Blessed ease!

"Drive the mokes faster so's we can get there sooner," I pleaded. "My back! Lean forward while I arrange this wogga over the back of the seat."

"Don't you worry, 'Ampshire," he further assured me. "Just now you're a bit run down like. You wants lookin' after. Marriage! A woman's lovin' hands -"

All that day we jogged along on the high seat of the buckboard which again contained the pedal-less bike in addition to the fencer's outfit. My partner swore he would never move without that machine. It had been his friend and his mistress in the days when he delighted - and had been free - to walk and push it at night in preference to the day.

It was early March and the still heat shimmering above the scrub-bordered track was terrific. In a kind of stupor I lived through the hours listening to the tale of a cool south verandah. That night we camped at a station dam. The next day it was hotter still. The dust rose behind us to hover motionless in the air. I was so stiff that every little jar tortured me.

"Gonna git a storm."

That aroused me to look up at the sky. The sun was a little after three o'clock. It was the colour of blood, semi-masked by a high, grey haze.

"Wind," ejaculated the Midnight Mail. "Hope it won't come till tomorrer. We'll keep going and get to Wilcannia about nine tonight. We'll 'ave a brush up and then we'll slip along to the Globe for a schooner or two."

"But the deck chairs - the verandah shade - the jugs of beer?"

"That'll start as of six in the morning. The pubs don't open till six."

We were watering the horses at the Government Tank about seven miles out of Wilcannia when the storm heaved itself above the long hill range to the west. So dark was the smother of sand that the hills themselves appeared to rise swiftly into towering mountains.

"Better camp," advised the man in charge of the dam.

"I reckon," agreed the Midnight Mail regretfully.

Removing the harness, we let the horses loose in a small paddock and rushed to the shelter of the dam-keeper's hut. The wind sprang up from the east. The sun went out - flick. The ramshackle hut swayed and rattled beneath the force of the east wind sweeping eagerly to meet the dust storm.

"Shut the door. Good job there ain't no winders," said the dam-keeper.

"Why in 'ell couldn't it 'ave kept orf till tomorrer?" growled my mate, slamming shut the door at the instant that daylight failed.

In the gloom, the dam-keeper crouched over the fire urging the billy to boil. There came a lull of grave-like stillness. Then the first buffet of the west wind, and the gloom was deepened by the sand and dust which hissed against the iron walls and roof, and entered through a thousand chinks.

We ate and drank. The damper and the slabs of salt meat were encrusted with sand, coloured a light reddish-brown, and on the tea in our tin pannikins lay a scum of dust. Later we rolled in our nap on the floor. When I was awakened, I asked the usual question: "Day breaking?"

"It broke two hours ago."

Two hours ago! It was as dark as the false dawn. All that day we were crouched on the floor expecting the hut to be blown from off us. We drank tea and ate the last of the cooked food. To cook more was impossible. All that day and night, and all the next day and night, the sandstorm kept us prisoner in the crazy hut. The third morning the sun rose as though such things as wind and sand never existed.

"Ah, now we shan't be long, 'Ampshire," remarked the Midnight Mail cheerfully. "We'll be lying in them deck chairs smoking and drinking cold beer before noon."

"What about a feed?" I inquired anxiously.

"Tucker! You bet! My ole woman can cook. I'll say that about 'er. Great woman on cookin'. She'll 'ave a feed ready fer us in five minutes. Whiles she's gettin' we'll send young Alf orf with a coupler jugs."

Eventually we arrived.

The verandah was unfloored. I saw no deck chairs. It was

occupied by three small children, seven or eight hens, a family of pups and two milking goats. As we drove up to the back door five other children raced out to greet us - half naked, healthy sun-urchins. The last to emerge from the warren was the Paroo Parrot herself.

"So you've come 'ome, 'ave you?" she demanded.

She was little and wiry, with small washed out brown eyes and rat-trap mouth. The back of her skirt almost touched the ground, and the front hem almost reached to her bare knees.

"Yes, dear, I've come 'ome," agreed her spouse. "A cheque's in me pocket and a good mate's alongside me." To a lanky youth the Midnight Mail added in a roar: "Alf, go along to the Globe and fetch a gallon of beer. Tell 'em that yer father's come 'ome and will pay for it later."

"That's right, Alf," agreed the Paroo Parrot with what struck me as sinister alacrity. Then she screamed at another youth: "Bill, you go and borrow the wheelbarrer of'n Mrs. Tinley. You others, you 'unt up a shovel. It's over there on the ash-heap, I think."

We unharnessed the horses, and a youngster named Enery took them to the town common. We approached the house at the same time as did the barrow and the shovel.

Within the house was a sandhill. In places the sand was a foot deep on the floor. Excepting the kitchen table and several jam cases, evidently used that morning for breakfast, every article of furniture, every wall projection, was loaded with sand as tree branches are loaded with snow on the highlands. The woman screamed at us; the children got in the way. The Midnight Mail laboured with the shovel, and I laboured with the barrow. I wheeled it out of the house and to the ash-heap at least seventy loads of sand.

Deck chairs! A shady verandah! Glass jugs kept filled with beer!

I was glad to drink out of a tin pannikin. We ate standing up and battled with the flies for the food. About three o'clock I grabbed my swag off the buckboard and made my way to the Globe Hotel.

The Midnight Mail turned up the next morning.

"There's a fencing contract going out on Grimpa," he said, his blue eyes sad, the corners of his mouth sagging.

"I am going to camp here for a week," I told him firmly.

"Aw, come on! Let's get out of town," he pleaded. "The ole woman's got me cheque."

"Hard luck! I'll lend you a tenner."

At that he brightened, and then gave indubitable evidence that already he had learned the married man's craft, or graft.

"Will you? All right. But I won't take it all at once. Gimme a half-note now and then."

I felt sorry for the Midnight Mail. His wanderings were over. His wings were clipped. Beer in glass jugs! A shady verandah! Marriage! Meals served by the "lovin' 'ands of a woman." I felt sorry, too, for the Paroo Parrot, living in that house after years of freedom spent on the great mulga lands west of the Darling.

We left for the Grimpa contract well within the week.

George's Accommodating Brother

"When we get round this bend we must step on it," George said as we approached a line of sand-dunes which, stabbing the river's elbow from across the wide, grey flats, recalled a different world to that of gum-trees, cool shadows and running water.

We were travelling southward, swags up, billies and waterbags empty. We were travelling light and fast, with cheques in our pockets and the alkaloids of a year's drinking of surface water coating our throats. Little more than one mile ahead was a supply of that which is the most efficacious remover of alkaloids in this world.

On reaching the summit of the sand-dunes physical effort was forgotten by the sight of One-tree Halt dancing and shimmering in the heat haze. Even the one tall red-gum growing in the centre of the township shimmered and jazzed.

"Come on!" urged George. "Step on it! Young Ted will be up that tree looking out for chequemen."

When a youth appeared frantically pedalling a bicycle towards us, George heaved a deep sigh. His swag was twice as big as mine but his body was only half as large. His red hair and wild whiskers rivalled any morning-glory.

"Hullo, Ted!" he cried when the youth dismounted.

"Day, Mr. West," replied the boy, grinning widely. From the basket on the front carrier he produced two bottles of beer and two thin glasses. "Mrs. O'Murphy sent me along to welcome you to One-tree Halt," he recited easily. "She sends her compliments, and she says as how she 'as your rooms ready.'"

"Take the empties back, and tell her we'll be seeing her in ten minutes," George said when he regained his wind. The boy rode off back with the empties and the glasses, and with even greater speed we moved upon the town.

On the outskirts were the usual mobs of goats fossicking round the usual bag-and-petrol-tin humpies; then the brick-built police station and the rambling Darling Hotel opposite. Beside the hotel was a store.

We plugged along the main street unmarked by sidewalks, and came at last to the home of our dreams - The Coach Exchange, owned by Mrs. O'Murphy, which stood in the shadow of the solitary gum-tree. Beyond, further down the street, was another store, a third hotel, the post office, more petrol-tin humpies and more mobs of goats. The next minute we were reclining against a bar counter, and were being served with deep-nose-ers by a diminutive woman of great age whose broad smile did not quite iron out the glint in her hard blue eyes.

"Well, this is a surprise, Mr. West," gushed Mrs. O'Murphy for the tenth time. George called her Ma. "Where have ye come from an' all?"

"Me an' 'Ampshire has been workin' - fill 'em up, please. Me an' Ampshire been up on Talarra for more'n twelve munse," George managed to say between swallows, and I saw the brain behind the blue eyes rapidly calculating the strength of our cheques. Time passed pleasantly.

"Now, you boys," chirped Mrs. O'Murphy an hour later, when a heavy triangle was beaten somewhere back of the house. "Go and wash. Dinner's ready. Your room's Number Eleven."

George stationed me at the door of our bedroom whilst he conducted a searching examination to discover an efficient plant for our money, we having agreed to pool our wealth and draw from it a fiver each every day. He had cashed his cheque with Mrs. O'Murphy before the haze thickened, and, by prising outward a section of skirting-board with a knife, he slipped my cheque and a roll of notes behind it. When the knife was removed, the board sprang back again against the wall, and imprisoned the wad.

Dusk was creeping over the peaceful town when the north-bound coach pulled out. I met Ted coming down the ladder nailed to the mighty trunk of the tree growing just outside the bar, and I asked him point-blank what work he did up there among its branches. Each freckle on his round face drew wider apart when he smiled, and one forgot the ragged trousers and the old shirt in the beam of that smile.

"I lives up this tree most all day," he stated with pride. "Old Ma pays me a quid a week and tucker to keep a lookout for chequemen. From the top of that tree I can see for miles. I can see everythink wot comes round Sandy Bend, as well as wot comes across Wide Flat to the south. When I sees a chequeman coming I reports to Ma, and she sends me off on the bike with a bottle or two of beer and a kind welcome. You see, all the chequemen 'as got to pass one or other of the other pubs before they can hit Ma's joint, and if they weren't met properly not one of 'em would get this far, Ma's pub being in the middle of the town, like."

Asked how he knew a chequeman from a stiff on tramp, he readily explained.

"I can tell that easy enough. If they're stiff they just ambles. If they're chequemen, they trots. Over the last two years I only made one mistake." He was about to depart with a shilling tip when he turned back to whisper: "You keep yer money well down south, or you'll be eatin' galah quicker than you'll have to."

Unenlightened on the subject of diet, I watched him till he disappeared round the building, and then waited to see the arrival of the south-bound coach drawn in by five weary horses and bringing four thirsty passengers. A person having but one eye attached himself to me with touching affection, and from him I learned that Ma O'Murphy's mother had been the founder of the hotel and of One-tree Halt. As the place grew around the pub and the yards for Cobb and Co.'s horses, in course of time a hotel had been erected on her either flank, taking from her hotel some of the cream of the business. Hence the employment of Ted, first to announce the coming, and then to meet all chequemen with refreshment before they could reach one of the opposition hotels. My affectionate friend estimated Ma's roll at £50,000.

It quickly became evident that George would not run away should Mrs. O'Murphy ask him to marry her, her husband long since having drunk himself to death. George had had his hair and beard trimmed. He wore his best clothes, and kept them well brushed and creased, and he refrained from getting properly drunk despite the fact that what he did consume would have paralysed an ordinary man.

For three consecutive nights did Ma O'Murphy visit us in the small hours. With a "Are you boys quite comfortable?" she sidled into the bedroom. Believing us to be asleep, she thoughtfully went through our clothes, and even slipped her hand beneath our pillows. As thoughtfully, she refrained from taking the loose change from the dressing-table.

In her dining-room we occupied places of honour at the long table, above which on the wall hung a full-length picture of the Iron Duke. At a smaller table were placed those guests who no longer were chequemen, whose money had been transferred to Ma's till, and who were living on credit whilst allegedly preparing for the track. Every mealtime Ma would first come round our table to ask if we would take a slice of beef or a cut of mutton. To those at the smaller table she would say: "Will ye be havin' a cut o' goot, or will ye take a bit o' galah?"

One to whom a little credit still remained might choose goat and get it. Should, however, there be any present whose credit had completely vanished, and who had the temerity to select goat, Ma would hiss: "Indade ye won't. Ye'll be havin' a bit o' galah."

We, in our state of affluence, were ever confronted by the ultimate "bit o' galah." Galahs were the inevitable fare of all chequemen staying at Ma O'Murphy's. It was as though they slid down a greased incline, tossing shillings as quickly as possible into Ma's till and eating beef and mutton until, having no more shillings to toss, they arrived at the bottom where many galahs awaited their mastication.

Down and down towards the galahs slid George and I. Our money plant was shrivelling with alarming rapidity. When Ma asked George how we were enjoying our rest from labour, he admitted that soon we would have to return to those labours if he could not induce his wealthy brother in Adelaide to send him some money. That afternoon he intended to dispatch an urgent telegram seeking financial assistance.

Into the beady blue eyes leapt the first flash of coldness that was so closely allied to a "bit o' galah," but the next morning, when the postboy brought George a telegram, and when on opening it George smiled and shouted snifters all round, Ma tried hard to see how much money had been wired, and she still smiled when George walked down the street to collect.

Without doubt George's brother in Adelaide was a trump. Every week George sent off a wire, and every week he received a telegram which took him to the post office. After many weeks had passed the goats and the galahs withdrew into the mists of improbability.

One telegram received by George, however, mystified me. I found it on our bedroom floor. It read: "Sorry. Cannot supply paint you require. - Icor and Company."

A week or so later I found another of George's telegrams. It read: "Regret unable to supply book asked for. - Book Marks."

The period of our alcoholic splendor extended to months. We were the most popular men who ever had stayed at Ma's pub.

Then there arrived one day on the coach from Cobar two city men who said they had come to purchase a site and to let the contract for the building of a branch bank.

Ma said that a bank had long been wanted at One-tree Halt. George was silent. I was not greatly interested because George's accommodating brother was going to live for ever. We sat on the verandah between drinks, idly watching the new bank going up, and the further it went up the longer lasted George's fits of depression.

Chequeman after chequeman was reported by the tree-dweller; was met by the tree-dweller with bottles of beer and Ma's compliments; finally arrived to be effusively welcomed. Chequeman after chequeman slithered down the money incline, tossing their shillings into the till, finally to be severely told: "Indade, ye won't. Ye'll be havin' a bit o' galah." Every time I heard that hissed into the ear of some poor devil I gave thanks to George's brother in Adelaide.

The bank building was at last finished, and on the day it opened for business we ate breakfast in an unusual silence. Afterwards, George and I sat on the verandah and watched the new manager go across to the building and let himself in. George muttered something about the crimson money monsters battening on the poor. Punctually at ten o'clock the door was thrown open, and that appeared to be the signal for Ma O'Murphy to walk out of her bar door with a well-filled paper bag clutched in her hands. She smiled at George, and then quickly crossed the track to the bank. When she disappeared inside George sighed as though in pain.

Two stiffs came and stung me for ten shillings. Ted came down the tree ladder in a great hurry with the news that another chequeman was in sight. Without waiting orders from Ma, he obtained a bottle of beer from the yardman who was looking after the bar, and a second later he was racing off on his bike. The policeman's dog chased a cat into the store opposite the post office, whence came a woman's screams, a man's oaths, smashing crockery and a dog's frantic yelps.

Through it all George remained in pensive gloom.

From that day we lived in a shadow. The flow of ale did not diminish, but henceforth George received no more telegrams.

At the end of the following week our decline came, and came swiftly. Ma was distinctly disappointed when George asked for a couple of deep-nose-ers and requested that a note of the transaction be made on the slate. That was during the morning. At lunch we were moved to the smaller table in the dining-room.

"Will ye be havin' a cut o' goot or a bit o' galah?" asked Ma.

George selected goat, and got it. I nominated galah, determined to get used to poultry as quickly as possible. However the following morning we rolled our swags.

"What! Are ye lavin'?" said the astonished landlady.

"Yes. We gotta knock up another cheque apiece. That brother of mine in Adelaide 'as gone an' died on us," George explained.

"Well, well! Ye'll be havin' a deep-nose-er on me afore ye pull out. An' ye'll be goin' along to the cook for to fill yer gunny-sacks for the track. My - my! What a time ye've had! I've enjoyed yer stay, and I'll be lookin' for to see ye again soon."

I ticked up a bottle of whisky, and, with exceptional care and restraint, eventually we regained normality and came to view the break at Ma O'Murphy's pub in its true perspective.

One evening when fishing, or pretending to because the fish wouldn't bite, George said, chuckling:

"We 'ad a good spin, any'ow. Some blokes would have gone too deep early in the piece. Moderation in all things is my motter."

"How much do you owe your brother?" I asked.

George grinned and winked. "Nothink," he said. "Sending away for stuff I knew them firms wouldn't stock and getting my reply-paid telegrams back was just a blind to keep nasty suspicions from giving old Ma insomnia. She give me insomnia once when she pinched me roll the first night I camped there, leaving me only six and ninepence on the dressing-table. That's 'er way of doing business, and I ain't cryin' it down. If a man's a mug he deserves a kick in the neck to remind him of it. This time, I does a bit of snoopin' round after the bar shuts down, and I seen Ma putting away her takings in a box wot she had in a hole in the wall behind that picture of the Dook of Wellington. After that I went to her plant every week to take out some of our money to spend over and over again. Ma 'ad 'undreds of pounds in that box, but I was honest enough only to take out enough to keep us going comfortably from week to week.

"Of course, when they opened that damned bank it meant good-bye to my dear brother in Adelaide, and a course of fifty-year-old galahs. That's the worst of being honest. An honest man never gets anywhere bar the long, long track. The night before the bank opened I should have taken all of Ma's roll, but I just couldn't be a thief."

Sunset Joe's Goanna

He lived, did Sunset Joe, in a stockman's hut on Telshe Station which, you might know, occupies the dead centre of South Australia. Its position has long been proven by Goanna Bill, who drew lines on a map of the State from its opposite corners. Where the lines crossed, there was the Telshe homestead.

Twenty miles west, or near enough to make no difference, of the homestead was Sunset Joe's hut, where he was lord of all he surveyed over about two hundred square miles. Sunset Joe lived alone most of his time, his nearest neighbours being a mob of blacks that lived a mile down the creek when not on walkabout.

The hut was twenty miles west of the homestead, and the station's western boundary was ten miles west of the hut. Half a mile beyond the boundary, at a place named Pine Ridge, Goanna Bill also lived in solitary state. Then nine miles to the south, well on a gibber plain, was Regan's Pub, which was built in the Year One. And a mile away from Regan's Pub was the township of Hell's Hobs, sprawled around the poppet heads of the mine which had been opened up in comparatively recent times.

In this district ten miles were but an evening stroll, but although they were near neighbours, Goanna Bill and Sunset Joe were not exactly neighbourly. When by chance they happened to be riding the boundary fence and met, the occasion was invariably marked by much sarcastic abuse and mutual invitation to "hop over here and see what you can do!" It was all rather peculiar, because when they met in Regan's Pub they were the closest of friends.

For many years these two enemy-friends held a two-horse race meeting every Christmas Eve outside Regan's Pub where the track is wide and straight. At each meeting, each invariably put up fifty pounds. The race began a mile from the pub and ended at the pub door, and the winner collected the fifty from the loser, and together they would breast the bar when the winner would hand over to Regan a hundred pounds with the command to shout it to the world when the money was cut out - if the police did not storm the place before that dread moment.

Here, then, were two remarkable men living on either side of a boundary fence, and this was their history up to the time I met Goanna Bill three days before Christmas Eve. At once I was charmed by the short, tubby, clean-shaven, white-haired and blue-eyed little man astride a bored roan mare. I gave the message to Goanna Bill which had been entrusted to me by Sunset Joe. It was to the effect that Sunset had a moke he was sure would knock spots off anything Goanna Bill could run this year.

The message was received in gloomy silence. In silence we rode either side of the fence for two miles. It could be seen that Goanna Bill was much perturbed by such a blatant challenge. Now and then he would remove his hat, all marked and burned by the red-hot handles of billycans, and scratch the back of his head.

"Me 'an Sunset 'as raced to Regan's Pub every year for the past twenty years," he said sadly. "I've won eleven times; he's won nine times. That narks 'im and pleases me. But this year I ain't got no 'orse wot would stand a chance against a keb 'orse. Whitefoot, wot I rode last year, went and got a stake in her offside fetlock only last week, and she won't be fit ter race for munse."

For another mile we rode in silence, and then Goanna Bill began to chuckle and to slap the old mare's neck.

"I got it, 'Ampshire!" he shouted. "You tell ole Sunset that I ain't got no 'orse fit to exert beyond a canter. Tell 'im I wouldn't fear no 'orse he's got if I 'ad a hanimile wot could gallop. But you can say that I've got a likely lookin' reptile wot I'll race against anythink in the reptile line 'e can run agin it. I'll 'ave my Melbourne Queen half a mile this side of Regan's Pub at ten sharp on Christmas Eve. Tell 'im that, 'Ampshire! Tell 'im that!"

"All right. But what kind of a reptile is this Melbourne Queen?"

"She's a real, proper, racin' goanna with plenty of toe and quiet enough to be 'andled by a lady," replied the little man proudly. "I picked 'er out of six wot I collected a month back. Yes - that'll 'ave to be it. Me and Sunset will race goannas this Christmas. If 'e don't like the idea, you tell 'im that I'll lay one 'undred quid against 'is fifty quid that my goanna will beat 'is."

Having heard of goanna races, but never having witnessed one, I agreed to convey Goanna Bill's challenge to Sunset Joe, and further agreed to leave Sunset's decision on a certain fence post at noon the next day. I had dinner ready when Sunset got home that night.

"Well, what did that pot-bellied skite have to say?" he demanded when he strode into the hut from the washing basin, and was drying his flaming hair and whiskers with a striped towel.

"He says that he hasn't a horse fit to race this year," I replied.

"What! No horse fit to race!" The giant's body was so stiffened by the effect of his astonishment that a push in the face would have knocked him backward like a toy soldier. "Why, we have raced every Christmas Eve for twenty years! It won't be Christmas at all if me and Goanna Bill don't race to Regan's Pub."

I allowed him time to set to on the grilled steak before I presented Goanna Bill's challenge.

"Stiffen the crows! What does he take me for?" Sunset roared. The fat of grilled steak made his brilliant whiskers gleam with fire. His enormous red-haired fore-arms encircled his tin plate like the jaws of red hot pincers. After exhaling a deep breath, he snorted: "Racing goannas! Racing nothing! If he ain't got a horse, I'll race him on foot."

"He offers to bet a hundred pounds to fifty that you won't produce a reptile fast enough to beat his Melbourne Queen," I murmured.

"Well, he's on a certainty. How the devil am I to get hold of a goanna?"

"How does he?"

"How does he?" Sunset echoed. "Why he's cracked on goannas. He tracks 'em, and snares 'em or digs 'em out of rabbit burrows, and then he lugs 'em off to his camp and makes pets of 'em. He understands goannas. I don't. I don't even know how to handle 'em. Anyway, how are we gonna keep 'em straight?"

"There's a netted vermin fence beside the track leading to Regan's Pub, isn't there? We set them going in the direction of the pub, and we ride beside them to keep them from leaving the fence and dashing off across the road," I pointed out. "A hundred for fifty is worth going after. Why not get the blacks down the creek to scout about to-morrow, and for them to bring in any they find. Surely they know enough about goannas? They ought to know more about them than Goanna Bill."

The next morning, Sunset Joe regarded the proposal of racing goannas with greater favour.

"You seen that Melbourne Queen?" he asked when we were at breakfast.

"No, but according to Goanna Bill she's got plenty of toe."

"Humph! There's one thing about Goanna Bill, and that is he can't train goannas to race like a man trains a horse. He can't make that Melbourne Queen run faster than her natural."

"Of course not," I assured him. "That's what makes it so fair a gamble. Trust the blacks to look out a likely-looking reptile for us."

After breakfast I rode away to leave the note of acceptance on the selected fence post, and Sunset departed down the creek to interview the blacks and bribe them with half a side of beef and a five-pound case of tobacco if they found a reptile that would beat the Melbourne Queen. When we met again at dinner, he was in high spirits, and he related how King James had guaranteed to bring him the fastest goanna in South Australia.

About sundown the next afternoon there arrived the entire aboriginal tribe. The blacks were so keyed to excitement that our pet galah thrust his head into an empty jam tin and kept it there. The din was terrific. Goannas were lugged along semi-strangled in the grip of bony black hands, or almost suffocated in the dark interiors of sugar bags.

"Cripes!" Sunset whispered.

Around the fowl house was a netted run put up when the dogs were bad. At this time the door was always left open and the hens could wander where they liked. Now they were converging to the hen house preparatory to early roosting, and at an order given by Sunset half a dozen naked urchins dashed into the run and shooed the birds out. Then into the netted run poured the flood of goanna catchers to empty their bags and release the hand-held captives. When they withdrew and the door was shut, there were, perhaps, twenty of the huge lizards. I could not count them. They moved round and round too fast.

"You wantum goanna feller lick hell outer goanna feller belongah Goanna Bill?" inquired King James, who was five feet high and four feet wide.

"Too right!" ejaculated Sunset, his eyes vainly trying to follow one of the darting green streaks inside the fowl run.

"Gibbit bacco!" commanded the king. Sunset proffered his plug. Half the plug disappeared into the king's mouth; the other half went into the pocket of a dirty pair of flannel trousers. The crowd became hushed. With difficulty the king spoke.

He said: "You takum feller wot runs his head kep' low. Goanna feller wot runs his head kept high ain't got no toe at all. You bin seen Goanna Bill's Melbun Queen?"

"No," admitted Sunset. "You take a pick outer this lot, and don't forget the half side of beef and the case of bacco."

The uproar broke out again, and the galah, which had waddled across to make inquiries, flew-and-waddled to the nearest empty jam tin for protection. King James and two of his bucks slipped into the run. Their bodies were blurred with greenish streaks. King James discarded his dignity when two of the reptiles fought for a foothold on his head and he was obliged to furrow the ground as though he were a plough share. Between them all they managed to bring out two.

The candidates were being strangled into submission when up along the creek came two stout fellows each straining at the end of a long rawhide rope having at its centre a noose through which was the neck of a ferocious monster - a perentie. Think of an alligator, reduce its size to half, and you will have an excellent mental picture of a Central Australian perentie.

The king chuckled, the mob yelled, and the perentie was halted for inspection. It was a little frothy about the gills, but otherwise seemed not to be inconvenienced by the noose. When he got his second wind, he began to raise himself high on his stiffened legs and to swell out his neck either side the noose to alarming proportions. When he opened his snout to yawn, there were revealed rows of teeth which would have shamed any actress.

"By cripes, Sunset, this feller go like hell," gurgled the delighted king when he had yelled for comparative silence. The mottle-green nightmare was trying hard to break the rope with its hind feet.

"Don't mind how fast he goes s'long as he don't come back to the startin' post, because that's where I'll be," Sunset said dubiously.

A sleepy fowl ran against the perentie in blind effort to find its accustomed roosting place. There followed a horrific snapping sound, and the hen was minus its head. Strong man though he was, Sunset shuddered. A lubra wailed, and the hunters holding the rope tightened the strain they maintained on it. The perentie practised tight-roping with some success.

"How are we going to get that thing to the course?" Sunset wanted to know. "You sure he's got plenty of toe?"

"Too right!" assented the king. "He'll go that fast that no feller know if he's comin' or goin'. Melbun Queen, she watch his dust all the way."

After a deal of guessing - for no living man could have measured that live perentie with a tape - there was constructed a kind of coffin without a lid. Trap doors with hide hinges were fitted both ends. After the green streaks had been liberated from the fowl run, the coffin was taken inside and put down against one of the netted walls, the door at one end being left open. Not without difficulty, the perentie was dragged into the run and liberated after having been made temporarily inactive by prolonged strangulation. On its recovery, it was stirred into volcanic action and poked about with sticks until it sought sanctuary by running into the coffin. The bravest of the blacks then sneaked into the run and securely fastened the prison gate. With the iguanas they had taken great liberties; with the perentie they took none.

At a quarter to ten on Christmas Eve, Sunset Joe was driving the station buckboard along the straight track to Regan's Pub. On the coffin behind us sat King James and four bucks. Seated in the stern of the vehicle were several lubras and two fat gins, and hanging on behind ran a number of youths.

Two miles ahead across the table-flat gibber plain was the sun-reflecting iron roof of Regan's Pub, and one mile to the east was the small and modern township of Hell's Hobs. The township lay off the track, but the hotel license had been continued because travellers not desiring to visit the mining town would thus be saved a distance of two unnecessary miles.

Another buckboard, several horses and a small group of men waited beside the netted vermin fence skirting the road at a point about half a mile from Regan's Pub, and when we drew sufficiently near to them to distinguish Goanna Bill and his native assistants, it was possible to make out, standing in front of the pub, Ted Johnson's tabletop waggon beneath the mountain of loading which masked from us the team of twenty-four camels. Naturally, Ted Johnson was inside the pub.

At the meeting, my two heroes glared at each other, and all hands waited to see either a fight or a bottle upended.

"Good day-ee!" drawled Goanna Bill, insolently eyeing his friend-enemy up and down. "Have a snifter?"

"Too right!" assented Sunset Joe, he apparently feeling generous to his already defeated opponent.

The king licked his chops and was given the empty bottles to drain.

"Johnson's team?" asked Sunset casually.

"Yaas. Ted's inside. Bin there orl night," Goanna Bill replied, without great interest. "Regan can't get 'im going, and 'is boss is ringin' up for someone else to drive the team on to Couldowie 'cos they're short of rations."

"Ted squiffy?"

"Well, not absolute. 'E can't walk, and, of course, 'e can't drive, but 'e can still talk, and 'e can still keep 'is eyes open. Any'ow, it ain't gonna be 'im wot drives them mokes to Couldowie, although the 'omestead is only three miles along the track."

By this time Goanna Bill's complexion almost matched the colour of Sunset's whiskers, and the moment arrived to discuss the real object of the meeting.

"Bring your reptile?" inquired Sunset, handing yet another empty to King James.

"I 'ave so. The Melbourne Queen's in that there box," replied Goanna Bill proudly, whilst he pointed to the coffin-like case set down beside the fence. "Wot's the name of your entry?"

Sunset hesitated. Then: "We calls him Australia's Pride," he said offhandedly. "Ready for the go? The sooner we get started the sooner we'll interview Paddy Regan. You're putting up a hundred to my fifty, aren't you?"

"Too right! 'Ampshire'll 'old the money."

A hundred and fifty pounds were in my pockets in less than ten seconds. The blacks lifted the coffin off the buckboard and set it down beside Goanna Bill's box.

"Wot you got in there? A crocodile?" he asked suspiciously.

"Not exactly. I like to give my reptile plenty of room. It ain't fair to cramp 'em too much this weather. How are we gonna get 'em started?"

Having thoughtfully regarded the two coffins, Goanna Bill offered several suggestions. Two boys rushed up from Regan's pub pantingly to ask if any one present was able and willing to drive Johnson's team to Couldowie.

"Blow Johnson!" roared Sunset. Then abruptly he subsided into gloomy retrospection. I knew what crossed his mind. We had made no mark to denote which end of the coffin Australia's Pride had entered and, consequently, we had no exact knowledge which end he would come out head first. Obviously, if he came out tail first he would lose a lot of ground getting away, even if the boys did manage to turn him in the proper direction.

We took King James aside and explained the handicap should the perentie emerge tail first, but that gentleman assured us that it would not matter in the least if Australia's Pride got a bad start, as it could easily overhaul any goanna in the country. In fact, it might be better if Melbourne Queen did get away first, and so give our lizard an encouraging lead.

As we had not thought to bring saddle hacks, we took out the buckboard mokes and mounted them barebacked. King James supervised the start. We noticed the police sergeant and one of his offsiders enter Regan's pub, without doubt to put the acid on Ted Johnson. A mongrel dog joined the party of blacks gathered behind the two coffins, from which, when there occurred a lull in the yelling, issued scratching sounds and thumps made by heavy bodies.

"All set?" asked Goanna Bill, now mounted on the old mare.

"Start 'em off!" roared Sunset Joe.

A wild scream rose from those crouched behind the coffins. Out shot Melbourne Queen. Then out came Australia's Pride, fortunately head first. Melbourne Queen kept going, but Australia's Pride stopped to regard the gesticulating blacks. He began to raise himself on stiffened legs and to swell out his neck, when from among the legs of the yelling blacks darted the mongrel. Australia's Pride decided to get going whilst the going was easy.

At the first furlong, Melbourne Queen was leading by twelve lengths. At the second furlong her lead was reduced to two. The dog was doing his best, but he lost a lot of toe through incessant yapping. The mounted spectators managed to keep level with the dog, but the pedestrians lagged a little. The reptiles kept to the fence in good order, and quickly warmed up to their work. At the third furlong they were running neck and neck.

Then the two policemen came out of Regan's Pub with Ted Johnson between them. They gazed with ecstasy upon the oncoming race and stood to watch. The sergeant shouted. Regan, his wife, the yardman, two maids and four semi-drunks emerged. By this time Australia's Pride was well in the lead and looked a certainty. Both reptiles were tiring, but the dog had got his second wind, although his yap-yapping never ceased. And then, at the foot of the fence post agreed on as the winning post, the hotel cat must needs get to her feet and arch her back at the approaching Australia's Pride.

There were no trees in sight, and both reptiles were looking for something to climb. Australia's Pride saw the camels, now on their feet and watching him with anxious eyes. For them he made. You could not see his feet moving, but you could see his snout wide open. The Melbourne Queen followed his course part of the way, but when he became entangled with the camels' legs she deviated northward and so passed round the rear of the waggon.

Twenty-four camels plunged and reared and roared, and somehow they all went into their collars at the same time, thus moving the waggon forward. It seems impossible, but Australia's Pride burst out from among the stamping feet on the near side of the team at the same instant that Melbourne Queen raced round the near rear corner of the waggon.

Old Johnson, over six feet and moon-faced, was left by his escort, who retreated at the gallop to the bar door, followed immediately by all those who a moment before had rushed out. Our champion followed them, but Melbourne Queen ran up Johnson's side, and her feet became entangled with his wild grey hair. For three seconds he stood swaying on his feet, his great face beaming with strange joy, before he realised that Melbourne

Queen was actually real. As the waggon moved by him with ever-increasing speed, he sprang forward, clutched at the loading ropes, and was last seen in the rising dust clambering to the summit of the mountain with the goanna still aboard him.

The cloud of dust departed down the track towards the homestead of Couldowie. Sunset Joe clapped me on the back. The yapping dog raced into the pub to add its meed to the rising crescendo of sound. Goanna Bill looked thoughtful. Dust, thin and attenuous, was beginning to float out through the front windows and doors of the old wooden building which had so successfully defied the white ants.

"'Tain't fair to run a alligator against my -," began Goanna Bill, when out rushed Regan himself at twenty miles an hour. He did not decelerate before reaching a point one foot from Sunset Joe's offside stirrup iron. He was trembling with emotion. Sunset dismounted preparatory to going into action. Regan hung onto the stirrup leather.

"It's all right - it's all right!" he managed to gasp.

To the uproar going on inside the building was added the yells of a female enjoying hysterics. Sunset, now knowing that Regan did not want to fight, made to stride off to the pub to rescue the screaming woman, but Regan turned from the stirrup leather and clung to the red giant.

"It's all right. It's only the old woman!"

"Mrs. Regan?"

"No. Her aunt. An' her cousin's in there, too. Let 'em screech. It's music in me ears."

"But that perentie'll chew 'em up," Sunset logically pointed out.

"No matter," Regan assured him, hanging on the tighter. "Let 'em bide. I ain't enjoyed meself so much in years - not since we buried Bill the Dog. Me an' the missus 'as 'ad them two females living on us for five weeks. We ain't been able to look at each other sideways since they been here. Trade's fell away to nothink, 'cos the boys says that their faces makes the beer sour in their mugs. Sunset, I'll never forget this day. Me 'ouse, everything that I've got, is yours fer bringing along that perentie."

His face expanded into joyous enlargement when the two policemen and several men appeared round an angle of the building. The sergeant strode to where we stood with the blacks massed in support.

"Who brought that reptile here?" he demanded to know.

"No wan, Sargint. You seen yerself how the hanimile arrived without no invitation," replied Regan, his face indicative of supreme happiness. "S'long as the pub don't fall down, no one's complainin'."

"But it's gone into a room where them two women relations of yours took refuge," the sergeant objected. "That must be them yelling. Whoever was responsible for driving that thing along the fence can now go in and bring it out."

"I wouldn't go in for all the tea in China," Regan said, to add belligerently: "And I'll wipe the ground with anyone who tries to."

"Well, you can begin on me, Regan, because I am going in," the sergeant challenged. "What's the meaning of it all, anyway?"

Goanna Bill hurriedly explained how the goanna race meeting had been convened, whilst Paddy Regan chuckled and slapped his enormous thighs, and now and then listened to the feminine yells. Then, with remarkable abruptness, all sound within the pub ceased.

"Well, that's that," Regan said. "The old woman 'as a diamond broach wot'll pay for the funeral. Five weeks of nagging 'as me and the missus 'ad to put up with, and now that there perentie 'as brought peace, perfect peace."

Sunset Joe chuckled and the mob roared when a swift cloud dropped its shadow on Regan's face. The change was brought about by the appearance of an elderly dame who trundled her own invalid chair out through the bar door. She was followed by a younger woman, gaunt of frame, white of face. One behind the other, they advanced upon us.

"Cripes!" murmured Goanna Bill. The sergeant said nothing. Neither did Regan. King James chuckled softly.

Then it began - twin, high-pitched, screaming voices giving a minute description of every one of us, of our progenitors and our possible descendants, of our future destinations, of all our sins of omission and commission. After that, the daughter began it all over again while the mother entered into a description of the innumerable ailments which had confined her to an invalid chair since before her second husband faded out with exhaustion.

The ceaseless stream of invective was terrible. The sergeant regarded Regan with an expression of deep sympathy. Goanna Bill looked stunned. Sunset tried to say something but failed. I looked at King James, and in his face read the regret that these women were not his lubras. Even the unclouded sun dimmed its light.

Then Mrs. Regan appeared, just outside the main door. She looked cool and determined. Only from her could help be expected. Only a woman could counter attack these viragoes, who could hold a crowd of rough men cowed with their tongues. Faintly, drowned almost by the screaming voices, there came to us the incessant yapping of the dog within the hotel.

The sergeant pulled out his watch to time the vocal performance, when out came Australia's Pride at full speed. The mongrel was close on his tail, and behind him came Mrs. Regan flourishing a broom. The perentie's great jaws were snapping in nightmarish fashion. Thinking we humans were tree stumps, he came at us like Campbell's "Bluebird."

"Look out!" someone yelled.

As though a four point-nine had exploded in our midst, we spread outward with terrific velocity. All save the invalid woman. She sat in her chair. The daughter tripped up and lay on the ground. The perentie ran over her the instant that she bounded to her booted feet, and the propulsion sent him a dozen feet into the air. Before he could land again, the daughter was streaking across the plain towards the township and the mother had bounded out of her chair and was following hard astern. Australia's Pride then steered a course for the fence and up along it to the north, and, after following for fifty yards, the dog lay down absolutely yapless. He, at any rate, had had enough for one day.

"Cripes!" murmured Goanna Bill again. The sergeant heaved a vast sigh of relief. Regan began again to chuckle and slap his thighs.

"The ole woman's gonna win!" he cried, his face once again lit with the lamp of a great joy. "The missus always said that she was putting the invalid stunt on, and that there was nothing ever wrong with 'er. Well, well! We didn't invite 'em 'ere, and we didn't ask 'em to go. Look at 'em! Crummy, don't they travel!"

"Hey, you, King James!" shouted Mrs. Regan from the door. "You and your mob run off after that perentie and fetch him back. We'll tie him up handy in case them two return and ruin our trade."

"It looks as though we done someone a good turn this Christmas, any'ow," remarked Goanna Bill.

"Still, we can't have these goings on," sternly interposed the sergeant.

"Now, now, Sargint, dear," cooed old Regan. "Everythink 'as panned out good-oh. Peace 'as returned to mine house. It's open to all 'ands for an hour, and so it is. Come on in now, and wet yer whistle."

"I suppose so," assented the sergeant.

Goanna Bill and Sunset Joe said nothing. They were the first to arrive, and not until New Year's Day did the Police Force have to cart them off to the jug in a bullock dray.

The Grousers

Salt beef hot; salt beef almost cold; salt beef and spuds with damper and strong tea. That was the standard menu for many weeks, because the station people would not kill a beast until the hot spell ended.

It suited Rooster Williams. All he had to do was to sling a junk of salt beef into a bucket of bore water and boil it from one to six hours, according to his mood. He was all right, lounging all day in the shade of a bough shed, but it was not fit tucker for three men working on contract raising the height of that vermin barrier known as the S.A. Border Fence. As Snooker Fred said more than once:

"A bloke on hard graft needs red meat at least once a day. We're losing money, we're that weak; all on account of that cross-eyed squatter being afraid to kill in hot weather."

Snooker Fred was the boss of the fencing gang. He was five feet high, three feet wide and two feet thick. Faded blue eyes habitually glared from twin open spaces in a whiskered face; and there was only one thing he could do better than build a fence, and that was insert a particular adjective between the syllables of words.

Then there was Long Tom, lean and lanky and tireless - Long Tom with his grey walrus moustache and one eye, and a neck like a ram. Being a fencer's offsider to these two was no bed of roses. It was even worse living week in and week out on salt beef hot, salt beef cold - or nearly cold. Life would have been less difficult had the meat been properly cold, but cold meat in a temperature which never falls below a hundred is not to be had.

The bough shed, built by Rooster Williams in his spare time, was situated some hundred yards east of the Border Fence. It was flanked on one side by the first Ford car that ever reached Broken Hill, now converted into an alleged ton-truck - alleged because more often than not it carried well over a ton. On the other side of the shed was the campfire where Rooster cooked according to his moods. From the branches of a nearby cabbage-tree were suspended the salt-meat bag and the loose rations.

Why that fence was ever erected and why it was carefully maintained was puzzling. They said its purpose was to keep South Australian vermin out of New South Wales, but the only vermin to be seen were the flies, to whom a netted mesh was no barrier. We saw no rabbits save three sitting on a burrow at sunset in New South Wales. We saw no emus, though one would have been preferable to the salt meat. In fact, in South Australia there was not a living thing, and by right South Australia should have regarded the fence as a protection from New South Wales.

The spring gales, having done their utmost to blind and choke us with the sand they raised, had given place to astonishingly still days and nights. Between sunrise and sunset not an ant was to be seen running over the red-hot ground, but from sunset to sunrise all were very much on the job, from bull-ants down to bright-red fellows no bigger than cheesemites.

Of course, the meat question had to reach a climax. Snooker Fred possessed but one virtue, which was never to work too hard on Sundays. Every Sunday morning he and Long Tom visited the homestead to purchase meat and rations - invariably salt meat. It was absolutely essential for Long Tom to go with Snooker, because Snooker could not steer the truck and play tunes on the box of four batteries fixed to the dash. According to the tune Long Tom played, so did the cylinders fire, and when he managed to fire all four cylinders in correct order the world knew about it. Two cylinders firing spasmodically represented Long Tom's average achievement.

One Sunday they returned from the homestead with no fresh meat, and when Rooster Williams learnt our fate he expressed a desire to stone the crows.

"If you was anything of a cook" snarled Snooker Fred, "you would go out and get a bit of fresh meat. You talk about us always grousing, but you keep your end up." (To get the full value of Snooker Fred's remarks it is necessary to interpolate an adjective at the most convenient spot in all words of more than one syllable.)

"Well, strike me pink, you're all right!" snorted Rooster. "Where in 'ell am I to get fresh meat?"

"There's them three rabbits in New South," Long Tom pointed out.

"Rabbits!"

"Yes, rabbits! A rabbit stoo would go better'n salt meat."

Rooster William examined Long Tom with eyes made glassy with horror, He tried to move, but could only repeat the one word "Rabbits!"

"Ain't y' ever seen one?" inquired Snooker with remarkable mildness.

"Rabbits!" again gasped Rooster Williams, and then leaned against the truck as though all strength had gone from him.

We turned to unload the truck, and by the time we sat down to eat the cook had partly regained composure. Glumly he carved the oily salt meat.

"Well, I'm the first bush cook since 1872 wot's been asked to cook rabbits," he complained, evidently deeply hurt.

"Yous blokes wanter remember I'm a cook, not a rabbit-oh. Any'ow, you get the flamin' rabbits, and I'll cook 'em,"

"How?" demanded Snooker contemptuously.

"Bile 'em, I suppose. How d'you think? I ain't never cooked no rabbits in me life."

"Ain't y'?" cut in Long Tom. "Well, you skins 'em first. Then you chops 'em up. Then you plants 'em in a pot of spuds and onions, and then you simmer 'em for an hour. That's the way my ole woman does 'em, and they ain't so bad."

For the first time hope was expressed in Rooster Williams' small black eyes. He said:

"All right! You get 'em. I'll cook 'em."

And so, instead of being permitted to try to cool off for the afternoon, we took shovels and proceeded to shift from twenty to thirty tons of sand to capture the three last rabbits in the Western Division. They were good examples of the survival of the fittest - three ten-year-old bucks more difficult to skin than a bullock. Huge iceberg-clouds lay aloft, but not one of them touched the sun or each other. There was no wind, not a breath, and this was singular, because cloud shadows produce eddies of air and willi-willies.

The rabbits were seized about three o'clock, and, on account of their age and sex, I suggested to Rooster that he should proceed instantly with the cooking. Despite his grunted objections, Long Tom overseered the job, determined that Rooster should not just "bile 'em."

When the sun went down that evening in a clear western sky, it lit to glory a vast and deep cloud mass lying above the Barrier Range about seventy miles from us. We had been obliged to wait for darkness to paralyse the flies before tackling the stew, for a stew is a more efficient flytrap than cold salt beef. While we lapped it up with noisy relish, we could see the lightning jazzing in and about that cloud mass.

Awaking about two o'clock in the morning, I found Snooker and Long Torn smoking their night pipes so carefully filled with tobacco and placed within easy reach before they went to bunk. I felt peculiarly exhilarated; gone was the heavy mental lethargy produced by high temperatures. About the camp a light wind was playing its music on the notes of the tree leaves. It was coming from the east. It brought the perfumes of paradise, and, instead of reaching for the cigarette makings, I lay breathing deeply with ecstasy. The wind was coming from the rain.

The Rooster crowed in the dawning, as was usual; and we rose to eat the remainder of the rabbit stew. It was quite impossible to chew the meat, but it was far better than salt beef cold - or nearly cold. No clouds formed above us this day, but the temperature was distinctly lower. Our failing hopes that the station people would now kill a beast mounted, and after a long day's labour the truck-driver and the battery player set off for the homestead. When they returned without any fresh meat, even Rooster Williams was shocked by their observations.

On the morning of the following day, life appeared in South Australia for the first time. Several hundreds of emus came marching down from the north, walking close to the west side of the fence and thereby delighting the fence-riders, because the birds kicked away from the netted barrier all dead rubbish blown against it. The Rooster shot one, and the others marched on as though nothing had happened. Long Tom and I preferred salt beef cold, or nearly cold, to the stew Rooster made from the leg of that bird.

From then on each day seemed determined to be hotter than the one before. The wind blew from the north and the north-east, and it shrivelled the black hair on Snooker's amazing chest and face. Other emu mobs passed south, hugging the fence like souls kept out of paradise.

We were now working about half a mile south of the camp, and late in the afternoon of the fifth day, after some three inches of rain had fallen north of Broken Hill, Long Tom abruptly dropped his pliers, seized a stick and gave chase to a rabbit that was determinedly following the emus' pad. It eluded him, and our hopes were dashed.

"Pity you couldn't aim a bit straight," groused Snooker Fred. "We could've had rabbit stoo again for breakfast."

We were returning to camp, walking over the monstrous ranges of sand, when from the allegedly dead heart of Australia appeared the army. Its leaders could be seen running eastward along one of the flats. We, having reached the summit of a sand-range, saw Rooster in South Australia rushing about and slaying rabbits with a hefty billet of mulga. At each kill, he tossed the carcass into New South Wales, and I when we arrived, to note his activities with admiration, he yelled:

"Stoo! Rabbit stoo! We're set for rabbit stoo!"

In the evening we walked across to the fence, to see rabbits gnawing at the netting; rabbits reaching up to find a hole big enough to slip through; rabbits lying bunched into masses covering many square yards. Rabbits ran and bucked about over all the ground in sight beyond the fence. Here and there against the fence, controlled by a strange law, they lay on top of each other, forming waves of fur to sink away here, to form again elsewhere. Not even a Jeans could have counted those rodents.

"We oughter be all right now for rabbit stoo," remarked Rooster.

The wind had died away, leaving the air stifling, In New South Wales was an unbroken silence, but from South Australia came to us a low, unearthly noise. In it was the murmur of the sea at great distance, the rustle of wind-stirred leaves fallen to a roadway, and the hissing of a gigantic snake. Above this sound, like objects floating on water, were the continuous squeals and screams of rabbits, high and piercing in note. We now could not see the fence but to us it appeared that South Australia was alive, stirring with life, no longer a tract of land.

They boast about Sydney bridge and they skite about St Kilda Road, as though these were marvels comparable with a rabbit migration halted by a netted fence. Men have related the passing of cats in vast hordes, followed by wild dogs that were in turn followed by blacks earning fortunes from dog scalps, and their gins following behind them waiting to snatch their scalp cheques to spend with the 'Ghan hawkers bringing up the rear. But when you see a rabbit plague boxed against a netted fence you wish, first, that you had a moving-picture camera, and, second, that you possessed a gallon of eau-de-Cologne.

Unlimited "stoos" faced us beyond the fence when day broke. The sky was empty of clouds, and the cadmium-coloured high level haze promised wind direct from the north. Before it came, the fence-rider of that section and the inspector, with their strings of camels, passed southward to the portion of the fence still to be raised to the new regulation height.

We ate rabbit stew for breakfast.

All the salted meat in the salt-encrusted bran-bag had gone blue-mouldy and recklessly Rooster Williams heaved it out. He was brilliantly cursed by Snooker Fred for not having "aired" it overnight by hanging it on hooks from tree branches, but he waved to the massed rabbits that could have kept the larders of all Europe well stocked for a year.

Smothered rabbits lay in heaps against the fence, and above them live rabbits were trying hard to reach up to the top of the barrier. The fence-rider's hurry was produced by just that danger where the barrier was yet only four-and-a-half-feet in height. Waves of rabbits washed up against the fence, to sink back and form again elsewhere. They were endeavouring to obey the single order which had started their migration: Go east, young man!

Now they were doing their hardest to obey the order, to go east to the miles of green feed promised by the recent rain north of Broken Hill. When we arrived at our work, when we had scaled the fence into South Australia to lash new posts against old ones and to net and wire the new topping, we had to slide our feet over the ground to get standing room.

There was no fear, no timidity, in those rabbits. They were driven by one desire, a desire which had ousted fear. We could pick them up, and on setting them down they would at once continue the frantic search for a way through the barrier. They gnawed at the wire-netting. They gnawed at the old fence-posts.

Strangely enough, they did not attempt to dig. As the day lengthened, so they massed even harder against the fence, to be suffocated in waves.

The hot wind came, and as the sun mounted it grew in strength. Like fleas jumping on the floor of a dog's kennel, so a never-ending succession of rabbits leaped high, screamed shrilly and fell back.

That night we again ate rabbit stew. Rooster Williams was improving with practice.

When darkness came, temporary reprieve was given to millions. From our bunks we could hear rabbits gnawing at the netting in a fearful assault on the barrier. The attackers were starving, and yet, because of the order to "go east," they never thought to return westward, even for a little distance, where they could still have found sustenance.

The next day the sun began its work early, assisted by a hot northerly. It was as though a windstorm had blown dead buck bush against the barrier, so high were the waves of smothered rabbits crested with living animals still reaching upward with outstretched forepaws. Little mounds of them lay everywhere, but not a rabbit lay further back from the fence than ten yards. The army had delivered its assault. To a unit it fought to death. Gradually, the number of rabbits jumping high in the death-leap diminished, until at noon that astounding manifestation of life was stilled. For forty miles there lay a festering horror.

The north wind brought with it detached fur fibres, invisible to eyes habitually semi-closed to withstand the sun glare. The fibres were caught by face bristles, and produced a tormenting itch. They were drawn up into nostrils, and produced violent sneezing. They were drawn down parched throats, and caused racking coughing.

From a warm, musty smell began the stench of death.

Came the carrion birds. The hitherto invisible eagles sank to the fence and neighbouring trees. They drew down with them eagles from adjoining areas, and in turn these drew eagles from further afield. The crows came out of space, and the daylight hours were shocked by their uproar.

And we, returning to camp, mentally unbalanced by the torture of the fur fibres, came to see Rooster Williams stirring the contents of a large billy.

"Come on!" he shouted cheerfully. "Rabbit stoo for supper."

And then Snooker Fred employed his adjective between words as well as between the syllables of words. After all, the Rooster deserved what he got. He was crowned with his rabbit stew.

Frozen Pumps

Hour by hour and day by day we drew ever nearer to Ma Slavin's pub; every day the distance dwindled between the pub and the line of fence we were building. Foaming schooners of beer grew ever larger and more numerous as the crimson February suns went to their rest.

The fence was begun at a point fourteen miles from Ma Slavin's pub, and it was destined to be finished a mile and a quarter from that haven of delight. The mile and the quarter was the width of the Paroo River. The new fence was to subdivide a paddock the eastern boundary of which skirted the Paroo, and from this boundary fence it permitted one to gaze across the flat, dry, grey bed of the river to observe the brown-painted, wooden building protected by pepper-trees growing on high land on the far shore.

As the Midnight Mail was eager to point out, twelve miles and six furlongs of fencing at eighteen pounds per mile would provide us each with 4,590 schooners of beer, less 600 schooners for tucker, leaving a balance of 3,990 schooners. He further pointed out, quite unnecessarily, that 3,990 schooners were not to be sneezed at in February. With a stick and two square yards of New South Wales, he showed that, in our then condition of bankruptcy, if we began work at the end of the job farthest from Ma Slavin's pub, we would not be so strongly tempted to draw schooners at every week's end, and that it was much better to handle 3,990 schooners at one standing, as it were, than in dribs and drabs.

"I've got the plant, 'Ampshire," he announced. "The boss'll let us draw rations and tobacco against the job. We'll start at this mark here and work across the paddock towards Ma's joint, and then when we reach the far side, here, we'll have the job done. All we gotter do then is to walk across the Paroo and tell Ma to ring up the boss to OK the cash and then begin serving us with our 3,990 schooners. I know Ma Slavin. D'rectly she knows the money's jake, she'll say: 'All right, boys! We lets 'er go.' And then we downs 'em, 'Ampshire, downs nearly 4,000 schooners. Think of it, 'Ampshire! Nearly 4,000 schooners!"

Like a tenth-rate fool, I fell for it. The Midnight Mail was wickedly wasting his time as a fencer - he should have been a land salesman. He was a tall, deceptive-looking man with stooping shoulders, weak eyes, flat feet and a walrus moustache. For years he had pushed a pedal-less bike loaded with swag and rations, choosing to do his travelling at night and at express speed. Then he married the Paroo Parrot, and, in exchange for her buckboard and team, he maintained her and her tribe of children for something like two years. Then there occurred an unofficial divorce, but the Midnight Mail retained the turnout, as well as the pedal-less bike, without which he would not move.

For the first three weeks we cut the posts, which the station bullocky laid along the line. When we started the post-hole digging and post erection on the first mile, I could no longer sweat. We began at daybreak, took one hour off for lunch, and continued until dark. As one hypnotised, I worked; but the Midnight Mail sang and whistled and constantly estimated the number of schooners already awaiting us at Ma Slavin's pub. He was a lightning ready-reckoner, and he always expressed values in schooners of beer.

"Now you just take 'er easy, 'Ampshire," he would say when night had vanquished the flies, and saws and hot irons were at work on my muscles. "You take 'er easy. I'll bake the damper and sling on a bit of a meal. A bloke's gotter get hardened up to this kind of work. Lemme see! Yes, we've gathered 1,537 schooners between us so far."

"Come on, 'Ampshire!" he would call when the sky only hinted at the coming day. "Breakfust's ready! We gotter pile up the schooners to-day. Tear into some of these chops and down 'em with sauce. There's nothing like sauce to put steam into a bloke, followed by a swig of painkiller just before he starts work."

In the dawning, we would leave for the job with my hands as stiff as leather, my spine a vast area of pain, my brain stunned by the need for sleep. The Midnight Mail constantly urged me to "take 'er easy," but never for an instant did he stop for a blow. Pride was a driver more relentless and cruel than a galley slave's master. The sun was a celestial hell; the ground was the lid of a stove; the flies were a million devils.

To leave a crowbar on the ground for ten minutes prohibited its use for an hour while it cooled in the shade of a mulga. Heat and friction blunted the auger bits. The mulga posts were like cement, the ground was like cement, the wire was a writhing, menacing monster devilishly desirous of flicking out an eye or strangling a man, but mile after mile that fence crept across the huge paddock towards Ma Slavin's pub, and day by day the tally of cool and foaming schooners rose higher and higher.

"Take 'er easy, 'Ampshire! We've earned 2,000 schooners to date," said the drawling voice from somewhere in that hell. "The first hundred schooners we'll pour down our gullets like water. The second hundred we'll lower gentle like, and from then on we'll let 'em slide acrost our tongues like lengths of silk ribbon."

When, at our work, we came in sight of the river that hadn't run its full course but once during the white man's settlement, when there were 130 schooners to be earned before we staggered joyously to paradise, the work became appreciably slower. It was impossible not to pause now and then to gaze across the wide, flat area of sunbaked mud rubble to the distant hotel cuddled by the green pepper-trees on the far shore. The unpleasant situation of the rich man in hell who was refused a drink by St. Peter or someone was no worse than ours.

It was about ten minutes to one in the morning when the job was finished, for we worked half that last night in the moonlight. If the ants had not been so bad, I would have camped at the new junction of the two fences. We lurched back to camp, there to drop on our stretchers and lie like the dead.

Recovery was slow, and, of course, mine was much slower than that of the Midnight Mail. Half a bottle each of painkiller partially restored me and fully restored him. A half-pannikin each of sauce almost restored me and more than restored my mate. He wanted to leave then for Ma Slavin's pub, but the limit had long been reached and passed.

"We'll leave the horses 'ere in this paddock, 'Ampshire," decided the Midnight Mail. "They'll be all right, and so'll the camp. All we'll need do in the mornin' is to roll a bit of a swag."

In a comatose state, I listened to the tale of nigh 4,000 schooners, sleep beaten back by exhaustion and that slow, drawling voice. Just to lie on the stretcher and feel the cool night air was heaven enough. It was, however, not to last. Directly day dawned, the Midnight Mail skipped about the camp, rolling his swag, cooking breakfast, stowing gear into the tent.

"Come on, Ampshire!" he called with annoying cheerfulness. "Come on now! 'Ave a wash and roll your swag. There's salt chops and damper for breakfast, but there's nigh 4,000 schooners waiting for us acrost the river. Hum-de-dum-dum! Hum-de-hum-hum!"

We ate the tasteless meal. The picture of foaming schooners was blurred by another of cold butter and yeast bread, coffee made with milk, and bacon and eggs. Red-eyed and weary, willpower destroyed by labour, sight almost gone through sandy blight, I could no longer listen intelligently to the tale of "Nigh 4,000 Schooners."

Yet, such was the effect of the Midnight Mail's optimism, I felt almost gay when we set off for the river and Ma Slavin's pub. We laughed at nothing - due, perhaps, to the last bottle of pain-killer - and we decided we would borrow two of Ma's bedroom jugs from which to take our first fifty schooners. The sun rose that morning with seemingly less heat. The flies were less tormenting. The mulgas looked beautiful. Age had fallen from us like a worn cloak. We strode through the half-mile of mulga to the Paroo like joyous children. We reached the boundary fence, to cling to it weakly - to gaze at Ma Slavin's pub across a mile and a quarter of water.

For the first time in memory the Midnight Mail was speechless. Slowly passing us was that mile and a quarter stretch of water, bearing on its rippleless surface the debris of years. It came lazily round a wide bend to the north, and as lazily passed from sight round another bend to the south. After a full two minutes, the Midnight Mail opened wide his mouth to curse. I expected an oration of remarkable force, but his mouth closed for another minute.

Then he whispered plaintively: "Stone the ruddy crows!"

He drooped. I thought he would collapse. Then he broke into a whirl of energy.

"Come on, 'Ampshire!" he shouted. "A mile below that bend a sand spit crosses the river. It'll keep back the water for a bit. It might still be dry t'other side. Come on! Come on! Never mind your swag!"

We ran down-river, the Devil of Desire prodding us from behind, and we yelled like lunatics when we saw dry land below a wide, white bar of sand. On reaching it, it could be seen zigzagging from shore to shore, a wall of debris grounded along its top side, here and there water trickling across it.

"Come on, 'Ampshire!" urged the Midnight Mail. "We'll cross a bit further down. Afore we could walk that sand bar the water would get too deep."

He led the way for half a mile below the sand bar, and then out along a tongue of sand which shortened the width of the grey rubble by three furlongs.

Grey rubble! Loose, iron-hard, baked-mud pebbles crowning wide stars of sun-baked mud, each separated by three-inch-wide, fathomless cracks. Our boots slipped on the surface rubble, gained no firm purchase for frantic feet hurrying, hurrying to Ma Slavin's pub and nearly 4,000 schooners. Above us, the relentless sun. About us, the already heated and motionless air. Below us, a strange gurgling noise as though there had come to the Paroo all the giant earth-worms from Gippsland. Winded, legs like cooling lead, I fell, crawled, lurched up, fell again, crawled, again lurched up to run after the lank man who never knew fatigue.

The water, banked up by the sand bar, had at last swept the line of debris across it, and now was bringing it down on us with deceptive speed, rolling it over and over some projection caught in the mud, sweeping it forward without apparent movement when temporarily there was sufficient water under it to float it along. We were half-way across when the sheen of water appeared half a mile down-river. The gurgling noise beneath us was growing ever louder, and then deep in the cracks could be seen the tarnished glint of evil water.

Up and up came those tarnished glints to melt like sugar the surface rubble on the great stars of baked mud. Here and there appeared water; first pools of it, then lakes and creeks, spreading, spreading on either side, behind and before us. Feet sank into new mud, clogging and sticky. Feet slipped off the stars into the leg-breaking cracks. Dry land melted like blotting-paper in brown ink. With a quarter-mile still to go, we became bogged like cattle.

It was as though we and the riverbed were sinking into the sea, and it would have been better had the "sea" been a mile deep.

"Lie down flat, 'Ampshire," shouted the Midnight Mail, setting the example. "Keep flat, 'Ampshire. When the water's deep enough we can paddle ashore over the mud before the current gets too strong. Look out for this mullock wave! We'll get acrost, all right. Near 4,000 schooners is waiting for us, 'Ampshire."

Fouled with mud, we lay flat in slime barely an inch deep, watching the tossing wall of debris - bush and grass and sticks - rolling towards us, and seeming to grow higher and higher every moment, an inch of slime in front of it, a foot of water behind it. To stand had become impossible, for the crown of each "star" was smeared with mud.

The long line of debris continued its advance, slowed here and there when projections on its underside caught in the mud, and then it would roll over with tiny crackling sounds when the water behind it pushed and heaved it forward. It reached us when but two inches of water covered the ground. At the last moment we stood up, our feet in cracks for purchase, and then we were fighting the debris, tearing it asunder with our hands to let it pass by and not over us. It was alive with ants and scorpions and centipedes. Here and there small snakes lay entwined. The mass of sticks and bush rose and fought us, creaking and hissing, pushing with terrific force. Insects bit and stung our hands. The ends of sticks prodded at our bodies, our faces. And quite abruptly it was past us, and the water was reaching our knees.

"Lie down again, 'Ampshire!" shouted the Midnight Mail. "Come on. We gotter paddle ashore afore she gets too deep and the current gets too strong."

With just sufficient water to float our bodies, we clawed our way towards the shore by digging fingers into mud. Semi-drowned, venomous insects floated against us. Dazed but angry whip and saltbush snakes wriggled through the water hoping to find dry land on our shoulder-blades. But we made progress. The cooling water invigorated lethargic muscles, and fear gave additional energy, fear of becoming entangled in the lantana a mile below us.

Presently the Midnight Mail shouted and lurched to his feet, and a moment later I felt not mud but the hard surface of a claypan under me. It gave us fifty yards of walking through knee-deep water, and then we had to swim for a hundred yards across a channel to reach the foot of clean, red sandhills.

"'Ad we bin an hour later, 'Ampshire, we'd have been blocked from them 4,000 schooners," calmly pointed out the Midnight Mail. "As it is, we've only to walk up-river for a mile and a bit to hit Ma Slavin's pub. Come on!"

No suggestion of a spell came from him. Spells were not to be thought of when "nigh 4,000 schooners of beer lay ahead." I staggered after the tall, sinuous figure of the most noted fencer west of the Darling, and, as though through a glass darkly, I came to see far ahead of us, on the rise of ground, the neat wooden hotel flanked with pepper-trees.

Already our clothes were dry and stiff with mud. Mud partially filled our boots, and, drying, bunched under toes and insteps. It was good mud, too. It was an excellent mud for the complexion, because it caked on the skin and defied the flies. Dogs came to meet us, evincing great joy, and the Midnight Mail's joy was no less. He almost ran up the rising ground, and if I hadn't run behind him I'd have fallen for keeps.

Ma Slavin came to stand on her front verandah to examine us with her beady eyes. There was distinct disapproval on her hard face. Two men came to life from beneath the pepper-trees, and they began to laugh. Behind Ma we could see the handles of the beer-pumps in the bar. A cockatoo screamed:

"Stone the crows!"

"Good day-ee, Ma Slavin!" shouted the Midnight Mail. "Me and 'Ampshire's just done that bit of fencing for old Marshall. Ring him up and get him to name the cheque. We got nearly 4,000 schooners each coming to us. Fill 'em up, Ma! Come on, you blokes! Come on, Ma! Fill 'em up for all hands!"

The men laughed. Ma Slavin's thin lips twitched.

"The pumps are frozen," she said coldly, triumphantly. "The teamsters have broached the loading down at Stephen's Creek, and they're dead-drunk. There isn't a drop of one schooner in the place. Come in and try the pumps for yourself if you don't believe me. They're dry, I tell you."

Why Markham Bought a Radio Set

Markham's antipathy towards wireless dated from that month's holiday he spent with relatives in Melbourne back in '25. According to reports of that holiday, his relatives were in possession of a wireless set which they kept going full blast all day long and half the night, even during meals, and when the children were mumbling their prayers before going to bed.

The one escape from wireless for Markham was to clear off to the corner hotel, and leave early in the evening to walk the streets before it was time to enter a theatre. Unfortunately he had chosen his holiday at that period of the year when Melbourne socially and climatically is at its worst, so that he was more or less ice bound, or rather cacophony bound, during four memorable weeks.

Not only was Markham unfortunate. His misfortune in striking a bad patch in Melbourne, allied with a family of wireless enthusiasts who deemed sound volume to be the appreciation of artistic taste, naturally fell upon us who lived with him on his station in northern South Australia, for not only would he not purchase a set, he threatened to discharge us if we jackeroos installed one.

"I like to hear myself eat," he often stated in defence of his fiat, "and I am going to hear myself eat in my own house. I am not going to be forced to yell like the bullock driver when driving his team when I want the salt passed. Have a wireless here - and it will be going night and day, including Sundays."

There was no persuading him to alter his decision, nor was there a sufficiently convincing argument we could raise to make him relent. We had to continue to be satisfied with the alleged music produced on an accordion by Tom Sawyers, and to follow the gee-gees from the two-weeks-old newspapers.

Then came the long drought of '31 when there was precious little time spent at the homestead, when it meant being out among the sheep week after week, camping with them; cutting scrub for them; yahooing them in to water and out again to the fallen scrub. By one and two the men were sacked, and eventually, when three-fourths of the sheep had died, the axe fell upon the jackeroos; and, beside the cook, only I was left with Markham to watch the last 5,000 sheep perish.

If you have never seen stricken sheep die, despite all your efforts to keep them alive; if you have never watched the brazen sky hour by hour and day after day for signs of approaching rain; if you have never seen a decent squatter's eyes reflecting the terror of creeping bankruptcy plus the horror of the paddocks; then pray your hardest you never will.

Save for his antipathy towards wireless Markham was a dinkum, dyed-in-the-wool bushman. When he sacked his men his lips were compressed into a straight line and his glance could not cross theirs. Some of them had been with him for twelve years, and there were three who had worked for his father before him.

Well, the sheep continued to die, the station hacks became apparitions, and Markham seldom spoke except to curse the country. The only living things about the place that maintained condition and equanimity were the blacks, who were permitted to camp beside a pool of permanent water half a mile down the creek. Like the crows and the hawks, the blacks had become fat and indolent - and from the same causes.

The fattest of them all was old Perentie, the king, lord, chief, head serang of a tribe numbering about twenty members; and these twenty blacks were intermittently supplied with tobacco and other luxuries by a half-caste who had "married" one of Perentie's daughters. He was called Motor Alec, for he owned a motor truck on which he transported his dogs, his dingo traps and scalps, his camp equipment, his children, and his wife - in this order of importance and precedence.

We knew the evening that Motor Alec arrived at the blacks' camp by the sounds of revelry which drifted up the creek to us after the merciful darkness had obliterated the terrible country of sand and dying scrub trees. Markham cursed himself for being a white man, and demanded to know why he was not born a lucky blackfellow. Obviously being unable to answer this pertinent question, I growled a "shut up!" and dealt him another poker hand.

After breakfast the next morning we found Perentie and Motor Alec waiting on the office-store steps, the half-caste announcing his desire to purchase tobacco and matches, and gunpowder with which to load his rifle cartridges.

The business having been transacted, old Perentie entered to cadge a little flour, tea and sugar, whereupon Markham directed me to give him a little of each, and on impulse said: "Look here, Perenite! You're a witch-doctor, and it's up to you to prove it. Get your bucks together, and make it rain good and hard, and I'll give you a full bag of flour, a case of jam, and a bag of sugar."

In Markham's voice was the note of desperation, the forlorn hope that by occult methods his station could be saved to him. The chief looked his doubt of success, but Motor Alec replied for him.

"Perhaps, boss," he said in his quiet manner. "You wait a day, or so. Old Perentie can make it rain if he wants, but you see when it does rain, or if he makes rain, the sheep will stop dying, and there will be no more mutton for the tribe."

"Ain't I always treated you fellers fair?" demanded Markham with the sudden rage of a sorely tormented man. "You make it rain, and I'll give you a sheep a week. Clear off now, and make it rain quick."

"All right, boss," replied the half-caste with such cheerfulness that in that place and tune it sounded like a man laughing at a funeral. "You wait! Old Perentie, here, will make rain. I'll make him make rain."

"Sure, too, boss. Bime bye I makum rain," agreed the fat and oily chief. "You gibbet sheep a week, eh?"

"Too right, I will," assented Markham.

"Orl ri. Bime bye, boss."

Three days later I went down to the blacks' camp to see if Motor Alec would truck a load of sheepskins to the railway at Maree. To my astonishment all the women and children were absent, and it was Perentie who explained that he had sent them all away whilst he and his bucks performed the Ceremony to the Rain God. When I put Markham's trucking job to the half-caste, the old chief was visibly relieved when Motor Alec stated his intention of remaining to assist in the ceremony, which might last two days.

In his dark eyes was a twinkle which then perplexed me.

They got to work making rain that evening; the chief, the half-caste and seven initiated bucks. At eleven o'clock when Markham and I threw in our last hand of poker and went to bed, they were going strong. Their yells and wailings we could distinctly hear. They kept it up all through the next day without cease, without taking time off to eat,

"If they make it rain they will have earned the reward," Markham said, grinning for the first time in fifteen months. "There's no more chance of it's raining for another year than my chance of winning Tatt's."

Rain! The sky was empty of clouds when the sun went down as usual in its wine-clear bed of crimson. When the wind dropped before darkness fell, when again we were playing poker for matches, through the open windows drifted the laudatory beseechings and pleadings to the Rain God.

"Silly fools!" growled Markham. "Still, I wish I was a black."

In the middle of the night I was seized and dragged outside.

"Look!" shouted Markham. "Am I mad or am I really seeing all that? Am I hearing rain?"

From the north-west was sailing towards us a cloud mass having a mile-deep face which glinted like dulled steel in the starlight. From the north-west drifted to us the smell of water sucked in by a thirsty earth, and the roar of water falling.

Markham was like a man demented. Wanting to dance, it was only with force that he was prevented from whirling me round and round. When later the rain began to thud on the iron roof of the homestead, Markham produced in me the shock of my life by broaching a bottle of whisky.

The new day revealed a drenched world to be seen through a pall of falling water. Long before it reached us we could hear the creek coming down a banker. It came, roared by the homestead, a wall of water five feet high carrying on its lip a whirling twisting mass of debris.

All that day it rained, and all the following night. It was still raining the next morning. At eight o'clock it eased a little, but towards sundown it rained harder than ever. Countless tons of water flowed down the creek, fed by thousands of water-gutters which drained the wide claypans.

Markham now was worrying about the remnants of the flocks. Weakened as they were by starvation, they now would be starved to death marooned as they were on the islands on what was now an inland lake. When at sundown old Perentie appeared, having crossed the creek by interlocking tree branches, Markham shouted at him:

"You stop it, Perentie. D'you hear? You stop it. We've had enough. You stop it."

"Good oh, eh, boss? You pay tucker; one bag flour, one case tea, one case jam? Me makum rain, orlright. Plenty rain, eh? You gibbit bag of sugar, me makum stop."

Markham glanced at the sky. There was no break in the racing wrack of cloud, no change of wind to the south indicating a break in the weather. Now thoroughly believing in the chief's occult powers to make rain - and stop it raining - he agreed to Perentie's hold up.

With a plug of tobacco and a few pounds of sugar on account, he called on the cook and cadged a couple of loaves of bread on the logical plea that to bake a damper in an open fire was then impossible.

The next morning the sun rose in a cloudless sky.

Markham paid the reward, and we rode out to estimate how many sheep were still alive.

A full week passed when again I walked down the creek to the blacks' camp to see Motor Alec about the trucking job. It was a day of high wind. Every member of the tribe was gathered about the half-caste's truck, and not one heard my approach. Drawing near, I heard a lively jazz tune. Then I saw the aerial. Then I saw light.

As I explained to Markham that evening, Motor Alec was mentally more up to date. The day that the half-caste arrived at the blacks' camp the Adelaide weather man had predicted a general rain extending over all South Australia, and, being less worldly wise than he, the blacks had been unable to understand the weather report even had they been sufficiently interested to hear it. Markham, offering the supplies of food the following morning before Alec could pass on the weather news, presented the half-caste with an idea and, being in league with Perentie, Alec had successfully urged the old fellow to conduct the Rain Ceremony on the plea that probable success would subsequently give him greater ascendancy over the tribe.

Markham saw it all more clearly when I pointed out that the weather forecasts for Central Australia are much more accurate than those made for the southern coastal districts. He was stung a little when I further pointed out that to be without a wireless set was to be less up to date than a half-caste who made a living - and a good one, too - from dog trapping.

Like a good salesman, having got the prospective buyer into the proper state of mind, I showed him the advertisement of the set I selected. I even brought the pen and ink so that he might sign a cheque and write an order.

The reason why I eventually left him was because he would have the set going all day long and half the night.

Hullo, Mate!

If the man in the tram had exclaimed, "Hullo, ole feller!" or "Hullo, cobber!" instead of saying "Hullo, mate" he would not have reminded me of a particular galah which was the greatest companion ever a man had.

Although Peter could not speak a word, he was as much governed by time as were the three camels which transported me along seventy-eight miles of vermin fence in New South Wales. At break of day he invariably bit the ear left exposed and screamed for breakfast, with raised comb and flapping wings. At noon precisely, from his perch on the front of the long iron riding saddle, he shrieked at the riding camel to turn off the pad to the nearest shade for lunch. Buller never failed to obey this order. And directly the top edge of the sun disappeared below the eternal mulga Peter screamed good-night from the summit of the object nearest the camp stretcher.

Along that section of fence there was only one hut, built on the shore of a large almost permanent lake, situated some sixteen miles from the opal diggings of White Cliffs. In the early 1900s two Chinamen had rented it from the station, and there raised vegetables with unlimited water for the gougers, but eventually one killed the other inside the hut and hanged himself from a cross beam, from that day unpleasantly influencing the superstitious. Yet abundance of wild fowl on the surface of the lake, and excellent fish below it, maintained a cynical indifference.

The three camels, the galah, Ginger the dog, and the boundary rider reached this hut late one autumn afternoon, when rain threatened. It began to rain about five o'clock, but by then wood was stacked in a corner, the fire was burning well on the open hearth, the slush lamps were ready for lighting, and the stretcher bed was fixed for the night at the opposite side of the single room. At six o'clock it was almost dark. The rain roared on the iron roof, almost drowning out the joyful cries of thousands of birds. Ginger lay before the fire, and Peter roosted comfortably on that roof beam used by the Chinaman.

Thankful for my fortuitous arrival at the hut that day, I washed the utensils while Ginger ate the scraps, and then rushed out to drive away the rabbits that came to the open door. I talked to the galah, and, when Ginger came back, to the dog. There was no one else with whom to converse, and six weeks had passed since last I had seen a man, black or white, to talk to.

At eight o'clock it was raining hard. The wind was veering from north to west, and rising. I could hear wavelets lapping the lake shore less than thirty feet from the hut door. From my stretcher, where I lay reading with the help of a guttering slush lamp, I could see nothing beyond the open door, so dark was the night.

"Hullo, mate!"

It was as though the wind carried the phrase all the way from England, for the word "mate" was seldom heard in Australia even in those days. I guessed that the long periods of solitude were making my ears play tricks. The two words were not printed on the page I was reading.

"Hullo, mate!"

This time there was no friendly surprise in the greeting. It was as though someone had called to a sluggard in the morning. I considered that a change of employment was a necessity. I was well along the road which every "hatter" had travelled. And yet, near the fire Ginger stood with tail between his legs, hackles stiff, fangs bared, a low growl in his throat, his eyes fixed on something beyond the door.

"Hullo, mate!"

There could now be no illusion. I had not spoken the words. Peter could not talk. I called to the man outside in the pouring rain to come in, and to my unwilling invitation he shouted back.

"All right, mate! Right, mate. I'm coming, mate!"

The repetition of the word "mate" proclaimed the proximity of a bush lunatic. That such a man should be there at all was extraordinary. The nearest road was fourteen miles distant, whilst the lake was not exactly between any two important centres. The nearest stockman's hut was nine miles away.

Although the dog remained fearful no longer did my flesh goose-flesh. Going to the door I demanded impatiently why the fool did not come in. To this he offered no reply. Only when I stood at the fire, which I had replenished with roots, did he appear. He was hatless and coatless. Over his shoulder was hung a cigarette swag. In one hand he held a billy; in the other a large butcher's killing knife. Black whiskers almost obliterated his face. Fading blue eyes peered everywhere but directly at me. Water dripped from swag and billy and knife, and from the frayed ends of his trousers.

"Good night," I said.

"Hullo, mate! It's all right, mate!"

I dragged Ginger across the room and pushed him under the camp stretcher, sitting on it then to make a cigarette. The prospects of a night's rest became nil. I said to him:

"You look wet. Help yourself to tea in that billy. There's meat and damper on the table. Eat near the fire and you'll dry off."

"Right, mate! All right, mate!"

I could not but note that never once did he put down the knife, or even change it from one hand to the other. After he had eaten I advised him to unroll his swag before the fire, and he did this with one hand, because the other was employed with the knife.

Of all youthful follies I did not then regret the purchase of a revolver. Whilst the hatter sat on a case silently staring into the leaping flames, I rummaged in a pack bag for the weapon and cartridges, and, when it was loaded, slipped it under my pillow. Presently, without trying to dry the blanket, he lay down upon it. The steam rose about him like the flames in a sacrificial offering. The wind buffeted the iron hut, and the rain roared on the roof. I thought he was asleep when, half-an-hour later, I piled fresh wood on the fire to assure light, and carefully attended the slush lamps. Lying down I determined to read till day dawned.

It was Ginger who awoke me by trying to stand up beneath the stretcher. He was growling fiercely. The fire flames were low, and, the slush lamps having gone out, the light was ruddy red. It etched in crimson the knife in the hand of the stalking hatter midway between his swag and me. Quite in the approved Deadwood Dick manner I bailed him up.

"All right, mate! Right-oh, mate!" he shouted, jumping to his feet and dropping the knife. "All right, mate! Yes, mate!"

With that he fled. Ginger rushed after him, barking furiously. Gaining the door I looked out into the darkness. The rain hissed on the sand and tinkled upon the water, for now the wind had gone. Ginger followed the visitor for a quarter of a mile before he turned back, and above the dog's barks I could still hear:

"Right-oh, mate! All right, mate!"

We sat up on guard until the morning came to show the rain steadily falling on the water and eleven ducks waddling about the shore but twenty feet from the door. I was taking aim to fire the shot which would gather for us five of the birds, when behind me I heard distinctly:

"'Ullo, mate!"

There was no one in the hut, but Peter gazed down at me from the fatal beam. With raised comb he flapped his wings and screeched for breakfast. I fired the shot at the birds from inside the hut. Peter fell to the floor, clawed his way up the table leg to the damper, and then, as a child wishing to learn a lesson, repeated a dozen times:

"'Ullo, mate! 'Ullo, mate! 'Ullo, Mate!"

Those were the only words he ever did say. Perched on the saddle before me as we swayed along above the fence he would cock his head aside to say those words with evident pride.

No one saw the hatter after that night. The police failed to track him. I wanted to keep the knife, but the sergeant was draped with red tape.

Rainbow Gold

Every year in June, Dr. Mark Death came to Weusanco. He came in his own motor caravan, driven by a silent man he addressed always as his Lazarus, looking at him with dark-grey eyes barely concealing a twinkle, as though his driver were an everlasting source of humour.

We knew little about Doctor Death and less about the driver. That the doctor was a clever medico was proved to us by the cure he affected in George Little, who had suffered delusions since before he came home from the war. We heard that he had a practice in Perth, a small practice; and that seemed strange for a clever man, almost as strange as a man retaining such a name when he became a doctor.

His visits to Weusanco sometimes lasted a month and never less than a fortnight. During each visit the doctor spent a day at the mine with old Six-Foot Jack, the manager, and entertained him some night after at the one and only hotel.

Of course, you all know that the Weusanco gold mine, out from Youanmi, was at first very rich. Old Mick Hogan discovered it on his own, and his original claim he called "We Us and Company," he having taken his dog into partnership. A syndicate bought him out, and Mick's name for the mine became one word. And now, when Dr. Death paid his annual visits, Weusanco was going down the long track to the devil, although it still was a distance from the bottom.

About six weeks after one of the doctor's visits, Harry Wontnor came into town from a trip out east with the report that he had struck it right. Harry, you know, had been chasing the weight for forty years without much luck, so it was time, we all agreed, that the old Dame gave him a spin. From what he said, he had found a second Coolgardie in the cap of a mighty reef studded with knobs of gold as big as your fists. At the time he was camped on an alluvial patch doing a bit of dryblowing, and every other afternoon drove his old horse and dray two miles south to a soak, fetching back to camp a fifty-gallon tank of water. From the soak he could see a mile further south, the top of a ridge peeping up above the mulga timber, and one day he left the horse and dray at the soak to set off to examine that ridge.

There was nothing on it worth dollying, but from it he could see several lesser ridges, and on one of them he found the reef of almost solid gold.

He was wearing a large red handkerchief round his neck and, to a close-by dead mulga stump he fixed the handkerchief, like a flag, so he would be able to get straight to the reef when he returned the next day. And when he did get back to the main ridge, he could distinctly see the red handkerchief fluttering in the wind, and, as I have said, he could see the main ridge from the soak.

You'd think that, without any trouble whatever, Harry Wontnor could have got back to the gold-studded reef, but he couldn't. He could not locate the reef or the handkerchief when he went back the next day. He never found either handkerchief or reef, although he hunted for them for weeks and weeks.

Stores running out sent him into Weusanco for a further supply, and he put in another six weeks hunting for that reef without success. The next time he came for stores, he formed half a dozen of us into a syndicate, and we prospected that lost reef, and never found it.

No one ever found it. At first some of us thought that Harry was playing some stupid kind of a joke, but seeing how dead earnest he was, knowing the man so well, we soon passed out that idea – and gave the reef another fly, with the same result.

That second trip busted the syndicate's finances. We went back to work in the old mine, but Harry stuck to his lost reef search, month after month, right through the summer and autumn.

In time, Harry's "strike" became known as "Wontnor's Lost Reef," but time had no effect on his determination to find it. Many of us shared his faith, small parties often going out independently with, however, the same result. Wontnor's Lost Reef was still a favorite topic of conversation when Doctor Death came again to Weusanco.

On this occasion he found me acting barman, Hogan having gone to Meeka on business. His coming did not add to my work, preparations to receive him being made by Mrs. Hogan and little Mary, but being barman enabled me to get to know the doctor pretty well. There was nothing about his outward appearance to compel respect, he mostly wearing an old grey flannel suit and tennis shoes, but we could not help calling him "sir," which none can say is a habit with mining fellows. It wasn't because he was standoffish, or that he was a clever doctor, or that he spent more freely than a man with a full shammy. It was something inside him, something behind the cold handsome face which clearly told me and the rest that we were worms compared with him.

Of a morning he would lounge against the bar counter, a tall, thin slab of a man, as though he had had lounged against pub-bar counters all his life, and with that amused twinkle in his dark eyes would yarn about gold mining and prospectors, and drink brandies and sodas without shedding a single tear till the cows come home. I can drink with the best, and old Bandy Legge, who can pour it down his neck day and night without stopping, is our champ; but the doctor could outdrink all of us without showing as much as a tinge of colour in his white face, the slightest redness of eye, or a single glossy black hair out of place.

It was the night before the mine pay-day, and business was none too brisk, when Harry Wontnor came in. At sight of him we local men looked him over quick to see if he had or had not found his reef, and the doctor examined him like you or me might watch a scorpion battling with a centipede.

"Any luck, Harry?" I asked first.

Shaking his head old Wontnor strode to the counter, when one of the others invited him to call for his poison.

"No, I can't find the blarsted reef," he said, with a note of despair in his deep voice.

All heads were looking at Harry, seeing the grime of travel on him, and the old hopeless expression which in a few days would give place to one of grim determination, indicating yet another trip to locate the lost reef. For once the doctor was ignored, and for him that must have been unusual for he always dominated any company. The next instant, however, he regained attention.

"What have you lost?" he asked in his distinctive but low voice.

That caused Harry's mind to shift from lost gold to our annual visitor.

"Oh! Good-night, sir. Glad to see you again. Jim" - to me -

"fill 'em all up."

"What have you lost?' repeated the doctor, in a manner so exactly like the first time that it seemed like an echo.

The weariness fell away from Harry. He appeared to get taller. He shook his white thatched head, and replied truculently: "I have lost a gold-bearing reef, sir, so rich that the gold in sight would make every man in Weusanco independent for life."

"Ah! Kindly explain."

So Harry told how he had found his lost reef, and detailed the fruitless searches for it, and while he was doing it Doctor Death was smiling faintly, not as though he did not believe a word of it, but as though he hungered for the gold Harry's word picture showed him. When Harry had done, he said: "The red handkerchief you tied to the mulga stump for a flag - was it the only one you possessed?"

"No, I bought six at the same time off'n the storekeeper here."

"Ah! Then possibly your gold is Rainbow Gold," the doctor said, like a judge putting a fellow away for ten years.

"Whatcher mean by that, sir?" asked Harry, hopefully.

"How old are you?" the doctor put, without answering Harry's question.

"Sixty-three, sir, but -"

"How long have you been a prospector?"

"Forty-one years last March; but what -"

"Did you secure any specimens from this gold reef?"

"No. I had no tools with me at the time, and I couldn't break off any bits."

"How many of the red handkerchiefs have you left?"

"I can't say for sure. Three, I think."

"And since you found the reef you have never seen it again, or the mulga stump, or the red neckerchief?"

"That's so, sir. But I will find it. I'll find it if I've got to search for the next twenty years, or till I perish."

"Possibly Rainbow Gold?" murmured the doctor.

"I don't understand. What do you mean by Rainbow Gold?" implored Harry.

The doctor emptied his glass and raised his brow to signal to me to refill it. He took a cigarette from his case, and lit it as though he had forgotten us all. Then, blowing smoke to the roof, he said: "It is something like this. When you left your horse and dray at the water soak, and walked to the reef of gold and back again, your subconscious mind noted a thousand and one things not noticed by your conscious mind. It would be possible, were you placed under hypnotic control, for your subconscious mind to reveal to us every step you took that day, reveal it so clearly that a subsequent search party could walk direct to the gold-loaded reef."

"You'd mesmerise me?" Harry demanded, pushing by a man so he could get closer to the doctor.

"No man could guarantee to hypnotise a particular subject," the doctor murmured, as though he spoke to a woman, "but if you wish it, I will try to subjugate your conscious mind, or personality, and bring out what lies deep in your subconscious mind."

"Right-o sir! Get busy," Harry said, as he might to a dentist.

Both old Wontnor and the doctor being keen, they decided to carry out the experiment right away. The doctor stipulated that they would use the bar parlor, and selected me and George Little to act as witnesses and be his professional prospectors. He did not say it, but we all knew that he did not want to be accused of self-interest, and yet could not have a crowd looking on.

With the door locked - and the bar locked, too, as I could not trust anyone - Little and I were made to sit in a corner. The doctor placed a low easy-chair in a corner near the window, and then got Harry standing with his back to the light facing him. He said: "I want you, Wontnor, to just try and think of nothing in particular. Compose yourself as though for an afternoon siesta. By the way, you do take a nap in the afternoon, eh?"

"Most times I has forty winks, sir."

"Excellent! I cannot help but remark what a wonderful climate you Murchison folk enjoy. So wonderfully dry and bracing and brilliant. That is right, is it not? Sleep - you wish to sleep. Ah - yes - yes - sleep."

The doctor was looking deep into Harry's eyes, and doing something with his hands before his face, and then he stepped back a pace, and Harry, as stiff as a wooden soldier, fell forward. The doctor caught him in his arms, and spoke so softly that we couldn't hear what he said. He helped Harry across to the easy-chair, and made him sit down in it. And with Harry sitting bolt upright in the chair Doctor Death mopped his forehead with a handkerchief before sitting down in another chair so close to Harry that their knees touched.

"Now, Wontnor, attention," he said softly. "Do you hear me?"

"Yes, I hears you," Harry answered.

"Good, I'll tell you where you are. You are at the water soak, taking a horse - your horse - out of a dray on which is an empty water tank. You have decided to prospect a ridge you have several times seen peeping up above the scrub about two miles southward. Now you have started on your journey. Tell me what you see."

"I can see the whitish-brown streak of the streak atop of the scrub. I am walking down a slope." From now on Harry made many silences but I will not again refer to them. "I can't see the ridges now, as I am on low country and walking through dense timber. Now the ground is rising. I am passing on my left a patch of white quartz chips. I am climbing the ridge slope. It is covered with loose ironstone. It doesn't look likely - the ironstone is too loose. There's a bit of a breakaway over to the left of me. I'm still climbing. Cripes! Wouldn't it be great if I find on the top a reef knobbed with gold as big as my fists! You never know. In a minute or two I might make my lucky strike. Now I'm atop of the ridge. Conglomerate stuff half a mile long. No gold here. It's pretty warm. Reckon I'll take a spell and have a smoke.

"I'm sitting down with me back to a tree. I'm cutting chips off'n me plug. Now I'm smoking and easing me legs. I can see above the trees growing on the slope falling away from me southward several other ridges not so high as this one. Well, having come so far, I'll walk across to them, and give 'em a look over."

Then it was that Harry jumped up, almost knocking the doctor over, and stood glaring down at the floor at his feet. His eyes were like walnuts. After a while he flopped to his knees, and made pretend he was hugging something on the floor. He shouted:

"Gold! Look at it! Gold - gold - gold! Jumping Moses! It's gold! Lumps of gold as big as me fists - paving stones of gold!"

Harry was grunting and pawing at the floor. "Come off it! I'll get some of it if I tear me nails off. Gold - ah, ah! I'm richer than Billy Hughes and Bruce rolled into one. Wasn't I a fool not to bring a hammer?"

He sprang to his feet and stared about. The doctor was looking at him, faintly smiling.

"I must get me back to camp. I'll shift over here early tomorrow. I'll drive in them spare pegs I made last week. My beauty! Gold - tons of it! Wontnor's Reef - that's what I'll call you. Me red neckerchief - I'll tie it onto this stump, and I'll see it from the big ridge. I'll make me way back now, just to be sure I can see the flag before it gets dark. There she is fluttering in the wind as clear as clear. And there's old Fred and the dray by the soak. Now -"

"Wontnor, wait!" ordered the doctor. "You have not told me how you walked, what you saw and did, after you left the main ridge."

"After I left the main ridge? Why I - I can't remember."

"I command you to remember. Remember, do you hear?"

"I can't remember - I can't remember."

"Very well. Listen carefully. You have not told me what you saw, what you did, after leaving the gold reef up to the time you got back to the ridge from which you saw the signal neckerchief. Tell me."

"I can't remember that. I must have been thinking of the gold and of nothing else. The gold - knobs of gold as big as your fists."

Doctor Death was smiling inscrutably when he said:

"Wontnor - awake!"

"Well, sir, did you find out anything?" Harry asked when he was brought to his senses.

Doctor Death expelled a great volume of cigarette smoke before he enlightened us by saying:

"Everything. As I suspected, your lost reef is Rainbow Gold. This is what happened. You sat down on the big ridge south of the soak to enjoy a pipe and a rest. For years you have been thinking of discovering a marvellously rich reef of gold, a reef with gold lumps in it as big as your fists. Sitting there on the ridge, you fell asleep. Your reef and your tying a red neckerchief to a tree stump were the incidents of a dream, so vivid that you were not conscious of awakening to realize that it was all a dream."

"But, sir -"

"You were able to describe to us everything you saw and did up to the moment you were smoking a pipe on the ridge," the doctor went on with patient calmness. "You could tell us all about the reef, and about your tying the neckerchief to the tree stump, but there was a blank in your mind connecting your actions and thoughts on the ridge and on the reef, and there was another blank connecting action and thought between the reef and the ridge. In reality you did not leave the ridge that day; you did not prospect the lesser ridges; you did not tie a red neckerchief to the stump of a tree. As I have explained, you dreamed all that.

"Your unshakable conviction of having found a rich gold deposit is coincident with the conviction held by a dozen or so other prospectors at different places and times. They went to the trouble to mark their great finds, but never again could they find them. As they did, you have for many years day-dreamed of finding such wealth, and then, without realizing it, you really dream it. You had more than one red neckerchief in your possession; had you but the one, that one found on your neck afterwards would have created a tiny doubt in your mind.

"There is no need for you to spend the rest of your life searching for that Eldorado; for, as I at first suspected, it lies at the foot of the rainbow - Rainbow Gold. Come, let us drink."

Mirage Water

He talked a shade too much. He was a little too anxious to be thought experienced, and Joe Longford wondered about him. That he knew how to ride and to lead a pack-horse, and that he had worked on well-known stations in New South Wales was proved by Longford's eyes and his knowledge of the bosses of those stations. And yet, there was the hint of over-reaching which made him suspect the stranger's bushmanship.

Having sought for and received the invitation to stay the night, the stranger announced his name as Charlie Dawson. At dinner he explained how he had travelled across country from Lake Elder, travelled due north and keeping about twelve miles west of the great dog-proof fence dividing two States, to reach Longford's hut situated on the northern boundary of Tilsha Station. It was his intention to leave early the following morning to proceed north-westward to Tinga-Tingana, away over on the Strezlecki.

It was roughly seventy miles from the homestead of Lake Elder to Longford's hut. There were no tracks other than those connecting Lake Elder with Quinambie, east of the fence; Tilsha with Yandama, also east of the fence; and Quinambie with the several bores on Quinambie country between Lake Elder and Tilsha. It was easy country all the way, for, beside the few tracks, the sand ranges ran east-west as did the division fences.

Had the Queensland-New South Wales Rabbit Fence been continued westward for another twelve miles, it would have separated Joe's bunk from the open hearth of his hut. The hut stood within stone-throw of Tilsha's northern boundary, beyond which lay open country - country unfenced, not taken up by the squatters. To travel across to Tinga-Tingana without hitting the back fences of Montecollina and Carraweena this Charlie Dawson would not see a fence or a track for at least ninety miles – say, three days.

It was an area of country adequately explored by no one. Somewhere in it lay permanent water, established by the fact that more than once good-conditioned, wild and unbranded cattle had run the Tilsha boundary fence. The Tilsha and Yandama blacks had penetrated into it a few miles, but they knew of no permanent water. They reported sandhills, gibber flats and grass plains, mazes of dry creeks and forests of dense mulga, but never permanent water. They revealed a marked reluctance to penetrate far or remain in it long.

Men like Joe Longford would not have hesitated, were the need urgent, to cross to Tinga-Tingana. They would know how to follow a dry creek bed to locate where to dig for a soakage, or how to get water by burning a needle-wood tree from the top. Joe's guest, however, was not of the Joe Longford's type, and of this Joe was almost sure, but not quite.

There is a wide margin between the cattlemen who go droving where fences are scarce, and the sheepmen who work on stations. They are the same under their hats, to be sure, but a sheep station man having forty years' experience might well be less a bushman than a boy of sixteen reared on a cattle station on the border of Central Australia. And, anyway, even an experienced cattleman would have to keep his head when crossing from Tilsha to Tinga-Tingana in March after a dry summer.

"You know your own mind best," Longford remarked at breakfast the next morning. "There's permanent water somewhere in that country, but just where no one knows. There was a lot of lightning away to the nor'-west the other night, but that can't be relied on for rainwater in the claypans. I wouldn't take it on until after the first general rain."

"Oh, I don't know!" countered Dawson, a heavily-built man about twenty-four years old. "If I strike water any time after two o'clock to-day I'll camp and start off from it early tomorrow. I'm loadin' eight gallons on the packhorse and that should see me through at a pinch. If I head true north-west I'll strike the Strezlecki below Tinga-Tingana, and, back at Lake Elder, I heard that there's plenty of water in the Strezlecki's holes."

"Still," Joe Longford objected, "you won't do much more than thirty miles a day. The crossing will take you three days. If you push your horses in this heat, and shouldn't strike water, they'll blow out on you. No, I'm hanged if I'd take it on before it rained."

"You needn't worry about me," Dawson said confidently. "I been knocking about this dust heap too much to be stonkered by ninety miles of open country. It can't be worse than from Lake Elder up here, while the Paroo below Wanaaring, is bad enough."

Joe's blackboy already had brought the horses to the yard, and now Joe accompanied his guest across the bare, sand-covered ground to the shed beside the yard in which was the traveller's gear. Dawson was talkative while he saddled up and loaded the pack-horse with water drums, rations and swag. From the neck and to the chest of the riding animal, he strapped a two-gallon canvas waterbag. The pack-horse was a powerful black gelding, quiet and intelligent. The riding horse was a brown mare, young and still nervous. Both were in excellent condition. Carrying on his side of the conversation in monosyllables, Longford escorted Dawson to the little-used gate in the boundary fence. Beyond the gate they shook hands, and then, the cattleman having shut the gate, he stood watching Dawson and the two horses until the mulga scrub closed about them.

At twenty-four, Charlie Dawson commanded the undaunted optimism usually to be observed in a boy of twelve. He was well up to thirteen stone in weight, dark-haired, fresh-complexioned, and blue-eyed. In himself he had supreme confidence. He believed himself to be much above the average station man in intelligence and general knowledge. He knew what horse won the Melbourne Cup and the English Derby, and what team won the Victorian League Football Premiership in any year one might care to mention. He prided himself in his ability to draft sheep. He knew that he could classify wool in any shed. He had never slaughtered a bullock, but he knew, without a qualm of doubt, that he could kill and skin and dress a bullock if called on to do the job.

It was the chief fault of those blighters like Longford, who lived too much alone in huts - that mental superiority of age and experience. They got that way that they came to think they owned the top wires of a station's fences. All he would have to do was to keep his block and head due north-west. He would show these crow-eating South Australians that nothing could stop him from going anywhere at any time. Why, if any of the blighters had guts enough to make it worth while - say a bet of a couple of hundred - he would track across to Broome.

Throughout the morning of the first day out from Tilsha,

Dawson kept his horses jogging at a smart pace through low, but dense, mulga of the thin-leafed variety, and across wide and shallow depressions supporting tinder-dry herbal rubbish. The flies, of course, were an eternal torment, whilst the heat in the meagre shade must have been in the vicinity of 118 degrees. The flies and the heat were nothing extraordinary to Charlie Dawson. He was inured to both.

At noon he camped for an hour among a group of cabbage trees. So far this open country was not in bad fettle. There was a fair amount of ground feed. The scrub was healthy, if stunted, and as yet no scrub-cutter's axe had bitten into it.

Dawson was sure that he had maintained a course to the north-west. Actually he had kept himself headed just west of north, but even so the fairly high standard of his bushmanship was proved in that he had maintained a straight line.

When many men would have remained at the dinner camp until three o'clock in order to save the horses, Dawson left at one o'clock, his action dictated by the idea of reaching water early and getting an early start from it the following morning. The idea was luckily profitable and sound enough in its way. Towards four o'clock, he cut several pads made by travelling kangaroos - pads converging upon box timber. Following them he found a shallow hole in which yet remained a little muddy water. He then had travelled about twenty-seven miles from Longford's hut.

To hear that old fence lizard talk about this open country, a man would think it was just plain hell. Of course there would be water for any bloke with brains to find. Nothing was wrong with this camp. All a man had to do was to use his eyes and put two and two together by watching for animals' tracks and noting which way the birds were flying. Of course a feller would have to go a bit slow like. He would not touch the water in the drums and the bag. He would make the muddy water in this hole serve.

Knowing his horses, he hobbled them out after allowing them to drink as much as they wanted. The sun was westering, but they would have a full three hours to feed before dark. After sundown he brought them back to camp where he let them go again with shortened hobble chains. The musical notes of their bells fell upon his ears before he slept, and he heard them close by when he woke as the day was entering on another round. By sunrise he was on his way.

Presently the mulga and the box-lined flats and shallow, empty depressions gave place to bare rising ground which took him to and over the edge of a wide, open gibber and sand-dune plain. Half a mile into this country, and the scrub trees behind him had vanished, hidden from him by the lip of the raised plateau. Although the sun's heat was no less than it had been the day before, it was cooler here than down among the scrub trees. Here the light breeze tempered the heat. Here was absent that "shut-in" feeling produced by illimitable scrub. Here a man could see to far horizons, long and level or slightly curved by distant sandhills. He camped for the noon hour beneath a solitary sandalwood tree.

Afterwards the sand dunes drew away behind as man and horses travelled steadily on a course west of north - but not north-west! The gibber patches were separated by equally extensive patches of spear-grass, and over the ground on all sides the mirage created lakes and lagoons of rippleless water. To the south the sandhills he had passed were now like red islets lapped by water, and the sandalwood, beneath which he had boiled the lunch quart, towered skyward, like Jack's beanstalk.

It was funny how blokes could think that mirage was real water. Why, it could not deceive a cook's offsider! It was a nuisance, though, hemming him in like it did. It prevented a man seeing what was ahead and to either side, and as he must have covered twenty miles before lunch, bringing him forty-five at least from the Tilsha boundary. He would have to keep his eyes open for water signs. For sure, at a pinch, he would have the water in the drums for the horse after taking out a gallon to put into the depleted water bag, but they would want feed. There was none here. He hoped to reach scrub country before sundown. If he found no water, the horses would have to go dry the next day until they reached the Strezlecki.

As the afternoon wore on the light wind dropped and the temperature rose. The flies became stickily persistent. The horses lathered freely - too freely. He was pushing them too hard in his growing anxiety to get off the plain before he would have to camp. He wanted a drink badly, but he kept thirst at bay by sucking pebbles between the hourly stops to drink from the water bag.

They were now descending a long and gentle slope on which the wind had carved the sandy sub-soil into statues and steppes and fantastic images. Water gutters, deeper cut still, were utterly without moisture. Arrived at the bottom of the depression, Dawson saw that when last it had rained the surface water had been carried in giant curves to the south-west. When it had rained! By the sand drifts laying across the gutters it had not rained for years.

He was tempted to follow the curving depression, arguing that it must eventually take him to lower land and scrub, but, putting it aside, he sent his horses up the opposite slope and to the lip of another wide expanse of plain. Nowhere could be seen a tree or bush, nothing but the gibber patches and the shrivelled, tindery grass. Low on the eastern horizon a range of hills thrust up their summits like blue-black rocks above the ocean swell.

The sun was low and the mirage lakes were drying up when Dawson saw a single old man saltbush surrounded by several acres of dead grass, tussock grass. It was away on his left, but it would, he thought, provide him with enough dry sticks with which to boil the quart; and, anyhow, it was more comfortable to camp beside a bush than on wide, open country. Accordingly, he directed his horses to it. Arrived before the high, silver-grey bush, he was in the act of dismounting - his offside leg was moving back across the saddle - when a dozing kangaroo bounded from the far side of the bush.

Both horses reared violently, and loudly snorted. Dawson was flung outward from his mount, his body parallel with the ground. As he fell he turned, and it was his back and the back of his head which received the impact of the ground. When he regained consciousness and groaningly lurched to his feet, the only objects within the far-flung horizon higher than a grass stem were he and the saltbush.

Anger - blood-heating anger - welled from his heart to his aching head. He would trounce that mare when he got her! Silly fool! As though she had never before seen a kangaroo! When on their tracks, he saw that the two horses had galloped away to the west. Well, galloping would soon shift the pack on the gelding. Those filled water drums and his swag and rations would either be scattered or the whole lot with the saddle would slide down under his belly, and then he would go to market. It meant walking like hell to get them again. And the sun was low, too.

Dawson, walking hurriedly over his horses' tracks, saw where they circled to the south towards Tilsha. When the sun had vanished, when earth and sky seemed one, he ran. He was walking and running when it became too dark any longer to see the tracks.

He then had plenty of time to consider his position, a position brought about by no emphasised carelessness, no fault of bushmanship - by pure accident. What had happened might have happened to the most experienced cattleman, though it was not probable, because the experienced cattle man would sub-consciously have maintained vigilance to guard against just such an accident.

He had tobacco and papers and matches. Other than his clothes, that was all he did have. How dry he was! He lay on his back on a hard claypan and smoked whilst he glared at the winking stars, without appreciation of their soft beauty, and of the kind night. He was in a blithering mess, for sure. Back at Tilsha, they would grin and whisper and make a song about it. Dawson was too angry to be fearful of his situation, too angry even to plan escape from this open country which had trapped him.

Had he but reasoned! Had he for but a few moments taken measure of himself!

From Tilsha he had come approximately sixty-seven miles, say sixty to be on the safe side. That left thirty miles at the farthest to reach the Strezlecki - if that old fool had been right in his estimate. Anger clouded reason: the pride of a know-all. Reason would have dictated walking all that comparatively cool night; it would have directed him to get as close to the Strezlecki as he could before sunrise. But anger demanded of him that he track his horses and take it out of the mare. Pride commanded him to retrieve horses and gear - so that none would ever know.

Instead of walking he slept. It was the heat of the sun that awoke him to the reality of a parched mouth and aching bones. That was about seven o'clock. At nine he was still tracking his horses. At ten the mirage water was spreading over the plain. At eleven he saw the horses away to the west, and, leaving their tracks to reach them by a direct route, he stumbled through the "water" only to find that the horses were two old-man saltbushes.

It was curious, walking through this mirage water and being unable to drink and drink. It was the heat, of course, that was making his eyes register splashes of blood against the silver mirage.

At one o'clock he was still trying to cut his horses' tracks, but an hour later that one idea which had tortured his shrivelling brain had been replaced by that of finding water.

Water! He must find water! It must be real water, not this mirage water lying all round him, lying in the claypans and over the patches of gibber stones. Well, he was not going to run here and there to those lakes and lagoons of mirage water. He was not that much of a newchum. He would have to keep right on, stop for nothing, walk and walk north-west to the Strezlecki. Of course he knew that the mirage would grow ever more enticing, ever more seductive.

Why, it was even splashing about his feet, wetting his boots, pretending to cool his feet! But he was not fool enough to be had by a mirage. Not he! He was no newchum. Go on, you mirage water, splash about, splash about! Mirage water in the claypans! Mirage water in the claypans! He couldn't shout it, but the phrase was loud enough within his brain. The claypans were full of mirage water, mirage water, mirage water!

Quite abruptly will-power failed. With its failure so failed his physical strength. He made one last effort to keep on his feet. Then he pitched forward on to sandy ground between two large claypans.

He was found by old Bill Mackay, who, with his blackboy, was attracted to the spot by the gathering eagles. A thunderstorm had dropped water along a narrow belt of country less than 500 yards wide, and Dawson had walked across several small claypans containing water half an inch deep before collapsing between two of them.

From then on he lost just a little of his overweening confidence in himself.

Bill Mackay's camels sucked up water from one claypan, and Dawson was revived with water taken from the other. At last he knew that a man could know too much.

The Stalker of Lone Men

The dummy post lay propped against the bark-topped, six-feet-high, netted barrier separating New South Wales from South Australia. The mulga post to which the dummy was to be lashed with wire was rotted below ground. It had done yeoman service for many years, and now the stubborn bark still clung tenaciously to the parent wood.

The boundary-rider's axe was lifted to the top of the post and the blade permitted to fall by its own weight behind the bark in order to make the dummy fit closely. The bark came away easily, too easily. The pressure of the axe behind it forced a long slab hard against Elder's left shoulder, and the reddish dust which had lain hidden behind it became a cloud to sweep into the man's eyes.

It was the dust of a long-dead fungus, a dust more potent than cayenne pepper. Like pepper it burned, and, again like pepper, it blinded.

Elder dropped the axe, swayed away from the fence, tore at his eyes and swore. With a sleeve of his shirt wetted with saliva, he endeavored to remove the dust from his eyes, but after a full minute of frantic effort, though the pain eased a little, he was still as blind as a day-old pup.

Because he had not turned round he was able to clutch the fence with one hand. The fence now was the only connecting link between him and the real world, a gateway, as it were, leading out from the dull-red darkness behind his tightly-shut eyes into the brilliant world of a July afternoon in far-western New South Wales.

Elder cursed the dust with the fluency of a man long accustomed to talking at inanimate objects and to himself. Then, sitting down with his back against the fence, he pressed his eyes into a shirt-sleeved arm supported on bent knees.

It had hurt like hell, that red powder. Its action had been swift. For a fraction of a second he had seen it whirling towards his face, but it had come so quickly that he had not had time to close his eyelids. In an instant the rotted post and the bark, and the red-brown sand lying beyond the mesh of the fence, had been wiped out by a fallen red curtain.

Through the utterly still air came drifting the musical tinkle of the bells suspended from the necks of his three feeding camels. Other than the ringing bells, the only sound impinging on the background of the silence was a blow-fly's faint, thin humming.

At long last the watching spirit of the bush had struck.

Elder had been working on the dog-proof fence where it crossed a narrow, rubbish-covered flat. On either side the flat was bordered by a massive range of sand footed with stunted mulga and crowned here and there with cotton-bush. This flat and the bordering sand-ranges were duplicated for miles to north and south; it was as though a mighty wind had risen the earth-like water into a raging sea, had blown up mile-long billows of clean sand, in the trough of which lay the narrow clay flats. Crossing this tremendous sea, keeping to the north-south boundaries of two States, the frontier barrier lay like a switchback railway track.

For an hour Elder, seated at the foot of the fence, worked on his useless eye with a shirtsleeve wetted with saliva, worked without achieving any result except to redden and make sore the inflamed lids. To lift them was possible only by using the fingers, and even then vision was not mastered, for he could see nothing but the dull-red curtain dropped by the fungus dust.

Clear understanding of his plight came slowly. A mile distant his camels were feeding in hobbles. Back along the next flat northward, amid a clump of mulgas, was pitched his tent. The nearest habitation was a station homestead twenty-two miles south of east. The nearest water supply was at Blackfeller's Bore, to reach which he would have to travel the fence southward for three miles, and then pass through a gate into South Australia and follow a faint track for seven miles.

Everything had been so right and safe in a crystal-clear world, and the bush spirit or banshee, or whatever you may care to call it, had appeared to be sleeping or absent on a long journey.

People who live at station homesteads, and those who explore Australia accompanied by a great retinue, do not believe that the bush has a personality, one that watches and waits the opportunity to strike at lone men. But the blacks believe it, and so do the few white men who, like Elder, live and work for long periods completely shut off from human contact.

The bush spirit does not trouble itself with men in crowds, for men in mass can defy it. It stalks lonely men and bides its time to prove its mastery. Made careless by the beauty of the day, Elder at last had given the spirit of the bush a chance, and it quickly proved that it was neither absent nor asleep.

It had caught Jim Matthews on that very fence. When Matthews had broken a leg climbing over the barrier, it had watched him crawl on one knee and two hands for slightly more than a mile, and then it had waited outside his tent during the full week in January until he died.

There was Mick Hogan. Hogan was patrolling the great Number One Rabbit Fence in Westralia when the bush spirit frightened the camels at the moment Hogan was climbing up into his heavy-hooded dray over one of the shafts instead of up the step at the rear. One wheel of the dray ran up a fence post and the dray tipped over to crush Hogan into the track and keep him there for hours before he died.

They who have been lured away by the spirit of the bush are legion. Those victims were shown the cunning and the malignance of the bush spirit or banshee. It lay at their feet sparkling sheets of water - in dry claypans. It painted for them in the distance pictures of beautiful houses and running streams and green gardens - at the feet of sun-scorched sand-dunes.

It stuck Elder on the S.A. Border Fence when least expected. It rendered him more helpless than it had Jim Matthews when he broke his leg. Although Elder could hear his camel bells, although by their aid he could have groped his way to them, he would still be helpless without one of the noselines hanging over a tree branch at his camp. And, had he a length of string or tie-wire to use as a noseline, it would be unlikely that his riding beast would take him to the nearest homestead, as its home was the twenty-one-mile section of fence now controlled by Elder.

For a little while panic raged through his brain. Then Sanity touched him with her cold and soothing fingers.

He must try to reach his camp, and to do that he must be, and he must remain, icily calm. Once at his camp he could doctor his eyes with Condy's crystals; once there he commanded water.

At all cost he must find his camp. It had been cold enough the last night to freeze into a solid block the tea remaining in the billy. It would be as cold this coming night. With him he had neither coat nor waistcoat. With him he had not a single match. If he did not find the camp -

Not without difficulty he created in his mind a picture of the next flat northward. It was about a quarter of a mile wide: therefore, it was about 440 yards from the edge of one sand-range to the edge of the other. The mulgas among which was his camp grew in the middle of the flat and about 600 yards back from the fence. Between those mulgas and the fence all was clear, hard ground except for a clump of the same trees growing towards the southern sand-range. Were he to walk beside the fence northward over the first sand-range to its far edge, and then take about 185 paces, he should arrive opposite his camp - about. Then by walking straight for 600 yards he would arrive at the clump of mulgas and the camp.

Curse it! There was too much "about" in these calculations. But he had to make the effort, and he had to keep cool, or the banshee would finish him before the morning. Fool that he had been ever to work at a job like this! Even the blacks wouldn't take it on.

There, there! He must keep cool. He would be lost if he didn't keep his block. There was no occasion to panic yet. He could still tell the direction from which the sun was shining, for when he turned his face to the west the red curtain was noticeably brighter.

Having reached the place which he thought to be opposite his camp, he stood with his back against the fence and squared himself with it by stretching out his arms and touching the wire mesh with the backs of his hands. Then he stepped away.

At once the severance of himself with the object made familiar to him during three years threatened to submerge his mind in the whirlpool of fear. He wanted to turn round and rush back to the comforting feel of it. It was the only gateway out of that appalling world of red-tinged darkness.

Then he remembered that as long as the sun shone, as long as the bells continued to tinkle, he could find his way back to the barrier.

Calm now, he stepped forward resolutely, counting the paces he took, estimating that at each step he would cover two feet six inches of ground. The camel bells were of great assistance in keeping him straight. The beasts were feeding north of east. He must keep the sounding bells at a point left of front.

When he fell the first time, tripping over a stick, his body received no hurt, but his mind was emptied of the number of paces he had taken from the fence. When he fell the second time, panic mastered him, although his mind triumphed to the extent of ordering him to lie still until he had in turn mastered panic. Thus, when again he stood up, he faced the same point that he had been facing when he fell.

After that the bush spirit began its real work on him. It played with him as though he were a mouse and it a cat. It tugged at his trousers, it scratched his arms, it prodded his out-thrust hands, and it whipped his unguarded face.

He found himself among timber and low, entangling bushes. There were no bushes among the mulgas about his camp.

Grimly determined, he ignored the teasing bush and plunged onward. At last he halted to swear loudly at his own foolishness in not immediately returning to the fence when he first knew he had missed the camp.

Obviously he must go back to the fence and start out again. Through his closed eyelids he found the position of the sun, and he did not have to tilt his head far back to do that. With the sun and the bells to aid him, he stepped cautiously, feeling with his feet for fallen timber and entangling bushes.

Then he was treading loose sand. Sand! How could sand come between him and the sun? Ah, he must be at the edge of the southern sand-range! Keeping the sunlight to his left check, he presently trod onto the hard clay of the flat. Then, when he was beginning to fear that he was again slewed, his fingers touched the border barrier.

He had regained the fence. That was something. He was given another chance to find the camp.

Far away the camel bells clashed most unmusically - and ceased to ring. The beasts had eaten their fill and had laid themselves down for the night. The outside world became strangely quiet. Before he heard the caw-caw-caw of the passing crow, Elder heard the swishing of its wings. When the crow had gone on to drink at the bore stream he was left in the silence.

Men flee from silence as they flee from pestilence. In the cities they find the quiet of an empty house too much for their nerves. The quiet becomes a stalking phantom. Lonely men in the heart of the bush pile wood on their campfires in order to beat back the silence with crackling flames. Other men living in huts play an accordion or a mouth-organ; and those in homesteads are blessed with squalling children or the radio or a piano. All men dread the silence, the silence absolute, the silence which thunders on a man's eardrums so that they hurt.

The mind is dwarfed by silence. The bush walls close in on one like the walls of the Inquisitors, or they fall back into infinity to leave a man naked and defenceless, like a snail without its shell. The silence of the bush is worse than the silence of a dungeon. The wretch in the dungeon can hear his own breathing.

Elder shivered when the silence fell about him like a cloak that he could feel. It was then that he realised his feet were cold. In a flash he turned to the fence. The sun no longer lightened the red fog before his eyes - not even when he lifted the lids with his fingers. It had set, and already the air was brittle with frost.

Now he could feel the presence of the banshee. He could feel it! It was all around him, waiting to rush into his mind and drive him on and on, anywhere, whilst he screamed for mercy and fought it.

Now - now! Steady! He had one more chance, although he no longer had the sun and the bells as compasses. Fool that he was to have wasted time hanging to the fence. He hurried along it to find the edge of the southern sand-range, then to turn and walk back for 185 paces to bring him once again to the supposed centre of the flat, keeping touch with the barrier with a hand drumming against the wire. With renewed hope, he left it on his second attempt to find his camp.

They say that a lost man walks in circles because he makes a longer stride with one leg than with the other. He had to chance that. He had to find the camp before the frost sent him to sleep for ever. The frost! Already the tips of his ears and his nose were tingling.

Then his groping feet trod on sand, fine, yielding sand.

He is a fool who says there is no sinister spirit of the bush, no banshee, to torture a man once it has him at its mercy. Now it spread beneath Elder's feet the soft pile of sand, and tempted him to lie down and take his ease.

He screamed defiance and stumbled on, and so came again to clay. Then the banshee led him to a mulga patch and tortured him with sharp-pointed sticks. It tripped him with sticks and whipped his face with a scourge. It sent trees marching against him to fling him back from the camp he must reach or perish.

The silence retreated every time he cursed the banshee, but it closed again like a vice when he ceased. The silence was not the banshee. Oh, no! It was the banshee's mate. It joined the banshee in this rough-house wherein a man played blindman's bluff for his life.

The reddish smear of colour was no longer before his eyes. Now it was dark - and cold. He struggled on, tormented by the bush, fighting it now on sand and now on hard clay. Just where he was only the mocking banshee knew. All feeling had gone from his ears and nose. Despite constant movement, the frost was attacking his heart, cramping his chest to the point of restricting his breathing.

When he tripped for the last time, and crashed headlong, he lay for a while sobbing with rage, his face pressed against one arm, the other stretched forward with the hand clenched.

He had had enough. He could do nothing more until the sun got up, and meanwhile he might as well sleep. He would never find the damned camp in the dark; he could make no fresh start to find it from the fence until the sun brightened the red curtain before his eyes.

Only in the hand of the outstretched arm did he feel any pain. The rest of him was numb, without feeling. The pain of the hand became worse. It prevented him from sleeping. It cleared his fogged mind before he could muster sufficient effort to move his arm.

Then he knew. His hand was being burned. It lay in a soft bed. With a strangled cry he lurched forward and plunged his other hand into that same soft bed. It was the ashes of his almost cold campfire. Beyond it, only a few feet beyond it, was the entrance to his tent.

Laffer's Gold

George Laffer, a boundary-rider employed by the Government of Western Australia, slid off his canvas stretcher and placed the half-filled billy of blue-black tea on the red embers of the camp fire. He listened for a sound, a particular sound, but the silence of the bush beat on his ears this morning more painfully than any uproar of hurricane and storm. Presently the billy began to "sing," and the sound was as morphia in the relief of pain.

The magic half-light of early dawn revealed a heavy, two-wheeled, hooded cart beside a narrow track that ran parallel with a netted barb-wire fence that stretched north and south as far as the eye could see. On the canvas stretcher-bed near the cart the blankets revealed the fact that the man had not slept in, but on them, the night having been hot.

While listening for the sound of camel-bells and sipping his blue-black tea, George Laffer felt no chill through his thin pyjamas. The singing billy having been removed from the fire, the silence again was portentous; but at long last, when the world lay bathed in the scarlet reflection of the sky, it was broken by the chatter of galahs in a distant swampgum.

"Another snorter!" commented the man to the low bush, hemming him in on all sides, unbroken in its dark greenness, almost devoid even of insect life. "Another snorter!" he repeated. "How sick and tired I am of this filthy heat! How long have I been out here? Twenty years - twenty years! And no better off now than when I first landed. Sunny Australia! Well, there's no argument. I'm not arguing."

Up from behind a long low ridge fifteen miles away the gigantic sun crept, magnified by the smoke of bush fires into an enormous single drop of blood. Before half its size had appeared the temperature began to rise, and when the whole of it was above the ridge the heat of an English midsummer noon filled all that world of desolation.

A few minutes later, dressed in cotton slacks, khaki shirt, and wearing a wide-brimmed hat, he took up the camels' nose-lines and left camp to track them. Making for a small, shallow, waterless creek bordered by gnarled swamp-gums, he found the winding snake-like trail formed by a length of chain buckled to a camel's foreleg. The large flat rubbery feet of the animal make tracks so very faint that a drag-chain is necessary by which to track them. Following the mark of the chain, it led him in a generally straight line to the north-east; and, whilst walking with long swinging strides, he talked aloud.

"Yes - twenty years. Twenty years of living on tinned dog and damper and tea, with an occasional visit to a city. And as poor this day as when I started. What's the good of health if you haven't money, and friends, and luxury? I'm that healthy I'm near starved to death for a good feed in a slap-up London hotel. Gad! Think of it! Bacon and eggs and toast and coffee set out on a real table covered by a snow-white table-cloth, and outside a proper London fog!

"And this! This for twenty years. Heat, heat, heat! A man's blood like water. A man's skin as parchment. No one to say good morning to. The sweat trickling into your eyes and gluing the shirt to your back. They call it life, the money-making city fellers. They call it freedom in the vast open spaces. And I'm tempted to sling in this dead-beat's job and rush to Perth, where I could smash a shop-window and go to gaol, and have the comfort of a roof over my head and four walls around me."

The sunlight falling on Laffer's right cheek burned it. He moved his hat to the side of his head to shade his face. It was reflected from the light-red ground and the gleaming bush foliage with an eye-paining glare. The wind, gentle as a zephyr, came as from between the bars of a northern furnace, and banished the silence with a million whispering voices.

Over the ground, winding between low scrub-trees and stunted bushes, laid the endless mark of the drag-chain. Laffer saw where the animals had paused here and there to feed from the unlovely bush of the desert. Desert! It was worse than a desert, this hundred-mile strip between the wheat belts and the northern pastoral country. He observed, too, the tracks of a giant monarch iguana, and later saw where a curious dingo had halted, circled, and then followed the camels' trail for a little distance. As though team bullocks were being driven to camp, a bird perched in a near gimlet tree imitated the clanging bell with ever increasing volume of sound. Laffer loudly cursed the bell-bird.

He had walked three miles before he heard ahead of him the genuine tinkle of the bells strapped to his camels' necks. It was then that he made a cigarette, and when it was between his lips, and then only, did he cease his everlasting monologue. More from habit now than from necessity, he followed the mark of the drag-chain.

A gleam of yellow light halted him, pin's head in size. It was as though the yellow beam was the head of Medusa and had turned him to stone. The world about him banished from his mind. The sun's heat was no longer felt. The succession of thoughts stopped at the one stupendous, flaring, fixed vision of gold.

Very slowly he fell on his knees, his gaze fixed upon that speck of gold, fearful that should it escape his eyes never more would he see it. Very slowly he put out his hand and picked up a piece of amber-coloured quartz. The camel's drag chain had turned it over, and its underside, clean and protected from weather, was studded with little knobs of gold.

Gold! Men toil all their lives to amass wealth, and seldom see gold, save in jeweller's windows. Men have toiled all their lives searching for gold, and never, never have they found it. And men, a very few, have stumbled on gold as did George Laffer one hot morning in early January. It has been found among the roots of wind-wrecked trees, in the sand rills of waterless creeks, and shot through and through great bars of stone. The mere sight of gold, not the quantity of it, has sent men raving mad, or made them caper as monkeys and scream with an overwhelming ecstasy, or stunned them with mental pictures of luxury and power.

For long minutes George Laffer knelt with the gold-studded quartz held in his two hands, and it was not visions of an alluring future which flitted across the curtain of his mind, but pictures of the years that were passed.

The home he had left. The old water-mill on the lovely, sparkling, green-banked river in Hampshire, adjoining which was the creeper-clad house wherein he had been born. Water! Running, glinting water had been the real companion of his youth. Young, strong, and keen, he had come to Australia to make his fortune. Time had stripped him of all illusions that romance and propaganda had created. He could have gone to work on a farm, he could, ere this, have owned a farm; instead, he went north among the stations, and there remained.

For twenty years Laffer had been satisfied to work for wages; but always had he dreamed dreams of England, suffered that terrible sickness which only the exile knows, because in his heart he could not become a good Australian. And now, with one blow, Fortune had set him free, had picked him up and set him down a winner in the race for success. Now he would return home, prosperous and self-assured, a living example of the great opportunities extant in Australia. No one would remember the twenty years of grinding poverty and failure.

The burning sun rose in a sky of brass, and still he knelt fingering the piece of quartz, the Aladdin's lamp, Balzac's wild ass's skin. He had read of the lamp, but not of the skin. He knew he had but to rub the lamp and the genie would appear to do his will; he did not know that every time he wished the ass's skin would shrink, and when finally it shrank to nothing he would be nothing as well.

It seemed almost that the gold in the stone did actually command the genie when rubbed, for now intruding among his visions came memory of his wandering camels, and, looking up, he saw them hobbling back over the trail towards him. Standing, he took one step towards them, intending to slip the noselines over the wooden plugs drawn through a nostril, before marking the gold-studded reef so that he would again easily find it. It was then that he stiffened with the horror of the thought that once he left the place he might not again discover it - a ghastly experience that had occurred to many before him.

He had to force his mind back into the calm channel of its habit, compel it to turn from its flashing pictures of affluence in glorious England, and concentrate on the shrivelling desert in this particular area of Western Australia. He nose-lined the camels and removed the hobbles, but left the drag-chain buckled to one camel's foreleg, so that when he took them back to camp it would make a double trail he could the more assuredly follow.

Having eaten a hurried breakfast, he took an axe and cunningly blazed a trail to his discovery; and there he cut pegs and paced out a claim. And his claim covered the cap of what proved to be an exceedingly rich reef.

Laffer sold his claim for £23,000 to a syndicate who hope to make four times that amount on the deal. He could not wait an unnecessary second to escape through a golden door from the bush he hated, yet which had enslaved him. And before leaving the bush he could not refrain from cursing its harshness and jibing at its inability longer to hold him, for the years had given him belief that the bush was a living entity possessing a malignant personality.

On February 21 he took possession of his private suite on a liner bound for London. During five wonderful weeks he revelled in sheer luxury and dreamed of the home he would buy overlooking a wide, beautiful river that never ran dry. His every wish was granted. Even the weather respected his desires and the sea was as smooth as a mill-pond.

At Gibraltar he had his suit of thick tweed and an overcoat brought out, and he was glad of the forethought he had shown in purchasing the heavy wool-lined coat when he stepped into the train at Tilbury out of a driving snowstorm.

Cold! He was never colder in his life. His blood was as thin as vinegar. How earnestly he wished for warmth! What a fool he had been to come away from the bush! But the ass's skin had shrunk to nothing, and three days later he was dead with pneumonia.

A Lovely Party

Like dark-green velvet rumpled in mighty folds, the Darling
Downs rolled away to the four points of the compass. Despite
the brilliance of the full moon, the world was calm and still in
slumber, and the noises made by the raised voices of men within a
room of the homestead were collectively like a virago's tirade
when a lover's whisper would have been more in keeping with
nature's mood.

Six gentlemen lounged about the clothless table in the dining
room at Muirraddin, before them bottles of old brandy, boxes of
cigars and a jar of Virginian tobacco, and now, at the hour of
eleven, they were in that condition denoting a too-long sojourn at
table after the departure of the ladies.

Arrayed in the tight-fitting, uncomfortable clothes of the
period - the middle 1840's - the gathering at Muirraddin was the
result of a statement issued by a person known as Jack Wilson,
the leader of as choice a gang of ruffians as ever appeared in the
pages of a tuppenny dreadful to delight the heart of a small boy.
Wilson had announced his intention of visiting the Darling
Downs and of making himself known personally to the rich
squatters who possessed the wherewithal of sustaining him and
his comrades.

Muirraddin Station was the largest and most prosperous in all
the wide district, whilst its owner, Mr. Henry Whitmore, was long
regarded the uncrowned king of this same district. He had called
together all his near and most influential neighbours to discuss
this Wilson fellow and formulate ways and means of
accomplishing his discomfiture should he have the audacity of
putting his threat into execution.

In deference to the feelings of those charming ladies, Mrs.
Whitmore and the two Misses Whitmore, the guests had parked
their armaments in the morning room before going in to dinner,
and at the close of dinner, when Mrs. Whitmore said that she and
her daughters would retire for the night and thus leave the
gentlemen to get along with their plans, the gentlemen had
reached that comfortable feeling when the exertion of re-arming

themselves would indeed have been a bore.

It must be recorded that the excellent dinner, topped up by the brandy, did not tend to defence-planning. To be sure, Mr. Whitmore had suggested that the best course for all to pursue was to hang together - meaning, naturally, to keep together, act in unison and not to be suspended together from a height.

"Dashed good idea," wheezed old Mr. Longman, mopping his round, red face with a huge silk handkerchief of royal purple. He was like a gasping fish out of water, and he found that the acceptance of ideas made by others was far easier than the labour of putting forth ideas of his own.

"Yes, we must - haw! - hang together," put in Captain Mayhew, who was tall and lean and leathery, beady of eye and Roman of nose.

It was now that the inaptness of the expression was realised by Mr. Champion, a gentleman who affected a lisp, drooping moustaches and long side-whiskers.

"He-he! Doothid good, that. I thay, doothid good, that. Hang together! Let us hope it will be Jack Wilson and his gang who will hang together."

A fleeting frown was portrayed on the big, weather-beaten, generous face of Mr. Whitmore. The fat and perspiring Mr. Longman wheezed when he stretched forward to reach the nearest brandy bottle. A chair scraped on the polished hardwood floor, and Lieutenant Anthony, on a visit from Moreton Bay, arose like a male Venus, with brandy dripping from his glass.

"Gentlemen! Gentlemen!" he called. "Be gad! I almost wish that this scoundrelly Wilson and his scoundrelly associates would turn up in this district. Aye, even at this very house. Be gad! Even now, to-night. We would give them a very warm welcome and, damme, if our own Jack Ketch would have much to do afterwards. Let us drink, gentlemen, to the good fortune of a meeting with the bail-up blackguards."

"To the meeting!" roared the company, and Lieutenant Anthony, a little wobbly, resumed his chair.

"I did hear, gentlemen, that Bushranger Wilson rides a brown filly reported as stolen from Mr. Wilder's station over towards Wide Bay. The filly is a descendant of that marvellous Saint George brought from Sydney on the *Shamrock* by our friend Mr.

Patrick Leslie." Every eye was turned towards the speaker, a hard-faced, muscular-bodied man of middle-age named Spinks.

Mr. Spinks, having captured the attention of conference, continued: "Gentlemen, I want that filly. Jack Wilson will not require her any longer after we have dealt with him and his gang. Besides, Mr. Wilder has announced that whosoever captures the outlaw may take the animal and welcome. Ever since I clapped eyes on Saint George in '42, I've sworn to possess one of his stock."

"I'll warrant Wilson's horse is no match for my Lovely Lass, who is descended from that same Saint George," loudly asserted Mr. Whitmore.

"That will make us happy to prove, sir," rasped Mr. Spinks. "Having dealt with this rascally Wilson and his followers, I shall be eager to run his brown filly with your mare, Mr. Whitmore."

"Good! Excellent!" shouted the company. "Lay a bet, Mr. Spinks."

The poker-faced Mr. Spinks and the smiling host regarded each other.

"We'll run 'em over the mile," suggested Mr. Whitmore.

"Agreed. Shall we wager a cool hundred guineas?"

"Yes. That will make the race interesting," assented Mr. Whitmore.

"Haw!" ejaculated Captain Mayhew. "I'm thinking I will back Lovely Lass to win. Who will take my ten guineas?"

Mr. Champion took up the captain. "I will, my deah Captain Mayhew," he said. "Yeth, I have the pleathure of accepting your wager. He-he! But first, Mr. Spinks, you have to get the brown filly. It - he-he - it might be a chicken that refuthes to hatch."

"I'll wager fifty guineas on Lovely Lass: be gad, I will," shouted Lieutenant Anthony. "Who'll take me?"

"What recklessness! Oh, what recklessness!"

The voice came from outside one of the three open windows. The gentlemen froze in their chairs. Fingers became clenched about the stems of brandy glasses. And then, as one man, they sprang to their feet to glare at the windows, upon the sills of which rested musket barrels, and above and beyond which were the faces of bearded and dishevelled knights of the track. Mr. Whitmore loudly sighed as a punter does when a dead cert fails to run the course. Captain Mayhew swore with unexpected violence. Mr. Champion tittered. Mr. Longman mopped up perspiration with the royal purple handkerchief, and Lieutenant Anthony appeared to be hypnotised.

The weapons were all in the adjoining room.

For several seconds the tableau remained perfect. Then the door was opened and the six gentlemen turned to it to observe enter a neatly dressed man, round of body and round of face; a small man nimble on his feet and quick in all his mannerisms; a cheerful, perky sparrow of a man. He was followed by two bewhiskered fellows who, in dress and stature, were his antithesis. He carried no visible arms; they were armed with muskets and pistols thrust into belts.

"Gentlemen! Permit me, I pray you, to introduce myself. Mr. John Wilson, gentlemen, entirely at your service." The notorious bushranger bowed with emphasised grace.

"I trust to find you all in very good health, gentlemen. Please remain seated. You see, my friends here and outside are very nervous fellows. It is their manner of living, you understand, that makes them so nervous. It is a peculiar condition, and one which had provided me with no small degree of interest, that the complaint is worse in their trigger fingers than in any other part of their bodies.

"So now, gentlemen, unbend - unbend! I will drink a glass with you. My friends will take it in turn to join us. We will make a night of it, gentlemen - 'deed we will."

Mr. Wilson now addressed himself directly to Mr. Whitmore. "Have no uneasiness concerning the ladies, Mr. Whitmore. One of my friends has slipped a wedge beneath their respective room doors, while another is on guard outside their windows. They will not be disturbed.

"Ah, excellent brandy, this. All the way from France, I'll warrant. They do say that a long sea voyage mightily improves brandy, and now I believe it. Drink, gentlemen, drink! Your good health, gentlemen."

But the gentlemen, haughty and stiff, tried to stare down the bushranger in the manner of that day - and failed. This Jack Wilson, despite his small stature and nondescript appearance, could not be successfully stared down. His geniality, his impish humour, countered hostility to such an extent that, as Mr. Champion afterwards declared: "How could a man long rethith such a light heart?"

A commotion came from without the door, and the urbane and smiling Mr. Wilson hastened to assure the gentlemen. "Sirs, be not uneasy. Some of my friends are bringing in the cook, and the servants are bringing in food. We will eat, drink and be merry. Again, gentlemen, your good health. Come, come, unbend gentlemen. Be merry, for, as the poet or someone hath said, to-morrow we die."

"If the 'we' refers to you and your associates, Wilson, then the poet or someone speaks true," rasped Spinks.

"Ah, that may be, Mr. Spinks," instantly agreed the bushranger. "To-morrow is a long time ahead, and before then many men could die. The thought saddens me when I would be merry. Ah, I was forgetting. A couple of my friends have gone out for all your horses. Thank you, gentlemen, for keeping them so handy. I have long had my eye on a mare named Lovely Lass. Yours, Mr. Whitmore? Well, I will leave with you my Gay Girl in exchange, so there will be no robbery in so far as concerns our horses. And now kindly permit me to withdraw for a few moments while the servants can prepare the board, as I wish to collect the weapons you so thoughtfully left in the next room. That done, we will set to in very earnest and make the welkin ring with our joy."

"Haw!" snorted Captain Mayhew. "The devil! We'll never hear the last of this."

Mr. Longman groaned. Mr. Spinks' face became even harder in expression. Mr. Whitmore vacantly regarded a bearded giant of a man whose tattered clothes emitted dust when he moved, and who now reached over the table to take up a bottle one third filled with brandy. He upended the bottle and drank the liquor as though it were water. Mr. Whitmore's curiosity overcame the stunning shock caused by this surprise visit.

The bearded ruffian drained the bottle and set it down upon the table with a thud. The gap in the whiskers widened when it could be seen that the fellow was smiling his appreciation, and now with one hand pressed to his stomach he bowed and leered upon the company.

"Ah - that there's a drop o' the real Malone," he said without a stutter. "Now, gents, take 'er easy. Take 'er easy, now. Mr. Wilson will be back in a jiffy. Meanwhile, being his first mate, as it were, I'm the bull in this ring, and the first gent wot gets to his feet is gonna go to hell."

Mr. Spinks flashed a glance at his host, and then, pushing towards the ruffian a half-full bottle of brandy, he said tauntingly: "I'll bet you a guinea, my man, you could not swill all of that."

The bearded man bellowed with laughter. "One guinea, eh! Make it two, mister. Show us yer money."

Mr. Spinks worked a hand into a tight breeches pocket and withdrew a purse both large and heavy. He was in the act of abstracting two sovereigns when the bushranger leaned further forward over the table and snatched the purse.

Silence fell upon this very mixed gathering. The six gentlemen seated about the table, stiff in attitude and stony of expression; the huge, bearded ruffian holding the purse on the palm of an outstretched hand as though, from its weight, estimating the value of its contents; the several tatterdemalions standing just inside the door; the sinister musket barrels thrust into the room across the window sills with the faint blotches of men's faces beyond them.

And then the silence was shattered by the giant's roar: "Ho-ho! I'll hold the stake money!"

The ensuing silence was broken by the cold and precise voice of Mr. Spinks, who said: "You snatch-purse, throat-cutting blackguard! However, as the purse contains nineteen guineas, I'll wager that to nothing that you fail to empty the bottle. You haven't the stomach for it, my man. Why, you are drunk already."

"Drunk? Me drunk?" gasped the outlaw. "Why, I'm as sober as a young gal. Oh, I see yer wheeze, mister, but it won't 'ave no effect on me. I can drink twice as much without battin' an eyelid."

"Of course you can," interposed the chuckling voice of Mr. Wilson, who had quietly entered the room and now edged himself to the side of the burly ruffian. "Of course you can, Mr. Barker. Proceed now, I pray you, to win the wager."

Barker's face indicated horror. "But, cap'n, the bottle's half-full brandy, cap'n, brandy."

"But, Mr. Barker, you can drink twice as much. You said so. We know you can. On behalf of the Knights of the Track, you have accepted the wager. You will not, I am sure, decline to uphold our reputation and our - er - honour."

"But - but -"

"We are waiting, Mr. Barker."

"But - Oh, all right. Gimme some water with it."

"Water, Mr. Barker? Water! You astonish me, 'deed you do. Water! Never in all my life have I heard of water being used to assist the swallowing of good brandy. Why, it would be murder, Mr. Barker. I never thought to hear you request the assistance of water to partake of your liquor. Come, now - we are still waiting."

Again silence ruled the gathering. There, beside the table, stood the giant, shaggy like a huge bear, unsteady on his feet from the spirit he had already taken. There before him stood the little, rotund, dandified Jack Wilson, a very terrier baiting a very bear. About them stood half a dozen other outlaws, dusty, unshaven, their clothes in rags. By the door stood the terrified house cook and servants.

Wilson was as much master of his gang as now he was master of the situation. "Mr. Barker, I fear you are wasting time," he said quietly.

Mr. Barker swore into his beard. Then he appeared to be on the point of revolt. He glared down at his chief, into the little man's eyes. What he saw in their depths swept away his opposition like a flake of snow fallen into a camp fire, and almost hastily he thrust the purse into a capacious pocket with one hand, and with the other snatched up the bottle, which he placed to his mouth and proceeded to drain in great gulps.

"Excellent, Mr. Barker. Done without a gasp. We are proud of you," Wilson remarked conversationally. "Dear me! Steady, Mr. Barker, steady!"

Mr. Barker was obviously experiencing extraordinary sensations. The pupils of his eyes turned upward so that only the whites were showing. His great body was swaying even more and more. Then his eyelids dropped and from his throat and nose issued a heavy snore. He pitched forward and would have fallen on Wilson had not Wilson stepped daintily aside to permit the gross body to crash to the floor.

"Be gad, the fellow's committed suicide," gasped Lieutenant Anthony. "Be gad, three-quarters of a bottle of old French."

"Sir," began the beaming Mr. Wilson, "nothing could kill our mutual friend save a rope or a bullet. Martin!"

While a tall, solemn person made his way through the crush, Wilson said to Mr. Spinks: "I take it unkind of you, sir, to attempt by a wager to lure one of my men - and my best man, too - into a condition of *hors de combat*. I shall remember you, sir."

To ease a situation which was fast becoming tense, Captain Mayhew hawed twice and begged leave to have a drink himself.

"My dear Captain Mayhew!" cried Mr. Wilson in affected horror. "Of course, of course! Gentlemen, fill your glasses. Come inside all bar Mr. Snooks and four men, who will keep guard for the first hour. Let the servants portion the food and set it before us. More glasses, there! More bottles from the cellar! Ha, Martin! Remove Mr. Spinks' purse from Mr. Barker's pocket."

"Certainly, sir."

The solemn bushranger stooped and obtained the purse, which he deferentially offered to Wilson. Wilson took it, opened it, and poured out the sovereigns into his left, hand. The coins he dropped into a side pocket. The purse he slid across the table to Mr. Spinks.

"Your purse, Mr. Spinks," he said gayly. "The money won by our mutual friend belongs rightly in share to every member of my command."

Quick in his movements, this sparrow of a man made room for himself between Mr. Whitmore and Mr. Longman, and sat himself down. The man Martin came and stood behind his chair.

Loudly Wilson coughed to gain attention, and, having gained it instantly, he said: "I am overwhelmed, gentlemen, by finding myself in such distinguished and convivial company. Martin, have the servants set food before us. Have tables brought in, and chairs, that our friends might take their ease, too. See that all receive food and drink. Only a little drink, Martin. Say half a bottle of brandy each. Should such a small drink overcome any man's gentlemanly instincts let him beware of Mr. John Wilson. Ah - these chicken look good. Nicely browned, too. Gentlemen, fall to."

The bushranger raised aloft his glass and gave a voiceless toast before draining it. Captain Mayhew and Mr. Champion involuntarily emulated him. Mr. Longman vigorously mopped up perspiration, although the interior of the room was not over-heated. Martin obviously was a born major-domo. He directed the servants, he instructed his comrades, and at the same time he managed to attend his chief. Following the example set by the gallant captain and Mr. Champion, the remaining gentlemen proceeded to sup. Even Mr. Whitmore was overcoming his concern at this invasion of his house, his larder and his cellar. If Wilson and his blackguards contented themselves only with stealing, then the consequences would not be nearly as serious as his imagination had been picturing.

And then for the second time the poker-faced Mr. Spinks committed a *faux pas*.

"I say, Wilson," he rasped, "what were you transported for?"

The beaming Mr. Wilson regarded Mr. Spinks with abruptly veiled eyes. "I was transported for snaring a rabbit on the squire's preserves," he replied lightly. "Martin, tell the gentlemen the reason for your transportation."

Martin, who had been a gentleman's valet, made answer in mournful and respectful voice. His face remained as impassive as a stone. "Sir, I omitted to pull my forelock when I awoke his lordship one morning."

"Thank you, Martin. Ask Mr. Jenks to step this way."

Once again silence governed the company whilst heavy and shuffling boots scraped over the floor. Beyond the table, opposite Wilson, there came to stand a thick-set, black-bearded ruffian whose mouth was a red gap and whose eyes were wild and evilly bloodshot. It was obvious that he was a half-wit. It was, too, obvious that he possessed enormous strength.

While engaged in picking the leg of a chicken, Mr. Wilson murmured: "Jenks, tell the gentlemen why you were transported."

The fellow looked at Wilson with dog-like devotion, the light of madness gone from his eyes. He spoke in thin, high-pitched tones. "Please, Wilson -"

"Mister Wilson, Jenks."

"Please, Mr. Wilson, I was sent out because I winked at squire's daughter. Squire had me whipped. I then strangled squire in the woods."

"And that was the only serious crime you ever committed?"

"Yes, Wilson, it was."

"Mister Wilson, please, Jenks."

"Yes, Mr. Wilson. Of course, I've strangled a few men when you asked me to."

"Of course! Of course!" Mr. Wilson agreed lightly, then to explain to the company: "My Jenks is a very obliging man. He will do anything I ask him to do. Jenks, remove Mr. Spinks!"

Mr. Spinks leapt to his feet and attempted to reach for a weapon in the shape of the nearest bottle, but with astounding agility Jenks was behind him. Mr. Spinks was whirled upward and out of the space he had occupied between chair and table. He began to yell, for even in those days the verb "to remove" possessed a sinister meaning. His voice was cut off like water gushing from a tap, and, steadily held by the throat and the back of his neck by Jenks' enormous hands, he was kneed forward towards the door.

Captain Mayhew half-rose to his feet and hawed twice. Mr. Champion tittered. He disliked Mr. Spinks.

"Jenks," Mr. Wilson called after the retreating gorilla, "kindly refrain from strangling Mr. Spinks. Such is not my wish. Merely keep him quiet."

"You shall pay dearly, you and your associates, for this outrage," exclaimed Mr. Whitmore.

"Now, now, my dear Mr. Whitmore," returned Mr. Wilson, an expression of pain clouding his round face, "unbend, sir! Unbend, I implore you! Martin, fill up all glasses. I have a toast."

Mr. Wilson's bonhomie was catching. It could not long be withstood. Mr. Champion filled his own glass. So did Mr. Longman. Mr. Wilson rose when the glasses were charged, to cry ringingly: "Gentlemen! To our good, kind and gentle friend, Jenks!"

Mr. Longnian drank as though suffering a mighty thirst, or as though determined that to die drunk was preferable to dying sober. So, too, did Mr. Champion and Captain Mayhew. Lieutenant Anthony and Mr. Whitmore declined, but they quickly consented when a pistol was pressed against them. Four toasts more were called by Wilson, and four toasts were drunk by every man there.

Now host and guests, bidden and unbidden, began to find the situation a little more colourful. Mr. Wilson voiced a sentimental ballad surprisingly well. A beardless youth among the bushrangers also sang really well. Mr. Champion was induced to recite a poem about a poor young maiden being lost in the snow. After a bout of community singing Captain Mayhew sang a sea shanty. It was all very nice and jolly. Towards morning Lieutenant Anthony believed he was a monkey and tried to climb to the topmost branch via a window curtain.

And then the solemn Martin whispered into the ready ear of Mr. Wilson the fact that day was breaking, whereupon Mr. Wilson, as steady as a rock, rose to stand on his two feet. Mr. Whitmore stood equally as steady.

"I am gratified, Mr. Wilson, to observe that you carry liquor like a gentleman."

"Sir, it gives me pleasure to be able to return that compliment," responded Mr. Wilson. "The evening has been quite successful. On behalf of my friends, I extend to you my appreciation and thanks. And now, as the time for our departure has arrived, there are several matters of business which must be attended to. However, while I must, regretfully, take all the money about the place, all the horses and weapons and powder and ball, and refit my friends with more serviceable clothes, I will leave with you the glorious Lovely Lass as a token of my respect. I will leave, too, my own Gay Girl, who is sadly ill conditioned, and will call for her on a future date when I am again in this district. Therefore we will be comforted by an *au revoir* and not good-bye."

To those of his companions able to stand, Wilson gave short and rapid instructions. The horses outside were swiftly bridled and saddled. Men ran to them with bags of food and rations to be strapped to saddle pommels. Mr. Wilson, attended by Martin, collected all the cash and jewellery, but did not enter the ladies' rooms. All the gentlemen, bar Mr. Whitmore, were stripped of their clothes, which were donned by the needy bushrangers. Old and tattered garments littered the verandah and front of the house.

The Darling Downs were being painted with browns and ambers and greens by the sun about to rise above a line of distant timber when, with much bustle and seeming confusion, Wilson and his fellows prepared to mount. Several of the bushrangers were tied to their horses, among who was Barker, still unconscious. Many of the unbidden guests were unusually smart in acquired clothes, while clinging weakly to the verandah rail of Muirraddin homestead were Mr. Whitmore's bidden guests, all denuded of coats and pants, the captain and Mr. Longman without even their shirts. None of them wore boots. Only Mr. Whitmore was still decently clad.

Now mounted, Mr. Wilson turned and waved his adieux.

"*Au revoir*, gentlemen!" he shouted cheerfully.

"*Au revoir!*" shouted Mr. Longman.

"He-he-he!" gurgled Mr. Champion. Mr. Spinks glared and swore revenge. Captain Mayhew groaned and bellowed: "Oh, curse it! What a night! What a night! Damme if I don't think I enjoyed myself."

John Wilson and his comrades rode away from Muirraddin Station - rode away to other parts and other adventures, and afterwards experienced the greatest adventure of all - at the hands of the hangman.

And so did the six gentlemen - five of them grotesquely arrayed - watch them go.

After dinner that evening they again met in conference and discussed ways and means of preventing reports of the party from becoming public property.

But the malicious Mr. Spinks proved to be a traitor.

Golden Dawn

At noon the only thing that moved in Golden Dawn was an ancient goat languidly chewing the upper of an old boot in the middle of the dust-covered track. To be sure there were Pat Hogan asleep on the broken verandah of his hotel, and Mr. Underwood lying on the flat of his back on the verandah of his store across the way; but these two gentlemen moved but rarely. Presently the goat found chewing a labour not to be borne, and, lurching to the store shade, flopped down and pretended to sleep, in company with a one-eared dog.

Behold, then, the township and inhabitants of Golden Dawn, Central Australia, all a-dance in the heat which shimmied and jazzed, as during summers long past it had jazzed and shimmied when the township consisted of three hotels, four stores and two dozen houses, all constructed of kerosene tins and hessian bags. But that was years ago, when much gold in the gullies and on the hillsides had created in a moment, as it were, a very famous town.

The gold had been worked out, the prospectors had departed either to fresh diggings or to that Valhalla which is made of gold, leaving a mere two hundred sinners in possession of the skeleton town - sinners whose one redeeming virtue is their sublime faith in the gold that is still to be found, given improbable luck.

The dog suddenly raised its one-eared head and growled. For a while it listened, and then ambled out on the road to gaze down the track where it ran straight over a vast salt-bush plain. What the dog saw made it raise its single prick ear and produce a half-hearted yelp. Mr. Hogan slept serenely on, but Mr. Underwood murmured nasally: "Shurrup, curse you!"

The cursed one's ear dropped, but its eyes still gazed down the track at a gently rising cloud of dust beneath which was something that looked like a pile of packing-cases on the back of a chestnut turtle. The nearer the object came the keener became the dog's interest, till at last it found continued silence unbearable and barked an excited welcome.

Mr. Underwood grunted. Without sitting up he removed one of his elastic-sided boots, turned his head to mark the position of his target, and heaved the boot over the verandah rail. The dog, observing the boot descending in a high curve as the shell from a Howitzer gun, stepped daintily aside and wagged its mangy tail. The goat, always interested in boots, left the shade to investigate the new arrival. But Mr. Underwood, unable to sleep, was uneasy. Remembering the goat's liking for leather, he remembered, too, that boots were a luxury even to the first gentleman of Golden Dawn. Rolling over twice, he clawed his way up the verandah post till he stood on his feet.

This movement brought the dog within view, and, noticing its fixed interest in something down the track, Mr. Underwood looked that way and saw what now appeared to be a horse-drawn dray. The driver was either asleep or drunk - the former, probably, because there were no "liquor bars" within a radius of a hundred miles from Golden Dawn.

From the store verandah Mr. Underwood descended to the track, ostensibly to retrieve his footgear. He was a tall man and painfully thin - so thin, in fact, that, when he stooped to pick up his boot with his left hand and a three-pound piece of rock with his right, he looked in grave danger of breaking in halves. The leading citizen had but one eye, but with this savagely red-rimmed optic he carefully judged the distance between himself and the corrugated iron roof directly above the sleeping Mr. Hogan.

The three-pound stone being sent on its mission, the thin man turned toward his place of business with the facial expression of one who, having set some piece of machinery in motion, had nothing to do with the results. He heard the rock crash on the verandah roof above the recumbent Mr. Hogan when he had taken two steps towards his store, heard it bounce at his third step, heard it thud on the track at his fourth, and at his fifth step heard a startled yell from Mr. Hogan. He did not see, and evinced no interest in, Mr. Hogan's spectacular rise from his slumbers. But, then, he was used to seeing the second citizen of Golden Dawn dressed in his habitual civic attire of cotton vest and dungaree trousers.

"Wa-cher-mean-be-that?" yelled Mr. Hogan.

Mr. Underwood turned round slowly with the dignity becoming his rank. Not a muscle of his gaunt, mournful face twitched, nor did his one eye so much as wink. Then, as though giving some mystic sign, he indicated the approaching dray with the thumb of his left hand. Seeing then Mr. Hogan's small, protruding, fish-like eyes turn in the indicated direction, Mr. Underwood continued his way to his own verandah, where he slipped on his boot.

Without further interchange the gentlemen awaited the advent of the conveyance. It was a large, cumbersome dray with a near-side wheel that wobbled, and was drawn by a horse poorly conditioned and markedly lame, for at every step the animal's head was thrown upwards with quite unnatural sharpness, and white streaks of sweat lined the edges of the harness where it touched the chestnut body.

Arrived in Golden Dawn, the horse looked straight at Mr. Underwood and Mr. Underwood's store, then examined with equal intentness Mr. Hogan and his hotel. Then he pulled over to the left and stopped before the verandah steps of Mr. Hogan's shanty, and promptly dozed.

The dog and the goat certainly appeared more interested in the dray than the inhabitants of Golden Dawn. This may have been for the reason that throughout the history of Golden Dawn direct questioning had been regarded as a breach of etiquette.

What the stranger was was fairly apparent. A man about sixty, with a greying full beard and brick-red complexion, wearing a large-brimmed felt hat and dungaree trousers, his general appearance stamped him definitely as a prospector. Had his profession been doubtful, the dry-blower, the cradle, the wash-pans and the picks and shovels on the dray with him would have been decisive. The only matter of doubt regarding him was the amount of his transferable wealth.

Since it appeared that the stranger had no immediate intention of waking, Mr. Hogan sauntered along his verandah and descended the three steps to the ground. It was noticeable that he carefully avoided the middle step, that step being dangerously broken. Of set purpose it was never repaired, the reason being that any visitor to the hotel during Mr. Hogan's occasional short prospecting trips would receive a nasty jar, and at the same time leave indubitable evidence of his visit.

Off the steps, Mr. Hogan drew from beneath them a board

which fitted exactly over the middle one, making that broken step perfectly safe. Drawing near to the dray, the publican examined the horse, the dray, and the loading in the manner of one who has unlimited leisure and appreciates it.

There was little among the stranger's effects that was worthy of much study, nor did a careful appraisal of the stranger's clothes reveal the locality of his wallet or gold-dust bag. And so again Mr. Hogan's eyes came back to the horse and finally rested upon the hind near leg, of which only the tip of the shoe rested on the ground.

No one studying Mr. Hogan's face would class it as keenly intelligent. A drunk once described it as a full-moon face, and one visitor who lost much money playing cards with Mr. Hogan described it as a twenty-to-four-o'clock face. Nevertheless, Mr. Hogan's face was his best asset. He was exceedingly proud of it, and was wont to look at it in a circular mirror and decide that it was a proper, regular Poker Face.

About the animal's lame foot he observed two things. One was that there was no swelling of the hock, and the other that the shoe was loose and appeared prised from the hoof on one side by some solid wedged between. Any unnecessary movement Mr. Hogan never made. When, therefore, he gave a swift glance at the sleeping traveller and then suddenly stooped to look more closely at the horse's foot, Mr. Underwood's placidity vanished and with long strides he crossed the road, and came on his fellow-citizen in the act of removing the laming solid with a blunt clasp-knife.

And then for probably a full half-minute the two gentlemen gazed with rapt earnestness at a piece of gold-studded pink quartz which lay on the palm of Mr. Hogan's hand. The position which the piece of rich quartz had lately occupied was proof positive that quite recently the horse had stood, probably feeding, on an out-crop bearing many, many ounces to the ton.

From the open hand three eyes rose and met avariciously. Mr. Hogan's head jerked sideways, toward the hotel, giving silent invitation to Mr. Underwood. For perhaps five minutes they occupied the bar engaged in conference, after which the one-eyed gentleman came out again, descended to the road, kicked the one-eared dog out of his way, and finally brought up against the dray-wheel, against which he negligently leaned.

"Do you think you'll be waking up to-day, mister?" he inquired, politely. The sleeper stirred and mumbled, but did not respond. The question was put again in a louder tone. The storekeeper saw then that his second effort was entirely successful, for the traveller opened a pair of deep blue eyes that regarded him with neither resentment nor surprise.

"Good day-ee!" he said, with a pleasant drawl. "Is this here the township of Golden Dawn?"

"It is. Come down, mister, and join me in a snifter."

"I was dreaming about one when you woke me up. Are you the publican?"

"Naw. I'm the storekeeper. Sell you anything from a bar of soap to a dry-blower. Mr. Hogan is the proprietor of the hotel. Here he is."

Leading the way to his bar, Mr. Hogan waddled round to his rightful side of the dilapidated counter and said: "Phwat's it to be?"

"Mine's a handle," answered the stranger, looking up from his occupation of cutting chips from a tobacco-plug.

Mr. Underwood nodded agreement, and, Mr. Hogan's taste in "snifters" being similar, he filled three glass pint pots having handles.

"Come far?" inquired the one-eyed man, casually.

"So-so."

"An' 'ow fer back may so-an'-so be?"

"Maybe a coupler mile - maybe twenty."

"Well-well! It's a dry argument. Again, Mr. Hogan."

For the next half-hour they indulged in many "snifters," discussing in the intervals the weather, the elections of last year, and the rapid manner in which Australia was rushing to the dogs. From taciturn the stranger became garrulous, and Mr. Underwood, with an oily smile, returned to the attack.

"You must have come a distance to-day," he said. "Your horse appears quite done up."

"Shouldn't be," the stranger said, a gleam of resentment in his blue eyes. "Camped at White Tank lars night. Only nine miles back." He seemed to ponder awhile. Then: "Well, mus' get on. Wanta hit Tolly's Tank to-night. Ten mile - ain' it?"

"Yep, about that," Mr. Hogan agreed. "Goin on ter-day, or is it ter-morrow?"

"Yaas - no dust to spend. Wot, again? All right."

"You camp long at White Tank?" asked the thin man, putting a hand affectionately on the stranger's shoulder.

"Only about a week," replied the prospector. "Going inter Dalby ter register claim. Foun' a leader - no, found nothin'. 'Scuse me, gen'lemen. Mus' go on. Help me inter dray. Orl ri', then. My bloomin' oath!"

Mr. Hogan placed the reins in the stranger's hands, and Mr. Underwood slapped the horse's rump with a "Ger-up, there!" The goat flapped her ears and the dog barked, more as a duty than from inclination.

Mr. Hogan and Mr. Underwood watched the lumbering dray until it disappeared among the mulga scrub half a mile distant. Then the thin man walked swiftly to the stable beside the store to harness his horse to a light sulky, and Mr. Hogan removed the board from the top of the middle step and carefully restored it to its hiding-place.

Meantime, the moment the stranger was hidden by the scrub, he appeared to recover his sobriety with amazing ease. Driving his horse into the shade cast by a giant leopardwood tree, he alighted from the dray and chained the wheel. After this he secured an empty flour-bag and went back to where he could view the township without affording a view of himself.

With a quiet grin of amusement he saw Mr. Hogan climb into the sulky with Mr. Underwood, and, whilst watching the two gentlemen of Golden Dawn driving off to White Tank in search of the gold-bearing reef, he attended to his tobacco-plug.

He gave them five minutes' start before walking back to the township, being careful to keep on the hard ground beside the road, so as to leave no tracks. He was careful, too, to keep to the patches of hard ground when near the hotel, and particularly careful not to tread on Mr. Hogan's middle step.

Crossing the road later to the store was more difficult, for the dust lay thick and even; but he did find a hard crossing a hundred yards out of town, and for a while was invisible within Mr. Underwood's place of business. When he emerged his bag was weighty in appearance and in fact.

At sundown, when the citizens of Golden Dawn returned to

their places of abode, they were in a highly disgruntled condition. They had found where the stranger had camped, and had tracked the horse's aimless wanderings in search of grass, but not a sign of any reef, or outcrop, or any pieces of pink quartz did they find.

And at sundown the stranger, sitting in his camp at Tolly's Tank, watched the billy come to the boil whilst engaged in mental arithmetic. He had the habit of many prospectors and other solitary workers of talking aloud to himself.

"A collection of rations, say, four pounds. Four bottles of whisky and two of gin, at fifteen shillings, is four pounds ten, making it eight-ten. Add a dozen bottles of beer at two bob, and we get a total of nine pounds fourteen shillings, less about fourteen shillings' worth of gold quartz. Them gents won't miss the afore-said articles, and I don't miss no piece of quartz. So we are orl quite equal, tired, and happy."

The Demijohn

It was a large demijohn. It had a capacity of three gallons.

Its history can be traced back to the year 1913, when a vast, bewhiskered person called Tiny bought it at Burracoppin, W.A., and packed it, along with stores and water, on a camel dray. He travelled that day as far as the Nine-mile Rock, taking the Government track northward along the new Number One Rabbit Fence in defiance of official prohibition. The beer being consumed during the first night out from Burracoppin, Tiny made the demijohn serve as a water container until he arrived at and camped near a rock hole eastward of the 227-mile peg and twenty-one miles north of the Mount Magnet-Youanmi track. Here he built himself a comfortable bough shed, and, when he was found dead in 1915, the police left the demijohn behind the back of the bough shed when they buried the body and removed Tiny's effects. No subsequent visitor desired the demijohn. It became Tiny's memorial.

The fact that Tiny camped for two years of his life at the waterhole, added to the fact that he purchased stores at Sandstone with raw gold, indicated to many that he had found gold in the vicinity. His standard of living during those last two years of his life was well above that of the average prospector. Yet, although many others diligently fossicked for Tiny's find, no one ever discovered it, and no one discovered Tiny's "plant" until Earle and Todd came along in 1929.

It does seem that the God of Chance, knowing of Tiny's demijohn, wrote a play about it, or rather around it, and then determined on two men to act parts in it. The god selected for lead a farmer who, feeling the first blast of the depression, decided to leave his wife in charge of the farm and use the partly-paid-for truck on a prospect for gold.

Arthur Earle was a slight man of about fifty - a neurotic, a whiner. He first tried his luck about Westonia, but, of course, he wasn't the man to be lucky enough to find gold. What he knew about prospecting was even less than what he knew about wheatgrowing, and what he did not know he never admitted even to himself. From Westonia he drifted east to Southern Cross, then on to Kalgoorlie and north to Laverton. He picked up Jack Todd on the road to Youanmi, and Todd talked about the long-dead Tiny and his alleged secret find. Seeing in Todd a man of abnormal physical strength, and recognising his knowledge of prospecting, Arthur Earle offered a mateship.

Todd was thickset, forty-odd in years, slow in action, humorous with a manner hinting at mental depth. He always chuckled at Earle's complaints and grumbling and outbursts of temper.

The mateship was formed fifteen miles out from Youanmi late one afternoon. It was arranged by the track side while the billy was being boiled. Into it was thrown a truck, tent and gear by the one, and twenty-four one-pound notes by the other. On reaching Youanmi after dark, Todd handed Earle eight of his pound notes, and he went along to the hotel to buy half a dozen bottles of beer while his mate purchased stores. They then drove west along the Mount Magnet track until they reached the gate in the Rabbit Fence at the 206-mile peg. There is a Rabbit Department hut near this gate and a large rock water catchment behind it.

The following day they drove north along the fence for twenty miles, and then they took a sandalwooder's track east into Tiny's country. At last the God of Chance had brought his cast to the stage, and the drama began before an audience of half a dozen crows and five emus.

"Yes, this here is where Tiny Evans got his water the two years and four months he was here," Todd remarked when, under direction, Earle stopped the truck at the edge of a big area of surface conglomerate.

"Where's the flaming water?" demanded Earle, as though his mate should have produced a second River Murray.

"Come on, I'll show you!" invited Todd, and he led the way across the rock "island" in the mulga sea until, near its centre, there was revealed to them a fifty-yards-long crevice. The width of the crevice was uneven, being a mere inch or so along most of its length and fully a yard for some ten or twelve feet towards one end.

"Gee! Water's a bit low," Todd said, standing and staring down. "But she goes deep and she never dries out. We can lower a bucket on a rope for as much as we want. By the water in that rock puddle back there it must've rained here within a week or two, but I've heard say that rain don't make no difference to the level of water down there. Yes - here's where Tiny got his water. Look over there. At the edge of the scrub. There's still the bough shed Tiny built. The roof looks a bit busted down, but we can soon fix 'er up and camp there."

"But that's where he died, isn't it?" stuttered Earle.

"Yes, that's where Tiny kicked off," Todd replied, as though the fact gave him secret pleasure. "Tiny wasn't nothing much to look at when old Bill Williams found him. There wasn't nothing the police could do bar dig a hole beside him and shovel him into it. But Bill Williams got Tiny's last two bottles of brandy. Close kind of bird was Tiny. Always was. If we can get onto his find, we won't be downhearted any more."

"Anyway, I don't much like the idea of camping in his hut," objected Earle. "He might be still hanging around like."

Todd flashed a quick look. His lips fell into a sneer. A strong man himself, he had no time for a weakling.

"Aw - come on!" he growled. "What's wrong with Tiny's camp? We can cut a few props and heave the shed roof level quicker'n we can build another. If it gets on your nerves after a bit, we can mark a place to build another. Tiny won't bother us. Blast me - he's been dead fourteen years."

When they had finished settling in Tiny's bough shed, the bronze-wing pigeons were whirring across the rock island to drink from the last half-inch of water lying in a shallow declivity. As there yet was water in the drum on the truck there was no necessity for the partners to visit the crevice hole that evening, and while Earle prepared a stew and baked a damper Todd went off with a gun and bagged several pigeons. These he plucked and cooked while Earle stared moodily at the campfire, and, thus engaged, Todd enlarged on Tiny's history.

"Tiny got gold around here somewhere," he said placidly. "I knew him, and he was never a bloke to stay in one place more'n a month unless he was on gold. Two years back I prospected for his find, but I couldn't stop long because I was broke. Now we'll comb this country fine. It'll be worth striking, for Tiny wouldn't have stopped here all the time just for a few 'weights, and he was the kind of bloke who'd be content to live in a place like this on good tucker and a bottle or two instead of having a fling down in a city no matter how much gold he had in sight."

"Well, we'll shift camp in the morning," Earle objected, his light-blue eyes aglitter in the firelight. "Dead men's camps ain't no good to me."

"Aw - why worry? When a man's dead, he's dead," argued Todd. "You don't want to hold with ghosts and things. They're last year's."

Earle sat like a man whose ears are tight to catch the slightest sound. His eyes constantly moved. The fingers which rolled cigarette after cigarette visibly trembled.

"Where did they plant him?" he inquired, and the placid Todd replied: "Plant old Tiny! Blessed if I know for sure. Somewheres around. What's the odds, anyhow?"

At middle-distance a curlew vented its long-drawn, screamed dirge, and the sound of it almost lifted Earle's body from the petrol case on which he was sitting.

"Curlew," grunted Todd, without looking up from the task of slicing chips from a black tobacco plug. "They ain't bad eatin' if cooked properly."

Earle's lean body relaxed, and he stared at the vague outlines of the truck as though half in mind to pack up and move right then. The shed faced to the south, and the soft east wind rustled the skeleton leaves remaining on the newly-propped roof, leaves on brittle twigs cut and placed there by the man called Tiny.

"We'll cut fresh boughs for the roof to-morrow," Todd said, noting his companion's quick upward glance. "Strange how the joint has weathered the years from 1915. Old Tiny must've made a good job of it when he put 'er up. P'raps he knew the gold was near here and he built her to stand for a long time."

He expected Earle to say something about moving camp the next day. By now Todd realised his mental strength over his mate, and he was confident that in this matter of a camp site, and in all other, too, he could and would prevail.

After breakfast the next morning, Earle volunteered to take the petrol-tin bucket to the crevice hole for water. With it he took a length of light rope, and as he walked across the island of rock he was watched by Todd. Todd saw him at the edge of the crevice and then he smiled dourly when through the still, sunlit air came Earle's vivid curses. His mate then came back with neither bucket nor rope.

"The wire handle came out of the bucket at one side. It slipped off the rope and sank," he explained stutteringly. Then he rushed to the truck, adding: "It's the only bucket we got. The blarsted handle would come out!"

Now, with a sneer about his mouth and his black eyes very small, Todd watched Earle pull from the truck a half coil of fencing-wire. Silently they strode over the conglomerate to the crevice, and there Todd bent one end of the wire and Earle straightened it as he paid it out from the coil and Todd began to fish for the bucket.

"Must be fifteen feet to the water," Todd said, to add: "Must be four or five feet of water in her still."

Demanded Earle: "Can you feel the bucket with the wire?"

"Yes, I've got her. The bottom seems to be flat and there's some rubble down there."

"Wave the wire around," Earle urged impatiently. "You can hook the free end of the handle."

Ten minutes passed before Todd gave a grunt of satisfaction, and Earle saw the dull glint of water break into ghostly bars of silver. Slowly the bucket, full of water, was drawn to the lip of the crevice, and then, as Earle grasped it, he gave a cry of amazement, and with furious energy tipped out the water and upended the bucket. From it dropped two small nuggets of gold.

Lips were parted and teeth revealed in fixed grins. Blue eyes encountered black eyes - four eyes, small and as hard as agates.

"Tiny's find must be down there," Earle said, breaking the silence.

"Don't think," countered Todd.

"But these two nuggets were down there to get into the bucket as you fished for it. There might be more, you fool," shouted Earle, his eyes now blazing.

Todd said calmly: "Don't get shirty. I reckon that's Tiny's plant, not his find. He got the gold some place else, and he put it down there for safe-keeping. He must've known that all he put down he wouldn't get back, but he didn't mind that, 'cos wot he put down was more'n enough. Come on, let's fish!"

By sundown they had retrieved thirty-two ounces of gold in small nuggets. Then, weakened by lack of food, they lurched off the rock to the bough shed, silenced by the reaction following the clamorous excitement. Not one cast of the bucket had failed to bring up gold.

"I'm going down into that water to-morrow," announced Earle as though thinking his mate would argue against it. "It can't be more than four feet deep. I'll cut down the handle of the shovel so's I can use it to scoop up the gold."

"Be worth a try, anyhow," Todd agreed, pouring water into the washbasin set on the ground. Earle was looking vacantly into space while Todd stripped off his flannel vest, and when again his eyes became focused he saw only the top of Todd's head as the man stooped over the basin.

Never in his life had Earle's brain worked so rapidly and so clearly. To it was presented a succession of questions like clear-cut screen shots of the one scene taken from different angles. He seemed lifted high on the wings of exultation, and with astounding swiftness into his vision sprang the tomahawk lying on the bush table. He need not divide the gold with this track hobo.

Without moving his feet, he reached sideways for the tomahawk and then forward to deliver the blow. After that he laughed shrilly like a woman. All the gold was his. No one would look for Todd. No one had seen Todd and him together; no one knew they were mates. Inexperience prevented him from seeing the difficulties of changing the gold into currency without answering questions as to where he got it.

The sun had gone. The warm wind was freshening from the north-east, and it disturbed Earle's sweat-plastered, scanty hair. In the gathering dusk he strode to the truck for the long-handled shovel with which to dig a grave. The dead man then was behind him. From behind him came a long-drawn moan of pain.

As though stung, Earle sprang about to stand and glare at the dim, sprawled figure of Todd. With a cry of fury, he rushed from the truck to snatch up the tomahawk, and then he stooped to batter in Todd's head. When he stood up he shouted:

"I'll bet all the gold here and all the gold down that crevice that's settled you!"

Again at the truck for the shovel, his body and his brain were frozen by the moan of anguish coming from the direction of Jack Todd. Rage burned through his veins like raw alcohol. Seizing the shovel, he rushed to Todd's body and began to dig a grave beside it - dig furiously, excitedly, like a dog close to a rabbit. Three feet down he went before he rolled the corpse into the hole and shovelled back the loose sand.

For years his mind had balanced on a knife-edge. The sight of gold had toppled it. Immediately he had finished the burial he began to regain a measure of calm. Chuckling and whistling by turn, he relit the campfire, filled the billy and then squatted on his heels before the blaze, his mind receiving pleasure from its task of making plans. Yes! He would change Tiny's gold into notes, and then he would make for Adelaide and Melbourne and have a hell of a good time. The wife could look after the farm. In fact, she could have the damn farm for keeps.

Then again came to him that terrible moan.

With the back of his head and neck frozen, Earle slowly stood up and as slowly turned round. The firelight reached the yellow mound which was Todd's grave. It revealed the sand particles and the mica particles. They were moving. Todd, under them, was moving! He was about to crawl out of his grave. He was moaning:

"Oo-oo-oo-oh! Ah-oo-oo-oo!"

Arthur Earle screamed. Turning, he rushed away, his body no longer controlled by a reasoning brain. Because it offered him clear passage, he ran to the island of conglomerate, raced across its uneven surface. Once he looked back - to see the flickering fire and the thing towering above and behind it. He was not to know that it was the swinging meatbag and not Todd standing up at the edge of the grave.

He screamed again. Then he stepped into the crevice above Tiny's safe deposit. Its opposite edge struck his chest, flung back the upper part of his body, so that as he fell towards the water the back of his head struck rock.

The billy boiled. Presently it was emptied of water and its bottom gaped. The fire died down to a red glow. At the back of Tiny's bough shed the demijohn squatted as though with studied comfort. The rising wind played about its unstoppered mouth.

From its empty belly came:
"Oo-oo-oh! Ah-oo-oo-oooo!"

A Waif on the Nullabor

Lena Harwood's life had been a long succession of escapades from which, hitherto, she had figuratively managed to land, firmly, if a little breathlessly, on her feet. She had long known she was too impulsive, and now realised that her latest escapade threatened an end neither romantic nor comfortable.

The present situation was, perhaps, not wholly her fault. Had not her brother-in-law been so free with his "don'ts" she might have listened to her reasoning sister, Stella. Now, both Stella and her husband would be frantically anxious about her, because she was utterly and bewilderingly lost on the Nullabor Plain. It was John's idea, this tour across Australia from Perth to Melbourne and Sydney, and, save for a puncture or two and getting off the straight road when driving through Western Australia's wheat belts, everything had gone on without incident until -

They had reached the abandoned town of Eucla early one morning, and because they were all anxious to see the famed Nullabor Plain, John had filled the water drum there, and they had crossed the three-mile strip of lowland to drive up the face of a tall cliff, and so reach the Plain and eventually halt for the night beside one of the underground water tanks originally constructed for the use of the linesmen patrolling the old Overland Telegraph.

After dinner John had begun to tinker with the car, and Stella wanted to lie down and read a novel. To Lena, the Plain was bitterly disappointing, for, despite what everyone said of it, it was not flat at all. The ground stretched away on all sides in wide swells. Lena thought that from the summit of the nearest swell she might see the flat part of the Plain talked and written about by everyone almost who had crossed it in the train.

Of course, John would say: "Don't go far."

Having made the summit of the nearest swell her objective, Lena had no intention of turning back before she had reached it. It was much farther away than she had thought, and she had not got anywhere near it when sudden realisation that the evening was advanced made her turn back. But the camp was not in sight, and she had no idea where it was.

Swift darkness found her running until she tripped over a limestone block. Remembrance of the stories of blowholes and yawning caverns kept her lying all night beside a blue-bush. Cold and weary when the sun rose above the horizon, she had started off confidently to find John and her sister, but after hours of walking she neither found them nor the track, nor did she see the telegraph poles.

Fortunately the weather was temperate. All day she walked and hallooed at intervals. All through the second night she lay sleeping fitfully on the comfortless couch offered by the bosom of Mother Earth, and when the sun rose on the second day her face was peaked with hunger and thirst, her stockings were laddered to ribbons, and her shoes were falling in pieces off her bruised and aching feet.

Had the Plain been flat, as people said, she never would have got into this hopeless plight. At first she reviled the people whose description had misled her, and then she blamed the Plain itself. Here it was stretching away to the completely circular horizon like a rumpled grey carpet. In all directions she could gaze across breathless space to the edge of the world supporting the dome of the sky. That was all she could see. There was not a tree; not a bush higher than her waist; not a single sign of the presence of human beings; not a bird, except one eagle planing so high that it looked like a mosquito. There were no fire smokes like those they had seen once when crossing the Hampton Tableland - there was nothing but a dreadful emptiness which made one feel so small and mean.

Panic surged through her like the soft wind meeting her face. What should she do? If only she could see the telegraph poles or find the road! At least she could follow the road. It would lead her somewhere, perhaps to one of the underground tanks where she could drink and drink. It now seemed so useless just to walk on and on, up a long ground rise, to see only wide ground troughs on all sides. It was her first meeting with the bush, and if only she could remember which was north and which was south she could try to keep in a straight line. She knew, of course, that the sun rose in the east and set in the west, and John had said that the railway line was to the north. But which was the north?

Well, she might as well walk on while any leather remained

under the soles of her feet as sit down and mope. Lena Harwood was no faint-heart. Standing up, there was the chance of seeing someone, or someone seeing her. Sitting down, the low bush hemmed her in. She elected to walk into the wind, because it smelt fresh and tangy.

Presently her little nose began to twitch. Surely she did not really smell frying bacon! It was absurd! Why, even though the land did lie in vast waves, she could see for miles and miles. Yet she could smell frying bacon. It was a too common, if delicious, smell to be mistaken about. The wind was carrying the aroma. It swept the lethargy from her mind.

If she continued to walk into the wind the smell would surely lead her to a camp. Unconsciously her hands fluttered about her wildly untidy hair as she hurried on. Fifty yards further and quite suddenly the smell evaporated. For a space she stood still, hands clenched at her sides, eyes burning with tears which would not fall down her tear-stained face. Then slowly she backed along the way she had come, and so came again to that delightful, if homely, perfume.

An absurd phrase raced back and forth through her mind. Follow your nose! Follow your nose! The smell of frying bacon could be caused by bacon frying, and by nothing else.

Again moving forward, she suddenly saw faint blue vapour coming up out of the ground. It was coming up through a hole no bigger than a dinner plate, and she went down on hands and knees and lowered her face close to the hole when, beside the smell of frying bacon, she could feel the warmth of the fire.

Then she heard a man's voice say: "How many eggs will you fellers have?"

"Three'll do me," another man said curtly.

"And me," added a third.

She heard a man whistling cheerfully. She heard a peculiar sound, something between a squeak and a sigh, and it was some little time before she understood that it was she herself who was making it.

From below, a man asked: "What the devil is that?"

"What's what?" demanded another.

"Why, that snivelling sound."

Then, from below, silence. Lena could visualise those men,

taut with listening. She flamed with anger. One had called her cries for help "That snivelling sound." The beast! Couldn't he understand that she had eaten nothing, drunk nothing for two nights and a day, and that she couldn't speak properly because her tongue was vilely sticky and simply wouldn't function? Beside the hole were several large limestone chips, and these she began to drop down the hole one after another. The fourth chip crashed into something metallic, and one of the men swore heartily. From the hole rose the hot smell of burning fat.

Then, from somewhere behind her, one of the men said with great emphasis on the first word: "Good morning!"

Weakly she turned over and partly raised herself. She saw a young man gazing at her with hard grey eyes. She pointed to her mouth and sank back to the ground.

"What's the matter with you? What are you doing there?" he asked. And then she saw his face soften. In the next instant he was on his knees beside her. "Why, you are all in! Are you bushed - lost?"

She nodded, trying to still her trembling lips, and then he rose with her in his arms. Reaction gripped her, and she wanted to cry but could not. No longer was she concerned with her grimy face and disordered hair, her tattered stockings and rent shoes. She was safe now - safe after those two horrible nights and the one staring day of torture. The sun went out. She felt herself being carried downward. Then the daylight waned, and she saw a ceiling of rock before it vanished. Darkness came, and then the darkness was relieved by a bright yellow light.

"What, another visitor!" exclaimed someone, and then the man who carried her laid her gently on what seemed to be a luxurious bed.

"Now," he said softly, "a little cold water for the first course. A little hot coffee with a dash of brandy for the second course. For the third course coffee, plain, and bacon and eggs and damper."

For a moment he left her. When he returned he carried a basin of water and a towel and a tin pannikin reflecting gold in the lamplight. Slipping one arm beneath her shoulders, he raised her and pressed the edge of the pannikin against her glued lips. Water, cold and clean, entered her mouth, and she swallowed and swallowed. He laughed at her eagerness and put away the pannikin just when she wanted more. He wetted one end of the towel in the basin and then began to sponge her face.

"In a pretty bad way, eh?" he said. "I thought you were putting it on at first. Now, now! All right, just a little more water, and then a little coffee."

Lena wanted to gulp the coffee - it was the most wonderful coffee she had ever tasted but she was restrained with annoying masterfulness. Grey-Eyes punched a pillow which smelled strongly of tobacco. She was permitted to lie back, and a rug was drawn up over her.

"Lie still while I fry some more bacon and eggs," she was urged. "Your brickbats ruined the last lot, but fortunately the supply is adequate. I'll not be long. Afterwards, perhaps, you can tell me all about yourself."

And then, before she was aware of it, she was asleep.

Lena Harwood was being carried on the back of a grey horse across a rumpled grey carpet. She feared it would trip her, and it did, throwing her to the carpet on her face. Abruptly the dream ended, and she found herself looking at a dark velvet sky from which, to her left, golden drops fell to splash on the floor near her bed.

"I say, miss! Wake up!" a man said softly.

Lena did not want to wake up. She stretched her toes and closed her eyes and began a hunt for the grey horse and the grey carpet -

"Try again, Jack," said another man.

Something solid dropped on her, but she was too sleepy even to be curious about it. She was searching for the grey horse, and fancied she saw him waiting for her in the grey carpet, when a hard object fell on her left cheek, stinging it. This made her open wide her eyes, and, with a cry, she sat up on the camp stretcher and stared at her surroundings, which were bizarre enough in all conscience.

On a case was set a brightly burning kerosene-gas lamp. Its yellow light showed her the smouldering ashes of a fire on a sandy floor, and a dull gleam of ghostly daylight silhouetting a shoulder of rock behind it. High above her was a circular hole through which she could see filtered daylight. She was in a large cavern, so large that one end of it could not be seen. Along the opposite wall bagged and cased stores were stacked high, and to her right were three magnificent stalactites, forming large pillars seemingly supporting the roof. Two men, each with his back against a stalactite, were sitting on the floor, the lamplight gleaming on metal encircling their wrists. They were neatly dressed, but their hair was tousled, and one of them badly needed a shave. This one whispered: "Come over here. Don't make a noise! Come quick!"

Still dazed with sleep, or want of it, Lena stood up from the stretcher and obeyed the order. She saw now more clearly that the two men were handcuffed, and that through the handcuffs and round the stalactites ordinary fencing wire had been passed and tied. The men could sit down, or stand up, but they were not free to leave the limestone pillars.

"We're detectives," one of them said, whispering. "We've been overpowered by a gang of crooks, and we're being kept prisoners. You see that box over there? Well, under its lid are two or three files. Go and fetch one, please. Hurry!"

Lena hesitated, and the fellow's dark eyes became ugly. Instinctively, she disliked him. When he again whispered there was menace in his voice.

"Go on - bring that file - in the name of the Law."

Mention of the law swept aside her aversion of him. She remembered something about a citizen being legally bound to assist the police if called on by them, and, without further hesitation, she slipped over the sandy floor to the indicated box, obviously a wooden tool chest. Under the lid, and attached to it by looped leather straps, were several files, while lying on the bottom of the box was a black sinister pistol.

One of the files she took back to the men, and he with the unshaven face held out his crossed wrists, saying: "Work the file on this wire. Hurry up. Don't lose time. We've got to be free before that fellow and his gang return."

Somewhat awkwardly, Lena began to saw through the stout, new fencing wire, and before she could file it quite through she was ordered to bend the wire either side of the cut she was making. It then snapped easily, and with pantherish agility the man leaped to his feet, snatched the file from her and sprang to his companion. As Lena watched him, first perplexity and then doubt assailed her.

"We've got to fix him before we can muck about getting off these bracelets. He'll have the key on him, anyway," said the unshaven, lanky man.

"Too right! We'll wooden him as he comes in," agreed the other. To Lena, he snapped out: "Get back to your bunk and pretend to be asleep. He'll come in any second, and we've got to arrest him."

Without a word Lena did as bidden. She lay down full length on the stretcher, but out of the corner of her eye she saw the men each obtain a case opener from the stack of stores. They then took up stations either side of the cave entrance, the manacled wrists held high above right shoulders, the iron bars ready to be used as bludgeons.

To the girl it seemed a long time that they stood thus, barely moving, sinister and menacing. Detectives! She wondered. She was sophisticated enough to know that detectives are usually promoted from uniformed constables, and constables, she knew, were big, soldierly men. The bearing of these two was not soldierly. Their movements were the antithesis of the steady, determined movements of policemen.

What it all meant she had not the faintest idea. She was still wondering, made gravely uneasy in her mind that she might have done the wrong thing in liberating them from the stalactites, when a man's footsteps on hollow-sounding rock came from without the entrance. The daylight silhouetting the corner of rock temporarily vanished, and after that her impressions were not so clear.

She saw the tall, broad figure of the man who had carried her down from the plain above and had given her water and then coffee. She saw the startled look of astonishment leap to his strong face. She saw iron bars describe high arcs and the big man sink to the ground beneath their blows.

"That'll keep him quiet for a while," predicted the man addressed as Fred. "Go through him for the keys of these bracelets."

The other went to his knees and awkwardly worked his

manacled hands into the big man's pockets. With a grunt of satisfaction he secured the key, and the next moment he and his companion were free of the handcuffs.

"Is he dead?" coolly inquired the lanky man.

"Dunno. Just as well if he is," replied the other.

They bent above the big man and roughly turned him over on his back.

"Alive all right. What'll we do with him?" one asked.

"Handcuff him and fix him like he fixed us. Then we'll get down to the beach and plant ourselves until the boat gets in."

Their callousness appalled Lena. Whatever they were they were certainly not policemen. She slipped off the stretcher silently to cross the sandy floor and so come unseen behind them.

"Give us a hand to haul him across to them pillars," ordered the lanky man; and, oblivious to Lena's close presence, they again stooped over Grey-Eyes and proceeded to drag him towards the stalactites.

Regarding their bent and grotesque shapes, Lena suddenly remembered the pistol in the small wooden box from which she had taken the file. Doubt had given place to terror. She thought to make her escape by running silently out of the cave, but her trembling knees cried out her bodily want of food, while memories of the Nullabor Plain were still too vivid to offer her even the possibility of escape.

Of pistols she knew nothing. She knew, of course, how one held a pistol from the manner in which people on the screen used such a weapon, and, with her old impulsiveness, she ran to the box as the men were joining lengths of cut wire together. Into the box went her hand, and she was made astonished by the facility with which her fingers closed round the butt of the weapon. Taking it from the box, her forefinger slipped through the guard and against the trigger.

In possession of the pistol, she wondered just what she would do with it. There was no pocket in her dress in which to conceal it. She thought of the tobacco-smelling pillow on the stretcher, and she was on her way to slip the weapon beneath it and to resume her position on the stretcher when one of the men sprang up, saw the pistol in her hand, and leaped at her.

His abrupt movement so startled her that she swung round to

confront him. Some reflex action of the nerves of her hand caused her to press the trigger. The pistol exploded with a reverberating crash. Her heart missed four beats, but the effect of the shot on the two men was ludicrous. Their hands reached for the cave roof.

"For heaven's sake, turn it the other way," pleaded the lanky man.

"Put it down," snarled the short man. "Put it down, I tell you. We're detectives, and I warn you that the consequences will be serious to you if you hinder us in the execution of our duty."

"I - I don't believe you are detectives," Lena said faintly.

The tall fellow swore, and with his hands still held above his head stepped towards her. So menacing were his eyes that the pistol in Lena's hand again exploded. The bullet went wide, but the man fell back beside his companion.

Now the girl was experiencing a new sensation. For the first time in her life she was feeling an inward power other than that given her by her sex. She had these two men whipped. She could see the fear glaring from their eyes. She could grant or take away their lives.

"Hold 'em, girlie, until I can get a grip on myself," said a voice made weak by pain. "Shoot 'em if they make a break."

Lena's heart again missed four beats. Beyond the two men she could see Grey-Eyes moving, and, coming to know that the girl's attention was diverted from them, the lanky man jumped. In a fraction of time, so it seemed to Lena, his two hands were within a foot of her throat. She forgot the pistol in her hand. She attempted to push the fellow back, and then the pistol exploded for the third time, and the tall man spun round in a full circle, sagged at the knees and collapsed.

White faced, she stared down at the twitching body, and then Grey-Eyes called out: "Look out, girlie! Look out for the other feller!"

When Lena looked up she saw the second man creeping towards her, but when he realised that her eye was on him he stopped and whined: "All right, don't shoot. I'll stay put."

"Keep him there for a little while longer," said the big man.

She felt, rather than saw, Grey-Eyes lurch to his feet and then circle so that he came behind her. Then his strong fingers took the pistol from her hand.

"Ah!" he exclaimed, breathing deeply. "Now, Fred, I've got the gun. Toss the keys of the handcuffs at this lady's feet."

Lena was to remember all her life the picture of two big hands crossed and the key held by her own grubby fingers. She remembered how the manacles snapped open, and then a black flood rose about her and engulfed her.

She found herself staring at the round hole in the rock ceiling, and once more twitched her nose to sniff at the delicious smell of frying bacon and eggs. Grey-Eyes was squatting on his heels at the fire engaged in breaking eggs into a frying pan. Beyond him one man was sitting with his back to a stalactite, and another lying on blankets over against the stores. At her movement, Grey-Eyes turned.

"Hullo! How do you feel now?" he asked cheerfully. "Ready to eat? There is a basin of water, a towel and a comb waiting for you on that box. Or would you like a pannikin of coffee before you get up?"

He had even provided a mirror. What a man!

A minute later she was seated on the ground near the fire, drinking hot coffee and watching him ladle crisp bacon and well-done eggs onto a tin plate. When he had placed this before her, with a knife and fork and a slice of damper on another plate, she smiled her gratitude and then, struck by a sudden horrifying thought, asked: "Is he dead? Did I kill him?"

"Don't worry," he urged. "Just eat and drink. Explanations can wait."

"But I want to know now!"

"You plugged him neatly through the shoulder. I have made him as comfortable as I can, and a truck will arrive at any minute to cart us all off to Ceduna. You see, I am a detective-sergeant. Wishhart's my name. For a month I have been playing a lone hand locating the gang who robbed the Trans train of £40,000 destined for the Perth banks. Everyone said I was a fool to think the robbers had their headquarters on the Nullabor Plain, but I couldn't see where else it could be, or what better place it could be in. I've had a wonderful time living for three months on the old man plain of Australia. I have found some amazing caves, and have explored 'em, too. Why, this Nullabor Plain is full of caverns that could hide an army.

"That's right!" he broke off to say. "Eat up! You can talk presently. The truck will be here at any time. When I finally located the gang in this cave I went back to my own headquarters in a cave a hundred times bigger than this one for a portable telephone which I took to the Overland Line and, through Nullabor Station, got in touch with the police at Ceduna. They are a little late in getting here, but they will have to drive slowly when they once leave the road. I marked the spot with a white towel. From that point they'll have white paper guides all the way."

"Those men told me they were detectives," Lena said with difficulty, because her mouth was full. "Like a fool, I believed them. In fact, I freed the first man. Indeed, I am sorry. It was a wonder they didn't kill you."

"My old felt hat saved me from anything worse than a thundering bad headache. Anyway, you made amends by shooting straight."

"You know perfectly well that the pistol went off of its own accord," Lena said hastily.

"Did it?" asked the sergeant, his eyes twinkling.

"You know the beastly thing did. It frightened me almost to death."

Lena then told all about the motor trip from Perth, and of John's "don'ts" and Stella's irritating attempts to reason with her. Then followed her adventure on the Nullabor Plain right up to the time she smelled frying bacon and eggs, and discovered the chimney of the underground house.

"I'm fearfully impulsive," concluded Lena, with entire frankness.

Detective-Sergeant Wishhart noted a spot of soot on her nose and wanted to brush it off.

"Impulsive, eh?" he said cheerfully. "Well, I am an impulsive kind of fellow, too. Look here, you will have to stay in Adelaide for some time in connection with this case, while, perhaps, your sister and her husband will want to go on to Melbourne. Why not stay with my sister? She's a good sort. She has only one fault: she will keep on trying to find a wife for me."

Lena regarded Grey-Eyes calmly. And then, as though to show

how impulsive she really was, she said: "If your sister asks me, I will be very pleased to stay with her."

Four Gold Bricks

Like a ribbon of white silk stretched across a rumpled green-black carpet, the twenty-feet-wide line cut through the bush goes endlessly on over the gigantic land-waves from the Southern Ocean to the Indian Ocean. Two feet west of centre is built the netted, barb-topped fence, along the east side of which is the track used by the patrolmen.

It is the great Number One Rabbit Fence in Western Australia, more than 1,100 miles long.

A few chains south of the peg marking the 128th mile north of the Perth-Kalgoorlie railway, a small, black leather portmanteau lay midway between the twin tracks of a motor vehicle. It was early one January morning. Three crows were watching the bag: one from a fence post; another from the edge of the track; and the third from the branch of a young sandalwood tree.

It was a well-made bag, strong despite its years of usage, and it lay on the track as though determined to lie there for ever.

The air was still and hot. Where the birds last drank only they themselves knew. Rule-straight, the netted and barb-topped fence maintained its exact position in the cut line, rising up a mile-long slope to the summit of the southern swell of land, continuing northward to disappear beneath the branches of mulgas, and to appear again beyond them, running up a long, two-mile slope to another land crest.

The position of the bag was lonely indeed. On the far side of the fence lies Earoo Station, its homestead eight miles distant through mulga forests and across saltbush flats. The southern wheat belts lie some seventy miles away, and the pastoral country forty miles to the north. Where the black bag lay was almost in the centre of a hundred-miles-wide belt of desert scrub.

The crow, perched on the fence post, began to gargle like a man being strangled. His comrade, settled beside the track, flew away into a mulga tree, the better to observe the coming from the south of two camels drawing tandem-wise a heavy hooded dray. The camels walked the sand-covered track with cat-like action and silence. The dray they drew made no more sound, save for an occasional thud when a wheel ran over a subterranean fortress built by white ants.

Once the camels stopped, and then the crows watched a man vault the fence and do something to it. When he regained the track side of the fence the camels came on again and the crows flew away with complaining caws.

Two hundred yards away, the leading camel saw the black bag. Her cat-like ears were pricked forward as much as they could be. Her big black eyes gleamed. Surely here was a grand excuse to bolt! Her swinging gait became slow and still slower. Knowing that something was amiss, the shaft camel strained his long neck to the off-side so that he, too, might enjoy and take advantage of any lucky diversion. Presently the leading camel declined to proceed further. From the rear of the dray appeared the section fence rider, Linton March. It was his job to keep rabbit-proof the 163 miles of fence between the Perth-Kalgoorlie railway to the south, and Dromedary Hill Camel Station to the north. He was of medium height, lean and lithe, and burned to the colour of mahogany by sun and wind. He spun round the brake handle at the rear of the dray until the wheels were locked, and then walked forward to the bag that lay in wait to offer him happiness and fortune.

For a short space he looked down at the bag, noting its nickel fittings, its stout leather handles, its appearance of determination to rest squarely and comfortably. Doubtless it had fallen from the rear of a table-top truck. That was indicated by its position in the middle of the twin tracks made by the motor vehicle that had passed him the night before when he was camped some distance off the fence at the 126-mile peg.

The weight of the bag, discovered to him when he attempted to lift it was astonishing. Strong fingers slipped back the nickel catches. The bag was not locked. Nor was it stiff. Its mouth sagged open readily, and within it he saw four large bricks of pure gold.

It is a significant mental phenomenon that a man living alone in solitude is able to think with greater clarity and rapidity than he who never is beyond sound of city traffic.

Within the space of three seconds, March's mind reviewed all the circumstances concerning this black bag and its contents. First passed the facts in review. One: That this track was not a public road, and travellers using it were liable to prosecution. Two: That several northern squatters in the vicinity of the township of Sandstone sometimes did use it to reach the main railway at Burracoppin. Three: That it was his duty to stop all travellers and note their names and addresses and the number of their car or truck, and that this duty was widely known to the general public. And four: That the track provided an excellent getaway for car thieves desiring to remove themselves and their stolen property to the State's great open spaces. More than once had he stopped a car containing police officers who were anxious to learn if he had seen and noted a particular car and a particular person driving it; and more than once had he stopped a south-bound car driven by a detective behind whom sat another officer handcuffed to their prisoner.

So much for the facts. Now for the assumptions. At a guess, inside the bag were 300 ounces of gold worth nearly £2,500 Australian money. Wiluna lay far to the north, and the management there undoubtedly consign their gold by rail to Perth. No gold was now being produced at Youanmi, and it was unlikely that any one of the small shows in the Eastern Murchison would allow so much gold to accumulate before dispatching it.

The chances appeared to favour the assumption that the gold in the black bag had been stolen. This fence track was not the usual route for gold consignments, but it would be a favourable route for gold thieves wishing to escape passing through gold mining centres where policemen are unusually wide awake.

Whether the gold was or was not stolen, it was certain that the driver of the vehicle from which it had fallen would return over his tracks in search of it. As has been stated, March had camped the previous night several hundred yards off the fence track at a rock-hole, and as he had not heard a motor pass along the fence track this one must have gone by when he was asleep, any time between the hours of eleven and five o'clock. He knew of its passing immediately he had driven the camels and dray onto the track that morning, and to him it was not difficult to establish the fact that the vehicle had been driven south.

That the driver had elected to travel at night may or may not have had significance. He might have chosen the night to escape the intense heat of the day; but he might have travelled in darkness in order to slip past the fence rider without being forced to give his name and the number of his truck. How far he might go before discovering his loss was problematical, but it was certain that he would return to retrieve the bag and its contents.

He stepped back a pace in order to gaze southward past the camels and the dray to the distant land-crest cleft by the cut line. At any moment now the black dot of a speeding truck would appear just below that cleft.

March's subsequent actions were controlled by an interesting psychological fact, for when all is said and done he was an honest man.

As most people will admit, gold-stealing in Western Australia is not considered a very serious crime by thousands of excellent fellows, who would be shocked by the thought of stealing a horse or taking a tin of bully beef from an absent prospector's camp. Gold is considered common property, and from many of the mines more gold has gone into the pockets of the miners than into the pockets of the shareholders.

It was, then, not unnatural that March's first thoughts were to secure the gold for his own uses. Gold was gold, and a plug of tobacco was a plug of tobacco. Gold, the gift of nature, was common property, but tobacco has to be bought by the individual. To steal tobacco was a heinous crime; to take gold belonging to a mining company or syndicate was not exactly theft. There could be no argument about it. If later he learned that the gold in the bag really did belong to a private party of prospectors, then it could be returned.

A swift glance to right and left assured him that the track was empty. He lifted out the gold, brick by brick, and set it down beside the fence. Bordering the cut line was close-growing, two-feet-high broom-bush, and, snatching up the black bag, he hurled it as far as he could off the track. It sank into the broom-bush as a stone sinks into water.

Walking back to the camels, he drove them forward so that their feet obliterated the indentation made by the bag. When the tail of the dray was level with the gold he halted them. To the tail of the dray was hooked a coil of wire for repairing purposes, and this he dropped on the site occupied by the bag. There were now his own tracks along the fence, made when he had walked forward to the bag and then back to the camels. They had to be concealed from, or accounted to, a man whose keen and anxious eyes sought a black bag containing between two and three thousand pounds worth of gold.

Having lifted the bricks of gold into the dray and covered them with an empty chaff bag, he took his tools and the coil of wire back over that fifty-yard section of double tracks, bumping the wire on the ground at every step, and when he was ready to call to his camels the veriest fool could see that he had stopped to make repairs to the fence.

The now-impatient camels eagerly broke into a quick walk, and, as usual, March strode along close to the near rear corner of the dray where he was within jumping distance of the brake and yet could examine each passing fence panel.

Constantly he looked back, expecting to see the returning motor vehicle, and eventually he arrived at the summit of the long land rise, from which the cut line could be seen crossing a twelve-mile-wide land trough, a brilliant white ribbon crossing the green-black bush carpet. Above, the cadmium sky seemingly filled by the fiery orb of the sun. Everywhere the drowsing bush - and the silence.

Here again he halted the team. The ground was free of the tell-tale sand, but he tossed wire and tools beyond the fence, and then put the heavy bricks of gold on the bag of tools. He took the bricks a hundred yards into the bush directly opposite a strainer post, and buried them beneath a bogeta bush. Back again at the strainer post, he cut every wire and repaired his breaks with new wire. What tracks he did leave merely indicated the work he had done.

And there, three miles away to the south, moved slowly a black dot on the ribbon of cut line. It was certainly a motor car or truck. It was almost certain to be driven by a man seeking a dropped black bag.

Glancing at the sun, then at the fence shadow, March decided that the time was half-past eleven. He called to the camels, and they began the long swing down the grade. The dray rumbled loudly when passing the cement-like belt of hard ground, and then fell silent save for the soft hissing of the wide iron tyres pressing into the sand. The low bush either side the cut line presently gave place to more robust scrub, which so sheltered the track that the heat was severe.

Occupying his usual position to the rear of the near side corner of the dray, March now did not look back. The long minutes passed. He cried a halt for a few seconds to enable him to pull from the fence a small wind-blown branch. Now and then he pushed at a post in passing, to ascertain if it were sound underground.

Then at long last came the expected. The camels abruptly broke into a trot which, if unchecked, would have become a gallop in two seconds. Swiftly he leaped for the brake handle, and swiftly he spun it round to apply the wheel-locking brake. Only when the dray was stopped did he hear the purring motor engine behind. When he turned round he saw a powerful touring car within forty feet of him.

Linton March had expected a truck, and here was a car. He had expected the driver to sound his horn, not as a request to be given right of way, for he had no legal right of way on that track, but as a warning to take precautions with his camels. For a moment March studied the now stationary car. With deliberation, he took a notebook and pencil from a canvas bag nailed to the inside of the hood, and, walking to the car, he jotted down its registration particulars. Arrived beside the driver, he said angrily:

"Haven't you got enough sense to sound your horn when coming up behind a camel team?" He found himself looking into a pair of expressionless and remarkably cold, blue eyes. "I want your name and address," he went on. "This is not a public road, and, as the notice on every gate clearly states, you are liable for prosecution for using it."

"Aw, don't be hard, dig!" exclaimed the driver, with an entire lack of warmth in his voice. "Sorry for not sounding the hooter, but I didn't know your mokes were touchy."

Appeased a little by the words, if not by the tone of the metallic voice, March said: "I'll not report you, because personally I'm only too glad to see someone now and then. But I must have your name with the number of your car. The inspector is somewhere up north, and if you meet him and he finds out I know nothing about you, I'll be in for it."

"It ain't likely we'll see him, any'ow," put in the man sitting beyond the driver. "We ain't going that far north."

March looked across at the passenger to take in details of a white-faced, black-moustached man wearing a black felt hat.

"You might meet the inspector within half an hour. I am looking for him to-day. Now, what name is it?"

"Powell," returned the driver, his face suddenly registering a scowl. "Out from Lake Grace. The post office knows where I live."

"All right!" March noted the name and the town, fiercely wondering if the black bag containing the gold had fallen from this car. Well, if these two hard-bitten men were looking for it, it was now their move. He turned to walk on his camels and so lead them off the track to permit the travellers to pass, for only by forcing the dray partially into the scrub could the car pass, when the driver called out: "Have you seen a black bag lying on the track?"

Neither man saw the gleam that leapt into March's eyes, and, when he swung about, faint interest only was signalled by them.

"No. Any idea where you dropped it?"

"Somewhere between the Camel Station and the Campion railway crossing."

"Was it on the luggage carrier?"

"No. It was in the back of the car but the bodywork ain't too good, as you can see, and the nearside door must have bumped open when we hit a pot hole. We didn't notice it at the time, because we were hitting the pace a bit, but when we pulled into the Campion store for petrol there was the door open and no bag."

"Well, I haven't seen it so far," March said casually. "If it fell from your car between here and the Camel Station it will still be where it fell out - unless the inspector picks it up on his way south. If you dropped it going through the wheat belt, then some cocky has picked it up. They are carting wheat at all hours down there, and they have permission to use the fence track in parts. Was that you went south last night?"

The driver nodded, his cold eyes staring at the fence rider. The other man was rolling a cigarette. Both of them appeared liable to commit murder for much less than four bricks of gold. March thought of his beloved .22 Savage repeating rifle in the dray . . .

"Where were you camped last night? We didn't see your camp or your fire," asked the passenger.

"You wouldn't. I was at a water-hole well off the fence. What kind of a bag was it?"

"A fair-sized leather grip. There's a lot of valuable property in it." The driver muttered a curse before he added: "Suppose we'd better push on as far as the Camel Station. About where are we?"

"The 138-mile peg is a few chains ahead. It will make twenty-five miles to the Camel Station. Did you call in there coming down?"

The driver shook his head, and again he examined the fence rider with his expressionless eyes.

The other man produced a watch, and then exclaimed: "Cripes! It's ten to twelve. What about boiling the billy?"

To March it was a peculiar suggestion from one of two men looking for a bag containing more than £2,000 worth of gold. It made him suspect that they thought he had found it, but he was on his guard and sure of himself. The driver's attitude became more affable, and, because it was natural for a lonely man to want to talk, March instantly agreed.

"I'll pull on a few yards opposite that quandong tree," he decided, and abruptly he left the car to reach the team and urge them forward and then off the track hard against the bordering scrub, thus leaving the track clear. Whilst the travellers made a fire and proceeded to boil the billy, he cut branches from the quandong tree to provide a snack for the ever-hungry animals.

With purpose now, he dropped the tailboard of the dray and took out the tucker box. The tailboard down, the gear within the dray was fully exposed, and, with the air of a man much interested in drays, the dark-eyed man examined the wheels and the body of this one. He even lifted the long lid of the box fixed to the front of the vehicle, seeing therein only a wheel spanner and two tins of grease. When he showed marked interest in March's rifle, the fence rider jumped up into the dray and so moved the gear as to convince the traveller that neither the gold nor the bag was hidden among it.

Both men made themselves pleasant during the meal of damper and tinned meat, talking of cricket and racing. Afterwards they drove on towards the Camel Station, their car disappearing where the cut line was hidden by the broad-leafed mulgas at the 144-mile water-shed. They left the fence rider smiling grimly, and now convinced that they were not representatives of any mining company.

At the water-shed, a corrugated-iron roof erected over two round iron receiving tanks, he took out his camels and let them go in hobbles. It was then two o'clock, and again he boiled the billy and took the tea with him into the dray, where he made himself comfortable. The breeze blew fitfully hot and cool beneath the high hood, and there he was removed from the annoying ants, although there was no escape from the sticky flies. Crows, the same birds that for days followed the dray up and down the fence, arrived from the lunch camp to settle in the near trees and patiently to wait for the scraps he would leave at this camp. Other than their mournful cawing, the only sound to relieve the silence was the passing of an occasional willi-willi. It was a silence to be dreaded by anyone used to the more dreadful uproar of a city.

Whilst he lounged in the dray smoking and trying to read, the flies a pest, the ground too hot for the ants to run over it, the camels contentedly camped in the black shadow cast by healthy indigenous pines, March noticed that he was strangely unexcited by the events of that day. He was at first inclined to think that the driver of the car was a policeman, but had he been he would scarcely have hesitated to say so.

There was something decidedly peculiar about the whole affair. Everything pointed to it. The fence track was not a direct route from any mine to Perth, but it was a good getaway for men travelling to the Eastern States to sell stolen gold.

They returned about three o'clock, disappointment writ plain on their cold faces. They asked March if he had seen anyone on the track other than themselves, and he told them he had seen no one for five days. Further, he assured them indifferently that, as they had not found the black bag, they must have dropped it somewhere in the wheat belt where a wheat-carting cocky had picked it up. Still they refrained from informing him of its contents, which was another point telling against them.

If they suspected him, they were careful to hide it. They knew that, without the certainty of regaining the gold, violence would be worse than useless, because, although the fence rider lived a solitary life, he travelled to a time table, and his absence at terminal points on certain dates would be at once investigated.

So they departed southward, and March again climbed up into the dray to drink tea and ponder on the matter until near sundown, when he took an axe and cut back the scrub for an hour, scrub which if not governed would, in a year or two, submerge both track and fence.

The next day he reached the northern terminus of his section, the Camel Station, with its stone-built homestead only a hundred yards west of the fence. He was due for four days' spell, one day for every Sunday he had spent and worked on the fence during the trip to Burracoppin and back. The man in charge of the station led a life as lonely as his own, and for an hour they shouted at each other just to hear the blessed sound of a human voice. March made no mention of the gold, but they discussed the black bag and the two travellers who had lost it. The station man knew the passenger in the car. His name was Newland, and he was one of those fellows always found hovering about mining shows, seeking to reap some advantage from the labour and the success of prospectors.

March was now convinced that the gold had been stolen, but so far the station man had heard of no theft of gold, which he certainly would have mentioned. Another peculiar fact presented itself. Why had not the travellers gone back further north than the Camel Station if they had come from farther north? They had passed the Camel Station sometime during the night, to be more exact, about three o'clock. The station man had heard them pass. And then, to cloud the matter still more, the fence rider, whose section began at the Camel Station northward, arrived, and he said he had seen the car and the driver at the 270-mile peg, but there had been no passenger in the car.

The result of all this was that when March left the Camel Station on yet another trip to Burracoppin, he was a sorely puzzled man. The northern fence rider would most certainly have heard of the theft of so much gold, and yet if the travellers had been genuine miners or the representatives of a mining company, or owners, would they not have said so and openly declared their loss?

As has been said, March's section of fence ran through a hundred miles of semi-desert country. Earoo's eastern boundary touched the fence on its west side for a dozen or so miles, but all the country east of the fence still remained to be taken up by a squatter. It was vacant because, while it had several tracts suitable for cattle, vast areas of it would not give a goat or a camel sustenance. Sandalwood getters had taken out all the suitable sandalwood, and the tracks of their drays, although many years old, still remained. Doubtless they had also prospected for gold among the scrub-hidden outcrops of ironstone and quartz, and doubtless there was gold yet to be found.

That the northern fence rider had seen only the driver and not the passenger when the car had passed him was the most significant fact of all. Nearly as important was the knowledge that the two men had not gone farther back on their tracks than the Camel Station. The idea presented itself to March's mind that somewhere east of the fence on his section a big strike of gold had been made, and that secretly the cream of it was being taken out before the announcement of the strike would start a rush. If he could only locate that secret strike he, as the holder of a Miner's Right, could peg a juicy claim. Thus it was that for the first time for many months he camped at the 135-mile peg two days after leaving the Camel Station. Here the fence ran over the broad back of one of the huge land waves. Just before the peg was reached the cut line passed over a belt of ironstone rubble masked by low bogeta bush, and at the peg itself, where the camp was made, waitabit and saltbush gave the camels excellent feed.

From the fence the great fall of ground to the east was hidden by this scrub, but he had only to walk 200 yards before coming out onto a low granite outcrop from which it was possible to view the horizon twenty to thirty miles distant. Below him stretched vast areas of scrub divided by rocky outcrops, almost unexplored land, vacant, and useless for pastoral purposes.

It was only one o'clock, and the inspector was still up north and might arrive at any time. It was a chance he had to take, but to give himself an excuse he cut and carried to the fence a dozen posts before starting off on a wide detour east and then north of the camp.

He knew the old sandalwood track immediately he came to it,

because he had seen it on several occasions, but this time his eyes gleamed and his mouth grew tight when he saw the fresh tracks of a dray on it. The track came up winding among the rock outcrops, and March knew that it would join the fence track along the ironstone rubble-covered ridge. Yet whilst a dray had lately passed along it, that dray had not been driven onto the fence track when he would have seen its wheel marks.

He proved that a man driving a horse and dray had come from the east to a point about 150 yards from the fence track. There he had tied the horse to a mulga tree. From there he had walked to the edge of the ironstone rubble which gave no tracks, and March became sure that he had deliberately selected that path to reach the fence track and to meet a car or truck driver. A second man, doubtless, had driven back the horse and dray.

So it had been here that the white-faced, black-moustached man had met the car and joined it with the gold in the black bag brought on the dray.

No longer nervous about the inspector, March walked to his own dray, from which he took his rifle and a handful of cartridges and a filled waterbag. Away to the east somewhere, men had found gold and were secretly mining it. They could not hold all the country, nor could they prevent him pegging out a claim. He determinedly followed the fresh tracks of the dray along the old sandalwood track, here crossing open, rock-strewn country, and now passing through bush of bogeta and mulga. The track led him for three miles, shouting up at him that the dray had made several trips along it. At the end of three miles he was encompassed by dense mulga; so dense, in fact, that the open space ahead promised blinding sunlight. Arriving at the edge of the open space, he was halted by what was presented to his astonished gaze.

To his front lay a 200-yard belt of open land covered with snow-white quartz chips. Beyond it rose the low rampart of weathered ironstone and quartz. A little to his left, three men were working at a face in this rampart, and where the scrub rounded to meet the rampart there were pitched two tents on the far side of a camp fire. Outside one of the tents a young woman sat on a case, her hands clasped about one of her knees. Two of the three men working with picks and shovels had rifles slung across their backs. They were so intent on their labours that they did not see him, and, in the positions they occupied, they could not see the girl. She rose like a startled kangaroo, and silently waved March back into the bush.

There was that in her action demanding obedience. He obeyed, stepping backward until the scrub hid all that open space from him. There he waited, and he had not long to wait before he saw the girl slipping through the bush to join him. She was slim and agile, and the sun had failed dismally to spoil her fresh beauty. Fearless grey eyes swept their gaze over him, and, when she stood close before him, strange excitement prevented her voice from rising beyond a whisper.

"Who are you?" she demanded.

"I'm March, the rabbit-fence rider," he told her. "And you?"

"I am Joan Ross," she replied hurriedly. "Listen, and then please act. I came here with my father five weeks ago. Before that he discovered a very rich vein of gold here, and he brought me to cook and look after him while he got as much of the surface gold as possible before making the find public. Then a man named Newland and his gang tracked us, and when they found the worth of father's strike, and that he had leased the ground around it, they made us prisoners. They have compelled father to help them steal his own gold, and they have threatened to shoot him if either of us tries to get away."

"I see," drawled March slowly.

"They would, too. They're desperate," the girl went on. "I am afraid. I think sometimes that when they have taken all they can they will kill my father and me to assure their safety. They could do it now, and hide our bodies, and no one would ever know or miss us. Newland is a beast - a cold, slimy beast - and you must be very careful."

"Where is he now? Is he one of those two carrying rifles?"

"No. He is away. He's been away for a week. He took over 300 ounces of gold in father's bag. The others are expecting him back any time. Oh, please, please, hurry back to your camp and go to Sandstone or Campion and ring up the police and tell them about us! Will you? Will you go at once without losing a minute?"

March hesitated. Then he said: "All right! But what about you?

You had better come with me."

"No, that would never do. They would kill my father if they knew I had escaped with you. They are desperate, I tell you. Oh, go! Go now and hurry!"

March thought of the inspector. If he got back before the inspector passed his camp in his ton-truck, a message could be sent to the police that night; otherwise it would take him four days to get into communication with them.

"I'll do it, Miss Ross. Leave it to me," he said cheerfully.

She nodded, thanking him with her grey eyes wide with hope; and she sped back toward the hidden camp.

He walked half a mile along the old sandalwood track when he abruptly halted. He swore softly, for had he not been within an ace of proving himself a mug? What was that trite saying? Oh, yes! A sucker is born every minute. Assuredly he would be proved a sucker if he did not himself handle this affair; if he rushed off to sool on the police; if he left this rich strike before pegging out a likely claim! Courage might win him a rich prize; lack of it would forever condemn him on riding a vermin fence. And audacity now might gain him a reward worth more than gold - a lovely face, an adorable mouth, and a pair of winsome grey eyes -

It was a desperate gamble, and March walked for another half a mile thinking it over before he came to a decision.

Then round he swung, and back he went - but not along the sandalwood track. He circled wide with expert bushmanship so that when again he saw the camp and the men working the claim, it was to slide his rifle barrel over the top of the ironstone mound and, behind its sights, look down on the three men and beyond them to the girl again seated on the case outside one of the tents.

"Put up your hands, you down there!"

Three startled men straightened up from their work. One spun round snatching at the butt of the rifle slung across his back. Without hesitation, March fired, and the fellow felt the wind of the bullet as it whizzed past.

"I won't give you another chance!" March yelled, every nerve in his body throbbing with excitement. "Up with your hands and turn round facing the tents."

Three pairs of grimy hands rose skyward. The girl came

running from the camp.

March stepped over the rampart and stood behind them.

"Which one of you is Ross?"

The man without a rifle at once answered.

"Good! Take that rifle from the man next to you. Don't get in front of my gun while you're doing it. I'll plug either of you two if you make a move."

The elderly, grey-haired man, whom labour had bent and exposure had toughened, with alacrity slipped the rifle up and over the head of the man standing nearest him. He had just taken the rifle when March's right thigh received, a terrific blow. To them came the crack of an automatic pistol. The girl screamed. The two men flashed about, the one still having a rifle whipping it off his back.

March staggered and fell, for his right leg was useless to him. The man with the rifle took a snap shot at Ross. He missed, but Ross did not. On the ground, March squirmed over onto his chest. He saw the girl crouched on the ground midway between them and the tents. Somewhere at the edge of the encircling bush lurked the man who had smashed his right thigh with a pistol bullet. He guessed it was Newland returned.

"Lie down, Ross!" March shouted, half-dazed with pain. But Ross, made almost mad by the treatment he had received at the hands of these gold thieves, reversed his rifle and felled the second bandit with its butt. Now, like an old lion at bay, he stood glaring across the open space, and the pistol expert fired again from the scrub.

Still Ross stood, on his feet, seemingly unhurt, defiant. He raised the rifle to his shoulder and pumped bullets into the scrub where the old track reached the clearing.

March, his eye squinting along his rifle sights, groaned with the agony of his thigh, and anxiously waited for an opening to shoot. He saw Newland partially masked by a tree. He was steadying his wrist for another shot at Ross -

The fence rider was feeling deadly sick. Low against the ground lay spread an ink-black mist. It surrounded him; it was rising about him. He knew what it was, and he knew he had to beat it, because Ross was so passionately angry that he scorned to take what little cover there was. He could now see Newland's white face, peering above the black object steadied against the tree.

Steady! His throbbing heart was causing the rifle sights to shudder. He held his breath, and then pressed evenly against the trigger.

The rifle uttered its staccato bark, and the face dropped to the foot of the tree. March tried to rise in order to escape the black flood, but he only sank into it.

The Fence Inspector, driving his ton-truck along the fence reached March's camel cart and the roped camels at ten minutes to four o'clock that afternoon. An hour before he had met and stopped a man driving a car, a man having cold, blue eyes and who said his name was Powell, and that he came from Lake Grace.

Having some urgent instruction to give his fence rider, the inspector filled in time by strolling about to stretch his legs and quite by accident crossed the sandalwood track on which were the fresh tracks of a dray's wheels. That decided him to follow the tracks of two men using it: those made by March, and those left by Newland. The distant sound of gun shots hastened his return to the truck which he drove over the ironstone rubble and then along the sandalwood track. He found Newland and one of his mates quite dead, the second bandit still unconscious from the blow given him by Ross, Ross wounded in the shoulder and March with an ugly wound in his right thigh.

March did not regain consciousness until the inspector's truck was crossing the wheat belt on the road to Merredin. The still unconscious gold thief lay on his one side, and on his other sat Joan Ross. Her father, a stoic if ever there was one, sat beside the inspector, and it was his roaring voice that first penetrated to the wounded man's groping mind. The first thing he saw was the dim figure of Joan, and the whiter oval of her face.

"Hullo!" he murmured.

"Don't try to sit up. Your thigh bone is smashed. Are you in much pain?"

"A little. So the boss arrived, eh? Where is he taking us?"

"To Merredin. To the hospital."

"You awake, young feller?" roared Ross. "Good on yer! You

got that Newland good and plenty. That'll lain him not to pinch 300 ounces of my gold, the dirty dog. Any'ow, I don't much mind that little parcel. There's plenty more where that came from, and, you bein' willin', I'm taking you in on a fifty-fifty basis when yer leg's right again."

March felt for and found the girl's hand. It gave him comfort.

"Tell your dad that the bandits dropped the bag containing gold on the fence track, and that I picked it up and planted it.''

Joan transmitted the message, and her father uttered his satisfaction with a bull-like roar. After that March tried hard to pronounce a name, but he gave it up when, just before he again sank into unconsciousness, he felt the firm little hand squeeze his own.

Lady, Stand Fast!

Cass Bennett was on his way to Broken Hill, but he had yet many hundreds of miles to cross before he could take his ease on the verandah of the Masonic Hotel. Not that he was addicted to alcohol, but, to any man living in Central Australia, such a spell on such a verandah in the proximity of such a bar represents the acme of bliss in a hot and dusty world.

It was the period of the year when the tourist route through the heart of the continent is deserted by motor car explorers and holidaying politicians: to wit, January. All he had seen when crossing the road following the telegraph line from the Alice to Pine Creek was one empty champagne bottle. He had been for a year or two mooching around the Arthur Hills, and he had crossed the road north of Ryan's Well to enter the great unknown country south and west of Aritunga. Although he could have travelled by train from the Alice to his destination he yet chose to ignore modern transport and proceed more or less in a straight line, using the transport that is older than the Pyramids.

Now the south-east corner of the new geographical division, named Central Australia, reaches that maze of small lakes and lagoons and creeks lying to the north of Lake Eyre, South Australia. On the maps they are coloured blue, representing water, but actually they hold water about once every fifty years. Here is hell situated on this earth. By comparison, the Northern Territory tableland is a health resort and the dry lands north of the Nullabor Plain lands of milk and honey. Here, among the stunted scrub trees, the sand-dunes and the flats and the tangle of canegrass, Nature writhes in eternal torment. A great desert is beautiful in placid death, the country north of Lake Eyre is utterly dreadful in its depressing ugliness. Heat, dust and winged pests are merely the minor devils.

Having made up his mind that he was due for a spell, an ordinary man would have left his camels at the Alice and taken the train, but then Cass Bennett was not an ordinary man even among those extraordinary men who prospect for precious metals and grazing areas, and thus blaze the way for the modern explorers. For one thing, there was no real necessity for Bennett to be wandering about Central and North Australia, even in the winter, because he had made a pile out of a show west of Mount Stanley in '24, and then another pile out of a show beyond the Plenty River in '29. But he was now too old to retire to a city. When a man reaches thirty it may be said of him that the bush has claimed him for keeps.

He had passed through the northernmost fringe of the land depressions, and this afternoon when the sun was westering, he was lazily sitting on his cud-chewing, riding camel in the lead of a string of five pack-beasts. His mongrel-bred cattle dog trotted ahead, while in his ears tinkled the light bell suspended from the neck of the rear-most camel. Should the bell stop its tinkling he would know instantly that somewhere along the string a break had occurred. Without the bell it was possible to look back and find half the camels missing.

Here the string wound in and around high, barren, red sandhills. Cass Bennett appeared not to note just what compass point he was keeping to, but nevertheless, almost sub-consciously, he equalised the unavoidable twists and curves. Presently, he reached a point from which there was no way round a battlemented rampart of sand. A cleft made by the last windstorm offered the easiest way over it, and to escape the discomfort of riding a swerving, sliding mount, he slipped to the ground and led the string up the lower slopes, choosing the grades over this mountainous sand-range.

When, eventually, he arrived at a position where he could see beyond the range, when he stood in the wind-created cleft, he was presented with an unusual picture. In the near foreground lay a jumble of low sandhills. Beyond them stretched the green-black maze of depressions bordered by gnarled box trees. Against the background of this picture was being acted a kind of war drama, arresting enough to seize Bennett's immediate attention. It caused him to halt while yet his camels were on the slopes behind and below him, and to look down with an interest containing a little amusement.

On the summits of low sandhills, separated by a wide claypan flat, two men were engaged in a rifle duel. One was wearing a red shirt, and the other one of khaki. It was a serious business, because bullets were kicking up little spurts of dust uncomfortably close to their heads, which snuggled against the sand. From the sounds of the reports, Cass Bennett knew that Khakishirt was using a high-powered rifle, and that Redshirt was working either a Remington or a Winchester.

One acquainted with rifles will know that Khakishirt held a definite advantage over his opponent - the advantage possessed by a warship mounting fifteen-inch guns over another mounting only ten-inch. And yet it was an advantage from which Khakishirt appeared not to profit. He retreated, slipping down the far side of his sandhill and racing back to the cover provided by the ridge of the next one. Redshirt immediately advanced, and it was obvious that he had the greater initiative and determination. He was a huge man and possessed of remarkable agility. Scrambling up the steep hill on his new front, he saw his enemy retreating up the slope ahead, and at once fired twice, placing his bullets about the feet of Khakishirt.

Khakishirt was evidently losing his nerve. He swung round before reaching cover and fired wildly - so wildly that Bennett could not see where his bullets reached ground, and then continued his retreat. Through the still air drifted Redshirt's bull-like roar. He raced after his opponent, and his opponent made the pace hot. Cass Bennett watched the protagonists as each came into his elevated line of vision on the summits of the lesser hills. Long after both had finally disappeared he could hear the reports of their rifles and Redshirt's roaring voice.

"Well, Hool-'em-up, what do you know about that?" he asked the brindle dog that stood beside him as interested as his master. "I would have thought it to be a little too warm for all that rushing about. Still, it is wonderful what the human body can stand. We will advance. The presence of human beings denotes water - unless those fellers are travelling with camels."

Passively, the camel string moved on behind him as he made his way down the sand-range by the easiest gradients. They crossed the tracks left by the combatants, continuing easterly through the jumble of low hills for fully a mile, and then quite abruptly they emerged onto a narrow flat bordered on its far side by box trees, which, in turn, bordered a creek. Having crossed the flat and passed through the trees, Bennett was astonished to find in the creek a wide and deep stretch of water.

He stood at the edge of the water while the eager beasts were taking in their many gallons, and thus he came to see at the northern end of the lagoon several bag tents protected by canvas flies. Smoke from a fire rose in a lazy blue spiral. Dogs barked. A human figure - it looked like a boy - stepped to the water and stared at him and his camels.

It is not bush etiquette for one traveller to make camp too close to another, and where he then was appeared to Bennett to be a suitable camp site for the night. There was plenty of herbal rubbish between the creek and the sandhills for the camels.

Whilst unloading the packs and removing the heavy saddles, Cass Bennett wondered. The two men engaged in the rifle duel - he still could hear the shooting - obviously belonged to this camp at the far end of the lagoon. It was obvious, too, that the camp was a permanent one, because the weather was too hot and dry for travellers to bother erecting tents. What the business of these people was, he could not guess. The country was not gold-bearing, nor was it taken up by pastoralists.

While he was still busy with the unloading, the boy from the other camp swiftly approached him, soon revealing to the surprised Bennett that she wasn't a boy at all, but a young girl dressed in the roughest of masculine clothes. About sixteen years old, she was well formed, and, despite her sun-ruined complexion, quite pretty.

"Good-day!" he greeted her, cheerfully.

She nodded. Her large, grey eyes carefully surveyed him: his stiff, wide-brimmed felt, the khaki drill shirt, the grey-green gabardine slacks, and the kangaroo-hide riding boots.

"Are you a policeman?" she asked.

"No!" replied he, smiling, "Why did you think so?"

"You look like a policeman, that's all."

"Trouble around here, apparently. What caused the shootin' match?"

"Me. Did you see them?"

"Yes. I didn't interfere. They were some distance away, and, anyhow, I dislike interfering in other people's business. Who are you?"

"Mavis Jacks. My father is one of the men shooting. Where are you headed for?"

"Broken Hill. You don't seem to he much concerned about your father."

"They're always quarrelling. So you are going to Broken Hill, are you?"

For a space they regarded each other: she seriously, he with twinkling blue eyes. Yes, she was rather nice looking, in spite of her complexion and lack of face adornment. She decided that his rugged features and compact and powerful figure indicated more than physical strength. Her brows drew closer together and her lips were pursed as though effort were needed to solve a problem.

Then: "Would you take me to Broken Hill with you? I could do the cooking or the camel-hunting, and in Broken Hill I could get a job at something. You see -"

"Mav-vis! I want you!"

Both turned to look toward the bag camp. Before it stood a woman.

"That's the old cow," the girl announced, with calm inelegance. "I shall have to go, or she'll knock me about. I'll try to see you again. If you would only take me to Broken Hill! So long. You go careful around here."

"But -"

She turned away and ran along the creek-bank to the woman standing like a tree stump, and as Cass Bennett's gaze followed her lithe figure the twinkle faded from his eyes. It was a thoughtful man who hobbled out the camels.

In Central Australia it is not customary among men to "pack a gun," although they certainly keep their rifles handy when in country inhabited by the wilder blacks. It was seldom that Cass Bennett actually carried a revolver in any part of the country, but here he foresaw the possibility of trouble with men - or one man if the rifle-duel ended fatally. Moreover, he was alone, and quite a lot can happen to a man travelling alone with pack bags containing gold.

When a revolver lay snug in a leather holster on his belt, he made a fire and set the filled billy against the blaze, watched by the dog that lay full length in the shadow cast by one of the pack-saddles. The flies were, as usual, annoying, and even tobacco smoke failed to keep them at bay.

Later, when he was sipping coal-black tea, he saw beyond the creek a man mounted on a fast-riding camel nearing the bag camp. With interest he watched the rider "hoosh" the beast down beside the camp, and he saw then the woman appear and stand talking to him as he removed the saddle and buckled on the hobbles.

Both man and woman then disappeared beyond the tents where the smoke spiral denoted the camp fire to be situated. Fifteen minutes later the fellow appeared again and came towards him. He was tall and shambling, bow-legged from much riding; his scant clothes were in rags. A pair of shifty, black eyes came to examine the lounging Bennett - eyes set in a sharp-featured, unwashed and unshaven face.

"Good day ee!" he drawled.

"'Day!" Bennett replied cheerfully. "Didn't expect to find a camp in this country."

"No! 'Taint eggzactly like the 'Awkesbury or the Yarra country. We ain't all millionaires who can foller the sun. We're doin' a little dingo trappin'. At least I'm doin' the trappin'. My ole woman says as 'ow Bill and 'Arry went orf on a rifle shootin' experdition. You seen 'em?"

"I did. Neither was registering any hits."

The shifty gaze roamed over Bennett's temporary camp and his equipment. The laugh he vented was more a snigger than an outburst of mirth.

"Good job they don't go in fer it when they're sober. They bin at the bottle," he said. "I 'ate diggin' graves this weather. Where you bound fer?"

"I'm working across to New South Wales."

"That's so! Well, you got a ways yet. Ain't travellin' alone, surely?"

Bennett nodded. He knew he was being urged to put down all his cards, and he expected the next question.

"Come far?"

"Been up in the Territory, and down through Arltunga. I crossed this country in '29, and there wasn't any water in this creek then."

"Suppose not. She got filled a bit from a thunderstorm last Christmus. Where jew stay at Arltunga?"

"I was only there a couple of days. Always put up at Hewitson's. You gettin' any dogs?"

"Plenty! When them other two takes an interest in their traps. 'Ere comes Bill Joyce now."

"What started the row?" Bennett asked sharply, when he turned from regarding the approaching giant.

"'Eat 'ad somethin' to do with it, I reckon. Then Bill Joyce's playin' around with the girl. 'Arry's daughter. Silly fool to bring 'er out 'ere, but 'Arry thought as she might be company fer my ole woman. Any'ow, the kid wants tamin' a bit."

In silence they waited for the huge man in the red shirt. He was built on the lines of a gorilla, and in one huge paw he carried a Winchester rifle. His small, very light-blue eyes were bloodshot, and, like his comrade, he badly needed soap and water. He planted his great bulk on naked, calloused feet that had not worn boots for months, and eyed Bennett.

"'Day, mister!" he said, with slight emphasis on the title. "Who you after?"

"Says 'e's 'eadin' fer Noo South," interposed Shifty-eyes, with a little haste. Bennett guessed that they, like the girl, thought him to be a policeman.

Redshirt said: "Oh! Flamin' 'ot. Spare a pannikin of tea?"

"Help yourself. Sugar in the powdered milk tin," Bennett assented.

Redshirt dashed scalding tea into a spare pannikin, added sugar, stirred the liquid with a stick he snatched up, and drank with grunts of appreciation.

"Thirsty work, a rifle duel," Bennett observed, lazily. There was no mistaking the bright red spots of blood on the blue drill trousers, but they might have been the blood of a wild dog butchered in a trap, on which the poison had failed to accomplish its purpose.

"You seen us?" demanded Redshirt, an ugly light leaping into his cold eyes.

"Yes. How did it end?" countered Bennett, casually. "It seemed to me that the heat haze was makin' the shooting poor."

"'Arry kep' me orf with his Savage. I 'ad only this Winchester. I got that dry that I 'ad to give in and come back," Redshirt growled, adding after short pause: "Me and 'im 'as a nargument now and then, and we shoots it out. Don't do no damage either side. 'Arry'll come back sometime to-night. Well -" He rose from squatting on his heels. "Well, dinner should be near ready. Come along up after and have a game of cards."

"Thanks. I'll not promise, though. I'm pushing on early in the morning."

Redshirt tried unsuccessfully to keep the satisfaction from his eyes. His lank companion got up, too, and, nodding, they departed for the camp, leaving Cass Bennett seated with his back against a pack-saddle and smoking between sips from his pannikin.

So that young girl was Khakishirt's daughter, this animal of a man wanted her, and Khakishirt was possibly dead. Sixteen or seventeen years old she looked, but she might well be younger. Her future, if Khakishirt was really dead, did not appear to be exactly bright. He decided that he could do nothing but await developments.

The sun went down at last beyond the great sand-range from which he had watched the duel, and he began the usual camp chores: filling the five-gallon water drums at the creek's edge; gathering wood for cooking purposes; and peeling potatoes to go with the tin of salt meat and the damper. That done, he kneaded the dough and set it to bake in the small oven he always carried, providing bread for the next day. At this time of the year damper had to be baked every night.

Still Khakishirt failed to put in an appearance. The sun vanished beyond the edge of the world, and a cloud of galahs came in to drink. When the dusk was deepening; when the celestial slaughter-house wall of western sky was being demolished by advancing night, he laid out his blanket roll and placed pack-saddles along both sides and at its head. Not till then, when the flies had been vanquished, did he eat.

As darkness fell, so did he allow the fire to die down. Khakishirt remained absent, and, if alive, he must by now be suffering torments of thirst. They were a queer crowd along there, where that bigger fire burned beyond the straight outlines of the bag tents. Here were no policemen on beat. Here were no widely-spaced squatters' homesteads, even. Here, men could do what they liked, even kill each other, and the law would probably never get to hear of it. Bennett knew men who were safe from the hangman as long as they refrained from entering the few settlements.

His own dog growled when the dogs in the distant camp barked. Perhaps Khakishirt was coming now, creeping to the creek for a drink, still fearful of the Redshirt. Then Redshirt at the camp roared at the dogs to keep guard, and Bennett's dog was ordered to "shut up." The hours passed, and the other camp fire died down so that presently the tent outlines became obliterated by the general darkness.

When his own camp fire was but a single red eye, Cass Bennett lay down fully-dressed on his unrolled swag, and the dog came and settled himself at his feet. Cass feared no surprise attack when the dog was there to give ample warning of it. Only such men as he know how faithful a dog can be.

Having implicit faith in the dog, Cass Bennett slept - to be awakened by the animal pawing him as it stood growling beside him. Sitting up, instantly alert, he peered across the pack-saddles into the encompassing darkness.

"Quiet!" he whispered, and the dog at once obeyed.

He saw the figure, blacker than the night, before it struck a match. A man! Probably Khakishirt! But why strike matches? He was coming through the trees from the direction of the camp, sheltering the tiny flame, and, when it went out, striking another.

"Who are you, and what do you want?" Bennett demanded.

"Oh! It's only me. I must speak to you -"

"Why the matches?"

"I - oh, I thought you might shoot, and I daren't call out. It might wake the others,' the girl said softly.

Cass stepped over one of the pack-saddles, and from force of habit began to load his pipe. Almost sub-consciously, he noted the position of the Southern Cross, and estimated the time to be about four o'clock.

"Come and sit here," he invited her. "What's troubling you?"

"Bill Joyce has killed my father. I heard them talking about it," she told him, the words tumbling from her mouth.

"He wounded father in the leg, and then he went close and shot him dead. Father's out there, among the dunes. I'm frightened."

"Wounded him in the fight, and then murdered him, eh?"

"Yes. And Joyce said it would be better for them all to kill you, too, and clear out for Queensland. He said you saw the shooting and would be bound to tell about it. Fred Brown's wife - I could kill her and be glad - backed him up, but Fred said that one killing was enough at one camp, and that you thought the shooting was a kind of joke, and that you were pushing off tomorrow early, anyway."

"Tell me straight, now - what caused the shooting match? You said the cause was you. Brown said the cause was due to booze. They were a bit drunk."

The girl paused. Then she said in a small voice: "Bill Joyce wants me, and father wouldn't let him have me."

"How did you come to be out here at all? How old are you?" Cass cross-examined.

"I'm seventeen. We used to live in Marree, and father and Fred Brown were mates for a while. Then this Bill Joyce told them where they could get plenty of dogs, and they agreed all to come out here. Mrs. Brown said she'd come, and then Bill Joyce and Fred Brown both said as I would be company for her. We've been here for ten months." The quivering voice became fierce. "Ten months here with the flies and the bad tucker, and the men getting drunk, and that old beast getting drunk with 'em, and they all turning on me. They kept on getting father drunk, and they got him so's he didn't seem to have any sense."

"Where do they get the grog from? They couldn't have brought ten months' supplies with them."

"Fred gets it from Charlotte Waters when he goes there in the buckboard to sell the dog scalps and buy tucker."

"Have you any friends in Marree?"

"No!" the girl replied bitterly. "I had only my father. The police sergeant threatened several times to take me from him and to send me to a home down at Adelaide. That was why we decided to join up with Bill Joyce and Fred Brown. Fred was all right until we came here. Now he and his wife have sided with Joyce. Oh - mister! You'll take me away, won't you? I'm scared. I can't stay any longer now father's dead. He wasn't much lately, but he was something. And I - I can't run away without a camel and tucker. They'd only track and catch me. But I've got some strychnine in a little bag hung around my neck, and I'll chew it off and swallow it if Bill Joyce tries to get me. I will so!"

Cass offered no immediate comment, nor did he further question the girl. The situation was one of decided delicacy, one that required cautious handling. The girl would not be allowed to leave with him without a lot of unpleasantness. He was alone; they were a woman and two men, one of them allegedly already a murderer. Then the girl was admittedly under age and not legally entitled to decide for herself. She had said she had overheard Joyce say he had killed her father, and she appeared to be true blue. But she might be playing a game for her own ends, or her father might not be dead, or even wounded. There was the possibility, although not the probability, that she was working a blackmailing stunt. He would have to have proof of Khakishirt's murder before he could wisely take the girl from the people to whom she obviously belonged.

"Do you know anything about camels?" he inquired at length.

"Yes. Oh, yes. Father had camels for years. I can load and manage them."

"And you would be willing to obey my orders - always?"

"Of course. I'd do anything to get away from here. Oh, please, you will let me go with you to Broken Hill!"

"Well, begin obeying orders right now," he told her. "Go back to bed, and in the morning stay in camp. Have your things and blankets so that you can roll a swag in a hurry, but don't roll it until I tell you."

"All right! I'll do just as you say."

"Very well. Now be off. And don't let them know you have been away down here."

"Thank you - mister. What's your name?"

"Cass Bennett."

"Cass Bennett," she repeated softly, and then slipped away into the night.

When the stars, low against the eastern horizon, were being dimmed by the light heralds of the new day, Bennett was out among the dunes and standing on the one from which he had seen the last of the combatants. There he waited until the light became sufficiently strong to enable him to discern the tracks made by one of them. Thenceforth he did not walk over them, but ran.

Time was all important, for he had to find Harry Jacks and be back at his camp with his camels before the occupants of the bag camp were astir.

It proved to be an easy task, for the tracks were plain. He found Jacks with a bullet-smashed leg. The man's tracks, as well as those made by Joyce, told the story without possibility of lying. Wounded and helpless, Jacks had either asked for a truce, or he had fainted, because Joyce had stood close to him when he shot him through the head, so close that the exploding powder had scorched the dead man's hair.

For a moment Cass Bennett stood listening. The early morning was cool and utterly still. Not yet was the eastern sky being tinged with colour by the sun. His dog, back at the camp, was not barking, and that meant neither of the trappers were near it.

Again he ran, doubling back to his feeding-camels. In camp he feverishly saddled and loaded them, and then led them further down the creek until the trees masked them from the bag tents.

When the woman emerged from one of the latter, the sun was showing. She was gaunt, slovenly, and dirty. She shouted for Mavis, and the girl crept out to be the victim of a torrent of abuse for not having got up earlier to light the fire. The big man, Joyce, appeared to lurch to the creek, not for a badly-needed wash, but to stare in the direction of where Bennett's camp had been.

"Hey, Fred! That bloke's gorn."

"Yes, an' it'll be a bad day for you 'as 'e 'as gorn," snarled the woman.

"You shut yer gob, or I'll shut it for you," threatened Joyce. "Hey, Fred! Wake up! That bloke's gorn."

The girl stood rigidly still with the kindling wood in her arms. She, too, was looking along the creek, big tears slowly sliding down her sunburned cheeks. So Cass Bennett had gone away and left her to these human wolves!

"Wot's up with you?" screamed the woman. "Light that fire or I'll gouge yer eyes out."

"You leave my little sweet'eart alone, or I'll do a bit of gouging on you," countered Joyce. "Come on, Fred! I tell you that bloke 'as gorn."

"Well, 'e said 'e was gonna push orf early. Wot's orl the excitement about?" demanded Shifty-eyes, stepping forth into the cruel light of day.

"You will oblige me by folding your arms," said Cass Bennett, stepping from behind the trunk of a box tree.

"Cripes! Wot you think you're up to?" asked Fred, when, with the others, he saw the levelled revolver in Bennett's one hand and the repeating rifle in the other.

The girl continued to stand like a statue, but her face slowly was becoming radiant, in her eyes an increasing inward glow.

"Mavis," Bennett said, "bring me all the guns in the camp. Woman, I'll shoot you like a dog if you move. You're on a par with the men."

"Wot's the game?" whined Shifty-eyes. "You can't go on like this. We ain't got nothink you can rob us of."

"No? You attempt to make a break, and you will find that you have your life to lose."

They stood, the three of them, with their backs to the tents in and out of which sped Mavis. When she brought Cass Bennett four rifles and a revolver, she was careful not to interpose herself between him and her former associates.

"I can't find father's gun," she said, pantingly.

"Where's that other gun?" Bennett asked.

"Planted where you won't find it," Joyce jeered.

"You wait, me girl," screamed the woman.

"Shut up, you!"

Joyce turned and sprang at her - not to strike her down, but to snatch her up in his arms and hold her like a shield. Then he rushed at Bennett.

But the shield was slightly smaller than the shielded, and Bennett's hobby was revolver shooting; a hobby that cost him a lot of money for cartridges. To a man able to bring down crows on the wing with single bullets, the margin of unshielded Joyce was enough. He placed a bullet in the brute's left shoulder.

Joyce yelled with anguish, and the woman shrieked when together they crashed to earth, the man to curse and groan, the woman to pour out a wild farrago of words.

"I'm looking at you, Brown!" Bennett warned. "Mavis, get your swag." To the others he went on, when the woman ceased her tirade for lack of wind: "I am taking the girl with me to Broken Hill, and from there I'll be sending her down to my sister in Adelaide. I shall, of course, report the murder of Henry Jacks at the first homestead I get to."

"It wasn't murder," snarled Joyce. "It was fair shootin' in self-defence. It was him or me for it."

"You got too close to him after having wounded him in the leg for it to have been anything else but murder. The girl heard you confess to killing him. Ready, Mavis? Then leave your swag with me. Take the guns, and, as you go along the creek, throw them one by one into the middle of the lagoon. Keep on going until you come to the camels, and then lead them away to the south-east. I'll overtake you presently."

Her face lit with the flame of hope, she nodded, snatched up the armoury, and danced away to do as bidden. Bennett remained standing, menacing the two men and the woman: Fred Brown, watching him with masked eyes; the woman, mouthing invective; Joyce, still on the ground groaning and cursing. The sun rose high, and still Cass Bennett kept them there. His dog, torn between duty to the camel-train and love for his master, deserted the former and arrived to stand by the latter.

"You gonna keep us 'ere orl day?" demanded Shifty-eyes.

"I think I'll be going now," Bennett replied. "You keep in mind this fact. Should you follow and play tricks, I shall shoot to kill. Be sure of that."

Backward then he moved for fifty yards, then to walk rapidly along the creek to pick up his camel's tracks, while constantly looking behind at the group near the bag tents. They hurled insults and threats after him, but they made no move to follow. Towards noon he caught up with Mavis, marching steadily to the south-west at the lead of the string.

"I was beginning to worry about you," she told him, with a quick smile.

"You need never worry about me. We'll camp soon and eat. Getting tired?"

"No!"

"But you will if you go on walking. Come, up you get."

"But -"

"You promised to obey orders," she was reminded. He made a step with his hands, and meekly she permitted herself to be lifted high into the long iron riding-saddle, while the camel growled its usual complaint. "Sit sideways," she was further ordered. "By sitting sideways you can maintain a lookout behind. They have your father's gun somewhere don't forget."

The following day Bennett began to think that Brown and Joyce - if the latter was able - had decided not to follow them, when, in the middle of the afternoon, a bullet fired from a high-powered rifle passed above his head and killed one of the pack-beasts. Fortunately, at the time both the girl and he were walking, and he had planned what to do if such an attack was made.

"Keep moving," he snapped out. "Try and spot him, and shoot as soon as you do."

Knowing that to go on would give the attacker the advantage of time and ground, and that the longer the issue was delayed the greater would be the chance of either the girl or he being hit, Bennett "hooshed" down the camels and lashed their bent forelegs with ropes. Another bullet sped over his head, and then the close report of an exploding rifle informed him that the girl was in action.

"Good kid!" he shouted. "Keep him occupied a while."

Feverishly he completed the roping of the camels and, that done, he unslung the rifle from his shoulder and glanced about to see the girl crouched against a mulga tree. Within two seconds he was behind another tree close to her.

"Where is he?"

"I saw his smoke," she replied, with astonishing calmness. "He's behind the clump of cotton bush on the summit of that sandhill. He's got father's rifle. I can tell by the sound of it."

"Which one is it - Brown?"

"Yes! That's who it is."

"I suppose Joyce is still nursing himself. What kind of a shot is Brown?"

"Only fair."

"What make of rifle does he usually use?"

"A Winchester. Father's is a Savage."

"That explains why he's firing a little high. I am going to rush him before he gets used to the high-powered gun. If we stay put he will understand what a fool he is to have started shooting with that wide flat to his rear, where there's no cover. We crossed it, remember. If I don't get after him now he will sneak round to one of our flanks among this dense mulga. You stay there. It's an order."

Before she could protest, he was away off on a darting zig-zagging course for the bare sandhill. Twice Brown fired at him, and twice she put a bullet into the cotton bush. She watched Bennett zig-zagging up the steep sand-slope like a snipe, and then he was silhouetted against the cobalt sky like a giant spider. He was there for a moment. Then he had disappeared.

After that, silence. She wondered if she should leave her tree-shelter and follow the man to whom she pinned her hopes of escape to a fairer and a cleaner world. Wondering, she heard two rifle reports, and, still undecided, she lived the year-long moments in fierce anxiety.

And then she saw Bennett on the sandhill; saw him walking upright and on a straight course. His upright figure meant only one thing. When he reached her, she said faintly: "Well?"

"That's that," he replied. "Now we can get along without worrying."

"Fred Brown?"

"It was," he told her, laying emphasis on the past tense. "I put the body into the lee of that sandhill and the wind will keep him well covered."

Mavis experienced a strange weakness in her knees. She was compelled to sit down while he was transferring the dead camel's loading to the others, and when he had removed the ropes, when all but the riding camel had risen, he walked to her and picked her up and carried her to the complaining beast, where he slipped her into the front part of the saddle, himself occupying the rear part. With a heave the beast got upon its feet, and making light of the double load began again the interrupted journey to Broken Hill.

"I don't think I want to go to your sister in Adelaide," she said presently. "This - this is good enough for me."

"You promised to obey orders," Bennett reminded her. "I shall expect you always to obey orders until you are twenty-one. You promised faithfully to do that, remember."

"Did I?"

"You know you did. The bush is no place for a child like you. And men's rough togs are not suitable for a young lady like you."

She was silent for quite a long time. Then swiftly she turned round to look at him and to say:

"Cass - I'll obey your orders - always - all my life."

Willi-Willi

It was seldom that Fay Stockbridge was to be seen behind the small bar of the wayside hotel forty-odd miles out of Wilcannia on the Wanaaring road. She was much more often found among the sheep on the selection which, as well as the hotel, was owned by her father. This day, however, he had had to take the spare pump engine out to the back well and replace it with the one there that had broken down.

This December day was warm and still. Even the blowflies sought the coolness of the low, bush-cast shade of the plain surrounding the rambling, low-built hotel. The passing track winding across the small blue-sage plain towards Wanaaring was empty and dustless, as it was to the south-eastward where, a mile distant, it ran into a line of tall gums masking a creek.

Fay was reclining in a long cane chair on the verandah outside the bar, for there were no customers this afternoon. In her lap rested a novel that had failed to win the fight with the heat for her attention. The wood-and-iron building faced the east and the two pepper trees beyond the track, whilst beyond them lay the level plain like a light-blue tapestry. Two dogs and several goats sprawled beneath the pepper trees and, in its large cage suspended from the verandah roof, Rastus, the white cockatoo, mumbled grumpily to itself.

Heavy footsteps came along the short passage reaching the main doorway beside the bar door, and there emerged a plump, square, plain-featured woman whose thin grey hair was drawn tightly into a "bun" at the back of her bullet-shaped head. She carried the afternoon tea on a tray, and this she set down on the small, bush-made table before lifting it to Fay's side and drawing up a chair for herself.

"I will be glad when Christmas is over," she said, mopping her face with damp handkerchief. "I always think we notice the heat more before Christmas than after. Was that Momba on the phone?"

"Yes, Aunt. Mr. Whaley rang up to say that there were four passengers on the Wanaaring coach."

"Four, eh!" echoed Mrs. Mason. "They will be finding it hot, but not as hot as it is here."

"Or where father is out at White Well."

"It'll be bad there, all right," Mrs. Mason agreed, pouring out the tea. "I suppose we're lucky being here on this verandah. It's mighty warm in the kitchen. Coach on time?"

Fay nodded, and smiled into the kindly eyes of her father's sister. She sipped her tea and ate the fresh buttered scones with evident appreciation. Across the northern track sped a drunken whirl-wind, or willi-willi, to whirl upward into its vortex the track's red dust, and to attract to itself a light breeze which slipped along the verandah momentarily to cool it. The girl's gaze followed the swaying, roaring willi-willi, and the thought occurred that days like this were much like human life, which ran quietly for year after year to be disturbed once, perhaps twice, by a willi-willi of passion, of tragedy, or of sorrow.

How like her life was this still day? The early years spent in Adelaide before her mother died. That was the first willi-willi to sweep through her life. The quiet years at the boarding-school had followed, years lived in quiet placidity. Her father then had been affluent and the manager of an important grain business. The second willi-willi had come then, sudden and fierce as all willi-willies are. Aunt Jane had arrived at the boarding-school to explain that her father had suddenly had to leave for Europe on confidential business, and that it had been decided Fay was to live with her in Sydney.

Her father leaving Australia without having come to say good-bye had hurt Fay deeply. Certainly he had written once through her aunt, saying that because of business interests, he had been unable to see her before leaving and explaining that he would be unable to write again until he returned.

That willi-willi had passed her by, and for three years life with Aunt Jane in Sydney had been still. Came then another willi-willi which had caught them both up and lifted them across the State to set them down at this wayside hotel where her father already was in occupation.

The business trip remained always a mystery. It appeared that it had been a dismal failure and that the firm had put her father outside its organisation. With the little money he had saved he had bought the selection with the license of the hotel, and together the hotel and the selection provided a living. Still, the trip to Europe ever remained shrouded in mystery. Her father evinced opposition in discussing it, and her aunt had said that its disastrous result made its discussion painful.

The quiet years after the removal from the city had then followed. Her father and her aunt had thought that the bush would have bored her to desperation, but she found it an endless source of interest. There were horses to ride, and the car to drive occasionally to Wilcannia. As time passed the management of the selection fell more and more to her and only when the two shearers, with their portable plant, arrived to shear the flock, or when the well-engine or a windmill needed repairs, did her father leave the bar to her.

Yes, her life had been just like this still day. Through it or across it had swept the several willi-willies, and looking back, she understood that, after all the willi-willies had been unimportant in her life compared with the whole as these real willi-willies were in their relation to the long, still December day.

"Now, if one of those willi-willies collides with this house before the coach passengers have gone the dinner will be spoiled," Mrs. Mason predicted. "You were out that day last month when one did. Bless me! The place was so filled with dust half an hour before the Wilcannia coach was due that the dinner was ruined."

"They are all right on the inside, Aunt," Fay said, smiling. "The other day I was eating lunch down at Far Corner and a slow one came along. You know, one of those little willies which move slower than one can walk. Well, Toby was tied to a tree, and when I saw the willi-willi coming I ran right into the middle of it and was easily able to keep inside it, too. When inside it I found it quite calm. I could see the circular wall of dust and leaves rushing round and round, and beyond it was Prince barking furiously because he thought the dust was solid and barred him from me."

"You be careful, Fay," urged the elder woman. "I once heard about a man who was caught by a big willi-willi and was whirled up into the sky. When it let him fall he was killed instantly."

"That was a fairy story, Aunt."

"It wasn't. It was true," Mrs. Mason argued indignantly. Fay laughed at her, and in pretended anger her aunt retired to look to the dinner for the coach passengers.

The hotel shadow lay far beyond the track when Fay Stockbridge saw the mail car appear from out the line of creek gums, when the westering sunlight was reflected by its headlamps. It came speeding towards her over the winding track, a long, dune-coloured, box-like thing zig-zagging above the intervening blue-bush. It sent upward a dense cloud of red dust as a warship creates a smoke screen. The rising hum of the powerful engine awoke Rastus. He yelled for a drink, screaming, "Cocky wants a booze!" The dogs ran out from beneath the pepper trees to bark, as though thankful that at last there was something to do.

Fay was standing behind the bar when the dust-covered mail car pulled up outside. Rastus yelled for a drink with increased determination, and men laughed at it. The arrival of a coach was always like that slow-moving willi-willi in which she had walked.

The four passengers entered, strangers every one to Fay. Two were patently stockmen returning from a city holiday, and the third might have been a commercial traveller. The fourth was a redfaced, heavy-jowled man, owning small, pig-like blue eyes and a coarse fat body.

"Good afternoon!" she greeted them. "Dinner is waiting."

"Good-day, miss!" chorused the stockmen. The commercial traveller echoed them. The fat man made no reply. His small eyes wandered from Fay to glance quickly about the bar before again directing their gaze at her.

"What are we going to have?" he demanded. "I'm at the end of my journey, so it's my shout."

Fay looked at him with increased interest. He most certainly did not look like a stockman come to spend his cheque. His brown suit and black velour hat spoke of city pavements, and his hands were white, if badly kept.

Then the mail driver came in loaded with mail bags and parcels. He was a red-haired youth, cheerful and carelessly free with the world, but of proved courage and tenacity in overcoming all difficulties to maintain his time schedule. The passengers, having quenched their thirst, departed for the dining-room. Fay signed the mail book for the bags destined for neighbouring station homesteads, and then she took charge of the parcels. The business completed, the driver consented to drink a full bottle of lemonade.

"The fat bloke reckons he's stoppin' here," he informed Fay in low tones. "Bit of a mystery, he is. Got to Wilcannia on the Broken Hill coach yesterday. Said he was looking for a quiet place to take a rest. All right, Rastus, I'll bring you out a drink in a sec. Yes, he told me that a friend recommended him to come here."

"Queer! Did he say who the friend was?" Fay asked.

"Nope. Excuse me! I'll give ole Rastus the remainder of this lemonade."

The Joyces arrived on a buckboard, the Paroo Station truck pulled up and a man and two boys on horses all came to get the mail from Fay. What with delivering the mail bags and parcels, selling stamps and drinks, she was kept busy for the next half-hour. Then the coach passengers came in for a departing drink, and after they had gone out at the driver's call the fat man leaned against the bar and leered at Fay in what he thought was an affable smile.

"I'd like to stay here for a week," he said. "I suppose you can put me up?"

"Oh, yes! I think so. I will take you to a room immediately I am free. My father is out on the run to-day."

Fay Stockbridge was quick to realise that there was something behind the coming of Mr. Edward Blake. His presence cast a shadow over the hotel from which there was no escape; no, no escape even when out among the sheep. The sun became hotter and fiercer, and yet it seemed less bright. As she walked behind the mob of sheep she had mustered and was taking to another paddock, Fay pondered on what was decidedly a puzzle.

It began, this puzzle, shortly after her father returned on the runabout with the broken-down pump engine. As usual, he had driven the vehicle straight into the motor-shed, and to him had gone the new guest. Always a great one for his tea - as Mrs. Mason put it - John Stockbridge and the fat man had remained fully an hour in conference. Sometimes an impatient woman, Aunt Jane grumbled at her brother's delay in coming in for dinner, and at last Fay had gone to call him. And before reaching the wide-open door she had heard the visitor say: "And that's the position, Jack. It doesn't do to kick at the rocks when you've no boots on your feet."

And then, when she entered the shed, her tall, gaunt father had said: "Oh, Fay! This is an old friend of mine. He will be staying with us for a week or two."

A week or two! It was now February and the fat man had been with them for seven weeks. Aunt Jane took his breakfast to him in his room. He never appeared before eleven, and only then to lounge on the verandah and smoke and drink. More often than not he demanded that his drinks be taken to him on the verandah, and never once had Fay seen him pay for them, or had even seen her father book them.

He was a monster, this Mr. Blake. She had come to hate the very sight of his red, flabby face and huge body. He was like a big fat spider, with his small blue eyes watching her father and her aunt and she as though they were flies in its web, flies it was too satiated to eat. Her father's buoyant spirit appeared to be crushed, whilst her aunt, usually well able and quick to get rid of a chequeman when he had over-stayed his welcome, crept about the place and waited on Mr. Blake as though he had whipped her. When approached, she had turned to Fay an expressionless face, to say:

"We've got to put up with him, dear. Being an old friend of your father's, we can't tell him to go. Besides," she added, as though clutching at some excuse, "besides, his bill will amount to a tidy sum, and business isn't that brisk that your father can turn away good money."

Yes, there was something very wrong somewhere.

The real still days of the year had come, when the willi-willies marched drunkenly across the scorched world with roaring defiance. Twice they had attempted to lift the roof off the hotel, and one had caught the house mill, to torture the framework and to snap off the heavy fan wheel.

Yes, life to Fay appeared like a long, still day, quite undisturbed by an emotional willi-willi. Nothing ever seemed to happen. The fat man loafed about the hotel verandah, never going for a walk, doing nothing but smoke and drink. He was become a kind of institution. When a mail coach arrived it was he who greeted the driver and passengers and invited them all inside to shout drinks for them, for which he never paid.

The happy laughter, the contentment, the mutual affections of pre-December days were no more. Aunt Jane lived silently grim in her kitchen. Her father moved about the premises or commanded his bar with anxious eyes set in a weary face. There had been never a hint relative to the departure of Mr. Edward Blake.

"That man has got some hold over my father," Fay told her horse when, having put the sheep through the paddock gate, she was riding homeward along the netted boundary fence. "I am sure of it, Toby. I'm sure of it. Perhaps he is even blackmailing him. Oh, but that's impossible! To blackmail a person shows that that person has once done something shameful. Why, father - it's impossible that father has done anything of which to be ashamed."

Arrived at a corner post, Toby began to hurry in his walk. The new line of fence skirted the main track, and track and fence could be seen mounting a line of sand-dunes beyond which, Fay knew, was the blue-bush plain and the wayside hotel in the middle of it. Sub-consciously - for she was still thinking of her father and the fat, spider of a man - her eyes noted every fence panel as it was passed, searching for rabbit-holes. She had no conscious knowledge of time and space until, when arrived at the summit of the sand-range, she saw, a quarter of a mile along the road, a stranded motor car and a man tinkering with one of the back wheels. A full mile beyond it stood the hotel.

It was evident that the motorist had passed the hotel, for the machine was facing in her direction. As she rode towards it she saw the man worm his way under it, and he was still under it when she, having climbed over the fence, crossed to him.

"What is wrong?" she asked.

"Hullo! Who's there?" inquired the partially invisible man. Then he began to squirm out from beneath the car and, on observing her, got at once to his feet.

She saw a tall, lithe but powerful man about thirty, clean shaven and fair of hair. Grey eyes twinkled.

"Crown wheel in the diff busted, I think," he explained

cheerfully. "Why it couldn't bust half an hour ago outside the hotel back there I don't know. I never did have much luck. You headed that way?"

"Yes. My father owns the hotel."

"You don't say! Well, I'm lucky, after all. I saw a car in the shed. Are you on the telephone to Wilcannia?"

"Yes."

"Good! Then would you mind asking your father to drive here and give me a tow back? I can ring up a garage in Wilcannia and tell them to send out a new crown wheel on the next coach."

"All right! But the next coach won't be coming until next Friday."

"Hum. Well, if there's plenty of tea and bacon and eggs and things, I shan't mind if the coach doesn't come for a month," he told her, boyishly grinning. "Your father will be able to put me up, I suppose?"

Fay nodded, finding the advent of this stranger not unpleasant.

"And can I borrow a horse and gallop all around the landscape?"

Laughing then, she found laughter come strangely to her lips.

"Why, yes! There is Tiger, if you want a gallop. He will either gallop or eat you, and he won't give you the preference if you are careless."

"Dear old thing," cried the traveller, patting his motor car. "Thank you kindly for breaking down. Oh, by the way, my name is Bill Mallory. Bill to my friends, Mallory to the boss, Mister Mallory to the fat man who lounges on yonder verandah."

For her the sun darkened. He saw her eyes freeze.

"You have met Mr. Blake?" she coldly asked.

He nodded. "I had a glass of beer with him when I called. He wanted to be the boss and to call me Mallory, so I was obliged to ask him for the 'mister.' Paying guest, uncle, or just plain bot?"

"The latter, I'm afraid," she replied with tight lips. "I'll go. Father will come back for you in the car."

"Pretty hot in the sun, Miss Stockbridge," languidly remarked the huge Mr. Blake when Fay stepped onto the front verandah. He was reclining in the long wicker chair which he had made his especial property, and on the small table at his side stood the inevitable glass.

"If I were you I'd go out in the sun and walk about a little," she flashed at him before passing through the main doorway to reach her father, then at work on his books in the sitting-room.

"Oh, Dad! That man who called a little while back in a car has met with trouble this side of the sandhills," she said, still irritated from her encounter with the guest. "The crown wheel has smashed, or something. He wants to be towed back here. Says he will have to 'phone Wilcannia for a new part to be sent out on the coach on Friday."

"All right! I'll go and bring him back right away," assented her father, white haired and lean, and by no means conforming to the boniface type. "You'll look after the bar? If Mr. Blake wants anything, serve him."

"Has he paid anything yet?" she asked levelly.

"No, but he'll settle when he leaves."

"When he leaves! Will he ever leave?"

Stockbridge forced a smile, and she knew it. Rising, he pressed her arm, and then was gone out to the motor shed.

Fay had removed her hat and was standing listening to the dwindling hum of her father's car when the guest called for a glass of beer. With a mutinous expression still markedly in evidence, she pulled the drink and took it outside to put it down on the small, bush-made table.

"Where's the boss gone?" he asked, little icy-blue eyes staring up at her.

"He has gone to bring back the man and the car who was here a while ago. The car broke down this side of the sandhills."

"Oh! Then I'll be having company in this dead hole. What with your father and your aunt and you - well, your faces are enough to drive all the trade away. They're nearly enough to drive me away."

"It's a pity they don't do it, then," Fay snapped with rising temper, as she turned back to the bar door.

His voice, low and sinister, halted her. "If they were that bad I had to leave you all," he said, "I reckon you would soon wish you had sparked up a bit. I'm an easy-going man, but I don't want and I don't intend to take any lip from you."

The girl's face swiftly lost its colour. Her eyes were blazing as she stepped back to the table. Here had arrived the opportunity to unload from her mind all the accumulated misery of the last two months. When again she stood looking down at him, his snake-cold eyes failed to cool her temper.

"And you, Mr. Blake, will get no more drink from me until you pay for it," she snapped. "You haven't paid for a thing since you've been here, and I can't understand father allowing you to stay."

The bloated body remained lying passively on its back. The red and shapeless face remained passive, too.

"The trouble, Miss Stockbridge, is that you want a holiday," Mr. Blake suggested softly. "I shall have to persuade your father to send you down to Adelaide for a month. You will ruin his business if he does not, because no business can continue to pay when its customers are insulted."

Reaching for the glass of beer, he drank its contents whilst continuing to stare up at her. Languidly he put down the glass.

"Take it away, please, and bring me a glass of whisky. I always drink whisky between two beers."

Then he added: "It would come hard on your father if I did leave you all before I am completely rested."

Fay now stood regarding the monster of a man, and slowly she nodded her shingled head before saying, with hate in her voice: "I thought as much. So you are blackmailing him. All right! I'll bring you the drink. When you blackmail father you blackmail me."

She quite expected that the use of the ugly word would bring him to his feet in hot denial, but he continued to lie passive, to stare up at her with cold eyes; actually to chuckle.

As usual, Mrs. Mason tapped the small Burmese gong exactly at six o'clock. She was a demon for punctuality, Aunt Jane, excepting on those evenings that a mail coach was late when, as she had no control over the drivers and they could not control the weather, she appeared never put out.

The new guest came quickly from his room to enter the dining-room through the passage door as Mr. Blake was hauling his bulk through the doorway giving exit to the front verandah. Fay, now arrayed in a cool-looking white frock, came hurrying in and, as from his position at table John Stockbridge could watch the bar counter, he, too, entered the dining-room. Aunt Jane at once served the soup from the sideboard.

"Trouble with your car?" inquired Mr. Blake.

"Yes. Crown wheel in the diff or an axle broken. I don't know which," Mallory replied cheerfully. "I'll know tomorrow when I pull the thing to pieces."

"Humph! Pretty awkward breaking down out here."

"It would have been much more awkward breaking down ten or twenty miles from this pleasant hotel. Are you staying long?"

"A week or so," Mr. Blake replied easily. "You see, I suffer badly from nerves. I find this place so peaceful and restful. There's no roar of traffic; nothing to worry me. Good food, plenty to drink and a soft bed. Now, what more could a man want?"

Stockbridge was eating quietly. He kept his gaze upon his plate. Mrs. Mason was attacking the leg of mutton on the sideboard with superfluous energy. Seeing that the new guest was observing this, Fay hastened to say: "I shall be glad when this hot weather is over. Sometimes it's so trying. The truly wonderful autumn and winter make up for it, though. Do you know this part of Australia, Mr. Mallory?"

Seeing her nervousness, he set out to dispel it.

"I have never been this way before," he announced. "In fact, I have never before seen the bush, the real bush of Australia. That's nothing to my credit. Its never-ending-ness awes one at first. You travel many miles every day for many days and there are still days of miles before you. It is difficult for a city man to appreciate the extent of this mass of land called Australia."

"What line do you follow?" asked Mr. Blake.

"Me! Oh, I'm attached to the law."

"The law!"

The fat man's body was tensed. Mr. Stockbridge looked up. Mrs. Mason stood with the gravy boat suspended over the meat on a plate.

"Yes," said Mallory. "What do you do?"

Fay thought that his question was put with undue sharpness. Mr. Blake hesitated to reply. He was like a man who finds difficulty in following a conversation.

Then: "I'm having a spell at present," he confessed. "I used to be a bookmaker."

"Indeed! I wish I had enough brains for a game like that," Mallory said. "In my profession there is too much jealousy. Your colleagues are always afraid you'll make a brilliant success of a case. Here I am chasing about after people, and there's you, a retired bookmaker, enjoying a well-earned rest in this delightful spot. Oh, well, perhaps some day I'll be able to retire."

"Chasing after people!" echoed Mr. Blake in low tones.

The younger man nodded carelessly and then determinedly engaged Fay on the subject of books. The others listened, or appeared to be listening. Stockbridge spoke only when appealed to. Mrs. Mason said never a word, but she appeared to find Bill Mallory a subject of great interest. With a slight snort of impatience, the retired bookmaker passed out to the front verandah, there to drop heavily into the complaining wicker chair.

Keenly observant, as he had to be, Bill Mallory saw that the discussion about books really interested the girl, that it brought a carefree vivacity into her large eyes. He saw, too, the dull look of worry return to them immediately Mr. Blake, from the verandah, called for a glass of beer.

When the blue-bush plain was being stained with gold and purple, when Rastus was mumbling his prayers and a pair of minah birds were twittering in the pepper trees, Bill Mallory stood in the centre of the track marvelling at the stillness of it all. For peace and quietness the fat man had chosen well. It was a place for quiet, solid happiness, and yet that nice girl, that homely woman and that cultured man were not happy.

Well, how could they be with that whale of a man flopped all about the place? He had an idea that he had seen the fat man somewhere and at some time. Perhaps he would remember the occasion. The corners of his mouth drooped ever so slightly. They had been known to droop when he was planning a rag in his University days.

"Beautiful evening," he remarked cheerfully as he stepped onto the verandah.

"'Tis so," agreed the fat man, his pig-like eyes almost closed.

Within the sitting-room, situated left of the bar, Fay sat at the table engaged with sewing. From her position she could look through across the passage into the bar-room. Her father was chopping wood somewhere at the rear. On Bill Mallory stepping into the room she looked up at him and he could not but fail to note the absence of what should have been a ready smile.

"What about a little radio?" he asked, indicating the cabinet in the corner.

"Why, yes! But the static is sure to be bad. It always is at this time of the year. Talk to me instead."

The quick glance through the verandah door where was to be seen the bald top of the fat man's head; the short, nervous laugh; the sudden physical strain to be seen in her firm, brown hands eloquently told the observant Bill Mallory that the wireless was forbidden, as well as who was the forbidder. He would have liked to comply with her request to talk, but then the corners of his mouth were still slightly drooping.

"We'll try it, anyway," he insisted stubbornly.

Switching on the batteries, he waited, grimly silent, for the valves to heat. Then he found a station that was smothered with cracklings and thunder-claps. On came the volume. Hideous cacophony spread outward from the building across the plain. Fay turned swiftly to remonstrate. She saw him fiddling with the dials, and the more he fiddled the louder grew the uproar.

Mr. Blake heaved himself from his chair, to stand at the door with wrathful protest writ plainly on his vast face. Bill Mallory found a station broadcasting a march tune beneath the crackling of 10,000 thunderstorms - and presently he turned round with a happy expression in his grey eyes. He saw the fat man at the door, flabby hands pressed against his ears. He saw the startled Fay, and he saw the grim Mrs. Mason with her arms folded and in her eyes a peculiar triumph.

Mr. Blake came into the room, and, bending above Bill Mallory, shouted the suggestion that a drink might go down well. He thought that that might stop the uproar. Every time thereafter, when he and the fat man went to the bar, Fay would turn down the volume and Aunt Jane would glare at her, and every time Bill Mallory came back from the bar he would turn on the volume and Aunt Jane would smile at him. And every time Bill Mallory did that the fat man suggested another drink to get him away from the wireless.

Between every two glasses of beer, Mr. Blake called for a

whisky. Altogether, Bill Mallory enjoyed himself.

He spent the first part of next morning taking down the car's differential, and found that it was the stripped crown wheel that had held him up at this pleasant hotel. Having washed his hands with petrol, he left the motor shed and sauntered round to the front of the hotel, where he found Mr. Blake not yet in evidence and Fay in charge of the bar.

"A glass of soda-water, straight, please," he called.

"Oh," she said, significantly.

"Yes, oh!" he mocked. "Where's our fat friend?"

At once her eyes hardened.

"He hasn't come from his room yet," she said, with that odd tightening of her lips.

"Room number four, isn't it? Near the telephone?"

Fay nodded.

"Good! I must ring up for a new crown wheel. By the way, what about a ride this afternoon? What about taking sandwiches or something and the quart pots, and having afternoon tea at some well or tank?"

"Well, it's coach day," she explained hesitantly, trying hard to smile.

"I don't suppose there will be that many passengers that your father couldn't serve 'em all."

"I'll see," she conceded, again trying to smile.

Smiling at her, and becoming annoyed by the fact that a girl could not smile properly when she wanted to, he passed from the bar and so reached the telephone fixed to the wall just beside the door of room number four. As he rang the exchange at Wilcannia he noticed that the fat man's door was badly warped by the heat.

"Hullo! That Wilcannia? Good! I want to call the Police Office at Broken Hill. Very well! I'll wait," he said loudly.

Whilst waiting he leaned against the wall and hummed "P.C. 49." He hummed it for five minutes.

Then he said, still loudly: "Ah! That Police Office? I want Inspector Lawton. All right!"

A pause.

Then: "Good-day, sir. Mallory speaking from Stockbridge's Hotel on the Wanaaring road out of Wilcannia. I've busted a crown wheel in the differential of the car. Will you have another sent out to me as soon as possible? I know that, sir, but the Wilcannia garage won't have it in stock. Yes, everything's all O.K. What? Yes, of course. Yes, two beers, one whisky. That's correct sir. Right! I'll keep my eyes open. Good-bye, sir."

Again humming "P.C. 49," he walked to the back door, passing Mrs. Mason, white-faced and decidedly anxious, to whom he grinned, and thence across to the motor shed.

Immediately after lunch, Fay and the new guest rode off to inspect White Well, Bill Mallory, mounted on Tiger, at once proving himself to be no mean horseman. To their saddles were strapped quart pots and packets of eatables. Like the days which had gone before, it was utterly still for long periods between the local disturbances caused by the marching willi-willies.

"Is this the White Well where we drink and eat?" he inquired as they jogged towards the windmill lording it above a set of sheep-yards and a horse-yard.

"Yes. Are you hungry?"

"Thirsty."

For a long moment she looked steadily at him.

Then: "You should drink less," she advised.

"What?" he cried. "Here's a lass telling me to drink less at her father's hotel! And after so manfully trying to keep up with Fat, too. It never varied. Two beers, one whisky. And I hate whisky."

"Then why drink it?"

"Perhaps because I wanted to check up on Fat."

"Are you a detective?"

"I beg your pardon?"

"You heard what I said."

"Did I? Well, well, well! Now, to tell you the truth, I'm blessed if I know whether I am or not. Here we are. What do I do? Grease the mill, dive down the well, or boil the quarts?"

"You can grease the mill head after you have put Tiger into the horse-yard. He can't be trusted to stand tied by the reins."

Engaged with the fire and the tea-making, she watched him run up the iron steps fixed to the mill frame and then she heard him blithely singing "P.C. 49" as he was screwing down the grease cups. How old was he? Sometimes he looked thirty, but when he smiled he looked not a year older than twenty. For the first time in many weeks she felt strangely happy. Perhaps he would arrest that Mr. Blake and take him away. But then - oh, she wasn't going to worry about it this afternoon. Detective or no detective, there was something most attractive about this Bill Mallory.

She had just made tea when he joined her, to pick up the blackened quart pots and the slip-in cups and to escort her to the shade cast by a splendid sandalwood tree. Seating herself against the tree she fanned away the small flies and watched his strong hands pouring out the tea.

Then, looking at her with twinkling grey eyes, he said gayly: "Madam, your tea!"

"Thank you, sir," she lightly countered. "It is so much better than whisky, isn't it?"

"As I agree, we cannot argue. As you are so observant, tell me why Fat never pays for his drinks, and why your father never slates them against him."

He witnessed the shadow again fall over her. He saw it in her eyes.

"That," she said slowly, "that is my father's business."

"Humph! I've an idea that he's sponging on your father, and that your father emphatically does not like it. Neither does your aunt."

"Oh, don't let's talk about the man. I loathe him."

"So do I. He's spoiling my young life. Mysteries sadden me."

"As for that, you are a mystery, too," she pointed out.

"A mystery! Me? Why, I'm as open as the day. Fat annoys me, I own. He doesn't like the statics and I do, and I have an equal right to listen to the statics if I want to."

Fay laughed, genuinely. "Do you like the statics because Mr. Blake does not?"

"I don't see what he has to do with my likes or dislikes. Have another cake? I can recommend them. Your aunt baked them."

Fay accepted the cake and looked down at the tips of her riding boots. He was playing with her, she felt sure.

Suddenly he said: "Excuse me, but I think there is an extra big willi-willi coming."

He was pointing to the west and when she, too, looked that way she saw a vast, brown cloud-bank reaching swiftly towards the sun.

"It's about three miles to home, isn't it?" he asked, now on his feet and holding the quart pots and cups in his capable hands.

"About that," she answered him calmly. Then, although it was the last thing she wanted to do, she suggested: "Shall we ride for it?"

"All right! We had better get going. Come on," he urged.

As they hurried to the horses he laughed, saying: "If Fat hasn't departed on the coach, and I can't listen to the statics to-night, I'm going to sit on the front verandah and howl like a dog, just to annoy him."

Then she was swept off her feet and she found herself on Toby's back. The reins were being pressed into her hands and in her ears rang his cry: "Ride! I'll catch up."

The hot air began to stream past her heated face as Toby got into his stride. Every nerve in her was thrilling. She felt peculiarly light-headed. Glancing back, she saw Bill Mallory leap onto Tiger's back within the yard, and then she cried wildly to her own mount. Toby set out to tell the world just what he could do. Another backward glance revealed Tiger and his rider coming on at terrific speed, with high above them the towering, mighty wall of sand.

No horse likes to be beaten, either on or off a racecourse. Toby quickly made up his mind not to be beaten by the savage Tiger, but Tiger was three times the horse he was. The faint track winding here through a patch of mulgas, now across a narrow belt of salt-bush, now over wind-swept, broken country, appeared to Fay like a road unwinding before a fast car.

With astonishing abruptness, the sunlight waned and vanished. Looking back for an instant, she saw Tiger and his rider close behind her and coming on fast and, seemingly only half a mile away, the sand-storm was eating up the world. It now hung suspended above them, like a mighty brick wall caught in the instant an earthquake was bringing it down to crush them to dust.

"Keep him in, Miss Stockbridge," shouted her companion, ranging alongside. "They can't travel like this for three miles. They'll blow out."

Of course the pace was too hot. She hauled on the reins and coaxed Toby back into an easy canter.

"Think we'll do it?" Bill Mallory shouted, grinning in his boyish manner.

"Hope so," she shouted back. "This is going to be a black storm."

Puffs of hot wind blew back into their faces, blew westward to meet the advancing horror. The willi-willies of the past months were fairies compared to this marching giant. At last they topped a low rise to see the hotel less than one mile distant; and now, above the thudding hooves, they could hear a sinister humming sound - the wind devil in the heart of the storm.

"Come on! Let 'em out now, or we'll be beat," urged Bill, and eagerly the animals responded.

They reached the yards behind the hotel when the foot of the sand wall was less than 300 yards away. Before it the air was crystal clear, but at its foot it was sucking into itself sheets of ground sand. Vision could not penetrate it. It looked solid. It reared skyward, toppling forward over the hotel itself. There was no time to unsaddle. There was time only to loose the panting beasts in the yard and then run for the back door.

It was opened to them by Mrs. Mason.

"You are just in time," she said, astonishing Fay by the smile widening her comfortable mouth.

The roof suddenly strained and creaked beneath the first powerful blast of sand-ladened air. The humming sound changed to a prolonged "woof." The daylight vanished, to be succeeded by an inky darkness. Fay felt a strong arm about her waist and the elemental pandemonium deafened her. The minutes dragged out their time periods.

Almost in one second the wind dropped. Gradually the light returned, to reveal Bill Mallory standing beside her and her aunt standing where she had been when the light failed. Mrs. Mason was still smiling.

Bill Mallory's second dinner was infinitely more cheerful than the first had been. Doubtless that was because Mr. Blake had decided he must transact urgent business and had departed on the coach for Wilcannia.

In the vacated wicker chair on the front verandah sat Bill Mallory, and beside him had come to sit his host.

"Be frank with me," pleaded Stockbridge, the desperation of worry writ plainly on his face, "are you a detective?"

"No. What made you think that?" Bill countered smilingly.

"You are not connected with the police?" Stockbridge persisted.

"Yes, by marriage. An aunt of mine is married to Inspector Lawton, at Broken Hill. I stayed with them a week before coming on."

"But - but -"

"Perhaps I should have been a detective," Bill admitted. "I wasn't here two seconds before I sized up the situation. Blake had you right where he wanted you. His presence was shadowing Fay's - I mean Miss Stockbridge's life. Mrs. Mason would have liked to kick him out but dared not. Problem: How to get rid of Blake and to remove the shadow without barging in on your affairs. I tried the statics, and a week of that would have driven him away, I feel sure. But I got a better idea. I thought I had seen Blake somewhere before, but I couldn't remember where, and the more I tried the more tangled up I got. Then, when I abandoned trying altogether, it suddenly came to me. Memory is like that, you know. I'd seen him in court once, in Adelaide, when he just managed to get off on a rather nasty charge, not because he wasn't guilty, but because the police just couldn't prove that he was to the satisfaction of the jury. So it struck me that if he'd been in bother of that sort once it probably wasn't the only time, and, as likely as not, he always went more or less in fear of the police. So all I did was to let him hear me ring up Inspector Lawton. I made it sound beautifully official - I don't know what Uncle Bob thought when I kept calling him 'sir' - and I threw in the 'two beers, one whisky' as though it were a sort of clue that I'd just come across. Uncle Bob kept saying 'What the blazes do you mean?' but when Blake heard it, it upset his applecart properly. He probably thought I was Sherlock Holmes himself."

"But you said you were connected with the law?"

"So I am. I'm a solicitor in Adelaide, having my first real holiday. Chase people? Oh, yes, I chase them all right. They'd never pay their accounts if I didn't."

John Stockbridge sighed. Then he said:

"I owe you a debt, Mr. Mallory. That man was ruining me.

You see - yes, I'll tell you. I once went wrong, and when I was paying the penalty I got to know Edward Blake. We were in the same prison. Afterwards, I - we - came here. I am not a criminal now, Mr. Mallory. My sister and I have done all we could to prevent Fay learning about my fall, and that man threatened to tell her if I did not give him all he wanted. He - he was blackmailing her aunt and me."

"Say no more, Mr. Stockbridge," Bill cut in. "I am not going to hurry away. Somehow I don't think that Fay would like me to. But of course I don't know. If you'll excuse me a moment I'll find out."

He rose and went into the sitting-room. Three minutes later Fay was whispering: "No, Bill, no! Someone will hear."

"Nonsense," said Bill, and turned on the wireless. As the statics gathered strength, he took her in his arms, and the sound of their kiss was drowned by something that vaguely resembled the "March of the Gladiators."

Henry's Last Job

M e last job! I was put to tramp after working close on eleven
years for old Iron McPherson what's managing Myrtleford
Station away up beyond Wanaaring. It was all through a character
called War Ace Bill what McPherson sent out to boundary ride
with me 'cos he reckoned ten years being alone was too much for
any man.

Now when a bloke's been working on his own for ten years,
with an annual spell of two weeks at Ma Murphy's pub, he sort of
gets settled in his habits. As I said, I was all right on me own. I
told old McPherson so, saying as how I had me pet sheep and
dogs and cats fer company at night at the hut. He used to come
out once a month with rations and papers, and although he was
the only bloke I did see, I could have done without seeing him as
all the hour he spent with me he groused about something or
other. Anyhow -

I ain't never heard nothing about this War Ace Bill until I finds
him in the hut when I come in from the paddocks one day. He's
cooking a dinner, and he's a character about fifty years old,
shortish on his legs, well set up and a bit stern looking.

I says to him: "Good day, mate!"

"'Day to you, my man," says he. "I am War Ace Bill, and I
have been commissioned by Mr. McPherson to take charge of this
sector of the front."

"Oh!" says I, sort of stonkered by such a character.

"I am Flight Lootenant Mitcham," say he. "And you?"

"I am Captain Henry, Seventh Batt.," says I, jokingly, thinking
that I could pull a leg as good as him.

This seems to rock him a bit, but he brightens up and says:
"Then, Captain, we stand on the same level. I feel sure we will
work this squadron smoothly. The maintenance of discipline is, of
course, essential. I would never have achieved my air victories
without ground discipline among the men."

Now this character throws it off his chest so well that I'm
more'n inclined to believe he was a flying officer in the war, and I
sees that, having told him I am a captain, I must play up to him.

That wasn't hard, because he insisted in doing all the talking. He tells me things about the war what I knew was right, me having really done me bit with the Seventh Batt. He tells me about the Jerries he shot down, and how he knocked 'em, and where.

Mind you, excepting for his haughty ways, he wasn't a bad sort of character to work with, me being easy going and not objecting to any man having his head when he wants it. Although he kept telling me we were officers and gentlemen, he never tried to wangle himself out of his share of doing the hut work. He could ride, too, and he knew how to manage cattle, and at the end of the first six months he was still telling new yarns of how he shot down the Jerries.

Came then the time for me to take me spell at Ma Murphy's pub, what's on the road to St. Albans, and I'm telling War Ace Bill I'll be leaving him next week, when he says, with his chest stuck out:

"It's impossible to grant you leave now, Captain Henry. I have a plan of operations which will demand your assistance. We will remain on this sector for three years, when each of us will have a million francs in our paybooks. We can then retire to a nice little estaminet down in Amiens, or rather I should say Brisbane. Being able to run the estaminet together, we will see cheques being handed across the bar counter to us instead of seeing 'em leave our hands to be grabbed by a publican who tells us to get off the premises when the cheque's cut out."

I see that is an idea what ain't exactly fresh to me, 'cos I've dreamed for years of owning a pub with barmaids and things to sort of give the place a standing. So I agrees to the idea put over by War Ace Bill, and in spite of a bit of bother I get over the Ma Murphy urge and settles down once more.

As you might guess, this War Ace Bill's as dippy as a goanna what got jambed in a netted fence, but he's sort of backing up the idea I've had about buying a pub, and although I haven't got no intention of going part-time with him I falls in with his scheme.

When me and War Ace Bill has been mates for a bit more'n two years, without a single spell away from the place, he's still telling me yarns about his air victories, and he's up to about his 300th battle when we has a duststorm what took the roof off the hut. He happens to see the roof disappearing into the fog, and this gives him an idea what he lays out when the wind goes down and we can breathe again.

"Captain," he says, standing straight, "I have a brain wave. To relieve the monotony of this quiet sector we will construct a glider."

"What with?" says I.

"With roof irons what's blown away," he says. "I have long thought I was losing my flying abilities, having been grounded since the war, and now I can see my way to keep my hand and eye in in readiness for the next war."

"But what about the roof?" I wants to know. "The summer storms will soon be here, and without no roof we're going to get wet."

"We can requisition for new roof iron from Headquarters," he says, impatiently.

"But Iron McPherson's the kind of character to get the roof iron back from wherever it's landed and put it on again," I points out, knowing the kind of character Iron McPherson really is.

To this War Ace Bills says: "I am not concerned with Mr. Ean McPherson. The first duty of an officer and a gentleman is to his king and country. We will find the iron roof, belt it flat and use it for the glider. We will begin operations first thing in the morning."

Now me, I'm all for collectin' the roof and putting it back. I knows Iron McPherson for the character he is, and I can see him charging us for the roof if War Ace Bill makes a glider with it, but there's no arguing with a character like War Ace Bill when he's set on doing something.

Next morning we takes the woodheap axes and the meat tomahawks with us. Account of the bore head and stream being only half a mile away, the whole place is in the middle of a big circular plain, cleared of scrub by the cattle. We don't find the roof on this plain, as I expected, and we find her among the timber in bits and pieces, most wrapted round trees and stumps. It takes a lot of work hammering the pieces out straight enough to satisfy War Ace Bill.

Most of three days it takes us to get the roof back to the side of the hut, and then the weather is looking cross-eyed and I seen it will surely storm in a day or two, and keep on storming for weeks, perhaps.

Anyway, War Ace Bill he draws plans of the glider on a bit of board and he gets things all set out for the job when he says he wants some straight lengths of timber. Of course there ain't any such thing in that country, the coolibahs not given wood straight for even an inch.

I tells War Ace Bill this and he says: "Difficulties are meant to surmount, Captain. We will use the roof rafters and frame."

No amount of arguing will shift that idea out of his head. I tells him again the kind of character Iron McPherson is, and that he's gonna charge high for the roof already without adding the cost of the rafters which is gonna be high too. But it's no use, and, being an easy going bloke, I gives in.

So down comes the roof rafters to be used as stiffening for the iron as there's no more corrugations in it after having been wound round trees and things.

I seen that War Ace Bill knows something about gliders, but he planned bigger than the material we has in hand, as he seen also when we'd built one wing and a bit. However, difficulties don't worry him, and he takes sheets of iron out of the hut walls, and every day the clouds banking deep and black telling of the rain that was due. The mornings were clear and hot, mind you, but towards afternoon the little puff clouds had grown to big ones that growled and shot lightning at each other.

When we'd all but finished the glider and I'm wondering what Iron McPherson will say when he sees the hut, or what's left of it, there arrives a character who says he's Flying Officer Delgarth.

There was no doubt about him being a flying officer because he arrived in a aireyplane.

We seen him first about ten o'clock travelling west. Half an hour later he comes back and, after circling round a bit, he lands between the hut and the bore head and finally stops his machine right near where we're working on the glider.

The character in the plane tells us he's sort of got sunstroke, that he's all queer like and giddy and burning like fire all over. So we get him out and carries him to the shade of the only wall of the hut left standing, and there I gives him a gill of painkiller, and War Ace Bill he makes a drink of tea for him and us while we talk things over.

The new character tells us he's making for Darwin, but he reckons he's pretty crook and must lie up a bit. Have we a telephone? I asks him if he knows a character named Iron McPherson and he says no. I tells him if he did he wouldn't expect to find no telephone away from the homestead.

Then he asks us what's wrong with the hut, and War Ace Bill explains how he and me took it to bits to make the glider. After that he sort of slept for a time, and when he comes to he says one of us will have to ride to the homestead to send off a report about him and his present position.

I seen then what was coming. War Ace Bill was getting another idea. He takes me away from the sick character and tells me that as it will take four hours to ride to the homestead and four hours to get back, it's likely that the character will be dead.

"We'll have to fly to Headquarters in his machine," he says.

"We?" says I. "Why me?"

"Because, Captain, I require you to act as my observer," he says. "I don't know the course. You do."

"But who's to look after the sick character?" I'm wanting to know.

"He'll be all right in the shade until we get back," says he. "Help me to lift the tail of the machine round so's we can move off into the wind."

He's all officer and gentleman is this War Ace Bill now he's met up with hero's work. We shifts the machine how he wants it, and he tells me to get up into the front seat and strap meself in. He gets into the other seat and begins to fiddle about with the levers and things, and the flying officer character he stands on his feet, waves his hands about, and then falls down again. Then the engine starts and things happen.

We slides across the ground at increasing speed, heading straight for the bore which is one of then shooting kind sending water up like a fountain for fifty or so feet. War Ace Bill don't seem to notice the bore casing and fountain. He's pulling levers and things like he was one of them railway fellers on a trolley, and he's doing it like he didn't seem to be enjoying himself.

Me, I'm looking back at him and forward at the bore, and I'm not enjoying myself either, because I know quite well the water's boiling hot. I wished I was handing painkiller to the sick character.

All of a sudden the bumping stopped and the fountain seemed to go down. I seen War Ace Bill still pulling out knobs and pushing 'em back, and he don't seem to notice anything else but what he's doing with the gadgets. Then I seen the fountain rise again, and I makes out that on the slant we're going we'd surely pass through the fountain just above the casting where the water's hottest.

But can War Ace Bill fly that machine? I should say. At the last moment the front end rises sharp like and we tips the fountain, the water slapping the keel as we passes over.

Then things get a bit more quiet with War Ace Bill. He's still pulling things out and pushing 'em in, but he doesn't seem so annoyed with 'em.

I takes a deck overside and sees the table and box seats on the floor of the hut, the sick character looking like he was dead, and the glider looking like a tree moth. All that seems to pass away, and I remember I'm not feeling too good and that we're a long way off the ground and over scrub.

Now War Ace Bill is banging on the side and I looks round at him. He's waving his arm in a Hitler salute, and I gives him the raspberry having been a good unionist for as long as I can remember. This seems to annoy him no end and I'm trying to concentrate my mind on him when the wind sets up a scream along the wings. And me, I seen we're headed right downward for the ground through the blur whats the propellor.

So I points to the earth, which is where it didn't ought to be, and War Ace Bill he stops giving me the Hitler salute and re-continues wrastling with the gadgets and things. I never knew a character so energetic as he was at times.

Any'ow, the earth goes back to its proper place, and we seem to be going up again higher than ever. And presently War Ace Bill he starts again hammering on the machine with his fist. I looks back and sees him doing the dictator act and I'm getting annoyed, being, as I said, a good unionist. He's speaking a piece what ain't poetry by any chance, but I can't hear a word on account of the engine, what's roaring and whining worse than the station truck.

Presently he gives in, and I'm very sick, and wishing I'd brought the bottle of painkiller, and then he starts again banging the side, and this time when I looks round I see he's holding up a writing pad, with writ on it the words: "Which way, you ruddy fool?"

I gets a deck now why he's doing the saluting, and I points a bit to the east. That satisfies him, and he keeps on until we can see the track to the homestead running across the bush like a brown snake, and leaving me to be as sick as I likes.

Now between fits I'm looking at the ground coming well up on my side and then disappearing under the machine for a bit and then coming again into view and heaving well up towards where the sky ought to be, and I think it crook of War Ace Bill to go on like this when I'm a terribly sick character. Either he's pulling my leg or he's a bit rusty on the flying, him having been grounded since the war, and you can bet I'm made joyful by seeing the roofs of the homestead and the outbuildings all looking like a bunch of unripe grapes on a carpet.

We takes a while to reach the joint, and then it's a long way down, and looking further away than a big black thunder cloud above us what's lit with lightning like it would bust. I'm feeling pleased with the prospect of getting me feet on firm ground, and then I see the earth all spinning round like a plate with the homestead just outside the dead centre.

All this ain't according to my ideas of flying, believe me. I'd seen plenty of planes in the war, and they mostly flew straight and on proper side up. This one was the first I'd been in and I wasn't enjoying it, although the man who was flying it was War Ace Bill himself. To make matters more unsettling the engine was roaring and spitting, and when I looks back it's to see me fellow character in holts again with the plugs and things.

We're going down all right. I see that by the way the homestead roofs are coming up and getting bigger. The place is still turning round like it was just outside the centre of a spinning plate.

I can now see people running round the big house fence and

waving their arms in welcome. I can even make out Red Lester, the men's cook, and old Iron McPherson himself, ziff and all.

Presently the engine stops altogether, and War Ace Bill is giving the levers and plugs downright hell. I looks over the side again, and then it occurs to me that it's us going round and round and not the homestead, and that we're like a drop of whisky sliding down a corkscrew. It don't seem that I'm pleased at the rate we're going down.

I can now see the colour of Iron McPherson's ziff. It's standing out straight from his face and I knows he's annoyed. I'm thinking of the money he'll be taking off my cheque for the material used in that glider. By this time we are low down the corkscrew, and I see that the point of the corkscrew is right centre of the Government House roof. There don't seem nothing that War Ace Bill can do about shifting the point away from the house, and I reckons it's a bit thick to have the cost of the roof piled atop the hut dismantlement.

With the engine stopped we're in a silence bounded by the whistling noise from the wings. I turns round to ask War Ace Bill to look where he's going, and he's looking downward and seem like he wants to be sick. I can hear Iron McPherson swearing terrible, and then the whistling noise stopped and I looks down, too.

From information received afterwards from Red Lester it seems that when we're getting near to the point of the corkscrew, the machine kind of rights itself and hangs fire right above the big roof. Then it drops down onto the roof.

Me, I gets a jolt up me back that stopped at me neck. I can hear brown paper tearing like mad, I see the chimbleys rock a bit. Then I hears a lot of crackling, and I see bits of the roof rising all around us and the chimbleys tumbling down. There were one or two other noises I can't describe because I never before heard anything like 'em.

Knowing old Iron McPherson for so many years, I don't like arriving like this, and I'm making up me mind that I'd not go mates with War Ace Bill any longer when I seen myself falling into a green sofa in what must be the best room. The next thing I sees is that I'm laying against a fence outside the house, and that the house don't seem too familiar to me. Somewhere about is Iron

McPherson telling War Ace Bill what a character he is.

It was a bit thick losing me job through no fault of me own. It was thicker still when Iron McPherson refused to give me a cheque, saying as how I owed 200 quid over and above what the station owed me on account of my share in the hut and the homestead. The dirty dog put me on tramp with War Ace Bill, and I've been out of a job ever since.

Me and War Ace Bill soon parted company, and about six months after I meets a character who tells me he knew War Ace Bill was never in the war. He tells me War Ace Bill couldn't fly a kite let alone a plane, and that it was them war yarns in the magazines what sent him cranky.

The Mover of Mountains

I'm boundary riding from Gray's Well, a sort of half-way joint between the main homestead and the out-station of Wombra, and cooking for me is a character called Murky Allen, who's a real artist on language. Mind you, Murky Allen's a good cook and we gets on all right together, but he's one of them round pegs in square holes and he ought to have been down in the city putting machinery out for sale and working on his inventions.

Anyhow, there's him and me living at Gray's Well which is comfortable enough as far as it goes, there being two huts built close aside each other and joined at the front with a cane-grass wall to keep the sand back. There's a new well sunk near the old one what caved in, and a good mill and proper stockyards, and heaps of stacked iron and timber what was once a shearing shed.

The job's all right if the boss is a bit flash and touchy. The riding horses is all right, too. The dust is the only cronk thing about the place, flying in clouds every time the wind half blows across a range of big sandhills to the north and west, and about half a mile away. Come a bit of a breeze and the air's like red fog and the cook's language is like the fog and the handle to his moniker. No matter what he does, there's sand in the bread and the tucker.

As I said, he's a misplaced character, being mad on inventing things. For instance, close to his bunk in the kitchen hut, and beside the winder from which can be seen the well and mill and the road to the homestead passing over the sandhills, there's a set of levers like them you can see in a railway signal box. You pulls a lever and the mill shuts off - you let her go and the mill goes on. You pull another lever and the gate across the homestead road this side of the sandhills opens wide, and when you lets go the lever the gate shuts. There's another lever to work the stockyard gates.

Then above this character's bunk is a board with bells on it. When a motor's coming from the homestead and getting near the sandhills a bell rings and gives Murky Allen time to pull the lever opening the gate. Another bell rings when the water in the tank feeding the troughs gets down to a certain level. A bell tells him when the bread's done baking in the oven.

He's got a electric light outfit worked with a small engine and dynamo and things, and he sends away for various kinds of painkillers and mixes them up to see if they'll do his rheumatism any good. That's how he spends his money, instead of going down to the Hill like you and me and drinking like a gent.

It's all nice and handy, I suppose, but I can't see much sense to it.

No, Murky Allen's no peaceful character to live with. His brain's always working hard as you can see by his black eyes what stares from a dead white face. He don't know the meaning of peace and quiet, and this sort of keeps me upset, because I loves peace and quiet, and longs for the old days when I uster live alone with me dogs and cats and things for company.

I'm out riding one day in the paddocks, and about two o'clock the wind gets up and comes on to blow sort of moderate. Immediately I gets in sight of Gray's Well, I can see the sand blowing off the sandhills right across the huts and blowing the usual hell outer what should have been a good camp. I hears Murky Allen living up to his handle while I takes the saddle and bridle off me horse, and when I goes into the kitchen for a drink of tea he says:

"A man oughta buy a coupler cases of high explosive and blow the joint to bits. I tells the boss that time the old well fell in, to sink the new one outside them sandhills, and to build a new hut with the shed iron and wood, but he says it would be too expensive. I'd like to see him here in a good sandstorm and hear him choking to death. The blasted sand's always getting into me dynamo and stopping it."

"Pity you can't make an invention to shift them sandhills," I says, without thinking.

I seen the rage leave his long face. Murky Allen comes to stand still, his hands raised like he was shaking his fists at me, and him looking at the pet galah what's perched on a roof rafter.

Then he says: "Joseph Henry, you are a inspiration. There ain't nothing impossible in this world. If I can't invent something to shift them sandhills down to Adelaide I'll - Yes, it can be done. It shall be done. Leave it to me."

"There's a few billion tons of sand in 'em," I reminds him.

"Yes," says he, and I knows the 'yes' ain't in agreement with what I said. "Yes, I will apply my mind to this problem of shifting them sandhills."

"With a million dam-sinking plants and five million men," says I, seeing a kind of glory on his face.

"Be quiet," say he. "What made them sandhills? I'll tell you. The wind made 'em. Well, I will compel the wind to unmake 'em."

After that he shuts up and won't hardly say a word for a week. His mind's that busy on shifting them sandhills that the tucker's crook for the first time. At night he's going like a scalded cat working on drawings, and blowing into a funnel thing he's made outer jam tins and things.

I gets home one afternoon to find him on his hands and knees on top of a small sandhill at the back of the woodheap. I can hear the dynamo running in the kitchen, and the engine going full steam ahead. There's a wire laid out to where Murky Allen's doing something with a sort of funnel with wings he's made outer shed iron.

"She works" he says, getting up and shaking hands. "Look at her."

I takes a bird's eye view. There's a lot of sand coming out of the small end of the funnel and flying high to be taken away by the wind. Presently the sand under the funnel sort of sinks and the funnel sinks, too, and goes on blowing sand. I seen that after a time the woodheap sandhill would be no more, but it's only a very small sandhill about five feet high, and I says: "The gadget's going to take a long time to shift all them real sandhills."

"Don't be silly," says he. "This is only a makeshift model to prove a principle. From it we will construct proper sand-shifting machines with all that iron stacked from the shearing shed."

"But the boss -"

"Blast the boss. Forget him."

"But he's a character what'll go dead cronk when he sees his iron gone."

"Forget him, Joseph Henry," snarls Murky Allen, getting real narked. "We're gonna remove the curse laid' on Gray's Well.

When we've done that, instead of going crook the boss will be highly delighted. Come on, we'll get dinner over and then begin work on the sand-shifting machines."

Now, me, I'm not over anxious to begin work. I've been riding in the paddocks all day, for one thing, and for another, I knows how the boss will go off when he finds the shed iron all cut to make sand-removers.

Still it's no use arguing with Murky Allen when he gets going, and after dinner there's me belting the corrugations outer the iron sheets, and there's him cutting it with tin snips and the axe. It's like that every night until after one o'clock: belting, cutting, rivetting. In the first week we constructs thirty long funnels. It takes us another week to make fans to go inside 'em, and a third week making sort of wings to be fixed to the bottom ends of the machines.

What with all this night work on top of me ordinary day it ain't long before I'm getting wore out, and I says to Murky: "What about having a spell for a week?"

"Spell!" he yelps, staring at me. "What-in-hell are you talking about?"

"I'm talking about a lay-in," I says. "I'm getting a bit tired like and could do with a week's sleep."

"Sleep!" he says, as though I suggest cutting his throat.

"Well, what about trying one of those things to see if it works proper. If one won't work the others won't, will they?"

"They'll work all right, don't you fret," says he. "When the next windstorm comes we'll have these machines all set, and then them blasted sandhills is gonna be removed to Adelaide where people like 'em for garden paths and things."

Just then the road bell goes off.

"Quick," he says. "Skid out and remove that last sand-remover behind the wood stack. It might be the boss."

It's the boss, sure enough, and he's on his way to the out-station and stops for a drink of tea.

This Hilary Markham is a chap getting on for forty. He's done his jackerooing on one of them Gov'ment stations, and he thinks he knows everything. He wears riding breeches and tops boots with spurs a foot long. He wears these spurs when he is driving his flash car and don't intend to do no horse riding. Times is changed all right from them days when bosses uster wear ordinary gabardine slacks and elastic sides in boots.

"The bullock waggon's on the way out and ought to be there tomorrow," he says to Murky Allen. "Old Mick's bringing Larry as offsider. The next day you, Harry, and Larry can load all the shed iron on the waggon, and, the day after, Mick and Larry can start off back to the homestead. I shall probably be back before they leave."

Off he goes in his flash car what's a brand new one, and Murky Allen says: "Come on! We gotta finish that last sand-remover and cart the lot over to the sandhills and fix 'em up before Old Mick arrives. If he sees 'em he's sure to blab to the flaming boss."

Now me, seeing the end of the job in sight, I gets kind of a last burst of energy, and I yokes a draught horse to the dray and one be one I takes them sand-removers over beyond the sandhills and dumps 'em where they're to be erected.

We works like slaves all that night and all the next day up to four o'clock, by which time we has the sand-removers set up and anchored with mulga logs. Being along the wind'ard side of the dunes north-west of the huts and mill they can't be seen from Gray's Well or from the homestead road. They're spaced a hundred feet apart, and they looks like anti-aircraft guns what's been partly melted by fire or something. When Old Mick and bullock waggon arrives I'm finished and me enthusiasm has gone down.

The next day's calm and hot, and me and Larry loads the remainder of the shed iron onto the waggon while Old Mick, being an ancient character, spends a hour or two telling Murky Allen how he can drive the bullocks. When the cook tells him to get out of the kitchen, he comes down to the waggon and tells us how to do the loading.

Coming on top of making all them sand-removers, this loading work about polishes me off, but we gets the job done just before Murky beats his triangle and we goes in for dinner. It's the worst dinner that ever Murky Allen cooked, and Larry tells him straight he's losing his punch. There's a bit of a argument, and this unpleasantness coming after all the work what I done spoils me digestive organs and I goes off and lays on me bunk.

About ten o'clock, when Larry and Old Mick is still grousing about the tucker, the boss arrives and comes into the men's hut in a hurry.

"Night!" he says, short like. "We're gonna have a almighty sandstorm. I'm camping here. Go and bring in my stretcher, Larry."

Well, as the night's quiet as a grave, and the moon's making it look like day, sandstorms don't seem right to me and I says so.

"Go out and look," yelps the boss.

So me and Old Mick, we goes out after Larry, and Larry he says: "The end of the world's coming."

We're out by the car in front of the canegrass wall joining the two huts, and we stand looking at the sky from the west right round to the north. It's like a black wall, and the moon's shining on it, and making it seem it was about to fall on Grays Well. The wall's getting higher and higher towards the moon, and we can see how it's bulging here and there, and leaning further and further over us.

"She don't look too good," says Old Mick, with his thin and piping voice.

We takes the boss's stretcher and valise inside. The boss is tearing some of Murky Allen's tucker into himself, trying to beat the storm, and he's doing it with a hurricane lamp to help him, because Murky Allen's disconnected the lights and is wrapping his blankets round the engine and dynamo. A minute later the boss comes into the men's hut, and Old Mick says cheerfully:

"'Taint gonna be as bad a storm as we had in '92."

"It's going to be the worst storm you ever seen, you old fool," says the boss.

"'Taint right ter go and call a working man that," pipes Old Mick, and the boss is on the point of saying something else when the storm arrives.

There's not much wind with this storm, but underneath what there is, is a low humming noise what don't please me particular. But there's plenty of sand in this storm, and the sand comes in through the cracks in the walls and the roof and falls down straight on us and everything. Doing a bit of spluttering, Murky Allen comes in and sit's down on the bunk beside me.

Presently we can't see each other, and the lamp looks like a kind of red star in a black sky. We can hear the sand falling on the roof like it was tiny hailstones, and beyond this sound the humming sound's rising into a low roar.

The wind comes like a train, and after she hit and rocked the joint, the air sort of got a bit clearer, so's we could see each other with towels and things being used to keep the sand out of our mouths and noses.

Murky Allen then leans close and whispers: "Them sand-removers will be going full blast, Joseph Henry. Time daylight comes the scenery is going to look entirely different, and the boss is due to have the surprise of his life."

I grunts that I hears him. The wind's blowing steady and screaming across the huts and round about 'em. The light goes dim like a red star again, and Old Mick says: "That's funny. The wind oughter have blown all the sand away in front of it."

"She's blowing sand off then dunes," says Larry, not knowing how right he was.

The lamplight gets that dark it's like a spark, and the place is so full of sand that I can feel it thick on me feet and on me head.

Sitting there and wondering how things was gonna end up, Murky Allen, he whispers to me: "It's them sand-removers. They're working all out."

The floor of the hut had been hard. Now it was soft. It's the worst sand-storm I ever knew, and I begins to think that Murky Allen must be right about his sand-removers being in action. Presently our feet is as high as the bunks, and we're sitting on sand; minutes after, the sand's higher than the bunks. All of a sudden Old Mick lets out a yell.

"I'm getting outer here afore the tide gets higher than the winder and the door and drowns us."

"Me, too!" yells Larry.

"Scram, you fellers," shouts the boss, after a fit of coughing.

There's a blind rush for the door. It's as black as the ace of spades, the lamp having been buried. I can hear grunts and curses over by the door, and then Old Mick he sings out: "Take your spurs off my face, boss."

"To hell with yer face," snarls the boss. "Get outer me way, you old idiot."

Me, I finds meself against the winder, or, rather, the top part of it, and I busts it open and crawls through and up a steep slope of sand. Me legs is pushing the sand downwards through the winder, and I hears Murky Allen sobbing curses at me as he follows me. We reached the top of a mountain of sand and there we stops for a breather, and presently Murky Allen he says:

"We placed them crimson sand-removers wrong. We didn't elevate them enough. Instead of them shooting the dunes high up towards Adelaide, they're aiming short and dropping the sand right here."

"What the boss'll say in the morning don't bear thinking about," says I. "I'm off to save me dogs from getting drowned."

I was only just in time, cos the chains went straight down through the sand what's got under the animals. Having let 'em go, me and them does a get for country free of the forming sandhills, and when a mile away we stops and thinks about things, the dogs rubbing against me and whimpering.

The air's clear out here, and the moon is looking good to me if she is a bit reddish. She's shining down on a kind of curved black cloud what begins where the sandhills were and what ends where Gray's Well is. I'm more'n pleased to be away from the influence of Murky Allen's sand-removers.

When day breaks the winds down and the sand ain't blowing no more. I'm thinking about breakfast but I don't see none in sight. There's about a thousand yards of sandhills misplaced from where they had been since the Year One to where Gray's Well is supposed to be. The huts are buried under those misplaced sandhills, and so's the two wells and the stockyards, and Old Mick's waggon and boss's flash new car. If it hadn't been for the mill head sticking a foot or two above a sand-crest you wouldn't have thought Gray's Well ever was.

I arrives at the edge of these misplaced sandhills and looks up and sees the boss walking up and down and waving his arms. There's Larry and Old Mick sitting down and looking as though they're admiring the scenery. The only ordinary character up there is Murky Allen, and he's nursing the galah and looking highly delighted, him telling me after that he remembered the bird when I told him I was going to save me dogs.

Then the boss he stands still and looks across to the thousand-yard gap in the sandhills. In this gap we can see the sand-removers looking like anti-aircraft guns what's been well bombed.

"What's them things over there?" yells the boss.

"Them's me latest inventions," says Murky Allen. "They're patent sand-removers what I invented and what me and Joseph Henry made and erected. We got sick of the dust every time she blew, and now when she blows again we won't get no dust."

"You'll get off the run, you lunatic," screams the boss. He's lost one spur and his silk shirt's all torn to bits. He don't seem particularly pleased.

Me and Murky Allen we're put on tramp, and we carries cigarette swags. We go looking for another job apiece, and we parts company when he gets a job cooking on a joint called Thunder Creek. The boss there offered me a job, too, boundary riding, but I thought better of taking it. Thunder Creek homestead's in the lee of a longish hill covered with loose rocks, and I'm thinking Murky Allen might try his mountain-removers on that hill. I likes peace and quiet, I do, and I'm looking still for a job where I can live, on me own with me dogs and a cat or two for company.

Henry's Little Lamb

Now me, I ain't got no time for them what says animals can't think; and I ain't got very much time for them animals what do think.

I'm remembering a pet sheep I called Orphan Boy, what I reared from a lamb and what lost me a good chance of going on the pictures, and no one can tell me that this Orphan Boy don't think. He thinks as good as any of them champions what plays billiards.

There's me living quiet and peaceful with me dogs and cats, and this here Orphan Boy pet sheep, at a hut on Marshall Downs, away up near Milprinka. I'm living in this joint for four years. The boss ain't too bad but he don't like to be asked for anything.

When I tells him the white ants and dry rot have chewed off the hut's corner posts below ground, and that a good windstorm is likely to blow her down on a man, all he says is to cut a few props and prop her up on the outside. The roof's all right, but the walls is made of pine logs what's become sort of powdery on the inside.

Any'ow, I props her up to stand against the westerly winds, and I don't worry because as I says, peace and quiet is everything.

Then one shearing time the boss sent out a half-caste to lend a hand moving the flocks, and this half-caste character, he sort of starts my bit of bad luck. He's about twenty, when they don't know what to do with theirselves, and he wears brown top boots and riding breeches and silly shirts and things.

At first he don't take kindly to Orphan Boy, who weighs something like 200 pounds on the hoof, and who follers him around like he's waiting for a chance to bunt. He don't know that Orphan Boy is follering him around in the hopes of picking up a cigarette butt, this pet sheep being nutty on tobacker.

After a bit this half-caste character gets to liking Orphan Boy, and he tells me he's planning to train Orphan Boy to do tricks, as Orphan Boy is a very intelligent sheep because he don't pick up cigarette butts till after he's put a foot on 'em to make sure they're cold.

He says there's no reason why Orphan Boy can't be learned to talk, but I says there's enough profanity from me pet galah without Boy adding to it.

When I gets home one evening I see this half-caste character has made a dummy man out of chaff bags stuffed with old papers. He stands up this dummy man well in the open, and then he walks Orphan Boy close to it and persuades him to charge it and bunt it yards. Every time Orphan Boy does this he gets a cigarette butt what the half-caste character has saved up every night.

Presently the half-caste character he erects a coupler posts about five feet apart, and he then plants the dummy man in front of the posts and tries to get Orphan Boy to bunt the dummy man clean through between 'em. At first Orphan Boy ain't too good at it, but presently he becomes a dabster at shooting goals, never missing and always getting his cigarette butt.

This half-caste character is Satan in disguise. When the shearing's over, he goes back to the homestead, and there's Orphan Boy asking me to put up the dummy man for him to score goals and collect cigarette butts off me.

He gets ratty when I can't be bothered setting up the dummy man, and when he don't get no cigarette butts from me as I'm a pipe smoker.

So what does he do? Why, what that half-caste character knew he would do. Orphan Boy waits outside me hut, and, when I emerges in the morning, he charges me an' sends me back clean through the doorway to lob on the kitchen floor. He fair shook me up, and when I gets me wind, I goes out and belts him for making a billiard ball out of me and pocketing me in me own joint.

He didn't come at me no more, but he picked his marks. He was like a billiard cue, and the kitchen doorway was like a table pocket. Orphan Boy pocketed a tramp what I asked in for a feed. He pocketed several of the hands. He even pocketed the overseer one morning, and the overseer wasn't particular pleased about it neither.

Never once does the gent to be pocketed hit either side the doorway. One second he's outside the hut, and the next he's on his back on the kitchen floor. I got to laying wool packs on the kitchen floor to ease the thud sort of. It was the surprise what annoyed 'em most.

In course of time, Orphan Boy gets famous. You see, there's a lot of creeks on this Marshall Downs Station, and if they're running when the shearing's on there's always trouble getting the flocks to cross the creeks by the narrow bridges. But there ain't no trouble at all when me and Orphan Boys lends a hand.

All I got to do is to let Orphan Boy smell me tobaccer plug. Then he follers me across the bridges, and the flocks they all foller him. Orphan Boy is the biggest sheep I ever seen time he's six-tus, and it's no good you telling me that terbaccer stunts the growth.

One day in early summer one year there comes a windstorm what threatens to blow me hut down, and I'm outside re-fixing the props to keep her up when the boss arrives.

As I mentioned, the boss is a very easy going character. He's a sixteen-stoner and always cheerful as long as you don't ask him for anything. He sees me propping up the hut, but he imagines he don't see me, and he tells me to foller him inside as he has important news for me.

When I'd made a drink of tea and got out me latest brownie, he says: "You ever hear of a great film producer named Carl Zalotta?"

"Course," I says. "I always reads the fillum news after the horses. He's the King Pin of the Modernistic Players Corporation. Ain't he on holiday in Australia?"

"He is," replied the boss. "He's written to me, saying he's heard of you and Orphan Boy. He reckons Orphan Boy and you might be able to act in his coming production what he's calling 'Sweethearts on the Saltbush'."

"Me!" I says, sort of stonkered.

"And Orphan Boy," adds the boss. "The great Carl Zalotta is arrived at the homestead tomorrow evening, and the next day he's coming out here to see if Marshall Downs will suit for his picture. Now you spruce up Orphan Boy. Make him look smart, and make a collar for him so he can be tied up when he's not wanted. Have a mob of sheep in the yards so that Carl Zalotta can see Orphan Boy and you herding 'em around. You might get a good engagement."

"Sounds goodoh to me," I tells the boss. "Me and Orphan Boy might earn a lot of money. I read where they pay thousands of dollars a week to pets and their trainers to act in pictures."

Off goes the boss looking mighty proud that Carl Zalotta is out to make a picture of Marshall Downs what's to be called "Sweethearts on the Saltbush." There's miles of saltbush on the place, and it's looking pretty healthy at this time.

And I'm doing a bit of a chortle to old Orphan Boy whiles I'm grooming him and, later on, fitting a pair of hobble straps for a collar.

I has him chained up with the dogs when Mr. Carl Zalotta and party arrives. Party is right. There's three cars of 'em, and the boss in his car looking as pleased as the dog with two tails. They all gets out and strolls around the place in a mob, and presently they sort of disentangles and I gets to know three of 'em special.

Mr. Carl Zalotta is a character on the smallish side. He's got a little black moustache with waxed ends and a long, narrer black ziff with a point. He wears a eye-glass, and he's got a squeaky voice.

Then there's a character what he calls Stan. This gent is very high and very narrer, and he chews cigars half a foot long, sort of running 'em backward and forwards across his mouth.

Another character is called Arthur, a namby-pamby squirt with no chest and a pasty-white face.

These three seems to be the bosses; the others are all yes-men.

"Ah!" says Mr. Zalotta to me. "So you are ze great sheeps trainer, eh? Well, well! What you tink, Stan? What you tink of our friend, here?"

"Oughta screen all right if he don't wash," says Stan, and I feels uncomfortable for I remembers that in the excitement I have forgot to wash that morning.

"Yes, yes, Stan, he'll screen well," says Mr. Zalotta. Then to me, he says: "Now where is your pet sheeps? You bring your pet sheeps, eh? Let us see what he can do."

So I unchains Orphan Boy and lets him smell my terbaccer plug, and I leads him over to the yards, where I opens up all the gates. The leaders of this mob all know Orphan Boy, and seeing him walking after me trying to get the terbaccer plug outer me hand, they follers him and the mob follers them.

We leads the mob outer the yard and into another, outer that and through the race and inter more yards. Then we leads them round the hut, and Mr. Zalotta he waves his arms and shouts: "Bravo! Bravo! How is that, Stan?"

And Stan, he says: "With a pair of trousers on him what ain't got no red flannel patch on the stern, that guy and his lil ole lamb is gonna make the fans weep buckets of tears."

"But I like ze flannel patch, Stan," says Mr. Zalotta.

"Oh, all right, boss, only it'll have to be white," says Stan, as though the subject don't interest him.

Mr. Zalotta, he tells me Arthur will make out the contract, and the boss he tells me to chain up Orphan Boy in case of accidents. Then me and the boss, Mr. Zalotta and Stan and Arthur, we all go into the hut, where Arthur sits at the table and gets ready to fill up a form.

This Arthur character he wants me name and address, the colour of me eyes and general appearance, and Mr. Zalotta he says to me:

"According to zis contract, my friend, you and your sheeps will work for the Modernistic Players Corporation for a term of three months, and ze said Corporation will pay you twenty dollars a week, and your sheeps ten dollars a week."

Now thirty dollars week for me and Orphan Boy don't sound in accordance with the fillum papers that I read, and I says so.

"Why, zat ess a good salary for you, my friend," says Mr. Carl Zalotta, the famous fillum producer.

"It's only seven quid and a half a week," I says. "What about Lovey Sunnygurl and her pet dog? She's drawing $2,000 a week."

"Say, bo," says Stan. "You don't want to go and believe the fillum papers. All them noughts after the figures is put in by the publicity agents. Why, we get bootiful society dames to pay us a premium to let 'em act as stars in our big mammoth productions."

All this may be so, and I might have been led astray by the fillum news what I read, but I don't intend to do no acting for next nothing, and I says so.

We all gets into a argument what is extended somewhat, and then Stan says: "Come on Chief! What's the use? This guy's been made nutty by the fillum magazines." Then out he goes.

I'm still laying down the law and the boss is enjoying it. Arthur is looking frightened and Mr. Carl Zalotta he's waving his arms and mixing up his languages. Then we hears a grunt and the hut rocks bad when Stan arrives back hard against the right door post.

I knows what's happened. Orphan Boy, he's got off the chain or slipped his collar. And for the first time he's missed pocketing the ball. I gets all hot with the shame of it.

Stan, he claws his way up the door post to his feet, a cigar still in his face and running back and across his mouth faster than ever. His eyes looks like empty bottles and he's saying something to himself. Then off he goes to argue it out with Orphan Boy. But he don't stay long. Back he comes to hit the right hand door post with a thud and the hut it shakes and sways so much that all the sand and stuff on the rafters falls down on us and chokes us.

Mr. Zalotta, he yells out he's smothering and he rushes to the doorway and jumps out over the body of Stan. We hears him let out a squeal and then he comes into view again to hit the right door post and flop down on Stan who's trying to be sick.

I don't understand. I can't figure out what Orphan Boy is thinking of making all them miss-hits. It ain't like him. It ain't as if he ever gets excited and off his game.

Then the Arthur character he gets windy. He scrams past the boss and makes for the doorway. There he jumps over Mr. Zalotta and Stan and does a bunk.

It seem that Orphan Boy is determined to pocket a ball and save himself from utter disgrace. He tries again, and this time he don't miss-cue. Arthur lets out a yell, and then he comes into view. He arrives clean through the doorway, and he continues right across the hut to bash against the back wall. I hears me props getting misplaced. I see the hut sort of swaying. Then down she falls and we all gets crowned by the roof.

Fortunately, when she lands the roof don't flatten out, and there's me and the boss, Mr. Zalotta, and Stan and Arthur, cooped up like a lot of fowls. It's hot in there, and the air ain't by no means pure, what with the dust and Stan's language.

Then we hears the yes-men outside, and I have to tell them to get the wood 'eap axe and belt off a sheet of iron to let us out. And when I gets out, there's Orphan Boy follering the yes-men around waiting for one of 'em to drop a cigarette butt.

That's how I don't get me contract to act for the pictures. Stan, he went off looking like he was unwell, and Mr. Carl Zalotta he tells me in ten different languages that "Sweethearts on the Saltbush" can go to the devil, and that his next picture is going to be "He Shot 'Em Dead" in which there won't be no pet sheeps.

The boss he laughed so much he sent out the carpenter to re-build me a hut, and one day I'm overhauling Orphan Boy and seen a grass seed in his left eye. It is this grass seed what made him miss his shots, and I gets it out and doctors his eye for a while. It's no wonder to me any more that he couldn't aim straight.

Time the hut's re-built Orphan Boy's eye is goodoh. I know this, for the next bloke he pockets, true and hard, is me.

Henry's Christmas Party

Lurid Len is a character named rightly Leonard Alphington Montrose, and I knows him when he's well over sixty and is growing a ziff down to his stomach. Me and him is boundary riding from a hut back on Yilgarn Station, and we decides to stay at home this Christmas so's to save our money for a proper bender down at the Hill at Easter time.

A day or two before this Christmas, Windmill Bill comes out in the station truck to fix the pump, and, as the Boss passes by the next day, he takes Windmill Bill in with him, and he leaves the truck with us.

Now me, I don't think nothing about this station truck. I've made up me mind not to spend any money this Christmas and I'm satisfied to forget all about Christmas. This ain't so with Lurid Len, who's a character not particularly strong in will power.

Christmas Eve is flamin' hot, a moderate wind seeming to come out of an oven, and when I gets home from riding the fences, I finds Lurid Len sitting in the truck and handling the steering wheel like a kid what imagines he is driving it. When he sees me coming he gets down and don't say nothing until we're having a drink of tea, it being then about four o'clock.

"I suppose the boys will all be gathering around Beaky Willi's joint by now," he says.

"Why talk about it?" I wants to know.

"Well, we got to talk about something ain't we?" he flares up. "Weather like this and us sitting here like a coupler dopey fowls when the rest is eating turkey and things and ripping cold schooners of beer down their gullets."

"What's the use of growling?" I asks. "We decides to go quiet this Christmas so's we can take a spell at Easter down at the Hill."

"Oh, I know that," he snarls. "But suppose we gets struck by lightning or something before Easter. Think what we'll have missed this Christmas."

"I don't want to think about that," I says.

"But I do," he tells me, savage like, his blue eyes gleaming and his ziff quivering. "Listen here, Joseph Henry. I got a plan. Beaky

Willi's pub is seventy-odd miles away, besides which we'd have to go through the homestead when the boss would see us passing. What about going down to Teddyrunta? We can take back tracks so's to miss the homestead, and, as usual, Paddy Grogan is throwing a free party at his place to begin at eight tonight."

"But Teddyrunta's close to sixty miles away," I argues. "And we can't expect the horses to do the trip after working all day in the paddocks."

"Well, what about the truck?" he wants to know.

"But you can't drive her, and you knows I can't drive her."

"No, but I'm game to try," he says. "I been watching Windmill Bill working her, and I know how he uses the levers and things. I shoved a stick into the petrol tank and she's nearly full. Cripes! It's hot, ain't it?"

Now me, I'm sore tempted, but I don't want to break me resolution. Besides, I can't drive this truck and I knows Lurid Len can't drive her neither. Teddyrunta and Grogan's pub sounds attractive to me, but the betting ain't in favor of us getting to the hall at Teddyrunta where Grogan throws his Christmas parties.

Any'ow, Lurid Len gets all heated with the idea, and he swears he knows enough about the truck to drive her, and the result is we changes into our city-going clothes and starts.

Now I seen that Lurid Len ain't too familiar with trucks. He's sitting straight up and hard against the wheel, what he is grasping like he's aiming a five-point-nine Howitzer. His ziff is falling down to his lap, and his eyes is staring and they don't blink. He's some considerable time getting a move on, although he does manage to get the engine going.

He's shoving in levers and things, and living up to his moniker, but nothing happens bar the noise of the engine and yelping of the dogs. Then all of a sudden the seat hits hard into me back and almost breaks me neck, but I'm not down-hearted because we're going at last although the excitement is no good for me heart what the quack said last year was on the weak side.

After the first two miles, Lurid Len gets in the proper gear for travelling, but there's steam coming out of the engine what I never seen when Windmill Bill is driving her. We're on a narrer back track and on our way across country to keep wide of the homestead and to hit a main road to Teddyrunta, and we knows there's five gates between us and the main road. There's also low mulga stumps sprouting close beside the track, and it seems to me that running over these stumps ain't going to do the tyres any good. These stumps seem to attract Lurid Len, for every time we nears one he has to slew the truck so's to run over it.

Still, he ain't doin' too bad for a new chum truck driver, and I'm thinking that with a bit of luck we might hit Grogan's party while she's in full swing. The country is passing us, meaning that we're not stopping still, exactly, but it sort of wobbles and gets blurred now and then, what makes me think we might be going a little too fast.

The backs of Lurid Len's hands is white from the grip they has on the steering wheel, and now and then the wind blows his ziff up and into his eyes - but we continues to go.

Then we draws near to the first gate. This gate is a wire one what I made meself a year or so back, fitting her good although it's me as says it. Naturally, I'm expecting Lurid Len to pull up so's I can get down and open her but he sort of speeds up and we passes through, wires and all.

I'm not pleased, this being my pet gate, and I says to him: "What's the idea of not stopping back at that gate?"

"Sun's getting low," he tells me. "We got to get to Grogan's before the party's all over."

"But if them weaners in East Paddock gets boxed with the ewes in this one the boss is going to go dead cronk," I argues.

"Don't worry," he tells me. "We'll mend her tomorrow on the way home."

I looks back to see the hole in the fence where the gate oughta be, but I don't see no fence. It's out of sight. All I see is the truck's tracks making a mark like a snake struck mad by the sun.

The situation ain't exactly reassuring, and I points out to Lurid Len that the next gate is a wood-barred one and pretty strong. She's painted dark-grey, and I reminds Lurid Len about this gate in case he don't see her in time to pull up.

When this gate comes into view, I tells him about it, and he don't say nothing and looks sterner than ever and keeps on going like he's seeing a paradise full of bars and pretty barmaids.

We duly arrives at the gate, a hefty barred gate kept closed with a hefty length of chain. We passes through this gate like it wasn't there, and the only things to remind us that it was back along the track is the bits of it lying across the engine bonnet and around the smashed windscreen. Them bits don't look natural to me, and I says so.

"We'll patch her up on our way back tomorrer," says Lurid Len.

I thinks this is going to be difficult when I takes a bird's-eye-view of the patch draping the bonnet, and when I suggests we stops to remove the wreckage, Lurid Len says it'll be safe enough where it is, and we can shift it to the body of the truck later on as he's anxious to cross Suicide Bridge before dark.

In this he ain't more anxious than I am. I have forgot this Suicide Bridge, or I would never have started. She's about a hundred yards long and only wide enough for one truck at a time. I see that the truck we're on isn't going to cross this Suicide Bridge if Lurid Len can't steer her straighter than he's been doing. The worst of it is that she spans a dry creek what is a full sixty feet below, and there ain't no side railings to make a bloke think he's safer than he is.

Time we gets in sight of Suicide Bridge I'm not feeling too good. I'm wishing I was back at home. I tells Lurid Len to pull up so's I can get out, because the speed is making me sort of sick, but he says the feeling will pass and the sun is getting mighty low.

I'm not pleased by the look in his eye, and by the way the wind is blowing his ziff up and across his face now and then. He ought to have tied it down to his middle with a bit of fencing wire.

In due course we arrives at Suicide Bridge. I expects Lurid Len to slow down so's to take this bridge carefully, but he's a character what can't see danger when it's gawking at him, and instead of slowing down he speeds her up.

Before I can argue about getting down and walking over Suicide Bridge, we're well on her, and the cross planking of the decking don't seem to extend more'n a foot either side the front wheels. Me, I'm looking down at this narrer decking, and I'm watching the near-side front wheel darting towards the edge and darting away before it's too late, and go on doing this sort of thing what I find is very bad for my heart.

I'm also watching the bed of the creek what seems to be a full mile below, and the view don't please me because down there is a lot of rocks and things. I forgets to understand why I ever come at all.

We're a bit more than half-way over when I hears Lurid Len doing some gargle-ing.

I screws him off and sees that the wind has laid his ziff across his eyes. He can't remove the ziff with his hands what are gripping the wheel, and the wind don't blow it off, so I've got to grab at it and pull it down so's he can see straight, and when I looks at the near-side wheel again it's running along the edge of the decking, and the only comfort I got is the thought of Grogan's party what we might attend if we're extra special lucky.

We're lucky enough to get off the bridge, any'ow, and I swears solemn that if ever I travels again with a driver having a ziff I'll deserve death and damnation.

Well, to shorten things a bit, we passed through the remaining gates, adding a baulk of timber and various lengths of wire to come trailing along behind us, to the wreckage still decorating the front. The sun's setting time we reach Teddyrunta, and I'm very glad to have arrived, even if I am a bit unsettled by knowing that Lurid Len has one great weakness in his driving.

I now see this weakness very clearly. He can steer all right, after a fashion, and he can keep the truck going at a good bat, but the weakness I'm speaking of is that he forgets to stop when he ought to. And I'm hoping he won't forget to stop at Grogan's place, after coming all this way.

We enter the only street at Teddyrunta. It is a wide street, and a long one, too. The houses and stores and things are all separated by vacant lots, and there's no front fences like there is down in the city. We're coming to Grogan's Hotel, what's just the other side of the hall what Grogan put up to rent to the dances and the pictures, and where he holds his Christmas Party.

Grogan is a character what believes in giving back a shilling for every quid he gets. He don't charge nothing for this party, and every station hand for miles around, and every man in the town, is made right welcome to his Christmas spread at the Teddyrunta Hall.

That the party is in progress is proved by the kids and their goat carts outside the front door. There's ropes of coloured paper and things hung up outside, too.

I don't see Constable Bilbey, and I know he's inside directing the band what he takes a interest in. Remembering that Bilbey don't like blokes without driving licences, I says to Lurid Len: "Better stop some distance this side of the hall so's the policeman will think Windmill Bill has drove the truck to town."

Lurid Len agrees with me and he begins stamping on the pedals and things. Every time he stamps on one of 'em the truck speeds up, and when he stamps on another pedal the engine roars enough to deafen a stone monkey.

The kids with the goat carts see us coming, and they belt their teams and get going. I'm yelling to Lurid Len to pull up, and he's carrying on something terrible. He's looking for more pedals to stamp on, and I'm looking at the kids and the goat carts. Some of them is going that fast that the wind is sending back clouds of dust made scarlet by the setting sun.

Suddenly the street sort of slides to the left, and I sees we're off the road and passing close to a house. Then we're on a vacant lot, and ahead of us is the side wall of the hall. I know this wall is coming towards us. It grows bigger and bigger, and I'm surprised to see that I can count the weatherboards from ground to roof and make 'em twenty-six.

Then with bits of gates and wires and all, we passes into the hall and comes to a stop just inside. There's a sort of tearing noise what smothers the sound of the accordion band and the singing of some of the gents.

I don't feel proud of this manner of entering a Christmas Party. There's rows of tables covered with white cloths and bottles and stands of cake and bread, and glasses and plates of plum pudding and bon-bons.

There's blokes lining these tables engaged in eating and drinking amber liquid. Up on the band stage is Constable Bilbey, and when he sees us the smile dies on his red face and his eyes sort of shoots out sparks. There is a dead silence, and Bilbey he steps down from the stage and advances towards us.

"Come out of it," he says.

Now me, I been wanting to come out of it for a long time. I has to shift boards and things off me shoulders before I can manage to get down to the hall floor, where I meets old Jack the Beanstalk what seems to be waiting for me with two foaming schooners of beer.

"Come on - you!" says the policeman to Lurid Len.

"I can't," Lurid Len say. "Me beard's jammed."

Everyone laughs bar Bilbey. We seen that the steering wheel has got shifted out of place and hard against the front at the truck, and between the truck and the steering wheel is Lurid Len's long ziff.

They got to fetch a crowbar to release him, and then Bilbey says, stern like:

"Drunk and disorderly. Driving without a licence. Driving to the public danger. Threatening to start a riot. Disturbing the peace. You two come along with me."

"But it's Christmas," says Lurid Len. "And I ain't had one yet."

"You might have one - some time in February. Come on now," orders Bilbey.

And then Paddy Grogan chips in: "Be shure, Constable Bilbey, it's forgetting you are it's Christmas an' all. Let the bhoys stay for dinner at me Christmas Party, for it's hungry they are and thirsty this hot day, and what's a wall or two on Christmas night, anyway?"

"Killed anyone?" Bilbey asks me and Lurid Len.

Lurid Len shakes his head and I seen that the off-side of his ziff is missing, and that his face's pretty sore.

"All right," says Bilbey. "You're lucky. You can stay on at the party, but you'll come along with me when the clock strikes twelve."

And someone yells: "Better hurry up, you two. You've only got three hours before you go back to Cinderella's. Come on now and get it."

Well, a bloke can do a lot in three hours, and Lurid Len and me did our best.

Pinky Dick's Elixir

I have a job boundary riding on Marlow Downs, and I'm being cooked for by a character named Pinky Dick.

Pinky Dick is getting along for fifty, when he ought to have been long past the age for boils. I ain't never before seen such a character for boils, for no sooner does he get one batch on the down grade than another batch sort of starts on the upgrade. You can understand a man having a boil now and then, but not keep on having 'em by the dozen, as though he likes having 'em.

Pinky Dick got his moniker on account of his pink skin, blue eyes, and seven hairs on the top of his dome. He's a good cook, and he's all there once he can be lured away from the subject of his boils. He says his boils are his cross.

When I first arrived at this job, Pinky Dick is engaged in drinking a course of medicine what he says an Afghan hawker recommends. There is two shelves over his bunk loaded with bottles from the previous courses, and he likes showing these bottles and telling how much morphia and strychnine is guaranteed to be in the medicines.

He tells me all these various medicines ain't had no effect on his boils unless to make them bigger and better. He's going to try mixing up the medicines to see how they work.

Pinky Dick tries out the mixings, and these mixings has strange effects on him. One mixing makes him cry all night for a week, another makes him giggle like a young gal, and another gives him the ding-bats. What they don't do is to cure his boils.

Then he hears on the wireless about a book called "Treat Yourself at Home." This book claims to tell how to cure anything. Pinky Dick sends for this book, and when she comes to light there's another book sent with it called "Twenty Thousand Recipes," what tells how to make everything from varnish to backache pills. But it's all money thrown down a gutter, because Pinky Dick can't get separated from his cross.

Still, life ain't too crook on this Marlow Downs. The boss is a decent sort, always bringing out vegetables and fruit from the homestead garden every time he comes our way. One day he brings us two petrol cases full of grapes, and me and Pinky Dick has lowered the tide in one case by the next day when the station truck arrives and unloads three more cases of grapes.

The truck is driven by a character called Windmill Bill, this character having got his moniker through doing nothing else for years bar look after the windmills and well pumps. He's a bit worse off than Pinky Dick. He's got two crosses to carry around: one being that he can't talk, having been hit on the head by a cricket ball when he was a boy; and the other being that, if anyone as much as says how good a schooner of beer would go down, he has to rush to the office, demand his cheque, and do a get to Beaky Willi, who runs a pub up the river a bit.

His unreliability is somewhat worrying to the boss, who says Windmill Bill is the best man with engines and things he's ever known.

Now Pinky Dick and me we don't want no more grapes. We are sick of grapes by the time Windmill Bill arrives, but Windmill Bill works with his fingers telling us he's not taking them grapes back to the homestead, and that if we don't like 'em we can throw 'em to the chooks.

We thinks it's a sin to throw good grapes to fowls, and we don't know what to do about it until Pinky Dick remembers the "Twenty Thousand Recipes." After Windmill Bill has gone, he says: "We'll turn all these grapes into good wine. The book says to extract the juice by stamping on 'em with your boots off, like they make wine in France."

"We ain't in France," I says. "Wouldn't the end of a nice clean glass bottle do better?"

"Perhaps it would, Joe," he says. "Any'how, to the juice of the grapes we adds plenty of sugar, and then we lets her stand for three days, skimming off the suds every hour. After that we bottles her up, and plants her for a month to mature."

So me and Pinky Dick gets down to making the brew, and when we reckon she's ripe we bottles her and ties down the corks with string. Then we plants the bottles three feet deep in the chook house in case Windmill Bill comes along and should happen to smell 'em.

When the month's up me and Pinky Dick has forgot all about the brew. It seems that a extra strong batch of boils has given Pinky Dick something else to think about, and I'm kept busy mustering fat wethers for the drovers.

It is three months when I remembers the brew, time I'm ridng for home one day in the beginning of summer and thinking how good a schooner of beer would go down me dust-lined throat.

So when I arrives I says to Pinky Dick: "What about about a bottle of that grape wine we has planted in the chook house?"

"Too right!" he says. "I have clean forgot that distillery. She ought to be prime by now. Go and dig up a coupler bottles, and I'll hunt up them two glass pots what I pinched from Beaky Willi."

So I takes a shovel across to the chook house, and I digs up a coupler bottles, and feels glad to see the white ants ain't et out the corks.

Back in the kitchen I holds a jug ready, and Pinky Dick he points a bottle at the roof and gently eases out the cork. But nothing happens. It's the same with the other bottle. The brew is as flat as water down a well.

"No good to me," I says.

"Nor me, Joe," he says, disappointed. "I don't understand it. According to the book this brew ought to be well matured and pretty lively."

"Perhaps we ought to have done the juice extractin' with our feet, as the book says," I tells him.

"No, that ain't it," he says. "What I reckon she wants is a start off with something. You know, something to get her fermenting, like I has to put a little old yeast in new."

"Well, we ain't got no old wine to give her a kick off," I tells him.

"We have not, Joe," he says, slow. "But I has medicines containing alcohol, and what this brew wants is a kick off with alcohol. You get in all them other bottles."

So we uncorks the entire brew and pours her into a basin, and Pinky Dick he adds some of his medicines while I'm stirring her round. Then, to make sure of giving her a real good kick, he puts in a box of pills what he says contains opium.

After that, in case he thinks of putting in more dope and spoiling her, I suggests we re-bottles her. This we do, and I replant her in the chook house.

It seems that this brew's got a hoodoo on her, for the very next day the boss orders a muster of all the flocks for a severe culling, and by the time this job of work is done, me and Pinky Dick has forgot all about her again.

February is extra hot, and the feed is all burned dry, and all the stock is coming to the well every evening to drink. There's 8,000 sheep, thirty-odd horses and a bullock team, and, because the wind don't blow continuous, we has to run the petrol engine and pump for sixteen hours a day.

Then the pump goes cronk. Ordinarily this would mean ringing up the boss and getting Windmill Bill out quick, but this time Windmill Bill is up at Beaky Willi's pub on a prolonged bender, resulting from a motor car explorer offering him a smell of whisky.

The situation ain't usual, by no means, and, when the boss runs up to Beaky Willi's joint, he has to kidnap Windmill Bill.

In due course the boss arrives with Windmill Bill, and Windmill Bill he shakes his head every time the boss asks him to go down the well and mend the pump. He can't say this with his fingers, because his hands are shaking too much, and the boss and us don't like getting too near him, because he has not washed all the time he has been away. No one can't say that Windmill Bill is normal. He's due for a bout of the ding-bats, and he knows it, and we all know it.

Me and Pinky Dick can't understand how it is that the boss is such a flaming fool not to have brought a bottle of whisky with Windmill Bill, to sort of keep him going until he has mended the pump. A man in his condition can't cut off sudden like, any more than an ordinary man can be cut off sudden like from air. And there's all them sheep and horses and bullocks fighting for water at the troughs when there ain't no water in 'em.

However, we does our best to persuade Windmill Bill to go down the well. He's sitting in the kitchen with his head between his hands, and he's so used to telling us he won't go down that he's shaking his head continuous.

There's the boss promising to take him right back to Beaky Willi's if he'll mend the pump. There's Pinky Dick offering him a pannikin of strong coffee laced with chlorodyne, what he won't take, and what I'm trying to persuade him to gollop down.

Then all of a sudden I remembers the wine we has buried in the chook house, and I says to Windmill Bill: "If I give you an extra good stiffener right now, will you repair that pump?"

He holds up his head, and in his eyes I seen the look of a famished dog being offered a round of beef. He tries to tell me something with his fingers, but he can't work 'em properly. Then he stops shaking his head and nods, and me and Pinky Dick we goes across to the chook house and digs up the entire brew.

Back in the kitchen me and the boss and Windmill Bill, we stands around Pinky Dick. He cuts the cork string, then he points the bottle to the roof, and then he eases out the cork with finger and thumb. Bang! The cork hits the roof. So does the wine. It rises like a fountain, and, before I can grab a jug, nearly all of it has gone.

"Ah!" say Pinky Dick. "She's got the kick of a mule in her. Hi, Bill! What-in-'ell you doing?"

We regards Windmill Bill with interest. He is running around the kitchen with his head well back. His mouth is full open, and he's catching the wine what's dropping off the roof. He looks peculiar to me.

Then Pinky Dick has an idea. He puts the next bottle in a basin, and holds her there with one hand while he loosens the cork with the other; meantime I'm holding another basin upside down over the bottle. In this way we gets all the brew into the bottom basin, and I must say she is flaming somewhat although she does look a bit green.

We has to grab Windmill Bill and stop him collecting drops falling from the roof. We sits him down and put a pint of our brew in his hands, and then we leave him to himself while he samples the wine.

I likes this grape wine. She tastes all right, even though she don't taste like any wine I ever has drunk. The boss says she's a good brew, and me and Pinky Dick agrees. So we all has another round, lapping it down like it was beer.

Presently Windmill Bill stands up and says: "Me life's saved. Gimme another, and I'll mend ten flaming pumps."

"No more till you've mended the one here," says the boss who is roaring with laughter at Windmill Bill. Pinky Dick is now doing a tap dance, and I'm surprised by the early effects the brew is having.

"Only one more, boss, and I'll mend that pump if she's down a well six miles deep," pleads Windmill Bill.

I'm looking at him, and I'm stonkered. For the first time in me life I'm hearing Windmill Bill speaking. I remarks about this, but no one takes any notice of me. So I grabs the boss and gets him to stop laughing, and then tells him about Windmill Bill speaking. Windmill Bill is now reciting "The Face On the Bar-room Floor."

"You're drunk, Joe," says the boss. "You're speechless drunk."

And I know he's right, although I can stand up, and I can see straight. I can open me mouth, and move me tongue, but I can't make no sound. It don't appear natural to me, and I'm not very pleased about it. So I tries another pannikin of wine just to see what will happen, and nothing does happen because I goes to sleep on the kitchen table.

When I revive I find the sun is going down. I can hear Windmill Bill reciting poetry. I can't see Pinky Dick from where I am on the table. I feels all right, and I can talk all right. I ain't had no dream about Windmill Bill getting the use of his tongue for there he is gabbling off poetry as fast as he can.

"Where's the boss?" I asks him.

He stops reciting long enough to tell me that the boss has gone back to the homestead. Then he tells me that he has repaired the well pump and that the engine is raising water for the stock. I asks him where Pinky Dick is, and he tells me Pinky Dick is outside looking for his boils.

I goes outside and I finds Pinky Dick standing in the red sunlight. He is quite naked and he's admiring himself with a mirror in each hand.

"What're you doing?" I says.

"I'm looking for me boils," he says, sort of hopeful.

I can't see no boils. They has all gone down. Pinky Dick looks like a sheep what's just been shorn. He's sort of dazed.

"It was that brew," he tells me. "I feels me boils going down when I'm drinking me second pint of that brew. She's the greatest boil-curer ever invented, Joe. D'you remember just what medicines we put inter her?"

I don't remember, and he don't remember. But he never has no more boils, and Windmill Bill he gets to be the greatest talker in the Outback. In fact, later on he gets into Parliament.

The Vital Clue

Now me, I'm carrying the old blue out from White Cliffs when I'm overtaken by a character called Communist Joe. Actually, he ain't no more communist than I am, and I knows this because me and him was in same batt. during the last World Argument. Even in them days he used to Hoch der Kaiser when a brass hat came along, just to annoy him. There's lots of characters like him; they must be agin the government.

Communist Joe has a utility truck what was born in the Year One, and what he give five quid for and made to go for another couple. He's looking for rabbit trapping, and a part of his stock-in-trade is eighteen alleged kangaroo dogs. He's going my way, and so there is me and him and the eighteen dogs and traps and gear all piled on to this truck.

Presently he says: "I'll have to be careful about the likes up at Wintersloe. Braid, the boss, has a habit of chucking out baits all over the scenery, and among me pack is a particular extra special tike what I wouldn't have poisoned for all the tea in China."

What he tells me about this Braid indicates that the squatter don't like dogs, and that Communist Joe don't like him.

"Ruddy capitalist," he says. "You wait till the workers of the world rise in their wrath and takes over the means of production and expenditure. We gonna make the bosses do all the work then. And if they won't work, d'you know how we're gonna make em? I'll tell you how we're - Why, talk of the devil! Here comes Braid now, headed for The Cliffs."

Now I see coming towards us another utility truck. She's not like ours, all lashed together with fencing wire and things. She shines and glints in the sun and I knows she is a Rolls Royce among utilities. Communist Joe steers our flying bedstead off the track and lets her stop, and the flash utility stops alongside.

"Good day, Mr. Braid," says Communist Joe. "Nice day, ain't it? Got any rabbits on Wintersloe you wants lifted?"

Now this Braid's character don't seem to please me. He's hard and lanky, and he's got a face like twenty-to-four, and eyes what are pale blue and never smile. He says something, but we don't know what because the stock-in-trade is all giving tongue at once. So he gets to ground and walks around eyeing the dogs like he don't approve of them, and then he says: "Them dogs all yours?"

"Too right," replies Communist Joe. "Everyone of 'em is a expert on catching rabbits. I trained 'em meself - plenty of stamina - plenty of toe - cast-iron feet. There's no poison laid along this track, is there?"

"Not that I knows of," says Braid. "Looking for rabbits, eh? Well, you can camp at my shearing shed tonight and see me in the morning. I can put you on to plenty of rabbits."

Off he goes, and after we get way on Communist Joe says to me: "Nice sort of bloke, Mr. Braid. Lots of these station bosses is given a crook name what they don't rightly deserve."

And he goes on telling me about good bosses until he remembers he's supposed to be a communist.

In due course we arrives at the boundary gate of Wintersloe Station, and we ain't gone two miles when we comes on a white-whiskered old bloke sitting on his swag beside the track and crying. We stops at this unordinary sight. Our mongs yap and bark, and the old bloke looks up at us and then goes on crying. So we gets down and asks the elderly character what's he's crying for.

The elderly character don't seem able to speak, but he jerks a thumb back over his shoulder and we then sees what seems to be a small grave.

After a bit, he says, between yowls: "It's me dog. She took a bait. I couldn't save her."

Then he hollers a lot more, and Communist Joe and me looks at him, then at the eighteen alleged kangaroo dogs on the utility. Then we sits down beside the old bloke and rolls a smoke to give him time to come to. Presently we hears the beginning of a serial story.

It seems that the elderly character once had a canine called Lizzie, and, this Lizzie being a pretty good sort of sheep worker, he's on his way to a shepherding job up near Wanaaring. He's highly delighted because it's going to be the first job he's had in ten years.

He meets Braid, and Braid stops and asks him where he's

going. He asks Braid if there are any baits along this public road crossing Wintersloe Station, and Braid tells him what he told us. Braid ain't out of sight when Lizzsie throws a fit and turns it in, in spite of all the old character does for her. Now without Lizzie the old bloke's chance of the job is Buckley's.

Having heard the end of the serial, me and Communist Joe arises and does a bit of prospecting. We locates right close about a dozen red-meat baits just beside the track what must have been chucked out by Braid as he was driving along. Probably he had a bucket-full of baits beside him, and scattered 'em with one hand, right and left of the track. When me and Communist Joe goes into conference about this, I get a sort of inside picture of what a real communist ought to be if he ain't.

"There ain't no law against a man chucking baits about on his own land," says Communist Joe. "But it ain't right for him to throw baits aside a public road crossing his land, no matter if there's a million wild dogs on his property."

"What shall I do?" yowls the old character. "Me and Lizzie's been mates for seven years, seven long years. We et together, and starved together. We -"

"You shut your gob, grandfer, and come along with us and camp at the Wintersloe shed," Communist Joe tells him. "I'll give you a dog out of my pack what's that intelligent that he'll round up a mob of sheep every time you spits. He'll do it without barking, too. And at night when everything's nice and quiet and you want a bit of mutton."

So the old bloke, he gets up with us and we arrives at the shed about an hour before sundown. We separates the stock-in-trade and chains 'em to stumps and things, and while I'm knocking up a feed, Communist Joe fills up the petrol tank from the drums he's carrying, and attends to the oil and things, all ready for the morning. The elderly character discovers five pups in a box, and he's sitting on the ground and arguing with the mother and the five pups as though he's enjoying himself. It's evident that he likes dogs.

Now the situation of this shearing shed is like so. You comes to a cross road and you takes the left turn to hit the shed half a mile from the main track, and this shed is built beside a creek, and being that it's late March the place is surrounded with dead leaves and sticks and fallen branches. It you takes the right hand turn at the cross roads you reaches the homestead in less than a mile.

We're eating dinner when Communist Joe says: "The dirty hound, throwing baits out along the track like he done. It's agen the law, but the law's on the side of the bosses every time. It we went to the police about it they'd call us liars and threaten to put us inside. Downtrodden, that's what we are. Slaves of the capitalists. They grow fat on the sweat of the working man, but the time's gonna come - Ah - I got a scheme."

I wants to know all about this scheme, but his trap gets shut, and I sees that his brain is working hard. The old character is feeding the pups and the bitch with one hand and himself with the other. I likes dogs, but not at meal time.

And when we goes to doss, the mother and her five pups all sleep with the old bloke what is talking to 'em like they was a lot of kids.

I see it is three o'clock in the morning by the stars when Communist Joe wakes me and Grandfer and tells us he has decided not to go rabbiting on Wintersloe Station, but make for the Queensland border. After breakfast we packs up and parks the stock-in-trade on the truck, and the pups in their box, and, when everything is Jake for the road, Communist Joe he goes into the shed and is there a bit. When he comes out I see he has left a dull light inside, and I'm highly delighted because I know he's left a burning candle on top of a pile of dead leaves and bits of greasy wool and oily wood and things. That bit of candle will give us a good start.

We all get into the utility, and Communist Joe winds her up and climbs up to the wheel. Afterwards I come to remember that immediately we starts we runs over a tree branch, and this branch snaps and a bit of it hit the underside of the truck pretty hard.

The old character is grumbling at the early start, but his mind is took off the subject by Communist Joe, who tells him to see that the pups in the box is all right. They gets talking about these pups, and I seen how artful Communist Joe is by taking the old bloke's mind off the light we left behind us in the shed.

We proceeds in good order, and I'm looking at the green dawning of the new day along the horizon when the engine splutters and finally conks out.

We've only come a mile and a half, and we don't aim to be held up at that distance from the bit of candle burning on top of a heap of oily rubbish. Communist Joe gets down and fiddles with the engine gadgets, but when nothing happens, me and the old character gets down, too.

Then the old bloke goes wandering round the back of the utility, talking to the dogs, and he strikes a match and lights his pipe, and then he throws the match, still alight, to the ground.

Things happen what I don't expect. There is a loud "woof" sound, followed by a terrible explosion. The bonnet of the truck falls down on Communist Joe's neck. The elderly character falls down hard, and the stern of the utility sort of sags somewhat. What I don't understand is the line of fire stretching back along the track we come from the shed. It is all very astonishing.

As there is a lot of flame under the truck, we all has to hurry to rescue the dogs, and the old bloke is in the way because his mind is on the pups in their box. We got no time to take anything else off the truck when the petrol drums explode like they was four-point-nine Howitzers.

From information received at a later date, it is these petrol drums what causes our misfortunes.

Braid, sleeping on his homestead verandah, is woke up by the explosion. He sees the glare of the burning truck in the sky, and he sees the reflection of the line of fire from the truck back to the shearing shed. This excites him a bit, and not stopping to dress, he drives his utility to the shed, where he finds the ground well alight at the place where our utility was parked for the night.

With a branch he manages to stop the fire spreading to the shed. Then he sees the light inside the shed and he finds the candle and does some thinking.

Having blown out the candle, all he has to do next is to follow the road on which there is still little puddles of fire, and so on until he arrives where we are thinking hard and quick.

Any fool can connect us with the lighted candle in the shearing shed. The stern looking character on the bench down in Broken Hill didn't find no difficulty, anyhow, and we all get six months for attempted arson.

It was that branch we run over at the start that morning. It put a hole in the petrol tank what laid a trail of petrol until the engine conked out. This trail gets all lit up when Grandfer dropped his match at our end of it.

Did he mind doing time? Oh no! Communist Joe tells him when we're all in the dock, that he can have the pick of the pups when we gets out again - plus that particular dog what rounds up a mob of sheep at night without barking, when a feller wants a bit of mutton.

Where DID the Devil Shoot the Pig?

According to my old mother, back in the Year One, the Devil went out on hunt for bad boys, and after travelling around for some time because I was in bed with the mumps, he sat down for a smoke and a drink of tea. He was thus engaging himself when he saw, not far away, a nice fat pig belonging to a character by the name of Pat McRory, and, being just the Devil, he ups with his gun and lets drive. It appears that the Devil is a rotten shot and after letting out a roar of anguish, the pig gets up to full speed and heads for home and glory, arriving with his nearside fore-trotter pretty badly wounded. He might have got over the effects of this wound if Pat McRory hadn't lost his temper and gone chasing after the Devil to beat him up - the result being that McRory didn't catch the Devil and found the pig dead when he got back. After that every pig has the marks of the gunshot on his nearside fore-trotter - according to my old mother who used to like pigs.

Now I'm telling this bit of history to a character called Paroo Jack. This Paroo Jack's boundary riding with me at Ethel Downs at the time. It turns out that his old mother has told the same yarn with the difference that the pig was owned by John O'Connor and was shot by the Devil on the offside fore-trotter.

He's a bit of a know all, this Paroo Jack, and he tries to tell me that all pigs bear the mark on their offside fore-trotters, not on the nearside fore-trotter, and that he has seen the marks on all the pigs he has taken a bird's-eye-view of.

"Bet you a quid to a shilling the mark's on the offside fore-trotter," he says, and me, being pretty sure the other way round, raises the betting to ten quid to one in favour of the mark being on the nearside fore-trotter.

Before we goes to bunk that night we're betting in thousands, and by the next night the betting has reached millions of quids. Eventually, to settle the argument, we decides the only way is to go and have a deck at Butcher Falk's pigs down at Willtonia about ninety miles away.

We are still engaged in this argument about a week later when the boss arrives, and we puts it to him to save further loss of energy. He tells us he ain't interested in pigs, and is most interested in sheep, and have we seen them on the run he's been paying us to see.

When he finds out that we have been too busy discussing where the Devil shot the pig to take time off to do any boundary riding, he loses his temper and takes us to the homestead for our cheques.

I don't like this very particularly, and I'm not pleased to have to walk ninety miles in February down to Willtonia to settle this pig argument and spend me cheque what I likes to save up big for a proper bender down at the Hill.

Time we're on the track, headed for Willtonia, I'm tired of pigs and devils and things, and I wish I'd never begun it and had never seen such a character as Paroo Jack. He gets a bit wearing, as the saying goes, and by the time we hits Willtonia we both stood to win or lose £10,541,000.

We arrives at Willtonia on the third day from Ethel Downs, about four o'clock, when the sun's red hot and the temperature up to around a hundered and eighteen in the shade what we haven't had any of. Naturally, at this moment the subject of pigs is not so important as is the subject of schooners of beer, and so we makes for the Willtonia Rose what's run by a character called Percy the Pirate.

It being a habit, so to speak, we hands our cheques across to Percy the Pirate, tells him to tell us when they're cut out, and calls all hands to assist us in lowering the temperature of our thirsts.

This having been accomplished, I says to the mob: "Where DID the Devil shoot the pig?"

There follows a short kind of silence, and then Ted Longbridge says: "Ah! I've heard that one. I have. The Devil shot the pig on the nearside rump."

"No, he didn't," shouts Paroo Jack. "He shot him on the offside fore-trotter."

"You're wrong," says a character, the name of which I haven't heard. The Devil shot him on the offside rump."

"I tell you it was on the nearside rump," shouts Ted Longbridge. "Bet you a level quid he did."

Now me, standing to win or lose more'n ten million quid, I

don't enter into this argument, but I notes that any time I downs a schooner of beer the betting is going up and up and seems like to get level with me own.

Then Percy the Pirate yells: "Come on you gory blanks. Time's up."

When the betting in general has reached about what Hitler and his gang has pinched, I suggests that we all go and have a look at some of Butcher Falk's pigs to settle this argument once and for all.

"But he ain't got no pigs," says an elderly character called Squinty Bill who can't never show you if he's looking at you or up the chimbley. "He took 'em all down to the Hill last week because of the rise in prices."

"But he didn't send the boar down," says Percy the Pirate.

"Betcher he did," yells old Squinty Bill.

"All right. I'll bet you -" begins Percy the Pirate, like he's wanting to be in the fashion, when who comes in but Butcher Falk.

He tells us that the boar didn't go down to the Hill with the other pigs, that this boar is getting on in life and is pretty sick. Notwithstanding, this animal is a prime pig what he values more'n his wife, and as this old pig has got in the habit of remaining inside his sty and dislikes being disturbed, he ain't going to be disturbed by no argumentative fools talking about what they don't know. Every young gal would know that the Devil shot the pig in the tail, which is why all pigs tails is crooked.

This don't seem to get us near to settling the bets, and as Butcher Falk got his moniker not because of his butchering business but because of his fights in the ring, no one talks out of turn with regards to his boar.

The dinner bell goes off, and those of us who's staying at the Willtonia Rose goes along for tucker, and to argue where the Devil shot the pig all the time we're eating. We then carries the argument to the bar, and continues while the sun goes down in the flaming red sky, and the mercury goes on up in the thermometer.

"Tell you what," says Squinty Bill. "I got one of them electric torches in me swag, and I votes that after Butcher Falk has gone to bed, and is well asleep, we all goes along to the boar's sty and ruxes him around so's we can take a bird's-eye-view of him to see just where the Devil DID shoot the pig. You'll see then that I'm right, and that the pig was shot just above the right eye."

We agrees that this ain't a bad idea, and we also agrees that we'll have to make sure that Butcher Falk is asleep before we examines his boar.

As per usual, the sergeant comes in to make sure only blokes staying on the premises is in the bar, and he has a couple, and says he don't take the slightest interest in pigs, and don't care two winks about pigs, except when they're on his plate in slices with a coupler eggs.

After he's gone old Squinty Bill does a bit of prospecting, and returns to tell us that the sergeant is in his cot, and that Butcher Falk is competing with his wife in the snoring line.

So away we go up along the only street where there's no lights in any of the houses what has all doors and winders open to let in the air. I find myself travelling alongside a corrugated iron fence, and through a hole in this fence, and across a fair-sized yard, to where I can hear the boar grunting and snoring at the same time.

I can also hear a sort of pumping engine at work close handy, and when I remarks to Percy the Pirate about this engine being at work at this time of night, he tells me it ain't no engine at all but Butcher Falk and his wife having a bit of shut-eye. All I can think of is that I'm mighty glad neither of 'em is boundary riding with me.

Anyway, to get on with the doings, I find myself against what is a pretty large canegrass shed in the corner of a small yard, and this canegrass shed has a roof on it to protect the boar from the sun. This roof is pretty solid and is kept down with fencing wire.

Percy the Pirate and Paroo Jack gets to shooing the boar out into his yard so's Squinty Bill can shine his electric torch on him, but the boar only grunts and does some low squealing like he's annoyed at the interruption. He don't come out, which is a bit annoying, so presently Paroo Jack says we'll have to make a hole in the low roof and prod him out into his yard.

This hole takes a bit of doing, but presently we has made one big enough for a man to stick his head in. Then we gives Percy the Pirate a stick, and he pushes this stick through the hole, and then we lift him up so's he can get first his arms and then his head through the hole, and so be able to prod the boar out into his yard.

We can hear the boar getting annoyed somewhat, and we can hear Percy the Pirate sounding like he's not enjoying himself in the position he's in.

We hears afterwards that the boar got his stern into one corner of his hut and wouldn't budge, and, when he grasps Percy's stick in his jaws and wrenches it out of Percy's hands, there ain't nothing else to do at this stage but to pull Percy out of the hole in the roof.

We goes into conference then, and Paroo Jack suggests that we pushes him into the hole with the electric lamp which he could shine on the boar, and so tell where the Devil shot the pig. This don't seem fair to me, and I says so. So we elects the strange character, who has no betting interest in the boar, to take a deck with the torch.

Squinty Bill shows him how to work it, and while this is being done they drop it and it goes bung.

"Shove me up," says the strange character. "I got a box of matches, and I'll see him with them."

We lifts him up by his legs, and he's got the matches in his hands, which has to go through the hole first before his arms and his head.

Presently he gets in the right position, and we can see through the cracks in the canegrass walls that he's striking matches, and we can hear him cursing at the boar to get it to turn round so's he can look at him properly.

Then we hears him give a low yell, and he begins to kick his legs around, and we think the boar has taken a running jump at him or that he's suffocating. Anyway, we hauls him out, and he is all excited and stuttering, and can't make us understand what happened.

Then we sees a light inside the shed getting brighter and brighter, and this unknown character he tells us he has accidentally dropped a lighted match which has set fire to the entire joint.

"I'm getting," says Paroo Jack.

"So'm I," says Percy the Pirate and the others.

We all does a get for the gate in Butcher Falk's yard, and when nearing this yard I remembers the situation of the boar, and thinks that it's a bit thick to leave him there to roast after having so rudely disturbed his slumber, as the saying goes.

Having arrived at this conclusion, I slips back and opens the sty gate, and I'm just getting away from this gate when I'm followed by the boar who don't seem to like the idea of the flames and things behind him.

Now in the light made by the burning shed I has a good chance to seeing just where the Devil did shoot the pig, but, you see, in this same light I also observes the boar's tusks and the look of annoyance in his eyes what are small scarlet disks. Having lost interest in the Devil's shooting, I makes a bee-line for the corrugated iron wall what is nearer to me than the yard door.

I'm on top of this iron wall when I seen the boar enter Butcher Falk's house by the back door. He's going pretty fast, and I'm very pleased to see his stern quarters and not his front part.

All of a sudden the steam pump shuts off. I hear Mrs. Falk let out a screech, and then I hears Butcher Falk emit a roar, and I thinks it best to get down from this iron wall and be satisfied with what I have seen and heard.

I hears behind me more screeches and Falk's roaring, and I hears a lot of crockery falling about. I can hear the boar squealing, and then I hears Mrs. Falk let out a extra special screech caused, I'm afterwards told, by the boar walking over her to get at the front door.

Me, I'm back at the pub and in bed in four ticks, and I refuses to pretend to be awake when the entire township is running up and down the street, some trying to capture the boar, others trying to get away from it.

In the morning I am told that the boar went bush, but I don't go out looking for him, it's that hot and the beer is that good.

They never find the boar from that day to this, although at odd times blokes have crossed his tracks away out on Shaw's Lagoon. I'm not really interested in pigs, and I wasn't sorry to see that boar do a get and so cancel all the bets laid on him.

In fact, I never did care where the Devil shot the pig. Sheep is more in my line.

That Cow Maggie!!

Now me, I'm working for a squatter called Lousy Lazarus, account of him being a bit mean with the men's rations, and it's this Lazarus and a cow called Maggie what puts me on tramp at a time when work's scare and the weather cold and nasty.

I gets took on as the station groom, and among the cows to be milked and separated is a cross between a Jersey and a Hereford, what behaves herself only when she's in the bail. Before and after she's bailed she's likely to charge a man and more'n once it's me for the yard rails at full speed, and no pause to light me pipe on the road.

Any cranky, vicious beast - no matter if it's a horse, a cow, or a camel - was made vicious in the first place by ill-treatment. They wasn't born vicious. After a lot of trying I got Maggie sort of fond of me by slipping her a spud or two at milking time.

Mind you, she never took to no one else.

The beginning of the unpleasantness came about when a new governess arrives to look after the boss's kids.

Me and Maggie and the other cows is making for the yards, kind of sauntering along the creek track what winds in and out among the box trees, and we're about a quarter of a mile from the homestead when Maggie gets a bird's-eye-view of the new governess.

She's sauntering along the track, too, but she's coming to meet us, and she's arrayed in polished top riding boots and riding breeches. It ain't the riding breeches and top boots what upsets Maggie, it is the scarlet hat and scarlet jumper.

She's a good looking gal, mind you, but no one can expect Maggie to know that when she's looking at a scarlet jumper and a scarlet hat.

I don't see this governess soon enough to draft her away. Maggie lets out a beller of rage and hate, wags her tail like a lion what's annoyed, and begins to shift.

Then I sees the new governess has seen Maggie, and the new governess can be active on her feet when she wants to. She don't pause any longer to admire the scenery, and she's up a box tree before me horse can get into a gallop, and before Maggie can arrive to beller and paw the earth and walk round and round the trunk.

I'm told to take the beastly cow away, but Maggie ain't the kind of cow to be taken away when she's getting an eye-full of scarlet jumper and red hat. It's no use yelling at her and flicking her with me stock-whip, and I gives up when she charges me horse and near horned her.

I might have managed her if I could have talked to her ordinary like, but I can't do this with the new governess in the tree listening to me, and Maggie don't understand polite conversation.

All I can do is ride to the homestead for a rope and a couple of hands to help me fix Maggie whiles the boss assists the new governess to the ground and tells her how sorry he is. He ain't that old he can't wink an eye at a pretty gal, and getting the new governess out o' the tree seems to please him a lot.

Any'ow, he takes her on back to the house, and when the others has departed I slips the rope off Maggie and makes a bee line for me horse, reaching the saddle before Maggie can get to her feet. After that it took me an hour to get her into the yard, but, once there, I had her in the bail in two ticks - with the help of a coupler spuds.

She's chewing these spuds and I'm milking her when Lousy Lazarus arrives to sit on top rail of the yard and tell me I'm to take Maggie to the butcher at Yundaroo, eighteen miles away. I am to get her started the next morning, meanwhile keeping her yarded and giving her a feed of chaff.

"Seems all right," I tells the boss, "but where am I to hand Maggie over to Butcher Neilson?"

"At the slaughter yards, of course," answers Lousy Lazarus. "He tells me he's hard up for beefers, and that brute is too dangerous to have around here any longer. You can take her through town. Neilson will have the street cleared until she's in the yards."

"I ain't going to manage her on me own," I argues. "What about someone to lend me a hand?"

"You can take Young Alec. I'll be wanting the other hands for mustering."

This don't please me, knowing Young Alec. He's nineteen and has no more brains than a galah excepting when he's planning a mischief.

We gets going next morning at sparrer-chirp, and it takes us three hours to get Maggie through the first gate what's only a mile from the homestead. By lunch time we still has fourteen miles to go. During the afternoon Maggie ain't too bad, and by five o'clock we come in sight of Yundaroo, where we has to pass through only the street to reach the butcher's slaughter yards.

All afternoon Maggie don't seem to be taking any interest in the scenery, but, once she sights Yundaroo, she wakes up. First she stops and glares at the place. I can see the hide along her back twitching. Then she paws the ground, and lets out a low, moaning beller of joy. Then she begins to trot forward like she's going to meet her calf.

Young Alec produces a grin of anticipation, but the prospect don't seem too normal to me. I knows Maggie too well.

So we nears the township at the trot. We seen people in the main street as we're arriving at the eastward end of it, and we seen all these people makes a dinny-aimer rush for the store and the Post Office and Police Station, they all being warned by Butcher Neilson, who's mounted on a piebald mare and who rides to the other end of the street so's to turn Maggie into his yards.

There's a pair of light draughts harnessed to a trolley outside the Police Station, and a bloke jumps up into the seat and gets that team going strong towards sunset. A fat man runs out of the store and across the road to where a flash motor car is standing and we don't see him no more. After that the joint looks like a Sunday morning.

By this time Maggie is looking for fight. She's travelling fair fast, holding her head low and bellering, and holding her tail out straight astern. We enters the street and, as she keeps dead centre of it, I hopes for the best.

"Better get her on the gallop," I says to Young Alec. "If she starts thinking, the pictures won't have a thing on her."

So we unlimbers our whips. The only thing Young Alec can do properly and be depended on doing good, is to crack his whip.

Our whips move Maggie onward, but she seems a bit too interested in the passing scenery to take any notice of us.

I can see four women and half a dozen kids looking at us over the top of an iron fence, and people looking at us from behind the pub winders. The sergeant and his two troopers are protected by the iron fence of the station. Too late do I see the fat man inside the flash car stamping on the pedals and trying to get it started.

If only he had kept still everything would have been jake. He kept on bobbing up and down while he's stamping on the pedals and Maggie sees him and becomes annoyed as is the usual.

We're just getting Maggie past the car when she turns sudden and rushes it, and don't stop until her horns have broke the side winder and her head's inside and she's blowing froth and bubbles at the fat gent. He shoots out of the other side to the sidewalk.

I don't understand why he stayed there, but it appears he can't make up his mind what to do or where to go until he views Maggie coming round the stern of the car. He makes for the store, although the pub is nearer. He's off like a rabbit, taking the street at an angle, and there's Maggie bellering and follering hard behind and doing all she knows to lick the back of his neck.

What can we do but yell and crack our whips? The street ain't wide enough to let a horse get into a gallop, and our mokes would have had to be galloping to catch up with Maggie and the fat man.

People in the store is watching the fat man arriving. They've got the door held ajar, and when the fat man arrives they swing it open and in he goes, and then they swing it shut.

It's only now that I'm aware of the 600 odd town dogs what's coming up hard behind Young Alec and me. I stops cracking me whip now that Maggie is facing a closed door, and I then hear the hounds right behind and reins in me horse.

But Maggie does not stop at the store door. She keeps going, and the next thing is that where the door was there's a large hole through which Maggie has passed. Now I'm sitting on me helpless moke watching the 600 dogs streaking through that hole.

There's Young Alec sitting on his moke like he's throwing a seizure or something. I can't see nothing to laugh at. The noise is terrible. Men yelling, women screaming, Maggie bellering, and all the dogs giving tongue; now and then a tearing, crunching sound; and then a dull sickening thud or two. All we can see is the dust coming out of the door.

The fat man comes out as he went in. He's follered by Mr. Mansfield, the storekeeper, apron and all. He's so excited that he can't say anything as he passes us. After that comes a dozen dogs, all yapping at his heels and thinking it's a great game. Then a coupler women appear with more dogs, and after that more dogs and more men. I don't understand it. It don't seem possible to me that the store could have held so many people and dogs and Maggie.

After a bit there's no more people and no more dogs to come out, and there we are waiting for Maggie. But she don't appear, and after a minute or two I gets off me horse and hands the reins to Young Alec with orders to hold him ready for quick mounting.

Nothing happens. I'm a bit careful approaching the hole, but presently I reaches one side of it and takes a deck inside.

All I can see is tins of foodstuff and brooms and rolls of cloth and frypans and things laying in a sort of heap of everything. Then I sees something moving, and I makes it out to be Maggie's tail. It's swinging gently from side to side and I can see her hind quarters. I don't see her head because it's held low, and I sneaks into the store and draws a bit near to her and sees what she's doing.

She's standing over a bag of spuds what's upset and chewing them up for all she's worth. When she sees me she gives forth a low beller of joy, like she was saying: "'Ullo, Joseph Henry. I've found my Paradise Delight."

It's wonderful what you can do with animals with a bit of kindness. All I had to do was to ferret out a few lengths of clothesline, make a halter round Maggie's head, fill me pockets with spuds, lead her out of the store and down the street to Butcher Neilson's yards.

But they didn't appreciate me as a animal tamer. No they wouldn't. They billed the boss with the damage Maggie done to the store and the fat man's car, and the boss goes and puts me and Young Alec on tramp when work is scarce and the weather cold and nasty.

The Great Rabbit Lure

Now me, I'm enjoying a short spell of peace and quiet boundary riding on Karpooroo, with old Rainbow Harry to cook for me, when out comes a character called Professor Hilary Death.

This Professor bloke is a sort of scientist, and he's dead set on killing all the rabbits in Australia what he tells us does fifty million quids worth of damage every twelvemonth.

Rainbow Harry tells him if that's his ambition in life he's come to the right place because within ten mile of the place is gathered all the rabbits in Australia, including them in the West what migrated over last winter.

When he goes to bunk that night, the Professor believes what Rainbow Harry tells him. After sundown we takes him out to see the beginning of the rabbits coming in to drink at the dam, and he's not the only gent present what's never seen so many rabbits before. Even me and Rainbow has been stonkered by the number of 'em.

The dogs won't look at 'em, and if I didn't stand over the hens with a waddy to keep the rabbits from pinching their tucker they'd have been starved to death long before.

Me and Rainbow don't take too well to this Professor character. We don't like the look in his eyes. He is tall and bony, and he has long-fingered hands like they was made to clamp on a man's throat. He looks at us like we was a pair of rabbits in a gin trap, and there don't seem nothing like home about the place any longer. As I read in a book once: he's a disturbing influence.

"I intend to tackle the great rabbit problem from an entirely new angle," he says while he's clenching and unclenching them long fingers of his. "The idea of exterminating rabbits by introducing a disease among them is bosh and balderdash, like making the tide rise by pouring a bucket of water into the ocean. My scientific colleagues are all men of small minds capable only of small ideas, and no one of them has thought to solve the problem of extermination by first studying the influences controlling their mass migrations.

"It is along this line of investigation that I hope to succeed. QUESTION: Why do rabbits abruptly migrate? ANSWER: Into the dry area made barren by a rabbit host the wind has brought the scent of new grass and watered earth from a distant place. IDEA: Produce a synthetic scent of new grass and watered earth. Place the origin of this synthetic scent within a vast wire-netted enclosure, and a rabbit host will be lured within to its final destruction. I think, gentlemen, I can produce the Great Rabbit Lure."

"Sounds all right to me," says Rainbow Harry. Then he pauses, lights his pipe and says: "As long as I ain't got to help make the trap yarding. It's much too hot to work in the sun."

"I shall require much netting and many men," says the Professor. "You lack imagination sufficient to visualise the size of a trap-yard capable of imprisoning all the rabbits in this locality. But first I must manufacture my lure and try it out in a small way. If that succeeds, then the experiment can be carried out on the grand scale."

After the Professor had gone to bunk under the nearby box tree, me and Rainbow Harry talks things over. He says, a bit narked like: "Live and let live is my motter. What 'arm's the rabbits done him, any'ow? I don't like it, Joseph Henry. What's the poor man gonna do without the rabbits tell me that?"

As I can't tell him that, I goes off to bunk and leaves Rainbow to make his bread batter for the next day. All that worries me is this interruption to me peace and quiet, for the very next morning the Professor begun to mess about with his bottles of dope and things. I has to bring in berries off'n the box trees what he boils all one day, and, what with this and the stuff in his bottles, the place seems to be surrounded by a vast stink what accompanies me all the time I'm riding me fences. What with the heat and the flies and this stink follering me around, life ain't worth living.

After a week of it the Professor tells us he has made his lure and will be trying it out the next day. He rings up the boss, and the boss tells me to stay at home the next day and help the Professor make his preparations. He'll be coming out in the evening to see how things are working

The next morning the Professor tells us he'll be wanting the use of the kitchen all the next afternoon, and that he'll be wanting a good supply of firewood inside and us to keep outside. And so it comes about that after lunch the next day me and Rainbow Hurry parks ourselves in the shade of the nearby box tree and waits for the circus to start, with the dogs and the four cats lying around us and panting in the heat. We're only a few yards off the kitchen door through which we can see the Professor going for the lick of his life with his bottles and things on the kitchen table and a roaring fire on the open cooking hearth.

"What's he want the bush fire for?" I asks Rainbow.

"He says he must have a chimbley," replies Rainbow.

"What's the chimbley for?"

"For the draught," replies Rainbow, quite narked. "He's made a bucket of thick paste what he's gonna put on a heap of red coals on the hearth. Reckons that'll produce a good smoke, and the draught will keep the fire from being put out by the paste. Any'ow, he's enjoying himself, and I'm not making no rabbit yards at this time of the year. Ratty, that's what he is."

All afternoon we lies around and smokes and waits. Now and then the Professor comes out to take a deck at the sun and the scenery, and then go in with another armful of firewood. It's hot enough where we are, and as the Professor ain't wearing nothing but short underpants and his eyeglasses it appears to be hot inside the kitchen, too.

About five o'clock, Rainbow says: "Looks like he's startin'."

Out of the chimbley is coming thick green smoke. We see this smoke rising about twenty feet before the very light winds gets a holt of it and carries it away to the east where it falls to the ground and goes rolling away like it was green water.

Out comes the scientific character, underpants and specks and boots. He looks for the sun to see the time, then at the surrounding scenery. When he seen the smoke coming out of the chimbley and rolling over the ground he begins to dance a jig and shout something about his great triumph over the nitwits what has been trying to squirt disease into rabbits down on some island or other. Then into the kitchen he goes and more smoke comes out of the chimbley.

"It doesn't look too natural to me," I says, spitting at a rabbit what's come to lie down with one of the cats. Me aim's crook and

I knows these goings on is unsettling me.

"I'm for the track in the morning and in for me cheque," snarls Rainbow. "I never did like Professors, and I don't intend to live with this one any longer. He's worse than a bloke getting off the booze. Pity he don't burn the ruddy place down. He will if he stokes her up much more."

We sees now that what wind there is has shifted round to the north and is carrying the smoke over the ground to the south as far as we can see. In less than half an hour the wind has done a full circle, and all around the trees and the sandhills is sticking up out of a green sea like they does above a mirage. The sun's getting low and I never seen the country looking like this before.

Rainbow says: "Look at them ruddy rabbits!"

I takes a deck at the rabbits in range and see them all sitting up and sniffing at the air like they do when the late summer rain comes. Our cockbird flies into the box tree and lets out a crow what he keeps up for two minutes without stopping, and as this is the first time he's crowed for nigh five months, me and Rainbow don't understand it.

After a bit the cats all begin purring and rubbing themselves against us. Then we seen the rabbits sort of drift into gangs and play chase-me-round-the-mulberry-bush. We hears the horses coming in to drink at the dam, coming in at the gallop, and after they has their drink they gallops out again, kicking their heels and neighing like they'd do if the end of a drought was coming.

I looks at Rainbow and he says: "Looks like that smoke stuff is gonna do the trick."

The boss rings up and wants to know how things are going, and, when I tells him they look to be going all right, he says he and the bookkeeper will soon be starting and hopes to arrive about nine o'clock. The Professor appears and regards the scenery in the red light of the setting sun. He does another jig and goes inside again. More green smoke comes bellering out from the chimbley.

The wind goes down and this green smoke falls down all round us and we can smell it. It don't smell too bad, either. Reminds me of watching a bloke cutting the grass with a motor mower down in St Kilda Gardens that time I'm taking a walk after a night before.

"Cripes! Look at the rabbits!" Rainbow says.

I am looking at 'em. Ordinary, they never gets on the move to come to the dam till it's nigh dark, but it ain't sunset yet and they're well on the run. There's something else funny about 'em, too. Other times me and Rainbow has often watched 'em running past the hut to the dam. This time they don't seem to be running to any particular place except running toward us through the green water covering the ground. We seen 'em coming from all directions, and the cock bird up the tree never stops crowing.

When the flaming sun sets at last, there ain't a breath of air. There's a sort of rabbit carpet all round us and the hut, and, to get a bit of peace, the hens join the cockbird in the tree and the cats they go up and join 'em. My old dog, Lizzie, comes and puts her nose under my arm and begins whimpering.

"Bust me insides!" says Rainbow, sort of stonkered like. "The old fool's dope is bringing all the rabbits in Australia straight to us."

Out comes the Professor to wave his arms and jump up and down with excitement. He's frothing at the mouth and yelling at the top of his voice.

"Success! Success! Success!"

Then in he goes again and, a second after, more green smoke comes pouring out of the chimbley. Now it's getting dark, and he lights the lamps inside the kitchen, and we can see the rabbits going in, too. Then he slams the door shut and we hears him shouting to himself with glee. The rabbits is getting that thick that when I spit I can't help hitting one. They're jumping over our feet and sniffing at our clothes. Two of the dogs finds they can't stand it any longer, and they lets out howls of fear and does a get for open country.

"Things is getting serious," I says to Rainbow.

"Too right!" he replies. "Seems to me the tide's coming up fast, and I've a good mind to foller them dogs while the going is still possible."

Now it's quite dark and all around us we can hear a noise I ain't never heard before, and the smell of new-cut grass is gone and in it's place we smell a strong animal smell like something - like something terrible big and rotten. All of a sudden Rainbow lets out a screech and goes floundering away from me, and I comes to understand that we been sitting surrounded by rabbits almost up to our shoulders. I had enough. It's me for home and glory, but not without me swag.

It's no longer a matter of walking over to the hut room where I camps. It means walking on rabbits, living ones atop rabbits what's been suffocated, and I'm slipping and falling and getting up and falling down again until at last I reaches me room door. When I opens her I nearly break me neck stepping down into the room from the mass of rabbits outside, but I lights me lamp and then seen the rabbits pouring into me room like they was a flood, and I remembers that the kitchen door opens outward and that the mad Professor is inside the kitchen still stoking up the fire and shovelling dope onto the hot coals.

I forgets me swag and gets outside again. I finds the rabbit tide is half way up the kitchen door what I can't open, and away in the distance I hears the boss hollering and Rainbow hollering back at him, and I knows they're wide apart and well bogged.

Things is getting serious. I can't open the kitchen door to warn the Professor. I don't know what to do, and whiles I standing there I hears the boss wanting to know what in hell's gone wrong and Rainbow Harry telling him what he thinks has gone wrong, and they're half a mile apart. It seems that both of 'em has decided to make for the homestead what's ten miles away, and neither of 'em knows where the car is. The bookkeeper seems to be somewhere in the opposite direction, and I wonder what he's doing away there.

Next thing I do is break open the kitchen winder. There's the Professor scooping dollops of his mixture out of a bucket with his hand and throwing it onto the fire what's roaring up the chimbley. He's talking something about showing the nitwits how to exterminate rabbits, and, when I tell him that if he don't quit at full speed, he's gonna be drowned by the rabbits, he picks up a chunk of firewood and heaves it at me.

What can I do? It's me for the open country as soon as I can get there and no pausing on the way to blow me nose. I falls down and the lamp goes out. I can hear the Professor yelling at the nitwits and their stupid ideas of squirting vaccines into rodents, but I'm taking less and less interest in him and more and more interest in getting clear before the arriving rabbits bog me and suffocate me.

For hours I climb hills of rabbits and roll down into the valleys. After a bit I don't hear the boss and Rainbow cursing the Professor and the rabbits any more. I get choked with fur fibres. I get bit on the face and hands every time I falls, and I suppose it's only me bushman's instinct that keeps me going straight till at last I gets clear and can run.

Time daybreak comes I'm five miles away to the north of the camp. All around me I sees rabbits running south towards the camp. Me three dogs has found me, and we all walk back to the camp to see what's doing, and to find the boss and the car and so get on to that homestead where there's me cheque's waiting.

But there ain't no camp. There's only a mountain of rabbits. Inside the mountain is the hut, and inside the hut is the dead Professor, suffocated as I told him he would be.

I joins up with Rainbow and the boss and the bookkeeper, and me and Rainbow gets our cheques and goes down to the Hill to recover from the shock we had.

Led by a Child

Detective-Inspector Morley swiftly surveyed this most regal apartment of Beechgrove College, the half-dozen reprints of the least innocuous of Hogarth's etchings, the cases of books reaching half-way up every wall, the luxuriously deep pile on the floor, the wide writing table set against one of the two tall windows, and, finally, the man seated at the table, sprawled forward over the papers - dead.

"I have given only a cursory examination, Inspector. I have not disturbed the body," stated Doctor Cummins. "Not in your sphere, I think. I have been expecting this, for Doctor Watts had suffered from heart trouble for the last two years. You see, I was his medical advisor."

"You think it was just heart failure?"

"Yes, I think so now. Of course, I cannot give a definite opinion until -"

"Naturally. Finished with your camera, Stevens? Very well. Assist the constable to carry the corpse into that ante-room. Let me have the result of your examination as soon as possible, Doctor."

Rigor mortis having already taken place, the long and heavy ebony ruler clutched in one dead hand was with difficulty freed, and placed on the writing table. It was laid down on the edge of a pamphlet, and thus received the impetus which sent it over the table edge, to drop with a soft thud to the heavy carpet.

Not one of the four men in that death chamber noticed this: the doctor, hurrying to the ante-room; the police photographer and the constable, engaged in their tragic task; the inspector, gazing out of the window.

With the interest of the trained investigator, he saw that this famous school building was planned in the form of a U. The building was three-storied. The room in which he stood, the late headmaster's study, was on the ground floor, occupying the inside corner of the left wing. Opposite, some fifty yards distance, was the inside extremity of the right wing.

The constable, emerging from the ante-room, was dispatched

for the maid who discovered the dead man. He left the door ajar, and a black cat came in. When he returned with the uniformed maid, she was politely asked to be seated on a chair near the door. The inspector moved a chair for himself, so that he came to face her.

"At what time did you discover your master?" was the first question.

"At seven-thirty, or perhaps a few minutes after. I took the doctor's morning tea to his bedroom, as usual, and found he hadn't been to bed. So I came here, and I - and I -"

"It must have been a shock," Morley said, kindly. "Never mind. Doctor Watts was married, wasn't he?"

"Oh, yes. But Mrs. Watts and the two youngest children are on holidays. You see, the school's closed as it is the spring term vacation. All the scholars are away, and the masters, too."

A slight noise behind Inspector Morley attracted his attention, but it was only the cat playing with the ebony ruler.

When again he turned to the maid, he said: "Am I to understand that some of Mrs. Watts' children did not accompany her?"

"Yes, that's right. Master John remained at home because he was naughty. He and the doctor were to have joined Mrs. Watts next week."

"Hum! All right."

The maid departed, the constable on guard at the door politely letting her out. Morley strolled towards the ante-room, his mind accepting the tragedy due to quite natural causes. And then he noticed the black cat lying at full length beneath the writing table, the ebony ruler but a fraction of an inch beyond its fore paws. It was still, significantly still. With hands clasped behind his back, the detective regarded the animal with pursed lips. Then he bent down closer to examine the cat. Without doubt it was dead.

The constable was outside the door talking to someone. The photographer was in the ante-room with the doctor. Morley placed the waste paper basket in such a position that it partially concealed the little animal. The ruler he did not bother with. For the first time in eleven years a cigarette was smoked in this juvenile holy of holies.

"It is as I first thought, Inspector," stated the medico bustling into the room. "Heart failure. I think it quite unnecessary for an autopsy. I am prepared to sign the certificate."

"Plenty of time. Did you notice anything peculiar about the dead man's right hand, the palm?"

"Yes, there is slight discolouration. Blood contusion due to muscular contraction clamping the hand round the ruler."

Morley nodded his dark head slowly.

"I suppose that was it," he said, a distinct pause between each word. "Oh, well, that lets us out."

The dismissed photographer followed the doctor, and, still in a thoughtful mood, Morley locked the ante-room door, pocketed the key, made sure the windows were fastened, and then passed out into the hall, there to lock the library door and pocket that key, too.

To the maid, who obviously had been talking to the constable, he said: "Is there a matron or housekeeper in charge of the domestic staff? There is? Please ask her to come and see me."

The housekeeper proved to be a coldly efficient woman above middle age, and Morley's first question to her was: "Do you know if Doctor Watts had an enemy?"

"Er - no," she replied, with slight hesitation.

"Come, now. With me you may be quite candid."

Seeing Morley's black gimlet eyes boring into her, her efficient manner relaxed.

"I - I am not sure, mind you," she said hurriedly, "but I believe there was an upset between the doctor and Mrs. Watts over Mr. Thomas."

"Oh! What about?"

"I don't rightly know, but we think Mr. Thomas was paying attentions to Mrs. Watts, and -"

"Mrs. Watts - young?"

"Oh, yes. Not thirty-five, and still good-looking. But, of course, we know nothing for sure. It may be -"

"What is this man Thomas?"

"He is one of the masters. They are all away on holiday."

From along one of the passages leading off the hall came the shrill voice of a small boy, and that of a woman scolding him. A maid and a little boy of perhaps six years came into the hall, halted to look at the group standing near the library door. Then the child eluded the maid's hand-clasp, and, running to the housekeeper, cried: "I didn't do anything very naughty, Mrs. Silver."

"What is all this?" demanded the housekeeper of the vexed maid.

"I was cleaning the upper sixth dormitory, Mrs. Silver, when I noticed Mr. Thomas' laboratory door open when it should have been shut and locked. And when I went to shut it, there I saw Master Eric playing with some of the - some of the machinery. He's been strictly warned -"

"I didn't do any harm. I only pulled down a lever," wailed the boy.

Inspector Morley smiled down at the tearful, chubby little face.

"Of course, you did not do any harm, son," he said gently. "You only pulled down a tin-pot lever. That's nothing. How long ago was it when you pulled down the lever?"

"I - I don't know. When I first went there. I was watching some bubbles going up in a red jar when I was brought away."

"All right, sonny. Don't cry any more. There is nothing whatever to cry about."

And then to the housekeeper, when the maid and child had departed: "This Mr. Thomas has a laboratory? He is, perhaps, the science master?"

"Yes. He is supposed to be very clever. He fixes the electric lighting and keeps the school's two wireless sets in order."

"Just now he is away on holidays?"

The woman nodded her head.

"Where?" demanded Morley impatiently.

"He went to Brighton, I think."

"You merely think? You're not sure?"

"Yes. Oh, yes. He went to Brighton. He took a furnished cottage there."

"Is he married?"

"No."

"Just between ourselves, he's in love with Mrs. Watts?"

Mrs. Silver nodded her head again, this time more vigorously.

Morley put to her another question. "In what part of the building is Mr. Thomas' laboratory?" he asked crisply.

"At the end of the other wing. Opposite the doctor's library."

Inspector Morley telephoned for Sergeant Telfer, the wireless operator of the night patrols, and on his arrival they were conducted to Mr. Thomas' private laboratory. The interior of this scientist's workshop entranced Sergeant Telfer, but at the end of an hour the inspector was becoming bored because he had found nothing of great interest, save an ebony ruler in one of the cupboards.

"Well, what do you know?" he snapped out at last.

"That the owner of all this is an astute bird, sir. He looks to me to be further advanced than Marconi. He's been concentrating on the transmission of wireless power. Looks to me as though he's connected with the electric mains. There is a bit of a mystery here, though. One switch is down when it should be in neutral."

"Be as well to put it back into neutral," Morley suggested. "A little boy pulled it down and killed a cat in Doctor Watts' library. We'll go down there now. I want to show you an ebony ruler just like this one - on the outside."

Mr. Thomas was astonished when they arrested him. It was proved to him, and later to a jury, that the ebony ruler Doctor Watts had been using for many years had been exchanged for a steel one painted to resemble ebony. From his cottage in Brighton, Mr. Thomas had surreptitiously entered the school after dark and watched from his laboratory window Doctor Watts at work in his library. When the famous headmaster was using the imitation ebony ruler - the steel one fitted with coils and electrodes - John switched on the electric power.

As Morley said, it was all very cleverly done. Brilliant scientific talent brought to the scaffold through illicit love not even reciprocated. It would have been the perfect murder had not a mischievous little boy opened the laboratory door with the key of another room, and then had impishly brought down that switch just in time to kill a rather nice-looking cat.

New Boots on Old Feet

People agreed that Marcus Budd's fall from grace was directly due to the pernicious influence of the crime story. His was not a case to attract wide publicity, and no criminologist of international standing ever devoted time to its study, but the thoughtful will probably reach the conclusion that it was not so much the detective novel as Budd's inherent vanity which prompted him to rob the one bank at Myme.

In appearance Marcus Budd was stockily built, and was, in these days of cleanskins, remarkable for his carefully trimmed blue-black beard, suggesting the sea and ships. Yet, had he removed the beard, the trick of closing his eyes for periods when talking would have supplied any policeman with ample means of identification. It was a mannerism betraying the vice of vanity.

This outback Australian rose from obscurity to local importance with the rise of the township of Myme, built near the Murchison gold mine of that name. BM, or before Myme, Markus Budd was, well, no one knew precisely what he had been. Those of evil mind whispered that he once had been a cattle duffer, and they pointed to his bow legs and mincing walk to support their nasty contention. Which, of course, was pure envy, for at the height of Myme's golden glory Marcus Budd owned the general store, the butchery and the ice works.

Comparatively abstemious for a mining centre citizen, Marcus Budd applied himself diligently to his various businesses by day, and usually spent his evenings with his fictional detectives and their super-villainous opponents. As the novels - always of the half-crown editions - finally entered his store library his reading cost him nothing.

Yet, from his reading, he profited nothing. He failed to learn the lesson of the crime story - reflecting that given by real life crime stories - that right triumphs over wrong mostly because all criminals are foolishly vain. For it is their vanity which creates the illusion that they can win a battle of wits with the law, armed by science.

That his favourite detectives always won their cases annoyed

Marcus Budd, as did the criminals who invariably committed stupid mistakes, which defeated them. When those mistakes were made Budd instantly saw them, and, figuratively, itched to lead the criminals by the hand and teach them how not to make mistakes.

Doubtless, from this thinking emerged the idea of robbing the bank. The owner of the general store, the butchery and the ice works was really not a criminal at heart. Vanity, not unbridled passion for gain, was the imp that drove him to disaster, for presently blazed determination to satisfy himself that he could successfully rob a bank.

And there was the Myme branch of an historic bank ready to his hands and brain, unprotected by a policeman, and often forgotten by the manager.

The eighth wonder of the world was the downward drift of John Abbott over the period of time which witnessed the rise of Myme and Marcus Budd. He was elderly, and he accepted the transfer to the Myme branch as banishment to Siberia. Without the sheet anchor of cultured society he drifted - downward. A more delightfully casual man never lived, even in those days when honesty was a virtue, and, in consequence, he was regarded with affection by all and sundry.

Now for the prospective crib. The bank building was a lock-up shop, situated opposite the store. It was frosted-glass fronted. The interior was divided by the wide plain jarrah counter, behind which stood a tallboy chest of drawers, containing the books, an ancient safe and a writing table, on which stood a mahogany cabinet, and two Windsor chairs. Beside the safe was the back door, opening up on a small yard enclosed with a corrugated iron fence, and during business hours throughout the summer this back door, like the front door, was securely wedged open.

There were many days of the week when the few streets of Myme were empty of life, save for the goats, during the bank's business hours, when all the men were absent at the mine, over the low hill, and all the women idled at home, and, as John Abbott had no liking for reading of any kind, there was only one avenue providing him with escape from boredom.

There were occasions when the bottle in the cabinet was empty. There were occasions, too, when a chance customer would suggest refreshment, and, the cabinet bottle empty or otherwise, poor Abbott would accompany the customer across the road to the hotel, leaving the bank doors wedged open and sometimes the safe unlocked.

It must be emphasised that Myme was just a sleepy little township, where everyone knew and trusted everybody, and the time when men were honest, the days before the universality of the crime story. Why, more than once John Abbott had to be called away from the hotel bar to assist collect the cheques and documents which a spiteful whirlie had blown out of the bank and along the street.

As all men in Myme, Marcus Budd was conversant with the bank manager's habits and failings. He knew that to the second, at noon and at three o'clock, John Abbott took refreshment between drinks at the hotel, and that usually between six to eleven in the evening he was holding forth in that same hotel.

As all men, Budd knew that the keys of the safe were often left in the lock, and that the bank doors were invariably wedged open during banking hours. And, as all men, Budd also knew that every Thursday morning at ten o'clock a clerk from the mine office would present to John Abbott an open cheque for some £200, with which to balance the mine's weekly pay sheet. And finally, as all men knew, Budd was aware that during Wednesday nights there was more money in the bank's safe than at any other time.

Having made careful plans, from which were excluded the mistakes in the plans formulated by fictional criminals, Marcus Budd selected a moonless and cloudy Wednesday night and robbed the Myme bank. He executed his plans without a hitch, and when, having disposed the money in a place of safety, he went to bed, he even more fully failed to withstand why stupid men shot their way again to freedom, only in the end to be caught and gaoled.

At half-past ten the following morning there arrived at Myme a police constable and a black tracker from Meekatharra. Thrilled, as never in his life had he been thrilled, Marcus Budd from the doorway of his store saw the constable enter the bank, watched him come out and beckon to the tracker. Later, Budd watched both policeman and tracker walk casually up and down the street, and finally disappear among the wind-tortured acacia bushes hiding away the low hill separating the mine from the town.

They returned about one o'clock. Whilst the tracker gazed pensively at the gutter in front of the store, the constable entered and pleasantly requested to be shown the stock of workmen's boots. He inquired if Budd did a large business in workmen's boots, and, on being assured that business in this line was fairly brisk, he and Budd strolled along to the hotel for lunch, followed by the black tracker, who still was controlled by the pensive mood.

At two o'clock Marcus Budd was arrested.

"What have you done with the money?" asked the curious policeman.

"What money?" Budd countered cleverly.

The constable sighed. "I suppose I shall have to explain it all to you," he said wearily. "One day - I don't know which - when Mr. Abbott was in the hotel you slipped over to the bank and made impressions of the keys which were carelessly left in the locks. You filed down blank keys to fit the impressions, and you were very careful that the filings didn't drop on the floor of your shop. You were careful that those filings dropped onto a sheet of paper, which you very carefully carried out of the shop and tipped into the gutter, where, this beautifully bright morning, they appear to the tracker like 20,000 Koh-i-nor diamonds.

"Because your foot size is number seven, you took from your stock a pair of number nine working boots, and you carried them to that large area of granite near the mine, where you changed them with those you were wearing. Wearing the number nines, you walked back to town over a little-used track, thinking we'd find those tracks easier, entered the bank when Mr. Abbott was at the hotel, pinched the money, and walked back the same way to the granite patch, where you changed back into your own shoes. To and from the granite patch in your own shoes you took the well-used road to the mine. You planned to cast suspicion on one of the mine workers."

"You've got imaginitus," Marcus said, sneeringly.

"Oh, yeh!" said the constable, who was a regular attendant at the Meekatharra pictures. "Well, I'll tell you some more. In those number nines you wore when robbing the bank there were seventeen hobnails in the right boot and nineteen hobnails in the left boot. In every other pair of your stock boots there are eighteen hobnails to the boot. I'll point out that bootmaker's error later, when you hand over the boots. The marks of the boots you wore are on the little-used track from and back to that granite patch, and the marks of the nails, Peter, the tracker, plotted in with indelible pencil on the wooden floor of the bank."

"Very interesting," Marcus Budd said, with his eyes shut.

"Too right," agreed the policeman. "Mistakes made by you clever fellers always interest me. I'll tell you a bit more, now that I'm feeling conversational, and then you can hand over the money and the boots, and we'll tool along to Meekatharra. When you first walked to the granite patch near the mine you was Marcus Budd, Esquire. You were Marcus Budd when you robbed the bank, and Marcus Budd when you walked back to the granite patch in the number nines and from there home in your own shoes. In fact, you were Marcus Budd all through the piece. You could change your footwear easily enough, but you couldn't change anything else, because you couldn't forget you were Marcus Budd. This unchanging Marcus Budd walks on the outside of his feet. His footwear gets the roughest doing on the outer edge and hardly any at all along the inner edge. Marcus Budd walks like that because he's bow-legged, having done a lot of riding when he was a boy. You see, Budd, you can't bluff the tracker. That's why the Force employs trackers. What did you do with the money?"

Marcus Budd admitted that the money he had taken from the bank's safe he had hidden behind some old ledgers in the tallboy chest of drawers in the bank. He said he robbed the bank only for a joke to impress on John Abbott's mind the looseness of his habits. He explained all this later to a judge and jury, explained it with his eyes shut for long periods, possibly to hide his failure-tormented soul and the hurt his vanity received at having been brought to his terrible position by a common police constable and not by a noted detective-inspector, by having, worse than even this, been confronted by mistakes the like of which these super-criminals in detective stories would never have made.

He got off lightly. He got a month - light.

The bank manager? He got the sack.

Wisp of Wool and Disk of Silver

It was Sunday. The heat drove the blowflies to roost under the low staging that supported the iron tank outside the kitchen door. The small flies, apparently created solely for the purpose of drowning themselves in the eyes of man and beast, were not noticed by the man lying on the rough bunk set up under the verandah roof. He was reading a mystery story.

The house was of board, and iron-roofed. Nearby were other buildings: a blacksmith's shop, a truck shed, and a junk house. Beyond them a windmill raised water to a reservoir tank on high stilts, which in turn fed a long line of troughing. This was the outstation at the back of Reefer's Find.

Reefer's Find was a cattle ranch. It was not a large station for Australia - a mere half-million acres within its boundary fence. The outstation was forty-odd miles from the main homestead, and that isn't far in Australia.

Only one rider lived at the outstation - Harry Larkin, who was, this hot Sunday afternoon, reading a mystery story. He had been quartered there for more than a year, and every night at seven o'clock, the boss at the homestead telephoned to give orders for the following day and to be sure he was still alive and kicking. Usually, Larkin spoke to a man face to face about twice a month.

Larkin might have talked to a man more often had he wished. His nearest neighbor lived nine miles away in a small stockman's hut on the next property, and once they had often met at the boundary by prearrangement. But then Larkin's neighbour, whose name was William Reynolds, was a difficult man, according to Larkin, and the meetings stopped.

On all sides of this small homestead the land stretched flat to the horizon. Had it not been for the scanty, narrow-leafed mulga and the sick-looking sandalwood trees, plus the mirage which turned a salt bush into a Jack's beanstalk and a tree into a telegraph pole stuck on a bald man's head, the horizon would have been as distant as that of the ocean.

A man came stalking through the mirage, the blanket roll on his back making him look like a ship standing on its bowsprit.

The lethargic dogs were not aware of the visitor until he was about ten yards from the verandah. So engrossed was Larkin that even the barking of his dogs failed to distract his attention, and the stranger actually reached the edge of the verandah floor and spoke before Larkin was aware of him.

"He, he! Good day, mate! Flamin' hot today, ain't it?"

Larkin swung his legs off the bunk and sat up. What he saw was not usual in this part of Australia - a sundowner, a bush waif who tramps from north to south or from east to west, never working, cadging rations from the far-flung homesteads and having the ability of the camel to do without water, or find it. Sometimes Old Man Sun tricked one of them, and then the vast bushland took him and never gave up the cloth-tattered skeleton.

"Good day," Larkin said, to add with ludicrous inanity, "Travelling?"

"Yes, mate. Makin' down south." The derelict slipped the swag off his shoulder and sat on it. "What place is this?"

Larkin told him. "Mind me camping here tonight, mate? Wouldn't be in the way. Wouldn't be here in the mornin', either."

"You can camp over in the shed," Larkin said. "And if you pinch anything, I'll track you and belt the guts out of you."

A vacuous grin spread over the dust-grimed, bewhiskered face.

"Me, mate? I wouldn't pinch nothin'. Could do with a pinch of tea, and a bit of flour. He, he! Pinch - I mean a fistful of tea and sugar, mate."

Five minutes of this bird would send a man crazy. Larkin entered the kitchen, found an empty tin, and poured into it an equal quantity of tea and sugar. He scooped flour from a sack into a brown paper bag, and wrapped a chunk of salt meat in an old newspaper. On going out to the sundowner, anger surged in him at the sight of the man standing by the bunk and looking through his mystery story.

"He, he! Detective yarn!" said the sundowner. "I give 'em away years ago. A bloke does a killing and leaves the clues for the detectives to find. They're all the same. Why in 'ell don't a bloke write about a bloke who kills another bloke and gets away with it? I could kill a bloke and leave no clues."

"You could," sneered Larkin.

"Course. Easy. You only gotta use your brain - like me."

Larkin handed over the rations and edged the visitor off his verandah. The fellow was batty, all right, but harmless as they all are.

"How would you kill a man and leave no clues?" he asked.

"Well, I tell you it's easy." The derelict pushed the rations into a dirty gunny sack and again sat down on his swag. "You see, mate, it's this way. In real life the murderer can't do away with the body. Even doctors and things like that make a hell of a mess of doing away with a corpse. In fact, they don't do away with it, mate. They leave parts and bits of it all over the scenery, and then what happens? Why, a detective comes along and he says, 'Cripes, someone's been and done a murder! Ah! Watch me track the bloke what done it.' If you're gonna commit a murder, you must be able to do away with the body. Having done that, well, who's gonna prove anything? Tell me that, mate."

"You tell me," urged Larkin, and tossed his depleted tobacco plug to the visitor. The sundowner gnawed from the plug, almost hit a dog in the eye with a spit, gulped, and settled to the details of the perfect murder.

"Well, mate, it's like this. Once you done away with the body, complete, there ain't nothing left to say that the body ever was alive to be killed. Now, supposin' I wanted to do you in. I don't, mate, don't think that, but I 'as plenty of time to work things out. Supposin' I wanted to do you in. Well, me and you is out ridin' and I takes me chance and shoots you stone-dead. I chooses to do the killin' where there's plenty of dead wood. Then I gathers the dead wood and drags your body onto it and fires the wood. Next day, when the ashes are cold, I goes back with a sieve and dolly pot. That's all I wants then.

"I takes out your burned bones and I crushes 'em to dust in the dolly pot. Then I goes through the ashes with the sieve, getting out all the small bones and putting them through the dolly pot. The dust I empties out from the dolly pot for the wind to take. All the metal bits, such as buttons and boot sprigs, I puts in me pocket and carries back to the homestead where I throws 'em down the well or covers 'em with sulphuric acid.

"Almost sure to be a dolly pot here, by the look of the place. Almost sure to be a sieve. Almost sure to be a jar of sulphuric acid for solderin' work. Everythin' on tap, like. And just in case the million-to-one chance comes off that someone might come across the fire site and wonder, sort of, I'd shoot a coupler kangaroos, skin 'em, and burn the carcasses on top of the old ashes. You know, to keep the blowies from breeding."

Harry Larkin looked at the sundowner, and through him. A prospector's dolly pot, a sieve, a quantity of sulphuric acid to dissolve the metal parts. Yes, they were all here. Given time a man could commit the perfect murder. Time! Two days would be long enough.

The sundowner stood up. "Good day, mate. Don't mind me. He, he! Flamin' hot, ain't it? Be cool down south. Well, I'll be movin."

Larkin watched him depart. The bush waif did not stop at the shed to camp for the night. He went on to the windmill and sprawled over the drinking trough to drink. He filled his rusty billy-can, Larkin watching until the mirage to the southward drowned him.

The perfect murder, with aids as common as household remedies. The perfect scene, this land without limits where even a man and his nearest neighbor are separated by nine miles. A prospector's dolly pot, a sieve, and a pint of soldering acid. Simple! It was as simple as being kicked to death in a stockyard jammed with mules.

"William Reynolds vanished three months ago, and repeated searches have failed to find even his body."

Mounted Constable Evans sat stiffly erect in the chair behind the littered desk in the Police Station at Wondong. Opposite him lounged a slight dark-complexioned man having a straight nose, a high forehead, and intensely blue eyes. There was no doubt that Evans was a policeman. None would guess that the dark man with the blue eyes was Detective Inspector Napoleon Bonaparte.

"The man's relatives have been bothering Headquarters about William Reynolds, which is why I am here," explained Bonaparte, faintly apologetic. "I have read your reports, and find them clear and concise. There is no doubt in the Official Mind that, assisted by your black tracker, you have done everything possible to locate Reynolds or his dead body. I may succeed where you and the black tracker failed because I am peculiarly equipped with gifts bequeathed to me by my white father and my aboriginal mother. In me are combined the white man's reasoning powers and the black man's perceptions and bushcraft. Therefore, should I succeed there would be no reflection on your efficiency or the powers of your tracker. Between what a tracker sees and what you have been trained to reason, there is a bridge. There is no such bridge between those divided powers in me. Which is why I never fail."

Having put Constable Evans in a more cooperative frame of mind, Bony rolled a cigarette and relaxed.

"Thank you, sir," Evans said and rose to accompany Bony to the locality map which hung on the wall. "Here's the township of Wondong. Here is the homestead of Morley Downs cattle station. And here, fifteen miles on from the homestead, is the stockman's hut where William Reynolds lived and worked.

"There's no telephonic communication between the hut and the homestead. Once every month the people at the homestead trucked rations to Reynolds. And once every week, every Monday morning, a stockman from the homestead would meet Reynolds midway between homestead and hut to give Reynolds his mail, and orders, and have a yarn with him over a billy of tea."

"And then one Monday, Reynolds didn't turn up," Bony added, as they resumed their chairs at the desk.

"That Monday the homestead man waited four hours for Reynolds," continued Evans. "The following day the station manager ran out in his car to Reynolds' hut. He found the ashes on the open hearth stone-cold, the two chained dogs nearly dead of thirst, and that Reynolds hadn't been at the hut since the day it had rained, three days previously.

"The manager drove back to the homestead and organized all his men in a search party. They found Reynolds' horse running with several others. The horse was still saddled and bridled. They rode the country for two days, and then I went out with my tracker to join in. We kept up the search for a week, and the tracker's opinion was that Reynolds might have been riding the back boundary fence when he was parted from the horse. Beyond that the tracker was vague, and I don't wonder at it for two reasons. One, the rain had wiped out tracks visible to white eyes, and two, there were other horses in the same paddock. Horse tracks swamped with rain are indistinguishable one from another."

"How large is that paddock?" asked Bony.

"Approximately 200 square miles."

Bony rose and again studied the wall map. "On the far side of the fence is this place named Reefer's Find," he pointed out. "Assuming that Reynolds had been thrown from his horse and injured, might he not have tried to reach the outstation of Reefer's Find which, I see, is about three miles from the fence whereas Reynolds' hut is six or seven?"

"We thought of that possibility, and we scoured the country on the Reefer's Find side of the boundary fence," Evans replied. "There's a stockman named Larkin at the Reefer's Find outstation. He joined in the search. The tracker, who had memorised Reynolds' footprints, found on the earth floor of the hut's verandah, couldn't spot any of his tracks on Reefer's Find country, and the boundary fence, of course, did not permit Reynolds' horse into that country. The blasted rain beat the tracker. It beat all of us."

"Him. Did you know this Reynolds?"

"Yes. He came to town twice on a bit of a bender. Good type. Good horseman. Good bushman. The horse he rode that day was not a tricky animal. What do Headquarters know of him, sir?"

"Only that he never failed to write regularly to his mother, and that he had spent four years in the Army from which he was discharged following a head wound."

"Head wound! He might have suffered from amnesia. He could have left his horse and walked away - anywhere - walked until he dropped and died from thirst or starvation."

"It's possible. What is the character of the man Larkin?"

"Average, I think. He told me that he and Reynolds had met when both happened to be riding that boundary fence, the last time being several months before Reynolds vanished."

"How many people besides Larkin at that outstation?"

"No one else excepting when they're mustering for fats."

The conversation waned while Bony rolled another cigarette. "Could you run me out to Morley Downs homestead?" he asked.

"Yes, of course," assented Evans.

"Then kindly telephone the manager and let me talk to him."

Two hundred square miles is a fairly large tract of country in which to find clues leading to the fate of a lost man, and three months is an appreciable period of time to elapse after a man is reported as lost.

The rider who replaced Reynolds' successor was blue-eyed and dark-skinned, and at the end of two weeks of incessant reading he was familiar with every acre, and had read every word on this large page of the Book of the Bush.

By now Bony was convinced that Reynolds hadn't died in that paddock. Lost or injured men had crept into a hollow log to die, their remains found many years afterward, but in this country there were no trees large enough for a man to crawl into. Men had perished and their bodies had been covered with wind-blown sand, and after many years the wind had removed the sand to reveal the skeleton. In Reynolds' case the search for him had been begun within a week of his disappearance, when eleven men plus a policeman selected for his job because of his bushcraft, and a black tracker selected from among the aborigines who are the best sleuths in the world, had gone over and over the 200 square miles.

Bony knew that, of the searchers, the black tracker would be the most proficient. He knew, too, just how the mind of that aborigine would work when taken to the stockman's hut and put on the job. Firstly, he would see the lost man's horse and memorize its hoofprints. Then he would memorize the lost man's bootprints left on the dry earth beneath the verandah roof. Thereafter he would ride crouched forward above his horse's mane and keep his eyes directed to the ground at a point a few feet beyond the animal's nose. He would look for a horse's tracks and a man's tracks, knowing that nothing passes over the ground without leaving evidence, and that even half an inch of rain will not always obliterate the evidence left, perhaps, in the shelter of a tree.

That was all the black tracker could be expected to do. He would not reason that the lost man might have climbed a tree and there cut his own throat, or that he might have wanted to vanish and so had climbed over one of the fences into the adjacent paddock, or had, when suffering from amnesia, or the madness brought about by solitude, walked away beyond the rim of the earth.

The first clue found by Bonaparte was a wisp of wool dyed brown. It was caught by a barb of the top wire of the division fence between the two cattle stations. It was about an inch in length and might well have come from a man's sock when he had climbed over the fence.

It was most unlikely that any one of the searchers for William Reynolds would have climbed the fence. They were all mounted, and when they scoured the neighbouring country, they would have passed through the gate about a mile from this tiny piece of flotsam. Whether or not the wisp of wool had been detached from Reynolds' sock at the time of his disappearance, its importance in this case was that it led the investigator to the second clue.

The vital attribute shared by the aboriginal tracker with Napoleon Bonaparte was patience. To both, Time was of no consequence once they set out on the hunt.

On the twenty-ninth day of his investigation Bony came on the site of a large fire. It was approximately a mile distant from the outstation of Reefer's Find, and, from a point nearby, the buildings could be seen magnified and distorted by the mirage. The fire had burned after the last rainfall - the one recorded immediately following the disappearance of Reynolds - and the trails made by dead tree branches when dragged together still remained sharp on the ground.

The obvious purpose of the fire had been to consume the carcass of a calf, for amid the mound of white ash protruded the skull and bones of the animal. The wind had played with the ash, scattering it thinly all about the original ash mound.

Question: "Why had Larkin burned the carcass of the calf?" Cattlemen never do such a thing unless a beast dies close to their camp. In parts of the continent, carcasses are always burned to keep down the blowfly pest, but out here in the interior, never. There was a possible answer, however, in the mentality of the man who lived nearby, the man who lived alone and could be expected to do anything unusual, even burning all the carcasses of animals which perished in his domain. That answer would be proved correct if other fire sites were discovered offering the same evidence.

At daybreak the next morning Bony was perched high in a

sandalwood tree. There he watched Larkin ride out on his day's work, and when assured that the man was out of the way, he slid to the ground and examined the ashes and the burned bones, using his hands and his fingers as a sieve.

Other than the bones of the calf, he found nothing but a soft nosed bullet. Under the ashes, near the edge of the splayed-out mass, he found an indentation on the ground, circular and about six inches in diameter. The bullet and the mark were the second and third clues, the third being the imprint of a prospector's dolly pot.

"Do your men shoot calves in the paddocks for any reason?" Bony asked the manager, who had driven out to his hut with rations. The manager was big and tough, grizzled and shrewd.

"No, of course not, unless a calf has been injured in some way and is helpless. Have you found any of our calves shot?"

"None of yours. How do your stockmen obtain their meat supply?"

"We kill at the homestead and distribute fortnightly a little fresh meat and a quantity of salted beef."

"D'you think the man over on Reefer's Find would be similarly supplied by his employer?"

"Yes, I think so. I could find out from the owner of Reefer's Find."

"Please do. You have been most helpful, and I do appreciate it. In my role of cattleman it wouldn't do to have another rider stationed with me, and I would be grateful if you consented to drive out here in the evening for the next three days. Should I not be here, then wait until eight o'clock before taking from the tea tin over there on the shelf a sealed envelope addressed to you. Act on the enclosed instructions."

"Very well, I'll do that."

"Thanks. Would you care to undertake a little inquiry for me?"

"Certainly."

"Then talk guardedly to those men you sent to meet Reynolds every Monday and ascertain from them the relationship which existed between Reynolds and Harry Larkin. As is often the case with lonely men stationed near the boundary fence of two properties, according to Larkin he and Reynolds used to meet now and then by arrangement. They may have quarrelled. Have you ever met Larkin?"

"On several occasions, yes," replied the manager.

"And your impressions of him? As a man?"

"I thought him intelligent. Inclined to be morose, of course, but then men who live alone often are. You are not thinking that - ?"

"I'm thinking that Reynolds is not in your country. Had he been still on your property, I would have found him dead or alive. When I set out to find a missing man, I find him. I shall find Reynolds, eventually - if there is anything of him to find."

On the third evening that the manager went out to the little hut, Bony showed him a small and slightly convex disk of silver. It was weathered and in one place cracked. It bore the initials JMM.

"I found that in the vicinity of the site of a large fire," Bony said. "It might establish that William Reynolds is no longer alive."

Although Harry Larkin was supremely confident, he was not quite happy. He had not acted without looking at the problem from all angles and without having earnestly sought the answer to the question: "If I shoot him dead, burn the body on a good fire, go through the ashes for the bones which I pound to dust in a dolly pot, and for the metal bits and pieces which I dissolve in sulphuric acid, how can I be caught?" The answer was plain.

He had carried through the sundowner's method of utterly destroying the body of the murder victim, and to avoid the million-to-one-chance of anyone coming across the ashes of the fire and being made suspicious, he had shot a calf as kangaroos were scarce.

Yes, he was confident, and confident that he was justified in being confident. Nothing remained of Bill Reynolds, damn him, save a little grayish dust which was floating around somewhere.

The slight unhappiness was caused by a strange visitation, signs of which he had first discovered when returning home from his work one afternoon. On the ground near the blacksmith's shop he found a strange set of boot tracks which were not older than two days. He followed these tracks backward to the house, and then forward until he lost them in the scrub.

Nothing in the house was touched, as far as he could see, and nothing had been taken from the blacksmith's shop, or interfered with. The dolly pot was still in the corner into which he had dropped it after its last employment, and the crowbar was still leaning against the anvil. On the shelf was the acid jar. There was no acid in it. He had used it to dissolve, partially, buttons and the metal band around a pipestem and boot sprigs. The residue of those metal objects he had dropped into a hole in a tree eleven miles away.

It was very strange. A normal visitor, finding the occupier away, would have left a note at the house. Had the visitor been black, he would not have left any tracks if bent on mischief.

The next day Larkin rode out to the boundary fence and on the way he visited the site of his fire. There he found the plain evidence that someone had moved the bones of the animal and had delved among the ashes still remaining from the action of the wind.

Thus he was not happy, but still supremely confident. They could not tack anything onto him. They couldn't even prove that Reynolds was dead. How could they when there was nothing of him left?

It was again Sunday, and Larkin was washing his clothes at the outside fire when the sound of horses' hoofs led him to see two men approaching. His lips vanished into a mere line, and his mind went over all the answers he would give if the police ever did call on him. One of the men he did not know. The other was Mounted Constable Evans.

They dismounted, anchoring their horses by merely dropping the reins to the ground. Larkin searched their faces and wondered who the slim half-caste with the singularly blue eyes was.

"Good day," Larkin greeted them.

"Good day, Larkin," replied Constable Evans, and appeared to give his trousers a hitch. His voice was affable, and Larkin was astonished when, after an abrupt and somewhat violent movement, he found himself handcuffed.

"Going to take you in for the murder of William Reynolds," Evans announced. "This is Detective Inspector Napoleon Bonaparte."

"You must be balmy - or I am," Larkin said.

Evans countered with: "You are. Come on over to the house. A car will be here in about half an hour."

The three men entered the kitchen where Larkin was told to sit down.

"I haven't done anything to Reynolds, or anyone else," asserted Larkin, and for the first time the slight man with the brilliant blue eyes spoke.

"While we are waiting, I'll tell you all about it, Larkin. I'll tell it so clearly that you will believe I was watching you all the time. You used to meet Reynolds at the boundary fence gate, and the two of you would indulge in a spot of gambling - generally at poker. Then one day you cheated and there was a fight in which you were thrashed.

"You knew what day of the week Reynolds would ride that boundary fence and you waited for him on your side. You held him up and made him climb over the fence while you covered him with your .32 high-power Savage rifle. You made him walk to a place within a mile of here, where there was plenty of dry wood, and there you shot him and burned his body.

"The next day you returned with a dolly pot and a sieve. You put all the bones through the dolly pot, and then you sieved all the ashes for metal objects in Reynolds' clothes and burned them up with sulphuric acid. Very neat. The perfect crime, you must agree."

"If I done all that, which I didn't, yes," Larkin did agree.

"Well, assuming that not you but another did all I have outlined, why did the murderer shoot and burn the carcass of a calf on the same fire site?"

"You tell me," said Larkin.

"Good. I'll even do that. You shot Reynolds and you disposed of his body, as I've related. Having killed him, you immediately dragged wood together and burned the body, keeping the fire going for several hours. Now, the next day, or the day after that, it rained, and that rainfall fixed your actions like words printed in a book. You went through the ashes for Reynolds' bones before it rained, and you shot the calf and lit the second fire after it rained. You dropped the calf at least 200 yards from the scene of the murder, and you carried the carcass on your back over those 200 yards. The additional weight impressed your boot prints on the ground much deeper than when you walk about normally, and although the rain washed out many of your boot prints, it did not remove your prints made when carrying the dead calf. You didn't shoot the calf, eh?"

"No, of course I didn't,' came the sneering reply. 'I burned the carcass of a calf that died. I keep my camp clean. Enough blowflies about as it is."

"But you burned the calf's carcass a full mile away from your camp. However, you shot the calf, and you shot it to burn the carcass in order to prevent possible curiosity. You should have gone through the ashes after you burned the carcass of the calf and retrieved the bullet fired from your own rifle."

Bony smiled, and Larkin glared.

Constable Evans said: "Keep your hands on the table, Larkin."

"You know, Larkin, you murderers often make me tired," Bony went on. "You think up a good idea, and then fall down executing it.

"You thought up a good one by dollying the bones and sieving the ashes for the metal objects on a man's clothes and in his boots, and then - why go and spoil it by shooting a calf and burning the carcass on the same fire site? It wasn't necessary. Having pounded Reynolds' bones to ash and scattered the ash to the four corners, and having retrieved from the ashes the remaining evidence that a human body had been destroyed, there was no necessity to burn a carcass. It wouldn't have mattered how suspicious anyone became. Your biggest mistake was burning that calf. That act connects you with that fire."

"Yes, well, what of it?" Larkin almost snarled. "I got a bit lonely livin' here alone for months, and one day I sorta got fed up. I seen the calf, and I up with me rifle and took a pot shot at it."

"It won't do," Bony said, shaking his head. "Having taken a pot shot at the calf, accidentally killing it, why take a dolly pot to the place where you burned the carcass? You did carry a dolly pot, the one in the blacksmith's shop, to the scene of the fire, for the imprint of the dolly pot on the ground is still plain in two places."

"Pretty good tale, I must say," said Larkin. "You still can't prove that Bill Reynolds is dead."

"No?" Bony's dark face registered a bland smile, but his eyes were like blue opals. "When I found a wisp of brown wool attached to the boundary fence, I was confident that Reynolds had climbed it, merely because I was sure his body was not on his side of the fence. You made him walk to the place where you shot him, and then you saw the calf and the other cattle in the distance, and you shot the calf and carried it to the fire.

"I have enough to put you in the dock, Larkin - and one other little thing which is going to make certain you'll hang. Reynolds was in the Army during the war. He was discharged following a head wound. The surgeon who operated on Reynolds was a specialist in trepanning. The surgeon always scratched his initials on the silver plate he inserted into the skull of a patient. He has it on record that he operated on William Reynolds, and he will swear that the plate came from the head of William Reynolds, and will also swear that the plate could not have been detached from Reynolds' head without great violence."

"It wasn't in the ashes," gasped Larkin, and then realized his slip.

"No, it wasn't in the ashes, Larkin," Bony agreed. "You see, when you shot him at close quarters, probably through the forehead, the expanding bullet took away a portion of the poor fellow's head - and the trepanning plate. I found the plate lodged in a sandalwood tree growing about thirty feet from where you burned the body."

Larkin glared across the table at Bony, his eyes freezing as he realised that the trap had indeed sprung on him.

Bony was again smiling. He said, as though comfortingly: "Don't fret, Larkin. If you had not made all those silly mistakes, you would have made others equally fatal. Strangely enough, the act of homicide always throws a man off balance. If it were not so, I would find life rather boring."

Breakaway House

CHAPTER ONE
Invitation to a Walkabout

For many years the house had never been so quiet, and not in years had Marie Bonaparte found herself listening to the clock in the lounge and that on the kitchen mantelpiece. Not for years had she noticed a passing train, and now when one did pass on its way to the city the noise thundered about her.

It had been like this since her last boy had married and left with his bride for a honeymoon at Sydney. Little Ed, now six feet two and an electrician, was boisterous, untidy, lovable. He had hugged her, kissed her, and for the umpteenth time told her she would be all right. She wasn't all right. It was now five months since her Bony had been home between assignments, and no woman could be satisfied with making just the one bed, dusting the dustless rooms, sitting at the kitchen table doing the daily crossword and reading. Just sitting.

She would get horribly fat leading this kind of life. She was cubical as it was. Her face was large and wrinkled, and the only feature she still had pride in were her feet, strong and trim. With dark eyes she gazed moodily beyond the front fence, across the road to the railway on which thundered a train from Brisbane to Sandgate. Patting her permed black hair she sighed and thought she might run into town to get away from her own shadows.

It was then that a powerful car stopped outside the gate, a police car and she knew the man who left it and came to knock on her door.

"Hello, Marie! Enjoying the spell or getting sick of loafing?" enquired Sergeant Dovey.

Marie Bonaparte beamed and invited the policeman to come in for a cup of tea. "I was looking forward to a good long rest and I'm sick of it already. All I do now is to look out the window. As Bony says, I'm a sailor's wife, and no doubt of that. Heard from him?"

"After I get my tea and those scones I know you have in the

cupboard. And plenty of butter. Know something?"

Marie turned from pouring water into the tea pot. "What am I supposed to know? You heard from Bony?"

"Looks like." Sergeant Dovey lit a cigarette, gave her the smile he reserved for his wife and children, and waited for his tea.

"The sailor's in West Australia, Marie. Mucking about, we think. Just got a fresh assignment. We have his orders - orders mind you, like give or else. We play ball or he's coming home."

Marie placed the tea before the visitor and provided scones, butter and jam. She sat facing the sergeant, knowing that to hurry him would be vain, and she picked up his cigarettes, lit one and blew smoke all over him and his scone.

"Now out with it, Mister Sergeant Dovey."

"Oh, yes, I forgot, Mrs. Napoleon Bonaparte. Ha, I thought I'd brought it. A telegram for you. Came this morning."

"He's coming home after all this time," Marie exclaimed, forgetting about the new assignment. Her fingers trembled as she opened the envelope and held the flimsy to read:

"Come awaltzing Matilda with me. Department will put you on plane for Kalgoorlie. Will have you met. Bring old fishing clothes and boots. All the real Australia is waiting for you to come home. If I don't say I love you you'll sulk, so I say it. Bony."

For almost a minute she sat with her head bowed, and Dovey saw a tear drop fall splash upon her forearm on the table. On looking up her eyes were full of sunshine after rain. She tried to speak and the sergeant relieved her of it.

"The wife and I know how you've lived in this house making a man of your Bony and men of your three boys, all the time eating out your heart for the bush where you came from. Well, here's the chance. You'll go? You can leave for Melbourne this afternoon, and catch a west bound plane early to-morrow."

Of course Marie had to find objections. There were the old clothes and boots to unearth and pack. There was the house to be looked after, and what would Little Ed and his wife say to an empty house? Besides what about the tradesmen, stopping the deliveries, and she'd have to pay a call at the bank for extra money. Oh no, she couldn't possibly go.

"Women!" exclaimed Sergeant Dovey. "You give 'em what

they been crying for for years and then they argue the ruddy toss about taking it. You pack those clothes and I'll get to the telephone."

Sergeant Dovey took her to Brisbane, entertained her at lunch in a fashionable restaurant, put her on the Melbourne bound plane. There she was met by another policeman who drove her to a comfortable hotel for the night, and then called for her and took her to the airport. She could have done all this for herself, but she was a policeman's wife.

On leaving the plane at Kalgoorlie, some 3,000 miles from her empty house, she was wearing a summery blue frock, a light plastic coat over an arm and a heavy suitcase. At the bottom of the disembarking steps she was accosted by a large young man having smiling grey eyes and face and hands burned almost black by the sun.

"Mrs. Bonaparte?"

"Have been for thirty-five years. Who are you?"

He had taken the case from her and was conducting her to the gate, and he said softly: "Constable Rockcliff, Mrs. Bonaparte. I've been instructed to convey you to a camp where, I know, your husband is waiting."

He flashed his credentials which she recognised, and a few minutes later they were by-passing the main town and driving north over a bush track. Marie was silent. The gimlet gums grew in clumps, and presently they were passing saltbush and bluebush and the much larger wait-a-bit shrubs. Marie breathed in deeply and held her breath as though the air was too precious to let escape.

When it did, she sighed and her driver said: "Tired, Mrs. Bonaparte? We could stop to boil the billy. Just say so. We've a long way to go."

"I'm not tired. Oh no, I'm not tired. Oh, it's lovely to belong, and I haven't belonged for years and years." The puzzled constable waited. "You see, Mr. Rockcliff, for thirty-five years I've been living on the outskirts of Brisbane. I've been from home all those years and now I'm back home again. Yes, I would like a cup of tea."

She was out of the utility before the driver, gazing about as a child in wonderland, breathing deeply, making no attempt to assist the policeman. He gathered a few leaves and then added dry sticks, and the smoke from his fire slanted gently away to the south and painted a bluebush purple. From the load on the utility he took down a tin of water and filled a blackened billycan, and looking up from it, he saw Marie Bonaparte standing in the smoke and enjoying it as though it were attar of roses.

Marie watched him bring from the vehicle a bushman's tucker box, and left the smoke on seeing he was observing her. Now she was smiling, a broad smile disclosing her teeth, and from her mouth issued a sound less like laughter than a gurgle of sheer happiness.

The constable tossed a handful of tea into the boiling water, left it for thirty odd seconds and lifted the billy off the fire with a stick. From the tucker box he took cup and its saucer, but Marie demanded a bushman's tin pannikin, and now sitting on the ground gurgled again like a small child. The policeman squatted on his heels, and opened the large packet of sandwiches he had bought in Kalgoorlie.

So this is Inspector Bonaparte's wife who reminded him of his mother. Minus affectation, minus the little bitternesses begotten by the years. Like his mother, this woman would never grow old. Damn it, when she laughed she reminded him of his own child splashing about in her tub.

Two hours later they could see the sun-reflecting roofs of a small township, and Marie was asked to bend low, when the policeman covered her with a light rug. Beyond the town, he explained.

"I've to get you to your husband without anyone seeing you on the road, Mrs. Bonaparte. Why, I don't know, but that was the order."

Beyond the township the flat land gave place to rolling dunes covered with dark scrub and revealing now and then a range of red sand. The track twisted to avoid steep grades, originally laid down by the old time bullock and camel waggons.

"I never ask him why he does anything," Marie said, and exclaimed delightedly when several kangaroos bounded across the track. "What he does outside the house is his business, but he tells me most of it. My business has been in the house, where I raised three boys, and now that the last has flown the nest, he and I are going on walkabout. The last walkabout was nine years ago, and that was only for a week."

"My wife wouldn't go walkabout for a million. We've two children: one three years and the other just a year," remarked the constable, and on being asked where he was stationed said it was at Kalgoorlie. "Don't get much bush work, and so I can enjoy a trip like this. We'll be coming to a wayside store in a couple of miles, and I'll ask you to get down again. We don't stop."

The bush store was a ramshackle conglomeration of slab buildings and, beneath the rug, Marie heard the barking of dogs and the shouted salutes of two men.

"They'll be wondering why we didn't stop," Rockcliff said. "Have to make up something when I go back tomorrow. Getting hungry yet? I thought we'd park at sundown."

"Go on and on and on for ever," Marie replied happily. "This is what I've ached for, this moving on, this going to some place or other. Strange, you know. At the end of this trip I'll meet my husband I haven't seen for eleven months, and I'm very happy, indeed. But it's the bush, this going on just to see what's round the next bend. It's tingling in my blood right now."

Eventually Rockcliff stopped the utility amid a grove of broad-leafed mulgas. The sun was setting, and all the shadows were tinted with red.

Then on again with the joy of coming home filling Marie's mind, and as the dusk passed abruptly the night made the headlight one great sword to pierce its black body. Presently she slept slightly, eventually recalling hearing voices on two occasions.

The policeman woke her: "Camp's just ahead," he told her, and there a short distance away were two flares of camp fires, and people all about them. Then she could see a tent to leeward of one fire, and two men standing close by. Finally at journey's end the utility stopped, and the door was opened and the firelight revealed her husband's beaming face.

She was being hugged and hugged in response. She was being kissed and gave back the kisses. She said, breathlessly: "Well, here I is."

"Same Marie. Same expression. Yes, here you is. Welcome to

the bush. Welcome to home. Come, dinner's ready."

He turned away to greet Constable Rockcliff. She noticed Bony's disgraceful clothes in which he appeared to have slept for a year. His straight black hair needed to be cut. The seat of his trousers was covered with patches, and his feet were bare.

The constable provided dinner and they ate and drank tea from pannikins in the light of the fire. Those about the second fire vanished into what she could see were wurlies, and there came one man to greet her. He was short and plump. He wore only a pair of dungaree trousers, a snakeskin band to keep his hair tuffed. The firelight gleamed in his coal black eyes. He could not be more than forty, and the cicatrices as well as the Mantle of the Devil proved him to be a Medicine Man.

He surprised Marie by his articulation of English saying: "The Begonia Tribe welcomes the wife of Inspector Bonaparte. He became our friend when my father was the chief. We hope now to repay something of the debt we owe."

"This is Chief Merlee," Bony explained. "He has offered to assist us, as I well knew he would. Tomorrow we go into conference at which you will be given a grounding in the job of work we have to do. Off you go to bed soon, for you have come a long way since early this morning."

Marie made no objection to being bundled off to bed. She was very weary but her brain refused to give up the delights of corning "home", and before sleeping she looked outside the tent to see her husband and the constable with Merlee at the fire. They were squatting on their heels, and Merlee was drawing on the sand with a stick.

On waking it was broad daylight, and when realising where she was felt vexed that she had missed the sunrise on this wonderful world instead of on house roofs which had been for too long her horizon. A breakfast of thick slices of bacon and eggs, together with yeast bread awaited her at the fire as guest of Constable Rockcliff.

"Our mutual hero says that it will be some time before you'll sleep off the ground again," he told her, smilingly. "He's away inspecting camels with Merlee. Seems that he plans to go on a kangaroo shooting trip. Wish I were going, too."

"You cook fine, Mr. Rockcliff. Yes, it's a wonderful morning. The smell of the cooking and the fire, the call of the birds, the aroma in the very air from all the trillions of trees, the scent exuded from all the pure sandhills. It's home for us.

"Could be home for me, too," conceded the constable. "What a hope! What with the town-loving wife and the kids, what a hope! I was born and reared on a coastal farm, but I can understand what you feel."

Marie saw that the camp was on the bank of a wide water-hole in a creek emptying into a great salt lake, when it ran, and that both banks were lined by magnificent gums. It was a flawless day in mid-March, and, although on the same longitude as Brisbane, lacked Brisbane's heat and humidity at this time of year.

"I was born in Queensland," she said. "For thirteen years I ran wild with other children. Then for three years I was in a mission. There came a man who looked at me with eyes like the sea on a bright cold day. He made me tremble inside, and after another year he came back to say he wanted to marry me. I trembled more than ever, and he pinched me till I said the words.

"Afterwards he carried me off to his camp close to a water-hole in a great area of tobacco bush taller than you. We stayed there for a month, just a wonderful month beginning and ending with the full moon. Afterwards he took me to a small house in the country outside Brisbane. He was away on duty when the first boy was born. He was with me when the second came, and away again when the third boy was born to us.

"He calls me his sailor's wife, and that's what it's been all these years. The countryside became a suburb of Brisbane. Deep down I grew to hate it. He promised and promised that one day we'd both go off on walkabout and stay together till death parted us, and now we are to go on walkabout, so he says, but not forever as he's still a policeman. D'you know what's it all about?"

Rockcliff shook his head. He said:

"I know only I've to collect the stretchers and other gear, and return to Kal to-day. I brought your husband here four days back. He had a pow-wow with the local chief, and I was then told to return to Kalgoorlie, load up with rations and second hand gear, meet you and bring you here." The constable grinned. "You're on walkabout all right, Mrs. Bonaparte. As I said before: lucky you."

"His eyes are still blue?"

"And how they can bore into a man's block."

Eventually he left her sitting on one of two rolled swags, a chipped iron camp oven, a rough tucker box, a sack she knew contained rations. There was an un-cared-for thirty-two calibre rifle, several boxes of cartridges, boxes of cake tobacco. There remained her own suitcase and another she recognised as belonging . . .

Printed in Great Britain
by Amazon.co.uk, Ltd.,
Marston Gate.